KEYED UP

SARAH ESTEP

For my friends, who pushed me, held me, and told me I could make magic.
I could not have done this without you.
I love you.

CHAPTER ONE

Foolproof42: I think the writers are trying to kill us. That's the only explanation for last night's episode.

Little_Teapot: I may not survive the next three episodes. Please prep my eulogy in advance of the season finale.

Foolproof42: Does this mean you're finally going to tell me something about yourself?

"Now do you see what I've been saying? He's been smiling at his phone. It's *weird*."

Graham Thatcher looked up from his phone and found Peter and Jordy watching him closely from their seats at his kitchen island. Peter looked a little smug, and Jordy was pensive —which were both concerning all on their own.

It was a beautiful Saturday morning. The sun was shining, the birds were chirping as they jumped from branch to branch on the small lemon tree in his backyard, and the only thing marring the blue sky was the layer of perpetual smog that hung over Los Angeles. Naturally, he had to ruin a perfect, early fall day by agreeing to host brunch at his house.

"I wasn't smiling," Graham insisted, tucking his phone back into his pocket. "And even if I was, it's not *weird*." He tried to copy Peter's inflection, but the actor had a way of adding layers of meaning to a single syllable. When Graham did it, it came out as pure sarcasm.

"It's a little weird," Jordy said.

It was Jordy's fault Graham's friends were at his house. If Jordy Taylor, veteran quarterback for the Los Angeles Phantoms, had moved a little to the left at practice yesterday, he wouldn't have been flattened by two of his linebackers and he would be on a plane headed to Cincinnati, not nursing a sore throwing hand in Graham's kitchen. Because it was still early in the season, the Phantoms' coaching staff had said it wasn't worth risking further injury on a non-conference away game.

And that decision had landed his three best friends in his kitchen.

Graham selected a knife from the block and put a tomato on the cutting board. Casual was the name of the game. "Why is it weird that I might be smiling at my phone? People smile at their phones."

"You don't," Peter said. "It's all scowls and frowns."

Graham frowned. "That's not true."

Jordy chuckled. "Yes, it is. It's always work, and work makes you cranky." He poured himself another mimosa. Jordy had the same beverage preferences as a bachelorette party, and two restaurants had revised their bottomless mimosa policy after he'd been there. "I think it's a woman."

The tips of his ears grew hot. "It's not a woman."

It was definitely a woman.

Under different circumstances, he wouldn't have been

dodging questions. If she was someone he was casually seeing, he wouldn't be embarrassed. But they weren't dating. He didn't even know her real name. Little_Teapot was a friend he'd made on a website called FanForum that hosted discussion boards for all kinds of things. Their shared interest was a TV show, *Claymore Abbey*, that Graham had discovered during a bout of insomnia.

Currently in its ninth season, *Claymore Abbey* was a romantic Victorian drama that followed the Bevingtons, an aristocratic family over-encumbered with daughters. Coincidentally, *Claymore Abbey* had been Peter's first acting gig when he was nineteen, long before Graham had ever met him. His character, Christian, was a stableboy for the Bevingtons. During the course of the first season, his star-crossed young love affair with the family's eldest daughter, Lady Amanda, had gripped the audience by their collective throats, and then the writers had lit the world on fire by sending Christian away on a boat to America during the season finale. Christian had promised Amanda he would return when he was worthy of her, but that still hadn't happened. It seemed like every time Peter was in London, new theories cropped up on the boards that Christian was finally returning to the show.

Graham knew better. Peter lived with him when he was working in Los Angeles. Surely there would have been a script left lying around since Peter had the housekeeping abilities of a raccoon. Graham could have asked, but that would have sparked too many follow-up questions from Peter. Why did he want to know? Had he seen the show? What was his favorite part? Who were his favorite characters? He had the persistence of a caffeinated kindergartner.

All those questions would have eventually led right to FanForum and Graham's dirty little secret: Little_Teapot.

He hadn't meant for their friendship to become so clandestine, but Little_Teapot refused to divulge any useful information about herself, like her name or where she lived or what she did, because that was how girls like her ended up on *Dateline* and then getting razzed on a murder podcast.

Her words, not his.

And because fair was fair, he kept his own secrets. Little_Teapot didn't know that he owned his own company, or that his three best friends were famous. Instead, they exchanged other, innocuous details, like how her favorite color was periwinkle and his favorite kind of pizza was pepperoni and jalapeño.

His friends wouldn't understand. Peter would spin it into something it wasn't, Jordy would ask if they were sexting, and Sam would be immediately and intensely suspicious that she knew exactly who Graham was and was playing him for money.

In his pocket, his phone buzzed with another notification.

"Well, we know which woman it isn't," Jordy teased, grinning at his own joke.

Graham didn't need him to clarify who he was talking about.

"My life would be easier if that woman would drop dead," Graham said as he slid his knife through the ripe tomato.

"You shouldn't say that," Peter told him. "Especially while holding a knife."

Graham sighed. He didn't like that Peter had a point. Making thinly veiled death threats while holding sharp objects wouldn't look good in court. But was it really a threat if he hoped a well-timed piano dropped on Eloise Price's head?

"It would make my life easier," he grumbled.

Eloise Price had started as an annoying pebble in his shoe and had grown into a boulder he could no longer ignore. When his great-uncle Edgar had died almost a year ago, he had left Graham half of his derelict hotel in quaint Crane Cove, Oregon.

The other half belonged to Edgar's hotel manager, Eloise Price.

Graham would have been content to let Eloise Price run the hotel with no interference from him. He didn't want the damn thing. No, *she* wanted his opinions and, more importantly, his money. Her first email had been a thinly veiled cash grab. Empty niceties that led to her asking for a non-specific amount of money to upgrade the hotel. Maybe he'd been in a particularly rotten mood that day because he wrote back that he had no interest in the hotel or putting any money into it. He'd thought he'd used strong, clear language to clarify his points.

He had been wrong.

Eloise Price was worse than a junkyard dog with a bone. She didn't give up. And the more she pushed, the harder he dug in his heels. Which had led to their current impasse.

Impasse wasn't the right word. Standoff with loaded shotguns was more accurate.

He wanted to sell and be done with it. She wanted to keep it. And thanks to a few quirks in Edgar's will, she had the advantage.

"It's going to be fine," Peter said, picking up the newspaper on the counter and snapping it open. He loved a prop. "Graham is going to go up there, they're going to sit down and have a chat like civilized humans, and we can move on from this." Peter flipped down the top of his paper to give Graham a stern look. "You are going, right?"

He sighed, scraping the diced tomatoes into a bowl. "Yes, I'm going. You finally bullied me into it. Are you happy?"

"What are we happy about?" Sam, perpetually half an hour late, asked as he set his canvas grocery bags down on the counter and began to unload.

Brunch was special to the four of them. It had bonded their strange little group together. Whereas Graham, Peter, and

Jordy enjoyed trying different restaurants in the Los Angeles area, scouring the internet and collecting recommendations from people, Sam preferred to cook when it was his turn to pick. The rock star didn't like paparazzi taking pictures of him while he ate. And none of them objected because he cooked well enough that if music didn't work out, he could've opened a restaurant.

Sam had also managed to convince Graham that his house was the most convenient location. It wasn't. It was just when Sam's social battery ran out, he wanted to be able to leave instead of waiting for everyone to vacate his own house.

"Graham is finally going to see that old lady," Jordy said, and held up the empty mimosa pitcher. "Can I get another one?"

"Does drinking an entire pitcher of mimosas count as resting?" Peter asked him as he folded his newspaper with crisp movements.

"Is your Bloody Mary on your movie diet?" Jordy shot back.

Peter was always on some kind of diet for a role. Bulk up. Slim down. It was a never-ending cycle. Peter normally didn't drink, but brunch meant Bloody Marys.

"Bloody Marys are basically tomato juice, and tomatoes are very good for you. They contain electrolytes, antioxidants, and tons of vitamins." Peter stirred the Bloody Mary Graham had made him with the celery stick garnish. "And they come with roughage."

"What about the vodka?"

"Vodka can increase circulation and blood flow, which decreases the risk of strokes and heart disease, and it can help lower cholesterol. This is a healthy drink."

Sam snorted. "Did your grandma tell you that?"

"For a gin distillery masquerading as a ninety-year-old woman, she's very convincing."

Sam passed Graham an onion. "Speaking of cantankerous old ladies, when did you decide to go up to Oregon?"

"Recently."

"You know, if you weren't such a stubborn asshole, you could have been done with this months ago."

"And if you keep being an asshole, the next restaurant I choose will be the Denny's on Sunset."

Sam shuddered as he put a pod into the fancy automatic espresso machine Peter had bought Graham as an apology for breaking the regular coffee pot.

If Graham was a stubborn asshole, it was because Eloise Price was an expert-level dodger. Every specific question about the financial health of the hotel was met with a non-specific answer. He didn't know if she was calculating or incompetent.

"When are you going?"

"Monday—and fuck, I need to call and change my reservation. I was supposed to go Thursday, but I have a meeting Friday, and I have a bad feeling this is going to take a few days."

"And I have a home game on Sunday," Jordy reminded him.

Sam put two pans and a pot on the stove. "God, I hope you lose just so you'll have to cut that fucking mop on your head."

Like most exceptional athletes, Jordy was a little superstitious. Some wouldn't wash their socks when they were on a hot streak, some needed to do the exact same pre-game ritual every single time. When the Phantoms were winning, Jordy wouldn't cut his hair.

Any of it.

"I'm not worried about his hair," Graham said.

"Thank you." Jordy gave Graham a thankful nod.

"It's the beard. Have you really been trying to grow that for four weeks?"

Jordy glared at him. "You know, I'm kind of rooting for the little old lady now. I hope she makes you cry."

CHAPTER TWO

"I think I'm going to have to kill him," Eloise announced early Monday morning. Stardust Coffee was empty except for herself, Sybil, and Connor.

"You can't tell us that," Sybil said from behind the espresso machine.

"Why not?"

The hiss of the steamer wand punctuated Sybil's sigh. "Plausible deniability. We need to be able to confidently say under oath that we had no knowledge that you were planning a murder."

Eloise pouted into her chai latte. If she couldn't plot the murder of one Graham Thatcher with her two best friends, who could she plot it with?

Kiki. Kiki would happily help her plot several gruesome murders while Eloise tried to make the accounting software she used to keep track of the Crane Hotel's finances produce more favorable figures. Kiki probably even had a coffin for the body. There had to be perks to having a goth as an employee, because having her work the front desk was not dispelling any of the rumors that the place was haunted.

"It's kind of disconcerting," Connor said, leaning against the counter, even though he knew Sybil hated it when people leaned on her counters. "You look so sweet and innocent, and then you spout off murder plans like you've just decided what's for dinner."

Eloise looked up at Connor. Way up. Like all the men in his family, he was obnoxiously tall and broad-shouldered, with thick blond hair cut in a style she called the Captain America. Actually, Connor kind of looked like what would happen if Thor and Captain America had a baby. Captain Thor. It was a shame that she only saw him as a friend. Sybil said she felt the same way, even if they had been voted Most Likely To Get Married their senior year of high school.

"I'm just saying that you could probably get away with it," Connor continued. "A jury might even call it justifiable homicide."

"Do not take legal advice from high school English teachers. His frame of reference is *To Kill A Mockingbird* and *Twelve Angry Men*." Sybil put his coffee down on the counter next to his elbow and flicked the back of his arm to try to get him to move. "And I really mean it about the plausible deniability. I'm trying to be the first Morgan to not end up in handcuffs. I won't be an accessory before, during, or after the fact."

"Leave you out of my murder plans. Noted." Eloise looked up at Connor again. "Want to help me hide a body later this week? His lordship has finally decided to grace us with his presence."

"I could finally catch up on my backlog of books in prison," Connor said thoughtfully. Sybil let out a frustrated groan.

"We had a plan," Sybil reminded her. "You were going to convince him to come here, see the hotel, impart your vision for it, and then spend his piles of money to make it happen. No room for murder, as satisfying as it would be. You can't use his money if he's dead."

Eloise sighed. That had been the plan a year ago when Edgar, her former boss, had died just as she was making some headway convincing him to do some much-needed renovations to the historic Crane Hotel. It had seemed like a great plan when she found out she had been promoted from manager to co-owner in Edgar's will, and it had seemed like a truly fantastic plan when she discovered that her co-owner was Edgar's great-nephew Graham, who was one of those obscenely wealthy tech guys with the funds to make all her wildest dreams come true. Yes, that had been the plan before Eloise had discovered that Graham Can't-Be-Bothered-To-Communicate Thatcher had no interest in the hotel, including chipping in for necessary—and very expensive—repairs and various disasters that plagued a hundred-plus-year-old building.

Sybil had a point, even if she didn't like it. He might be a year late, but Eloise needed his money. The check engine light she was doing her best to ignore reminded her of that every single day. Whatever monetary gains they had made during the summer tourist season and the popular Cranberry Festival were immediately eaten up by expenses.

"I don't see why he needs to show up at all," Eloise grumbled as she picked up the very large and very sweet cold brew Sybil had put on the counter. "My life would be easier if he would just send me a blank check. With interest, for being such a dick."

"Eloise Price, I think that's the meanest thing I've ever heard you say about anyone in public." Sybil beamed at her. "I'm so proud."

"Check back with me later this week. I'll probably have more rotten things to say." Eloise touched her head to Connor's shoulder because her hands were too full for a hug, and gave Sybil an awkward pinky wave. "I'll see you both later."

It was a beautiful morning, cool and crisp, and Eloise tried to count her blessings to restore some positive energy before she tried to start her car. She was employed, she employed others, this season of *Claymore Abbey* was the perfect mix of swoony and bonkers, she had wonderful friends, and lived in a town so quaint she wanted to pinch herself to make sure she wasn't dreaming.

"Please start," she whispered before putting the key in the ignition. It clicked once before turning over, and her shoulders relaxed. Once she could scrape the money together, she would take her car to Dale to triage the repairs that needed to be done.

Once she had the money. That had been her line for the last three years since she had moved to Crane Cove to become the manager of the Crane Hotel. The salary hadn't been enough to get ahead, but it had been enough to get by, and at one point she'd had money in her savings account.

It had been a while since she'd had money in her savings account.

Eloise sipped her chai latte as she waited for her turn at the stop sign. A car at all four signs counted as the morning rush hour now that tourist season had passed. It was a good thing Sybil didn't charge her for coffee since things would be slow until Spring Break.

Her brain buzzed with what needed to be done before Graham Thatcher arrived on Thursday. It wasn't an inspection, she kept telling herself, but she wanted the hotel to look its best. There was a lot riding on this meeting.

The drive was short, less than two miles, which was not a lot of brainstorming time. Flowers on the front desk would be a nice touch. She could get the lobby throw pillows dry-cleaned. A thorough dusting could be completed during her morning shift at the front desk. By the time she parked near the entrance of the grand hotel, she was almost cheery again.

Almost.

Eloise put the large iced coffee down on the front desk and frowned at the girl behind the desk. "You look like Wednesday Addams."

Kiki looked up from her book, which had a black-and-red cover and screamed "Danger!" to Eloise's brain, and smiled sincerely. "Thank you. That's exactly what I was going for."

Eloise could feel the first throbs of a headache coming on. "But I thought we talked about dressing a little more...cheerfully. For the guests."

"Oh, that reminds me. Room 313 checked out at about three a.m." Kiki placed her bookmark between the pages, and Eloise made an effort to avoid looking at the title, which probably contained the words "blood" or "murder." "Elias must have been feeling frisky last night."

Eloise definitely had a headache now. She circled behind the elegantly carved mahogany front desk and opened a drawer, taking out a bottle of ibuprofen and popping two into her mouth. She shot a glare at the portrait on the wall. Despite the overactive imaginations of the locals, Eloise did not believe that Elias Crane, the founder of Crane Cove, was haunting the hotel that he had built. She was absolutely positive that ghosts did not exist. Just like she was absolutely positive that the eyes of the portrait did not follow her around the lobby.

Eloise took a few steps to the left. Then a few steps to the right.

She was *almost* positive the eyes of the portrait weren't following her.

"I tried to tell them that he's a friendly spirit, even if his wife did murder him."

"Kiki," Eloise groaned. "You shouldn't be telling guests that there's a ghost, period, because there is definitely not a ghost."

"He's never hurt anyone before."

"Because he doesn't exist."

"They said they heard bumps—"

"And I hope you reminded them that our property is over one hundred years old and makes plenty of noises, especially as the weather gets cooler."

"Well," Kiki began thoughtfully, and Eloise braced for the other shoe to drop. "Even if I had, I don't think that explains the voices."

Eloise wished she had something stronger than over-the-counter pain medication. During the summer, when the tourists poured into Crane Cove and the surrounding towns that dotted the Oregon Coast, it was easy to play off any of the bumps, thumps, creaks, and voices a guest might have heard and attributed to the definitely-not-real ghost. But it was low season. A quick glance at their reservation system would have told her that they were below half capacity, and the adjacent rooms were likely unoccupied to provide quiet and privacy to the guests they did have.

"Oh! And we got a call—"

Eloise put her hand up to silence Kiki. "Please. I can't handle any more disasters this morning. Unless I've won the lottery, I don't want to know."

"If you say so, boss." Kiki picked up her large iced coffee and her purse to head out. "I'll see you later. Try to stay out of trouble."

Eloise opened her work email and made a show of checking it until she was certain Kiki was gone. One more surreptitious glance around the lobby to confirm that she was alone, and she pulled up the FanForum homepage. In the upper right-hand corner was the little envelope with a message notification. Her breath caught, and she made a concentrated effort to steady it.

He had messaged back.

Of course he had. Foolproof42 almost never made her wait for replies. She felt guilty by comparison, since she could only really check her messages when she was at work or somewhere with decent Wi-Fi, and then she was trying to hide her clandestine correspondence from Kiki, her other employees, and her friends. Even with terrible cell phone reception, news spread quickly around Crane Cove, and Eloise engaging in anonymous emails with a man would be News. By the time the story got back to her, she would be writing sexually explicit emails for money. Which, upon consideration, might not be a bad way to raise money to fix up the hotel if Graham Thatcher kept stonewalling her.

> Foolproof42: I'm going to be on a business trip for at least a few days. I don't know how active I'll be on here while I'm gone.

Eloise sagged, all her joy at having a message rushing out of her life a balloon losing air before it could be tied off. It was silly to be sad. Logically, she knew that. But logic played a very small role in her relationship with the mysterious Foolproof42. It was the logical part of her brain that kept her from revealing details about her life that could identify her in a Google search. Where she lived. What she did for work. Where she had grown up and gone to school.

That didn't stop her from telling him other things. He knew about her teapot collection that was collecting dust in her parents' garage. He knew her favorite color was periwinkle, just like the blouse she was wearing today. And just the other day she had told him that Christmas was her favorite holiday because her grandmother sent a giant box of cookies every single year.

It was entirely her fault that, even after months of talking almost daily, they didn't know even the basics. If given the chance, Eloise was sure Foolproof42 would tell her more about himself. Men didn't have the same internet safety rules.

She typed out a response.

> Little_Teapot: Trying to give me a taste of my own medicine?

Eloise was about to exit the chat to start crossing items off her mile long to-do list when she saw the three little dots that indicated he was writing a response.

> Foolproof42: Never. Unlike Christian, I wouldn't leave and NEVER COME BACK. I'll write on my journey. It just might not be as frequent.

> Little_Teapot: You should write an impassioned letter to Peter Green and the showrunners. Justice for Lady Amanda's love life!

> Foolproof42: I have half a mind to do just that. It would be so much more fun than the work I'm supposed to be doing.

Eloise's fingers hovered over the keys. She could ask. What would it hurt if she knew a little bit more about him? She knew *she* wasn't a deranged stalker/murderer.

> Little_Teapot: What do you do?

The wait for the three little dots was agonizing. She forced herself to minimize the window, because the longer she stared, the more she was convinced she'd overstepped. If she checked her work email, she bargained, she could check to see if he had answered her question.

Eloise wished she hadn't opened her work email. Sitting at the top of her inbox, like a letter from the IRS, was an email from *him*.

Ms. Price,

Per my last email, I would rather discuss the property when I arrive. We've remained at an impasse despite our correspondence this last year. Either you'll convince me this place is worth saving, or I'll get you to agree to sell.

Regards,

Graham Thatcher

Dickhead.

Eloise decided one email from Graham Thatcher deserved a reward. There was a message waiting for her.

> Foolproof42: If I was a smarter man, I'd hold out until you told me something else about yourself. But I'm not. I own my own business.

What kind of business did he own? The upside to the slow season was that it left a lot of time for daydreaming. In her fantasy, he owned an overstuffed used bookstore, with a shop cat curled up in the window, sunning itself among the display. And he wore knit sweaters and always had a cup of tea nearby.

Eloise let the warmth of her fantasy about Foolproof42 carry her through her morning catastrophes.

Buying the property when Edgar had been ready to retire had been her dream from the moment she first saw it. Now that she owned it—or at least half of it—it was more of a night-mare. The quote from the electrician just to *look* at the flickering lights made a sizeable dent in her mood. She had a sickening feeling that the quote from the plumber to try and find the cause of all the leaks was going to be just as bad, if not worse.

Was this what it felt like to be the captain of the *Titanic*? Was she doomed to have her dream sink beneath her, helpless to stop the rising level of the water, even as she asked the band to keep playing bravely on the deck?

She hadn't replaced any of the summer staff, and she'd happily accepted their cook's resignation because it meant she had a good excuse to shut down the dining room. Not ordering food that would get thrown out because no one was eating it saved her money.

The budget just needed a little tweaking to account for more repairs. She could tweak.

This is fine. I'm fine. Everything is fine.

"Hello?"

Eloise jumped, barely catching herself on the edge of her stool before she fell. Her pulse was hammering, and her hand came to rest on her chest to make sure her heart was still safely in her ribcage. With a steadying breath, she looked up at the voice that had startled her... and promptly forgot how to breathe.

A man looked down at her, one eyebrow slightly raised in casual amusement. His hair was dark enough that she couldn't tell if it was brown or black, and it looked recently cut. Eloise remembered her own split ends, and she wished she had spent a little more time getting ready this morning. In an effort to stop admiring his hair, she forced her gaze down, settling on his mouth, which was her next mistake. Eloise did not have an abundance of free time, but she would have happily dedicated every single spare minute to the exploration and study of that mouth.

Stop. Staring. Look him in the eye and say something.

His eyes were her absolute undoing. Eloise didn't know how long she spent deliberating the precise shade of green, but when he cleared his throat, her cheeks flamed.

"Um, hi," she stammered, trying to be graceful as she got off her stool, but only succeeding in half stepping, half falling. Eloise caught herself on the front desk, her face getting hotter by the second as the beautiful stranger in front of her fought to keep the corners of his mouth from turning upward.

"Was it interesting?"

She had no earthly idea what he was talking about, and she fought to keep down the panic that he had said something while she'd been gaping at him. "Was what interesting?"

He gestured to her computer, and Eloise got a little light-headed. He had rolled the sleeves of his black shirt up so his forearms were bare. They were strong without being overly muscular, his white skin sun-kissed tan.

"What you were reading. You seemed invested."

Eloise needed to pull it together. Nearly swooning over forearms was an activity she saved exclusively for *Claymore Abbey*. Though, as she took another moment to appreciate his face, he did look a bit like Lovingford, the Duke of Walston. Tall, dark, and positively sinful in black.

"I guess you don't really do small talk," he said, resting his forearms on the front desk. The muscles there flexed, and Eloise swallowed hard. "Any chance I could check in?"

Oh, if only a hole would open up in the carpet and swallow her whole. Or maybe the chandelier that hung in the lobby could do her a favor and come crashing down. That would be an excellent distraction from the fact that every single one of her people skills had abandoned her in her time of need. This man did not have a single safe spot on his body for her to look at.

"Yes," she finally managed, turning her attention to the ancient desk computer. "Sorry, the reservations program is more advanced than this computer, so it takes a while..."

"It's fine."

Even his voice was attractive. Eloise wished she had never stood up because her knees had the structural integrity of a popsicle stick house built by a five-year old.

"Are you from around here?" There. She could make small talk as long as she didn't look at him. Her brain regained some functionality the longer she looked away.

"No. I'm from California," he answered.

"Ah. I would have guessed New York."

"What makes you say that?"

Eloise couldn't resist looking at him. He was like a magnet.

"That looks like an expensive haircut, you're wearing black, and I know that's not a cheap suitcase."

There was a beat of silence, and Eloise's stomach dropped as she was certain she had said too much. Then he chuckled, dropping his head like he was trying to hide his amusement. The sound was deep and warm, heating her from the inside out.

"Is that funny?"

"A little. My friend told me I looked like a New Yorker when he dropped me off at the airport this morning." He smiled, and a dimple appeared in his left cheek. *Fuck.* "I just thought he was being grumpy because it was so early."

"Must be a good friend to take you to the airport."

"Well, I let him crash at my house, so he owes me."

"Owes you? Doesn't he pay rent?"

The man shook his head. "No. Then he would *live* there, and Peter, well, he's kind of like a stray cat. I made the mistake of feeding him once, and now he won't stop coming around."

Eloise laughed and was rewarded with another brain scattering smile.

"At least you got a chauffeur out of it," she teased, unable to stop grinning.

"But the thing is, Peter is a terrible driver. Two-star rating at best. One of those stars would be because he's obnoxiously nice and could hold a meaningful conversation with a wall."

Eloise's cheeks were starting to hurt. She smiled at people every day, but she hadn't smiled this much or this hard in a long time.

She turned back to the computer that had finally loaded their reservation system. "So, what brings you to Crane Cove?"

"Um, business, actually."

There was an awkward hitch in his voice that hadn't been there before. What kind of business did he have in town? Usually Eloise knew if someone important was coming to stay.

"Oh?" Eloise hoped that was enough to prompt him.

Before he could answer, the phone rang. Eloise gave him an apologetic smile. "Sorry. Do you mind if I grab that?"

"No, not at all. I have nowhere else to be."

With her most chipper customer service voice, Eloise answered the phone. "The Crane Hotel, this is Eloise. How may I help you today?"

The stranger's eyebrows came together in a frown.

"Eloise!" It was Kiki.

"Kiki, shouldn't you still be asleep?" Eloise glanced at the clock and was surprised to find that morning had slipped into the afternoon while she had been trying to rework the budget.

"How could I sleep? I need to know how it went!"

"How what went?" Eloise gave him another apologetic smile, but the cryptic frown he'd developed didn't shift.

"Graham Thatcher! What is he like in person? I'm dying to know."

"Kiki, Graham Thatcher isn't supposed to be here until Thursday. And since I do not smell brimstone—"

"No. That's what I was trying to tell you this morning." Kiki sighed heavily. "You haven't even been into the office yet. I left you a note. Graham Thatcher's assistant or someone called this morning and said his plans had changed and he was coming today. He should be there by now."

Eloise felt cold all over even as heat rushed to her face. She could hear her brain connecting the dots. The expensive suitcase. The impeccably tailored clothing. That he was in town on business and no one had bothered to call her for a favor.

"Kiki," she said hoarsely. "I'm going to need to call you back."

Eloise set the phone down on the receiver and hoped he didn't notice that her hand was shaking.

"Brimstone, huh?"

Dammit. A small, eternally and hopelessly optimistic part of her had prayed that he may have been afflicted with a sudden and temporary case of deafness and had not heard any of that. But he had. And through the buzzing in her ears, Eloise was having a hard time telling if he was amused or annoyed. She would have bet the meager funds in her bank account that it was the latter.

"I, um..."

"Don't get shy on me now. You were just getting warmed up. Why don't you call her back and you can mention my cloven hooves?" His jaw tightened. "The pitchfork would have been a dead giveaway, but TSA confiscated it."

"Should have checked a bag," Eloise muttered, and turned her full attention back to the computer to avoid those intensely green eyes. Of course the gorgeous stranger she had been trying —and likely failing—to flirt with had been Graham Thatcher. Of course he would change his plans at the last minute to suit himself and no one else. And as she typed his name into the reservation system to pull up his information, all her careful planning from that morning went up in smoke.

"You're not what I was expecting," Graham said, his eyes darting around the room.

"Sorry to disappoint." Eloise looked at the room the system had assigned him. Four twenty-three. She hoped he enjoyed erratic heating and a window that rattled when the wind blew.

No. She should change that. The hotel needed to put its best foot forward.

He straightened to his full height. "No need to delay the inevitable. Let's step into your office and get to work."

Eloise's heart shot up into her throat. "We can't."

His frown deepened into a scowl. "Why not?"

"Because I'm not ready."

"How is that possible? You knew I was coming."

"On Thursday." Eloise took out a blank keycard from the drawer and put it on top of the machine. "It's Monday. I can't drop everything because you decided this was more convenient for you."

A muscle in his annoyingly perfect jaw twitched. "What am I supposed to do until Thursday?"

"I don't know." Eloise wrote down his room number on one of her periwinkle sticky notes, stuck it to his key, and held them out to him. "You're smart. You'll figure something out."

Silence swirled around them. If this had been a western movie, the locals would be ducking inside the nearest building for cover. Eloise was not a confrontational person, but Graham Thatcher brought something out in her.

With a heavy sigh, Graham took the key from her. Their fingertips brushed, and a jolt of awareness sparked from the point of contact straight to her belly. With anyone else, she would have considered it pleasant, but with him, she hoped it was static electricity.

She forced a tight smile. "Have a nice stay."

Graham returned her forced smile with one of his own—no teeth—and then turned on his heel, suitcase rolling helpless behind him as he stalked toward the elevator.

It was after she heard the ding announcing the arrival of the elevator that Eloise realized she had never switched his room. Graham was headed for the infamous room 423. She opened her mouth to shout for him to stop, but then closed it. A year's worth of resentment whispered in her ear to let him suffer for one night. Maybe that would convince him how dire the situation was.

She hoped his room was haunted.

CHAPTER THREE

It wasn't so much an elevator as it was an antique death trap that moved upward at a shuddering pace. Graham wished he had updated his will before getting inside.

He leaned against one of the mahogany walls and closed his eyes. How had this day gone so utterly and completely sideways?

Probably at the exact moment he'd realized Eloise Price was not a stern matron with half-moon glasses perched on the end of her nose, dressed in gray wool cardigans embroidered with flowers or cats. That was his fault for performing one perfunctory Google search and abandoning it when he got busy. His punishment was a lush angel that frowned at him with a full mouth. When she had smiled at him—a genuine smile, not her customer service one—all the blood required to power his brain had rushed south.

Graham rubbed his chest. It was oddly achy. What was the matter with him? He didn't completely lose his mind over women, especially women that ranked him with the devil.

The doors finally opened at the same halting pace as the elevator had risen, and Graham resolved to avoid the thing for the rest of his short trip. He was just up here to convince her that they should sell the hotel and then he could put hundreds of miles between himself and Eloise Price's perfect, distracting mouth.

Graham put his key card in the door and withdrew it quickly. The light blinked red. He glared at the door and tried again. Red. Resisting the urge to grind his teeth, Graham reinserted the key and drew it out slowly. This time it blinked green.

Finally.

He turned the handle and...nothing.

The door would not open.

Graham allowed himself a frustrated groan before trying again. And again. He was beginning to have vivid fantasies of burning down the building, or at least taking a wrecking ball to it, when a combination of quick entry and slow withdraw with a forceful twist of the handle finally granted him access to his room.

As he stepped inside, he shivered. He'd been in walk-in coolers with more warmth. His simmering temper was enough to keep him warm as he stalked over to the thermostat, which had been turned off, and after finding just the right way to touch the buttons to get them to work, he heard the ancient heater by the window kick on with a groan.

Rubbing his hands together, Graham turned in a slow semicircle to assess the situation. The room was...small. Which was surprising, given the age of the building. Edgar had boasted that The Crane Hotel had been built around the beginning of the twentieth century and had been a thoroughly modern building in its heyday. Not much had changed. The lobby reflected that, and the rooms did, too. A hodgepodge of several decades worth of half-hearted and poorly funded renovation attempts made the hotel look shabbier than it probably was.

"Uncle Edgar, what were you thinking?" Graham muttered,

taking his cell phone out of his pocket. The one flickering bar was not going to do him any good. Cell service had dropped off on his drive; he assumed it would resume once he got into Crane Cove, but he had been wrong. He needed to check in with work, and by this time he was sure Peter would be researching how to call out the National Guard, the Coast Guard, the Park Service, and the highway patrol because he hadn't given him a call to say that he had made it safely. Peter had been watching slasher films for research and was convinced Graham was going to get a flat tire and be abducted by a hillbilly who wanted to wear his skin as a waistcoat.

His stomach growled. He needed to get some food, maybe some coffee. Then hopefully he could find a signal before the search and rescue team descended on Crane Cove. Maybe by the time he got back, his room wouldn't be the same temperature as an ice-skating rink.

A plan grounded him. He felt secure with a plan. With a plan, he might even be able to handle Eloise Price and her beguiling mouth and big blue eyes. Though he'd probably need something on par with Eisenhower's designs for D-Day to conquer that hurdle.

———

There was no parking in historic downtown Crane Cove. There was no *driving* through it either.

The street was closed off at either end, presumably to preserve the brick pavers. As a business strategy to get tourists to stroll past shops they may have never glanced twice at, he had to admire it. As someone who had left his raincoat in his room and had been too embarrassed to turn around and walk back up the grand staircase to get it, he did not like it at all.

The storefronts were uniform, with carved wooden signs

hung from wrought-iron arms above the doorways. There were a few other people out, all appropriately attired for the unpredictable weather of a Pacific Northwest fall. Graham was damp all over, like he had stood directly under a vegetable mister. A drop of icy rain slid down his spine. He looked up at the darkening clouds that were threatening more than a gentle pitter-patter and ducked into a large white building at the end of the street.

He blinked a few times as his eyes adjusted to the dim light, and he took a deep breath. Yeast and pine filled his nostrils. Leather-topped stools were lined up along the bar, with a few small high tops positioned along the other wall. It was empty, but a classic country song he couldn't remember the name of was drifting through the kitchen doors. At least he hoped it was a kitchen. His stomach growled.

Graham sat down at the bar just as a man that his attorney Athena would have described as a "bear" pushed through the swinging doors. He was likely several inches taller than Graham and had at least fifty pounds on him, almost all of it muscle. His blond curls were pulled back into a bun, and he looked at Graham for a long moment.

"You haven't been there long, have you?" he asked, stepping behind the bar.

Graham shook his head. "No, I just sat down. Needed to get out of the rain."

That earned him a friendly grin. "I'm going to guess that you're not from around here."

"What gave it away?"

"Besides the Beverly Hills Johnny Cash look?"

"The what?"

"Johnny Cash. The Man in Black. You've heard—" He gave an exasperated sigh and pointed to some unseen speaker.

"Johnny Cash. This man. 'Walk The Line.' 'Boy Named Sue.' 'Ring of Fire'. Ringing any bells?"

Another man came out from the back. He had the same blond hair, but his was cut short. If it hadn't been, Graham didn't think he would have been able to tell them apart.

"Cole, the joke isn't funny if you have to explain it." The second man held out his hand to Graham. "Chase McMahon. Welcome to Crane Cove and Cranberry Brothers Brewing."

Graham had always thought Jordy had large hands, but Chase McMahon was giving him a run for his money.

"Cranberry Brothers?" Graham asked once Chase released his hand. Cole slid a slim paper menu in front of him. "Where did you get that name?"

It was Cole who answered as Chase filled a pint glass with a dark beer. "Our family owns a cranberry farm. It was the best thing we could come up with."

"Beat out Bog Brothers by a mile." Chase put the beer in front of Graham and nudged it toward him. "Here. I've got a knack for guessing what people like."

Graham took a tentative sip. Normally he wasn't much of a beer drinker, and when he did, he preferred to stick to the lighter varieties, like pilsners, but this was incredible. It was deep and complex, with notes of chocolate and some fruit he couldn't quite place, and it was smooth with only the slightest bite from the hops.

"Holy shit. This is delicious."

Chase gave Cole a smug grin. "The streak continues."

Cole rolled his eyes. "Everyone likes that beer. Our mother likes that beer."

"Still counts," Chase crowed, and Cole pointedly turned his focus back to Graham.

"Are you hungry? Lunch is kind of light during the week, but if you come back Thursday night, we do barbecue."

"I'm starving, actually," Graham admitted, taking another gulp of his beer. "And not picky right now."

Cole nodded and went back through the double doors. Chase rested his forearms on the bar, and Graham wondered if he had gotten this big from owning a brewery or if he ripped apart trees with his bare hands in his spare time.

"So, what brings you to town? You missed the Cranberry Festival."

"There's a cranberry festival?" Graham could not have heard that correctly.

"Yup. It's the last big event of the summer tourist season. We've got a Cranberry Queen and everything."

"A Cranberry Queen..." Graham felt like he had stumbled into a quaint 1950s television show. "I'm, um, here on business actually."

"Business?" Chase's eyebrows rose. "Tell me more."

"I don't know how much there is to tell."

"Where are you staying?" Chase was persistent when it came to making small talk.

"The Crane Hotel."

Chase's expression brightened, the grin that always seemed to be hiding in the corners of his mouth widening into a full-blown smile.

"That's great! Eloise will take excellent care of you. She is, and I don't think I'm exaggerating here, the world's nicest person. I actually brewed that beer for her."

Graham frowned, looking down into his half-empty pint glass. Maybe there was another Eloise at the hotel. "There is no way we're thinking of the same person."

"Sort of short, kind of curvy, brown curly hair, big blue eyes? Kind of looks like one of those Renaissance angels?"

Dammit.

Naturally the world's nicest person would hate him. And

Graham didn't know what he hated more: that she didn't like him, or that he cared now that he'd met her. Because she did look like an angel from a Renaissance painting, and he needed to nip the jealousy that flared instinctually right in the bud.

"Sounds about right," Graham bit out, draining the rest of his beer. "How long have you been open?"

"About three and a half years."

"How's business?"

"Pretty good, actually. Can't complain."

Cole came out from the kitchen as Chase refilled his beer. He put a chicken salad sandwich with potato chips in front of Graham.

"Are those cranberries?"

"We try to sneak them in wherever we can. This is our grandma's recipe. Passed down through several generations of beleaguered McMahon women who needed to find creative ways to get rid of extra cranberries." Cole put a jar on the bar. "Pickle?"

"Please." Graham took the spear from Cole, biting into it while he thought. The brewery seemed to be doing well, and the town looked like it was able to support a variety of businesses. But a brewery or a coffee shop were less expensive to run than a hotel. And they were starting in the hole with all the repairs and updates the building needed. Selling it made the most sense. Let it be someone else's problem.

He just had to convince Eloise.

CHAPTER FOUR

"You didn't actually say that, did you?" Sybil asked, filling her wine glass beyond the halfway mark.

"I did. And then I gave him the one room in the place that even makes me wonder if the hotel is haunted."

Eloise sighed and sipped at her merlot as Sybil cackled gleefully. Mondays were for Wine and Whining, a tradition between her, Sybil, and Connor. After the day she'd had, she needed her friends more than ever.

"He deserved it," Sybil said, picking out a chocolate-covered almond from the charcuterie board she'd assembled for the night. "And frankly, I'm proud of you."

"Did he?" Connor countered, not even flinching at the icy glare that Sybil shot his way. "It sounds like you were getting along before you knew who he was. Is it possible he's not quite as bad as you thought?"

"Connor!" Sybil snapped. "Whose team are you on? We don't like him."

"I haven't met him," Connor pointed out, snatching the almond Sybil was reaching for out from under her fingers and tossing it in his mouth. "You're really very suspicious of people. Did you know that?"

"Better to be suspicious than murdered."

Eloise had to stifle her laughter in her wine glass as Sybil and Connor sniped at each other.

"Anyway," Eloise said, holding out her glass for Connor to refill, breaking up the spat before it got bloody. "That's enough about me. How's school going?"

"It's fine." He shrugged as he picked up his red pen and the stack of quizzes he had been grading while Eloise relayed her tale of workplace woe. "I must have been too nice to my AP kids last year because they're really phoning it in right now. I'm plotting their demise for next week."

"Do you enjoy terrorizing teenagers?" Eloise asked, settling back into Sybil's big, comfy blue velvet couch.

"It's my favorite pastime." Connor grinned at her, his blue eyes sparkling with glee. "I'm making my team do hills tomorrow."

"Why anyone willingly runs without being chased by an axe murderer, I will never understand," Sybil said.

"Some of us enjoy it," Connor argued. "It's good for you. Releases endorphins."

"I'm with Sybil on this one. Running is the worst."

Connor rolled his eyes. "I can't with you people."

"You have to be nice to us. We're volunteering at your cross-country meet on Saturday," Eloise reminded him. "Who else will hold the clipboard and the stopwatch?"

"I could always offer some of my students extra credit."

"And ruin your sparkling reputation as a hard-ass?" Sybil teased, pouring the remnants of the wine bottle into his glass.

Eloise discreetly pulled out her phone. One of her favorite things about having Wine and Whining night at Sybil's—and it was always at Sybil's because Connor still lived with his parents while he saved up to buy a house, and Eloise didn't want them knowing where she was living—was that Sybil had good Wi-Fi. So, while Sybil and Connor rehashed some old drama from high school that she wasn't privy to because she hadn't grown up in Crane Cove, Eloise checked to see if Foolproof42 had responded to her last message.

> Little_Teapot: What kind of business?

> Foolproof42: Something dark and mysterious. Does that make me cool? I'm shooting for cool.

> Foolproof42: Today has been really weird. I think I've been adopted by some locals. Or kidnapped. It's hard to tell if this is a hostage situation. Send help.

"What's so funny?" Sybil nudged Eloise's leg with her foot.

"Hmm?" Eloise looked up from her phone to see her friends studying her.

"You're smiling at your phone. Did you decide to try dating again?" Sybil tried to take a peek, but Eloise clutched her phone to her chest. "I hope you're not using an app. That's how you get murdered."

"No," Eloise answered, typing out a quick response once Sybil looked away. "Can you imagine the results around here? They'd all be McMahons."

Sybil laughed, and Connor groaned.

"Can we not discuss dating? My mom has been particularly insufferable lately." Connor drained his wine glass. "She acts like you were her last great hope, Eloise."

"Me? What about Sybil?"

"I'm a lost cause. All of her boys see me as a sister. We crushed that dream ages ago."

"Bitsy would have made a good mother-in-law," Eloise mused as she nursed the last few sips of her wine.

"I have two more brothers," Connor offered. "Chris is in vet school, and Clark does... something for the government. You could still get invited to Christmas."

"Oh no. Chris and Clark are far too eligible. My mother would be proud of me, and then where would I be?" Eloise looked down at her empty wine glass and wished there was more. Her mother was a two-bottles-of-wine conversation, not a glass and a half. "Do you think if I begged, Bitsy would invite me to Christmas? Or maybe Thanksgiving, as a trial run?"

"The cranberry sauce is unrivaled," Sybil said reverently. "I would highly recommend begging."

———

Little_Teapot: Send up smoke signals and I'll come find you.

"That position cannot be comfortable," Cole said, passing Graham the bowl of pretzels that a silent and extremely intimidating bartender the twins had introduced as Moonie had just refilled.

"If I hold my arm like this, I get cell phone service," Graham told him, shoving a handful of pretzels in his mouth in a vain attempt to soak up some of the alcohol he'd imbibed trying to keep up with the twins. "Barely."

Graham wasn't sure exactly how it had happened, but he had spent the entire afternoon with Chase and Cole. Then the afternoon turned into the evening, and they had taken him to a pizza place that made him feel like he was in New York—which meant it was incredibly small, questionably clean, and served what was possibly the best pizza he'd ever had. He was going to go to sleep dreaming about that sauce.

From there they'd given him a short and colorful tour of downtown Crane Cove. Who owned what, who they were related to, how long their family had lived in town, and the Cranberry Festival feud of 1968 that had lasted for forty years. The crash course on local history was illuminating and overwhelming. The tour had concluded at the Neon Moon, a dive bar that either got its name from the bartender or vice versa.

The moment Graham had gotten even a smidgen of cell service, his phone had begun vibrating with texts, emails, and voicemails. He was still trying to read through the group chat he was in with Peter, Jordy, and Sam. Peter had spent most of the day speculating on what had happened to Graham and all the ways he could have died. He had also taken the opportunity to change the name of the chat to Brunch Bros.

Peter: I'm giving Graham until the morning to respond or I'm getting the jackets made.

Jordy: I need a frame of reference. T-Birds or Pink Ladies?

Sam: T-Birds seems cost prohibitive. Silk bomber jackets are definitely in right now.

Peter: I feel like we could all pull off a blue or a green.

Graham: We are not getting Brunch Bros jackets.

Peter: He lives!

Peter: You were supposed to call.

Peter: How did it go? Were you charming?

> Peter: Jordy, I need clarification. Grease or Grease 2?

> Jordy: There was a Grease 2?

> Peter: Michelle Pfeiffer. It has a bowling number.

> Graham: It did not go well. Cell service is shit. I'm at a bar with twin Vikings.

> Jordy: Do I need to watch it?

> Peter: Do you enjoy campy goodness?

Keeping up with the rapid-fire nature of any text conversation that included Peter was futile so long as he had to send all of his messages twice. It didn't help that he was getting their responses in bunches as his phone dipped in and out of service depending on the angle of his hand. Graham would have to call Peter in the morning to catch him up on his strange trip.

"So, has Keeks told you the hotel is haunted yet?" Chase asked.

The word "haunted" caught Graham's attention. Eloise had never mentioned ghosts in any of her emails. He didn't believe in ghosts, but he could understand how some people might mistake the natural creaks and moans of an old building for spectral guests. Still, the hotel was over one hundred years old. If there had ever been potential...

"What is a Keeks and exactly how haunted?"

"Kiki," Cole said, shooting his twin a look that bordered on exasperated, "works at the hotel."

"You haven't met Kiki yet?" Chase was gobsmacked.

"Um, no. I don't think so?"

"Trust us, you will know Kiki when you meet her." Chase chuckled like he was privy to an inside joke. "Keeks tells everyone the hotel is haunted. And coming from her, I kind of believe it."

"Kiki thinks the hotel is haunted because the guy who built it died there," Cole explained.

"Murdered," Chase clarified, flagging down Moonie for another drink.

A shiver slid down Graham's back, and he frowned. "Just because someone died there doesn't mean it's haunted. People die in places all the time and you'd never know."

Chase leaned in close, pitching his voice into a low stage whisper. "People hear things. Moaning. Footsteps. Things move. TVs turn on by themselves. Doors shut when no one has touched them."

Cole gently shoved his shoulder. "Stop it. You're going to scare him."

Chase sat up straight and grinned. "No, I'm not. I bet Graham doesn't believe in ghosts. Right, Graham?"

"I don't," Graham confirmed, but added, "So is it haunted?"

Cole shrugged. "Don't really know. You'd have to ask Keeks."

Graham sighed and ordered a water. He needed to get back to the hotel and get some sleep. It had been an incredibly long day, and he was exhausted. In the morning he could try to be friendly and talk to Eloise about the hotel and maybe even be on a plane back to LA by the evening.

———

Graham was proud of himself when he opened his door on the second try. He took two steps inside and stopped. It was a sauna. Sweat immediately formed on his forehead as he marched to the window and forced it open. He shoved his head outside and gulped the crisp night air like it was water.

He remembered turning on the heater before he left, and now he knew why it had been turned off in the first place. After a few more deep breaths, he went to the thermostat. Strange. It read sixty-nine, but if he had to guess, it was ten to twenty degrees warmer in the room.

Graham pressed the down arrow. The display did nothing. He pressed the up arrow. Nothing. Graham pressed every button with no results. The light breeze from the window was only helping marginally. Beads of sweat slithered down his back.

Maybe if he snuck up on it...

Down. Down. Down.

Nothing.

Graham rested his forehead on the wall. It was late. All he wanted out of life was to take a shower and then fall into a nice, eight-hour coma. No dreams. Just sleep.

He could go downstairs and ask for a new room. This one was rather obviously Eloise's idea of payback. Graham had to give her credit. As far as revenge went, alternately trying to freeze him out or roast him to death smacked of evil genius. The door that needed dinner and a movie before it would open was a particularly nice touch. He should be annoyed, but there was a sliver of respect for the level of pure pettiness.

Tomorrow, he resolved, he would do better.

BANG!

Graham jumped more than a foot in the air. When he came back down, he felt like his organs were still suspended mid-air. His heart had relocated to his throat, and his stomach was definitely up in his ribcage. Slowly, he turned.

It was only the window. Somehow, it had slammed shut, though it had felt secure when he had lifted it a few minutes ago. The hair on the back of his neck stood up as he recalled the twins talking about the man that had been allegedly murdered in the hotel.

"Ghosts do not exist," he said, mostly to convince himself. The window probably didn't work anymore, like everything else in the room.

Saying it didn't make him feel better. He sat on the bed and reached for the phone. Sam would be awake. He had terrible bouts of insomnia. And Sam wouldn't ask a lot of questions or spin his imagination further out of control, unlike the other two. It was why, after he found out he had inherited a hotel he didn't want and couldn't get rid of easily, he had talked to Sam first. Yes, Sam would calm him down.

Graham put the receiver to his ear, and then dropped the phone like it had burned him.

That was definitely not a dial tone. And he definitely could not stay in this room.

———

"Could you describe the noise?"

At the front desk, Graham searched his brain for a relevant comparison. The young woman behind the desk—Kiki, he assumed from the McMahon brothers' vague description—leaned forward, her delicate chin resting atop her laced fingers, dark brown eyes unblinking as she waited for his answer.

"It, um..." Graham shifted. "I guess it was kind of like a demonic dolphin. Maybe?"

"Could you recreate the noise?" she asked, indifferent to what he'd said.

He had stepped into the Twilight Zone. In a normal hotel, a guest coming down to the front desk in the middle of the night with all their belongings complaining that their room was potentially haunted would have been cause for concern. At least a gasp of surprise. But here, an elegant goth merely quizzed him about the details like they were talking about his last vacation and she wanted to go next year.

"Uh...no."

Her burgundy mouth turned down at the corners. "Drats. I've never been able to hear it before." She turned to the front desk computer, which groaned in protest as she clicked through a few different pages. "I suppose you'll want a new room. Can I get your name?"

"Graham Thatcher."

Dark eyebrows rose and she swiveled her high stool back toward him slowly. "*You're* Graham Thatcher?"

Graham could feel the blush radiating from the top of his head down to his neck. The way she looked at him made him want to squirm. Acute fascination mixed with morbid curiosity, like he was part of a sideshow at a traveling circus.

"Yes?"

"You don't sound very sure."

"I'm pretty sure." He leaned on the desk, exhaustion permeating his marrow. "You're Kiki, right?"

Her eyes narrowed suspiciously. "How did you know that?"

"Cole and Chase McMahon told me to look out for you." He raked a hand through his hair as she sized him up. "Has anyone ever told you that you kind of look like Morticia Addams?"

"Well, aren't you an absolute doll." Kiki smiled widely, her pale cheeks flushing. "I think I'll forget half the rotten things I've heard Eloise muttering about you."

"Only half?" Graham teased, trying to remember the bullet points of the lecture Peter had given him on being charming and polite, even if he didn't want to be there. He might be able to get further with Eloise if her employees liked him. "What exactly has she been saying about me?"

"It can get quite colorful, but she normally only says them when she doesn't think anyone can hear her." Kiki's blood red nails flew across the keyboard. "Hmm...what can I get you...Ah. How would you like a room with no neighbors? Should be nice and quiet."

"As long as it isn't haunted."

"It should be relatively ghost-free," Kiki responded cheerfully, making him a new room key. "But Elias does like to wander."

"That does not make me feel better," Graham said, taking the plastic key from her.

Kiki laughed, and the sound had a light, melodic quality that was at complete odds with the image she portrayed. "He's a friendly ghost, I promise, despite the circumstances that led to his demise. He just likes to make sure his hotel is running smoothly."

"Is it running smoothly?"

In the past year, Eloise had been rather elusive about the hotel operations. She would tell him that they needed to make repairs, or that renovations would be welcome, but very little about the health of the business. When he asked to see the books, she had sidestepped his request entirely. His response had been to stonewall. Graham had no interest in funneling cash to someone who might be trying to rob him blind.

"Eloise is a really good boss," Kiki began. "She covers for everyone, makes sure there's a cake on your birthday, actually listens if you have a problem." She pressed her lips together. "It's just been a rough year. She and Edgar were really close. And she loves this place, so the way things have been going has been, like, compounding trauma, or something."

"Right." Graham frowned. His relationship with his mother's family had been non-existent except for his great uncle Edgar. Edgar had always been there for him and his mother if they needed him. Hell, they'd lived with him when Graham was really little, before Edgar had taken the manager job at the Crane Hotel. They had been close until Graham's business had started to take off ten years ago and Graham got progressively worse at returning phone calls. Graham had been downright resentful when Edgar used the money he'd given him to buy the hotel instead of retiring. Why had he left the hotel to Graham and a woman Graham had never met until this afternoon? Edgar had talked about Eloise before, but clearly Graham had only been half listening, since he'd assumed the woman who'd kept Edgar in line the last few years had been so much older than she was. How many times had Edgar asked him to come visit? To come see why this place was so special? Guilt and regret fused into a heavy weight at the pit of his stomach.

"It's not your fault," Kiki said quickly. "I didn't mean that, if it came out that way. I'm just taking this psychology class, so I'm thinking way too much about this stuff, and I've got a lot of time to think at night..."

Graham was, for once, grateful to have someone word-vomit all over him.

"A psychology class? Are you in school?"

Kiki nodded. "I'm taking online classes through the community college. Though I'm still holding out hope that a rich woman will come in one night, fall madly in love with me, and ask me to run away with her. So if you know any eligible bachelorettes, send them my way."

Graham grinned. "I'll ask around. Goodnight, Kiki."

CHAPTER FIVE

Oregon.

He was in Oregon.

Eloise didn't know what to do with that information. Should she tell him that she was in Oregon, too? Would he want to meet? Did she finally want to meet her secret internet friend that she had the vaguest hint of a crush on? What if her fledgling feelings weren't returned in any capacity? Or—possibly worse—what if they were?

Watching reruns of *Claymore Abbey* hadn't helped. The season where tall, dark, and broody Lovingford had been brought to his knees—literally and figuratively—by shy wallflower Olivia had been on, and they were the couple that had bonded her and Foolproof42 on the forums.

Eloise tossed and turned, rotating her pillows to keep the side against her face cool. She put on an audiobook she'd listened to before on a half-hour timer. She added an extra blanket to her bed for the weight. Nothing helped. There was an aching emptiness between her thighs that had been there since the afternoon. She hated that her mind kept wandering back to Graham, his stupid dimpled smile, and those leanly muscled forearms.

"Oh, goddammit," she cursed, rolling onto her stomach and yanking open the top drawer of the nightstand. Her trusty vibrator rolled to the front. If she couldn't sleep, she might as well take care of her other problem.

The hum of the battery-powered device sent goosebumps skittering across her skin, and there was a rush of heat in her underwear. Yes, she'd had some good times with this particular toy. Lord knew she hadn't had any action in the last few months.

She pushed her silk pajama shorts down her legs and undid the top half of the buttons on her matching sleep shirt. Her nipples hardened in anticipation. If her body was this primed and ready to go, she'd needed this more than she thought she did.

Eloise relaxed into the mattress, closing her eyes to sink into a fantasy. A certain co-owner bubbled to the top of her mind. She sighed and tried to shove his image away, but it wouldn't budge. The memory of his deep, throaty chuckle warmed her all over again, and with a grumble, Eloise allowed Fantasy Graham into her space.

His hands were large and handled her firmly but gently, and she palmed her breast, pretending it was his fingers that plucked and pinched her nipple. She whimpered, teasing herself with the vibrator, running it through her wetness and grazing over her clit. In her fantasy, Graham lifted her onto the desk in the manager's office, his fingers caressing her through her soaked panties, while his other hand freed her breast from her dress— the green velvet cocktail dress in her closet, because it was her fantasy and she was going to look hot, dammit. His teeth scraped her throat, while he told her that he was going to get what he wanted, one way or another, except what he wanted now was her impaled on his hard, throbbing—

The vibrator died. And she was out of batteries.

She threw the vibrator to the side with a frustrated growl. Vibrators weren't supposed to get her all riled up and then leave her hanging. That was what regular men were for.

At least her fingers couldn't die on her.

Where had she been? Oh, yes, Graham had been telling her to turn over and put her hands on the desk so he could fuck her from behind. Eloise rolled onto her stomach, drawing her knees up to give herself better access. The first touch made her moan into her pillow. Doing this manually wasn't ideal, but she was so spun up that her orgasm was on the precipice.

Fantasy Graham teased her entrance with the tip of his cock, and Eloise moaned again as she worked her clit. So, so close...

The muffled sound of a door closing in the next room stopped her cold. No one was supposed to be in that room. No one was supposed to be in this part of the hotel. It wasn't even on the cleaning schedule anymore. Eloise knew because she was the one who made the cleaning schedule.

Living at the hotel had started as a temporary solution that past winter when she had lost the room she was renting to her landlord's elderly mother. It had been impossible to look him in the eye and say, "No, I have a lease, you can't kick me out." That had happened right after Sybil had told her that she needed to stick up for herself and demand that Graham deal with his half of the hotel responsibilities, so instead of asking to crash at her house, Eloise had taken up residence in the hotel.

When things were slow, Eloise conveniently closed this part of the hotel, consolidating guests to shorten the time it took to clean the rooms. During tourist season, she had hung the Do Not Disturb sign on her door. No one had noticed. And as her bank account had dwindled trying to keep the place running, living there had become indefinite. How could she afford a deposit on an apartment when she couldn't even afford to fix her car?

Eloise pressed her ear against the wall. She could hear someone moving around the room. Maybe it wasn't who she thought it was. It could be someone driving down the coast who had decided to stop for the night. And Kiki, trying to be helpful, had put them in the quiet part of the hotel so they could get some rest.

Yes, that had to be what happened. Because if Graham Thatcher was her new neighbor, Eloise was well and truly fucked.

———

"Coffee." Kiki reverently picked up her morning cold brew like it held the elixir of life. "You are still my favorite boss."

Eloise snorted, then frowned. "Favorite boss? I'm your only boss."

Kiki shook her head. "Technically, Graham owns half the hotel. So, if you think about it, he's my boss, too."

"Try not to get too attached. Lucifer won't be sticking around very long."

"I don't know. He seems to be acclimating." Kiki began to gather her things. "He met the twins, which if you ask me, is much scarier than Elias haunting the room next to his."

Eloise's grip tightened around her chai latte, and she tried very hard to keep her voice even and uninterested. "You don't think Elias is haunting 423?"

Kiki giggled as she shouldered her bag. "That was mean, putting him in there. No, I had to move him last night. Poor guy looked spooked."

"Why does he think that the room next to his is haunted?"

"He said he heard someone moving around early this morning. Oh, and there was some moaning last night. He asked if there was anyone next door, but there isn't."

Eloise took a deep breath and pinched the bridge of her nose. This could not be happening. The universe could not be this invested in fucking up her life.

"I know you had that part of the hotel closed off, but I just wanted him to be comfortable. So he'd like the hotel." Kiki's brow furrowed. "Was that wrong?"

"No. It's fine. Really." Eloise bit back a sigh to keep Kiki from feeling worse. "Where is he now?"

"In your office."

Her pulse jumped into overdrive. "How did he get into my office?"

Kiki flinched. So much for keeping her emotions in check.

"Well, he asked to go in, and I said no because I didn't think you'd like it, but then he pointed out that he was, technically, also my boss, so..."

Eloise could not quite smother a groan as she took off for her office at a pace that fell just below a run. She threw open the door. Graham didn't even look up from the computer, which was probably a good thing, because Eloise felt her entire body blush.

It wasn't fair how gorgeous this man was at seven o'clock in the morning, after they had both been up late. Plus, she looked like a natural disaster. Her hair was twisted into a hasty bun that was falling out, and she had grabbed the first dress she'd seen, a dark blue vintage silhouette dotted with large magnolias she thought made her look a bit too pale, but her cousin Annie had insisted she buy.

But Graham? He somehow made a forest-green knit sweater and a pair of khaki chinos look erotic. And for an added layer of torture, he was wearing glasses, like a slender Clark Kent.

"Good morning, Eloise," Graham said, finally looking at her. Between his sweater and the glasses, his eyes were even more intensely green. The entirety of her interrupted fantasy came rushing back to her, and Eloise gripped the door frame with her free hand, because her legs were not doing a great job of keeping her upright anymore. His eyes dragged down her body, and it might as well have been his hands because she would have sworn under oath she could feel it.

Breathe. In and out. Swooning because of a look was embarrassing.

Graham let out a rough breath and pursed his lips before looking back at the computer.

Well, so much for that.

"Your computer is password protected," he said tersely, and the undercurrent of ice cooled Eloise's lust momentarily.

"Of course it is." She walked to the other side of the small office and set her drink on top of the filling cabinet. "You never know who is going to strong-arm their way into your office to go snooping."

"Is it snooping if half of this office is mine?" Graham glanced up at her and quickly looked back at the computer. The lockout countdown was nearly done. How many passwords had he tried?

"Which five feet do you want?" Eloise snapped, and took a deep, calming breath so she wouldn't say something she would regret. That was a mistake. She didn't know if it was his cologne, shaving cream, or soap, but the infuriating man smelled so good it took all her willpower not to bury her nose in the inviting curve where his neck met his shoulder.

He looked around the room. "Do you really think this closet you've commandeered is ten by ten?"

Thank God he remained irritating.

"I have absolutely no idea. I haven't picked up a measuring tape to check. But I'm definitely going to be keeping the door locked from now on." Eloise leaned back against the filing cabinet, which was the furthest she could get away from him without standing in the doorway again. She would not cede an inch. "Why are you trying to get into my computer?"

"Records, Eloise."

"And you need them because...?"

"It makes no logical sense how this place is still running. It costs too much. Or it *should* cost too much." Graham frowned, stroking his chin. "Given our current occupancy rate and price per night..."

"Oh, so suddenly you're interested in the hotel? Where were you a year ago?" Eloise snapped, and crossed her arms before she gave into the urge to dump her chai latte over his head.

Graham's color rose as he typed another unsuccessful password. "I'm here now."

"You're fucking late. And stop with the passwords. You're never going to get it."

"That's not necessarily true. There are ways—"

"No! You're going to lock me out for the rest of the day, and I have work to do. Give it up, Graham."

Like a Bond villain, Graham slowly turned the chair until he was facing her. He leaned forward and rested his forearms— which were mercifully covered today—on his thighs. It was hard to maintain eye contact, especially after last night, but Eloise refused to lose their staring contest.

"Um, can I go home?" Kiki asked cautiously from the doorway.

"No," they answered in unison, not breaking their stare down.

"Okay…"

Eloise's nostrils flared as she let out a long breath. She pushed away her second vivid fantasy about him in less than ten hours, but this time it was about stabbing him with her letter opener. "Kiki is my employee, not yours. You can't tell her what to do."

"Actually, she is my employee, too. And I would prefer there were witnesses."

"For what?"

"My murder. You're plotting it right now." Graham's mouth quirked upward on one side. "Has anyone ever told you that you have an extremely expressive face, Eloise?"

Eloise's fingernails dug into the soft pad of her palm as her pulse drummed in her ears. The final straw was when Graham casually covered his mouth, clearly trying to hide a smile as her frustration reached its boiling point.

"Has anyone ever told you that you're an arrogant jackass?" she asked, and then marched out of her office, slamming the door behind her, enjoying the way the sound reverberated in the lobby.

After an hour organizing and reorganizing the linen closet, Eloise felt like she could go back to the front desk and not tear into the first person who made the mistake of saying good morning to her. There was a pang of guilt that Kiki had been waiting this whole time to go home. She would find a way to make it up to her. Maybe an extra night off. Or some new red nail polish.

But as Eloise rounded the corner, it wasn't Kiki behind the desk, but Graham, sitting on her stool like he had always been there. He was hunched over, the long fingers of his right hand threaded through his dark hair while he wrote something down.

He was left-handed, she realized, and hated how endearing she found that. Determined not to let him see how much he affected her, she quietly came behind the desk and tried to peek over his shoulder.

"What are you doing?"

"Making a list."

"What kind of list?"

"All the ways you could kill me and make it look like an accident," Graham said casually, and Eloise bit her lip to keep from smiling.

"If you could make me a copy, I would appreciate it. I'm absolutely bereft of ideas."

Eloise looked at the giant chandelier that hung in the lobby so she wouldn't stare at him. The chandelier bordered on gaudy, dripping with crystals, and Edgar had told her that it was original to the hotel. It seemed Elias Crane had enjoyed flashy things.

"Where did Kiki go?"

"I sent her home. Promised I wouldn't touch anything but the phone." Graham looked at Eloise just as she ventured a glance at him and her heart stuttered when their eyes met. "So, I'm an arrogant jackass?"

"I cannot be the first person to call you that."

"And you won't be the last." He folded his list and tucked it into his pocket as he stood. Even with a modest heel on, Eloise had to tilt her head to look at him. "Are you going to tell me your password?"

"You can keep guessing." Eloise sat on her stool. It was warm from Graham and her stomach did an impressive swoop.

He rolled his eyes, but Eloise caught a shadow of a smile on his lips. "Alright, Rumpelstiltskin."

Eloise tried to not watch him walk away. She really did. But she was helpless against the siren song of a well-fitted pair of pants. The way they hugged his thighs and ass made her want to write the designer a thank you note. Maybe even send a fruit basket.

He passed under the chandelier and took his phone out of his pocket, and Eloise got a good, long look while he stood there.

"Oh, Eloise?"

She quickly looked back at the computer like she had not been objectifying him and said a quick prayer to whoever was listening that he hadn't caught her staring.

"I'm going to figure it out."

"Figure what out?"

"How exactly you've been spinning straw into gold." He gestured around the opulent lobby before he turned on his heel and left.

CHAPTER SIX
<hr>

It was small, petty, and quite possibly the stupidest thing she had ever done, but Eloise was desperate.

Graham Thatcher could not occupy the room on the other side of the thin wall.

She had spent her entire front desk shift trying to figure out a solution. Moving her stuff wasn't an option. There was too much of it, and she might get caught by either Graham or her staff. She could explain the mini fridge, but not the armloads of dresses squished into the closet. Once Graham knew the hotel was such a money pit that it had drained her savings like a vampire on a bender, it was all over.

The idea struck her while she was having her midmorning staring contest with Elias Crane's portrait. Graham believed in ghosts. Maybe not in the same way that Kiki did, but enough that he had shrugged off her moaning as spectral. There was a chance that if he thought the ghost didn't want him in that room he would move again. He had done it the last night on less evidence. Well, less evidence and a potentially possessed phone.

Armed with the housekeeping cart and a hazy recollection

of too many *Scooby-Doo* episodes, Eloise had casually broken into Graham's room, tossing the Do Not Disturb sign behind the door.

Was it breaking and entering if she made a key?

The housekeeping cart was her cover. If Graham came back from wherever he had gone, she could say that she was tidying up. Not that there was a lot of tidying up to do. His room looked barely touched. Half of the bed was still perfectly made. Apparently, Graham was a still sleeper. Every morning Eloise's bed looked like she had gotten into a wrestling match with the sheets and it was unclear who the winner was.

Eloise did a slow turn, surveying the room. "Think like a ghost...think like a ghost..."

Graham's expensive suitcase was open on top of the collapsible luggage rack. Even though curiosity killed the cat, it was satisfaction that brought it back. And needing to know what a billionaire brought on an intimidation trip was going to kill her if she didn't find out.

The answer turned out to be packing cubes. Matching in color, variable in size packing cubes. Some of them were empty, so Eloise went to the closet. She pulled open the doors and hummed with satisfaction. Her hunch was right. Graham was the kind of person that hung up his clothes in a hotel room. Two button-down shirts, and another sweater. Two pairs of slacks. So he'd planned on this being a quick trip.

A ghost, Eloise decided as she divested the hangers of his clothes, would help him pack. She quickly refolded the pants and the dress shirts and dropped them back into the suitcase. Ghosts couldn't be too neat.

She picked up the sweater from the bed and brought it to her nose. That morning in her office, she had gotten hints of his smell, but couldn't figure out what it was without getting closer to him. It had bothered her all day. She inhaled deeply. His scent clung to the wool, embedded in the fibers like it had been woven in during the spinning process. Warm spices, something like leather, and a possible splash of vanilla. A pleasant, giddy tingling originated in her stomach and spread outward, up through her chest and down her legs. A full body fizz, with an unexpected warmth between her thighs.

Eloise threw the sweater into his suitcase like it had bitten her. If smelling his clothes was going to turn her on, she really needed him to leave so she could finish what she started last night. An uninterrupted orgasm to clear her head. Scratch the itch herself before she tried to scratch it with someone she would regret. Like Graham.

It wasn't her fault that he had snuck into her solo time. Yes, he was a frustrating jerk, but he was also undeniably attractive. That dark hair, paired with those eyes... What if, instead of dictating to her from her chair like a bored prince, he had stood and pressed her back against the filing cabinet, letting her find out for herself if he felt as solid under her hands as he looked? He could have gripped her jaw firmly, not enough to hurt but enough to let her know he was in control, and then captured her mouth...

Eloise shook her head to erase the image that was forming. No more office fantasies. And she needed to stop rewatching the season where Lovingford and Olivia got together. Their first kiss had nearly burned the fandom to the ground. It had certainly set Eloise's imagination on fire.

She picked up the remote from the nightstand and turned on the TV. It had been left on one of the news channels that focused on business. A few clicks got her to the static input channel, and then she cranked the volume to full blast before turning the TV off. That should scare the ever-loving shit out of him later.

The bathroom was as tidy as the rest of his room. Towels

had been hung back up on the rack instead of left in a soggy heap on the floor, and that made Eloise like him more than he deserved. The bar was getting too low if towels impressed her. His toiletries were lined up neatly next to the sink. There was an open black leather dopp kit off to the side, with the letters GKT embossed in gold on the side. What did the K stand for? Eloise hadn't pegged Graham as the kind of person who got his stuff monogramed. He was too understated for that. Maybe it been a gift, and if so, who was it was from? A former lover? A current girlfriend? Those possibilities left her with a heavy, unsteady feeling near her sternum. Eloise gathered up his toothbrush, toothpaste, razor, and shaving cream and dropped them into the bag unceremoniously.

Eloise pulled the towels off the rack. Leaving him with only hand towels was an excellent poltergeist prank. She wadded them into a slightly damp ball and turned to take them out to the cart.

"What are you doing?"

She screamed, the towels falling to the floor with a muffled thud. Graham was standing in the bathroom doorway, one eyebrow half-cocked. How had she not heard the door?

"Fuck," she cursed, pressing a hand to her chest like she could calm her pounding heart. "You scared me."

The eyebrow went fully up. "That didn't answer my question."

What had she been doing again?

"Cleaning. I was cleaning."

"So, the Do Not Disturb sign is a suggestion?"

"It wasn't on the door," she lied, stooping to pick up the towels. Graham crouched down at the same time and their hands brushed. Eloise snatched hers back quickly. "I've got this."

"Do you always clean rooms in your nice clothes?"

"I do what I have to do to make sure the hotel is taken care of." She grabbed the towels and stood up quickly, holding them against her body like armor.

"Is that why you packed my stuff? To take care of the hotel?"

"I didn't pack your stuff," she said, stepping around him and out of the bathroom. Small spaces and Graham did dangerous things to her brain. "It was like that when I came in."

"Uh-huh." He didn't sound convinced.

"Strange things happen in this part of the hotel."

"I wanted to ask you about that earlier." Graham followed her to the door and opened it for her. "Last night, I heard some things. And then again this morning."

"Kind of like someone was in the room next door?" Eloise suggested. She shouldn't bait him. The potential for this to backfire if she went too far was astronomical.

"Yes."

Play it cool. She shrugged, dropping the towels into the linen hamper. "I personally don't believe in ghosts, but I know some people have had...experiences. There's only one thing to do when there's something strange in the neighborhood."

"Ghostbusters?"

She didn't want him to see her smile, so she took her time selecting four clean towels for him. By the time she turned around, she had regained her composure. "I think they're in the phone book."

Graham held out his hands for the towels. "I didn't know they still made phone books."

"We have one," she said, reluctantly handing over the stack. "Everyone around here still has a landline because of the—"

"Unfathomably shitty cell service?"

"I was going to put it more diplomatically, but yes."

There was an awkward pause where she could see him

trying to piece together what he was going to say next. Inside his room, the phone rang, and they both jumped. An embarrassed laugh passed between them.

"I should get that," he said, still lingering in the doorway. "I've been playing phone tag with someone all day."

"If you answer the phone, are you it, or do you win?"

Why was she trying to prolong this?

Graham chuckled, the sound rolling through her body like a late summer thunderstorm.

"I don't know. I'm going to have to think about that." The phone rang again, shattering whatever strange spell this moment held over them. "I'll get back to you."

When the door shut firmly behind him, Eloise groaned, putting her face in her hands. Screw getting him to move rooms. She needed him out of the state, maybe even out of the country. Graham Thatcher was a menace to her mental health. If he didn't do something irritating soon, she was in real danger of finding him charming.

Maybe rereading some of their emails would help balance the scales.

———

Graham leaned against the closed door for the length of one ring to catch his breath. Eloise Price did things to his brain. On a normal day, he thought he was a decently intelligent man in firm control of his emotions. He shouldn't like her. He shouldn't find her amusing or cute. Her stubborn refusal to cede even a single inch to him when it came to the hotel had forced him to take several days away from work to deal with her.

Hell, he'd spent most of his day driving to Eugene and back to get her a new front desk computer.

It was an olive branch with a state-of-the-art processor. That was how he justified it, anyway. Not that he'd had a compulsory urge to fix her problem the first time he saw her struggle with it. It was only a computer. The old one had offended his delicate technological sensibilities anyway. He wasn't going to read anything into the deflating disappointment he'd felt when he got back to the hotel and Eloise wasn't behind the desk.

Instead he got to deal with Rochelle, the daytime front desk clerk, who was about as helpful as a "Be Back Soon" sign with no return time. He couldn't fathom why Eloise hadn't fired her yet as he tried to copy the files from the old computer onto a flash drive and Rochelle gave herself a manicure. Kiki was at least pleasant, even if she was spooky. Ten minutes with Rochelle really made him appreciate the charming goth.

He was going to buy Kiki a present. Like a cookie. Or a coffin.

The next ring snapped him out of his murky thoughts and feelings, and he crossed the room in a few long strides. If he missed Athena's call again, she might be too annoyed to help him.

"Hello?"

There was a husky chuckle on the other end of the line. "Hey, stranger."

"Sorry. I've been running errands." Graham sat on the side of the bed and tucked the phone between his head and shoulder so he could untie his shoes. "This place has no cell service."

"Are you ready to shrivel up and die?" Athena asked. "You've been pretty attached to your phone lately."

"I have not been attached to my phone," Graham rebutted, frowning.

"Uh-huh. How's it going up there?"

"I am part owner of the world's worst hotel."

"That bad?"

Graham didn't know where to start.

"The girl who works the front desk at night looks like she's going to turn into a bat and fly away." He had a feeling Kiki would appreciate his description.

"Oooh. Sounds sexy. Is she single?"

Graham rolled his eyes. "Keep it in your pants, Athena. I don't think she's old enough to rent a car yet."

"I could be a cougar. You should give her my number."

Graham fell back on the bed, studying the stain on the ceiling that looked like an ink blot test. He needed to keep Athena on task if he had any hope of making it out of Crane Cove.

She was probably billing him for this call anyway, and she charged by the minute.

"Did you get a chance to look over everything?"

After Edgar had passed, Graham had had Athena look over the will in hopes of finding him a quick exit out of Edgar's terms and conditions. There wasn't one, unless he wanted to take it court. Athena had cautioned him against that. Lawsuits took time, and a reporter on the courthouse beat was bound to turn him suing Eloise Price into a giant story. She recommended that he deal with the matter himself.

Dealing with it himself had still landed him in Crane Cove, and Athena had gotten involved anyway. Now he was paying her to look through his emails.

"I did. What's she like in person?"

"She's..." Graham's vocabulary failed him. Gorgeous? Ethereal? So sexy when she got riled up that he couldn't help but try and irritate her? "Not what I expected. I don't know."

"Graham Thatcher, are you hedging my question?"

Yes, he was, and he did not like that she noticed. Though not surprised, because Athena was a hawk for details.

"It's nothing, really," he assured her. "Do you think you

could quietly float the hotel around to some of your real estate friends? The sooner I'm back in LA, the better."

"I can, but do you think you're going to be able to get her to sign off? Remember that I've read your emails."

"I will find a way to make her sign, okay?" Maybe an offer in hand would be enough to push her over the edge. It was hard to say no to a few zeroes.

"Do you want me to dig around a little on her? Find some leverage?"

Graham thought about that morning in Eloise's office. What was on that computer that she didn't want him to see? Why wouldn't she share the financial records for the hotel?

"Can't hurt. She's hiding something."

"That's for sure. She's dodgy as fuck in your emails," Athena said, her nails clicking against the keys as she typed.

"Call me when you've got something."

"Will do. And Graham, pass my number along to the vampire girl, okay?"

Graham rolled his eyes. "Maybe if you make my life a little easier."

He hung up the phone and took off his glasses, rubbing the tiny indents on the bridge of his nose. What was he going to do? Eloise was hiding things, that was obvious. Did it go beyond the computer password and the financial records for the hotel? Was she a sinister mastermind with big, blue eyes he wanted to swim in? Or was she really "the sweetest person on Earth" like the McMahon twins had said, and he just brought out her murderous side?

God, he liked her murderous side.

That morning she had blown into her office with the force of a hurricane, and he had let the storm happen because it was beautiful to watch.

Not that he had been able to look at her for very long.

One glance—her hair slipping from her bun and her skin flushed—and he'd gone to half-mast. It had taken every single ounce of his rapidly declining willpower not to pin her against the filing cabinet and kiss her until she forgot why she was mad at him.

And that dress...It was going to be a long time before he could look at white flowers without getting hard.

Thinking about her made him feel hot all over, and if he didn't do something with all the pent-up energy in his body, he was going to go out of his mind. Or he'd do something stupid, like hunting her down to find out if she felt this crackle of electricity between them, too.

He needed to go on a run.

In one of his packing cubes were his workout clothes: a Los Angeles Phantoms T-shirt Jordy had given him during their white elephant gift exchange two years ago and a pair of shorts. He could re-unpack his bag when he got back, assuming he didn't run all the way home to LA before he felt better.

The lighthouse was a bit further than he had anticipated. He had spotted it from the hotel, proud and lonely on a protruding cliff, and decided that he would run there and back. His smartwatch told him that he had already run five miles, and he had been all but crawling up a brutalizing hill for at least half a mile.

"On your left!"

Graham barely heard the voice over his music and the sound of him sucking wind. A tall blond man with broad shoulders passed him like it was nothing. Even though his legs were screaming at him, Graham pushed himself, trying to chase the other man down. He finally caught up to him at the lighthouse.

"How...who..." Graham put his hands on top of his head,

trying to make his breathing deep and even, though he wanted to gasp like a fish tossed up on land. He narrowed his eyes at the other man, who was sweaty but otherwise unbothered. It wasn't fair.

"Do you need to sit?" he asked, checking the stopwatch he had looped around his neck.

"No," Graham panted, even as his legs shook beneath him. "What are you doing?"

"Waiting for my team to catch up."

"Are you a football coach?" Graham guessed from his hulking physique.

The big blond man shot him a glare that looked familiar. "Cross-country."

Graham gave up and sat down on the ground before he fell down. His run had accomplished its goal: it was impossible to think about Eloise while his lungs were on fire like this.

"I thought coaches just sat back at the school and waited while other people did the running."

"I said if they could beat me to the lighthouse, I'd cancel practice on Friday. They thought they could, so now I get to try and figure out what we're doing on Friday."

"Seems reasonable enough." Graham studied the other man closer, a nagging sense of familiarity forming. "You wouldn't happen to be related to Chase and Cole McMahon, would you?"

The man rolled his eyes. "Those are my baby brothers. I'm Connor."

"Connor," Graham repeated, trying to cement the name in his brain. "Nice to meet you. I'm Graham. Just so you have a name for my headstone when I die right here."

Connor studied him with a slight frown. "You don't look like pure evil, but Eloise isn't known to exaggerate."

It was hard to laugh, but Graham managed. The sound was

dry and hoarse. "My reputation precedes me. I'm guessing you're a friend?"

"The nicer of them, yes."

Thick silver clouds were gathering to form a heavy blanket across the sky.

"It looks like rain," Graham commented. He rolled up into a sitting position. "Isn't it kind of evil to race a group of teenagers?"

Connor smirked. "It is. But hubris must always be punished."

"Ah, so you're a vengeful god."

"With dashes of benevolence." Connor held out a hand to help him up. "You should really walk around a little so you don't get a cramp."

"Thanks. Can I ask you something?"

"Shoot."

"Do you know the password to Eloise's computer?"

Connor laughed. "Well, I know it isn't I Love Graham Thatcher."

"Yeah, I tried that this morning. Right after Die Graham Die." Graham paced in a small circle as the first few lanky teenagers bounded down the gravel road. "She really doesn't like me?"

"She's frustrated," Connor answered diplomatically. "Though if you see her with a shovel, I'd run the other way."

"I guess I'm a dead man then," Graham joked. "I think I'm going to be crawling back to town."

"Do you want to run back with us?" Connor offered as the last of his team trotted up to the group.

He let out a short laugh. "No. My pride could not handle being shown up by a bunch of high schoolers."

"Suit yourself. Don't expect Eloise to send a search party."

Connor gathered his team, and they began a slow, leisurely

jog back toward town. Graham waited for them to disappear down the hill before he sprawled out on the soft green grass.

An incessant buzzing in his pocket alerted him that he had some cellphone service again. Despite what Athena had alluded to earlier on the phone, Graham was enjoying the break from being constantly connected to the world. Sure, he missed his friends. Peter had left him more than a dozen short voice memos that morning, asking questions and then reporting back when he found the answer, so it was nice to know at least one of them missed him, too. But most of all, he missed knowing exactly when Little_Teapot had responded to one of his messages.

Foolproof42: I'm in Oregon, whenever you want to mount the rescue mission.

Little_Teapot: Ah, so you're getting warmer.

Foolproof42: How warm am I?

Little_Teapot: Basically burning up.

Graham stared at his phone. Was that an invitation to more? Or was she just teasing him? Even his online love life was hopeless and confusing.

Foolproof42: Do you want to meet?

There. He'd said it. The ball was in her court now. And since the stress of waiting for her not to answer was going to kill him, Graham pushed himself up and began to jog back to the hotel.

CHAPTER SEVEN

He wanted to meet.

He had actually typed the words "Do you want to meet?" and then sent them to her. It had been fine when he was an abstract sweater-wearing bookstore-owning idea of a man, but the reality of meeting him was overwhelming. Eloise rubbed her chest in a vain effort to soothe her racing heart. Chickens in the mouth of a fox were calmer.

What had she been thinking telling him they were close? She hadn't been thinking. Or, she had been thinking about Graham I-Have-No-Business-Being-So-Hot Thatcher. Hot, bothered, and confused Eloise should not be allowed to send semi-flirtatious messages to a stranger. This was how she got into trouble.

"Don't take this the wrong way," Sybil said as she put Kiki's usual morning jumbo cold brew on the counter, followed by a second one instead of her usual chai latte, "but you look exhausted. I don't think chai is going to cut it today."

Eloise was exhausted. She had been up all night, tossing and turning, unable to string more than two hours of sleep together.

Between Foolproof42's message and Graham next door, she couldn't relax. Around three a.m., she realized that he could take a leaf out of her book and make a key to investigate the noises in her room, and that gave her stress dreams when she was able to sleep.

"Couldn't sleep." Sybil's eyes narrowed, and Eloise knew that hadn't come out as light and breezy as she hoped.

"Is it that rich asshole, because I can—"

"I met him yesterday," Connor said, cutting her off. "He didn't seem that bad. Kind of funny, actually."

Sybil snatched back his coffee that she had just set on the bar. "Traitors don't get coffee."

"I am not a traitor because I don't think he's the Prince of Darkness." Connor crossed his arms over his chest and fixed Sybil with the same glare that got rooms full of rowdy, hormonal teenagers to be quiet.

"Sybil, it's fine." Eloise looked up at Connor. "You're allowed to like him as long as you promise not to rat me out to the police if I give in to the urge to strangle him."

"Stop discussing your murder plans in public." Sybil put Connor's cup back on the bar forcefully. "Here. Take your stupid coffee, you overgrown bookworm."

"Thank you." Connor picked it up before she could take it back again. "Are you still coming over for dinner? Mom is making pot roast."

"Yes."

As Sybil marched into the backroom to finish out her huff, Eloise decided she was never going to fully understand their friendship.

A light drizzle had started to fall as Eloise got into her car. She inserted the key into the ignition and turned it.

Click click click.

"Oh, come on. These are not shoes I can walk back in," she

said to her car, and turned the key again. After some complaining, the engine roared to life, and she relaxed.

Eloise needed to figure out what she was going to write back to Foolproof42. How did she say, without sounding like a pathetic loser, that she was afraid expectations on both sides would not be met if they met? What if he was not who she imagined he was, but someone who snapped his fingers at waiters? Or smacked his lips after he slurped his soup?

Or, worst of all, what if he was perfect and *she* wasn't what he had been expecting?

Eloise was in a fog of indecision when she walked into the hotel and handed Kiki her coffee.

"Don't take this the wrong way," Kiki said, "but you look exhausted."

Eloise sighed and sat down on the stool. "I am clearly not getting my money's worth out of my concealer. What's this?"

"That," Kiki said with a flourish that would have made any *Price Is Right* model proud, "is our new front desk computer. Graham bought it and set it up last night."

Eloise blinked. This had to be another stress dream. She had been shopping for new computers for the hotel, so she knew that the one in front of her was out of her budget by miles.

Her stomach twisted into a Gordian knot. If he expected her to reimburse him for this, she was screwed.

"He did, did he?" Eloise wiggled the mouse, and a login screen came up. She frowned. While she had password protected the office computer, she didn't lock the front desk computer because it had proven too hard to keep rotating staff from accidentally locking themselves out.

"Kiki, what's the password?"

"Did he actually lock it? I thought he was kidding about that." Kiki leaned in, like being closer to the screen would help. "Maybe he wrote it down on the sticky note."

"What note?" Eloise looked around the desk and found one of her periwinkle sticky notes next to the phone. Scrawled on the small piece of paper in spiky script was a list of what could be passwords. "What exactly was Eloise80085 supposed to mean?"

Kiki laughed. "Oh, that's supposed to be boobs if you wrote it on a calculator. I thought it was funny. Is that what he picked?"

"I don't know. This is a list, not a single password," Eloise explained, showing Kiki the note.

"Ah. That might be his list for your computer in the office. He was trying to pump me for information last night. Even brought me one of those giant cookies from Gilda's as a bribe."

Eloise narrowed her eyes. "What did you tell him?"

"Not much," Kiki answered, picking up her bag. "The only thing I could really think to tell him that might be helpful was that your favorite color is purple."

"Periwinkle," Eloise corrected. "Have you seen him yet today? I need to get into the computer."

"He stopped by about ten minutes ago. Asked me where to get coffee, so I sent him to Sybil."

Good. Sybil would take Graham down a few pegs for her. And when he got back, she was going to make whatever Sybil said to him look like a pleasant chat.

The phone rang and Eloise waved Kiki off. With a deep breath and her best customer service voice, she answered. "The historic Crane Hotel, this is Eloise."

"Good morning, Eloise."

Eloise put her head in her free hand. It was too early in the morning to be dealing with her mother. Especially on no sleep. She had been successfully dodging her calls for a few weeks, but Sandra Price was not easily deterred.

"Hi, Mom. To what do I owe the pleasure at seven o'clock in the morning?"

"Well, if you'd return my calls, I wouldn't have to call you at seven in the morning," Sandra returned in a clipped tone. "Are you coming home for Thanksgiving this year? Flights are filling up."

"I don't know, Mom," Eloise sighed. "Hotels don't exactly close down for the holidays."

"I don't understand why you are wasting your life in that town, with that hotel." Eloise could hear her mom rolling her eyes from across the country. "You went to the University of Pennsylvania, for Christ's sake. The Wharton goddamned School of Business. With your degree and resume, you could show up anywhere and—"

Eloise settled in for the usual lecture about how she was wasting her potential. How she could walk into any corporate office in America and get a job in their finance department. That being in the hospitality industry was so far beneath her it might as well be the Earth's core.

As her mom reached the midpoint of her speech—guilt about all the money she'd spent on her education—Eloise looked at the periwinkle paper stuck to her finger and read the list of passwords Graham had written down the night before.

PurplePeopleEater. Rumplestiltskin. GrahamThatcherSux. ThePriceIsRight. Eloise60065. BossyMcBossPants. Eloise snorted and covered her mouth to stifle the laugh that was trying to erupt.

"Eloise, this isn't funny. This is your life."

"I know. I'm sorry. It wasn't you," Eloise promised, taking a calming breath. "How are Maddy and Henry?"

While Eloise didn't want to hear how her golden younger siblings were conquering the world, it was a topic her mother enjoyed, and it was less painful than hearing all of her own shortcomings laid out at her feet. Madeline, her younger sister, had graduated from medical school the previous spring and had started her internship at a prestigious hospital. Harry, her baby brother, was starting his second year of law school. They would both be at Thanksgiving, and the way Eloise didn't want to hear their Harvard versus Yale rivalry bullshit...

Her eyes wandered back to the list. A blush warmed her cheeks.

AngelEyes. EloiseAtThePlaza.

He'd guessed the book she was named after.

"Eloise? I asked you a question."

"Hmm?" Eloise put the Post-it back on the desk. "Can you repeat that? I think you cut out."

"I said," her mother continued in the exasperated tone Eloise knew so well, "that I saw one of your old coworkers at Monica Brooks's wedding. Don. Or was he your manager? Because he said that if you ever wanted your old job back, it's yours. All you have to do is call. He said you have his number."

All of the warm fuzzies she'd gotten from Graham writing down "angel eyes" and guessing the origin of her name evaporated at Don's name.

"I'll keep that in mind," Eloise said tightly.

"Promise me that you will think about Thanksgiving," Sandra pressed.

"I promise that I will think about Thanksgiving."

There was some background chatter on the other end of the line, and her mom hung up without saying goodbye. Eloise hung up her phone. It wasn't a lie. She would think about Thanksgiving. She would think of all the excuses she could give to get out of going.

CHAPTER EIGHT

It was small, petty, and possibly a little stupid, but Graham hadn't been able to resist. Eloise was going to be furious about the password, but that was most of the fun. Still, he had wanted to be out of the blast zone when she found out. He could handle a simmering snit after the initial boil had settled. A quick trip to Stardust Coffee in town, the place Kiki said Eloise went to every morning, seemed like the perfect way to kill some time.

Warmth and the smell of freshly ground coffee wrapped around Graham like a hug when he entered. He inhaled deeply and looked around. It was bigger than he would have expected from the outside, with a few small tables to his left and a large, L-shaped bar to his right. The room continued behind a corner, but before he could go peek, a woman came out from the back-room, summoned by the small bell attached to the doorframe.

"Are you going to order?"

Graham was taken aback by the brusqueness of the question. Almost everyone he had met in Crane Cove so far had been so kind that he wasn't sure what to say. His mouth opened and closed a few times like a fish, but no sound came out.

"The bird-watchers are going to be here in about five

minutes, so if you want something, you need to order now before I get swamped." She tucked an auburn curl that had escaped her French braid behind her ear.

"The bird-watchers?" Graham frowned, confused.

The woman sighed and pushed the sleeves of her oversized red cardigan up her forearms. "We have a large retiree community. They find ways to occupy themselves."

"That sounds ominous."

"It does, doesn't it?" She grinned. "It's mostly harmless. Just don't come in on Tuesday afternoons when the romance book club meets. Things can get a bit heated."

"I will keep that in mind." Graham stepped up to the counter and looked up at the menu. "Is there something you recommend?"

"Everything, or I wouldn't have put it on the menu."

"That is very helpful," Graham said flatly. "How about just a regular coffee?"

"Great choice." She plucked the largest hot cup from the various stacks and went to a carafe to fill it. "So, are you visiting?"

"Kind of," Graham said. "I'm in town on business."

"Now that sounds ominous." She opened a small fridge under the counter. "Do you want any milk?"

"A splash of cream." Graham took out his wallet and then, remembering that Eloise came here every morning, asked, "Do you know Eloise Price?"

"That really depends on who is asking," she said, securing a lid on his coffee before handing it to him. "If you're a cop, she didn't do it, even if he had it coming, and I know absolutely nothing about it."

Graham narrowed his eyes. "How do you know she didn't do it if you know nothing about it?"

"Dammit," she swore under her breath. "I have got to practice that. What did you want to know about Eloise?"

Everything.

"Not much. Just curious about her and the hotel," Graham said, trying to be casual as he handed her a ten-dollar bill for the coffee.

She examined it. "If you wanted information, this is kind of a tiny bribe."

"How much would it take to get you to talk about Eloise?" he asked, trying to remember how much cash he had in his wallet.

She shrugged, putting the bill in the till without giving him his change. "Again, that really depends on who's asking."

"I'm not a cop, if that helps," Graham offered, and she smirked.

He took a tentative sip of his coffee, and his eyes widened. He had been to every overpriced coffee place in Los Angeles searching for the perfect cup of coffee. If he had known that perfect cup existed in Crane Cove, he would have visited years ago.

"This is amazing," he said, and the woman behind the counter gave him a smug smile. "How is it possible that the best beer and the best coffee I've ever had come from the same town?"

"Because this is the Pacific Northwest, and our two major food groups are coffee and craft beer," she told him. "I'm Sybil, by the way."

"Graham. Nice to meet you."

Sybil's eyes narrowed. "Graham Thatcher?"

Graham could feel the frost forming around her words. "Um, yes?"

Sybil reached out to snatch back his coffee, but he held it over his head, far out of her reach.

"Give that back," she demanded. "Asshats don't get coffee."

"No. I already overpaid for it."

"You can afford another coffee from somewhere else," Sybil ground out between clenched teeth as a group of senior citizens with binoculars, cameras, and walking sticks filed in through the door. They were chattering about the birds they had seen, and Graham took a few steps backward out of self-preservation.

"I could, but I'm really enjoying this one," he said, and grabbed the door, holding it open for a few white-haired women. "Have a nice day, Sybil."

Graham entered the hotel, his heart hammering half in fear of Eloise's reaction to his little prank, and half in excitement because he was going to see her. He really needed to get out of Crane Cove and back to LA before he changed his mind about owning a hotel that was falling apart at the seams.

His heart sank when there was no one behind the desk at all. She was probably in her office, and he knew from experience that being trapped in small spaces with Eloise was dangerous. And not just because it gave him less space to run away.

With a little effort, Graham pulled one of the large, wing-back armchairs from in front of the fireplace, and then one of the small, round side tables to the spot under the chandelier he'd been able to get cell service before. As soon as he got settled, his phone rang.

"Good morning, Peter," Graham said, picking up his coffee and taking a sip. Damn, it was good. There had to be a way to get it smuggled to him since he doubted Sybil would willingly sell him any.

"Is there a trick to turning on the stove?"

Graham choked on his coffee. The stove was gas, and Peter, who could remember lines from roles early in his career, often forgot what he was doing in the moment. Not to mention he could not cook to save his life. Graham had come home to several well-meaning kitchen disasters.

"Why are you trying to turn on the stove?" Graham asked, trying to keep his voice calm even if his panic level was rapidly rising.

"I wanted to make breakfast," Peter said. The clicking of the pilot made Graham's heart clutch.

"Peter," he began slowly, "do not mess with the stove. Just make some cereal or have a yogurt."

"But I wanted eggs."

"Then go to a restaurant."

"I don't have time. I have to go to work soon. It's just the stove, Graham. What could go wrong?"

"The fire department—"

"Has shown up once!" Peter interrupted. "And that was the grill, not the stove."

Graham groaned, looking up at the gaudy chandelier. "I think I'm still traumatized from the picture you sent me last night."

Before leaving for this trip, Graham had made a casserole that Peter should have, in theory, been able to put in the oven, bake, and then pick at for a few days until he got home.

"In my defense, you weren't available to explain how this space-age oven works."

"How do you get bake and broil mixed up?"

Graham didn't hear Peter's explanation because Eloise floated out of her office, her pink polka-dotted skirt swirling around her legs. And while he was pretty sure he had never noticed what kind of shoes a woman was wearing before in his life, Graham was developing a deep appreciation for the cute little ankle strap on her matching pink heels.

Eloise spotted him and glared.

"Peter, just eat a grapefruit or something. Do not fuck around with the stove. I've got to go," Graham said, and ended the call before Peter could try and convince him that his house wasn't going to burn down in his absence.

"Boobs? Really?" Eloise held up the sticky note he had written on the night before when he and Kiki were setting up the new computer. "Are all billionaires as immature as you, or did I just get lucky?"

"I'm not technically a billionaire," he corrected, getting up from his chair. "The company is worth that. I'm just a multi-millionaire."

Graham leaned against the desk and peeled the sticky note off her index finger. Her off-the-shoulder white top was making it hard to concentrate on anything but resisting the urge to memorize the curve of her shoulder with his tongue.

"Would you believe me if I told you that boobs was Kiki's idea?" he asked innocently.

Eloise crossed her arms and fixed him with a stern look that was supposed to be chastising, but it just made him grin instead.

"So, no?" Graham scanned the list. "Did I get close at all? I thought this was A-plus work last night."

"Nowhere near," Eloise told him, and pointed at the computer next to her. "What's the password for that?"

"Tell me the password for the one in the office, and I'll tell you the password for that one," he bargained, but she didn't budge. "You have to tell me eventually, Rumpelstiltskin."

"I have to work, Graham. What if someone wants to check out?" Eloise raised her eyebrows to emphasize her point.

"Then I will be sitting right over there," he told her, pointing to the chair and table he had moved. She gave a small, defeated huff, and sank down onto her stool.

"Did you have to rearrange the furniture?"

"It doesn't look that bad."

"Your interior decorating skills could use some work." Eloise picked up a pen and one of her purple Post-it notes and began making a list of her own. Graham leaned a little further forward to try and see what she was writing, but she put her hand over it.

"Stop it."

Graham raised an eyebrow. "Are you always like this, or is it just me?"

"It's mostly just you," Eloise answered, shielding what she was writing with her free hand. "You could inspire a saint to curse."

"I personally like to think Saint Anthony said fuck a couple of times."

Graham felt a swell of pride—and a swell further south—as Eloise sank her teeth into her bottom lip to keep from smiling.

"I've got some questions about the hotel."

"Oh, goody."

"Why are you cleaning rooms?"

She didn't look up from her writing. "Because housekeeping is short-staffed."

"Why don't we hire someone else?" he pressed.

Eloise sighed, glancing up at him briefly. "I'm handling it."

"Forgive me for being concerned since your version of handling things has a girl who could be replaced by a paperweight working the day shift at the front desk."

That had possibly been too far. Eloise looked up at him again, her blue eyes ice cold.

"Don't act like you care about staffing decisions. You'd be happy if we folded."

"I just think—"

Eloise pressed the Post-it to his chest, digging her fingers into his sternum, then got up and marched back to her office, slamming the door behind her.

So much for that conversation.

Graham peeled the note off his chest.

GrahamCracker. HailLucifer. MrImpossible. GoAwayGraham. ArrogantJackass.

CHAPTER NINE

Sabotage had become necessary.

Eloise didn't want to break something. It seemed counter-productive, since she would be the one that needed to fix it. The last thing she wanted to do was create more problems. The hotel did that all on its own.

But Graham showed no signs of wanting to switch rooms. He had been wholly undeterred by her little ghost act. So, between wishing the chandelier would fall on his head, and some half-hearted guesses at the front desk computer's password, she researched how to switch shower knobs from hot to cold.

It had definitely looked easier in the videos.

Eloise checked her watch and hoped that Graham liked to take long runs. A casual marathon would work out in her favor.

The timing had seemed so perfect. Graham had unlocked the front desk computer and told her he was heading out. When he strolled through the lobby in a T-shirt and running shorts, Eloise knew it was her chance. Rochelle would be there soon, and the front desk would survive unattended for a few minutes. It wasn't like they had anyone scheduled to check in.

It had been almost half an hour, and she only had one of the knobs off.

"Stupid...mother...fucker..." she growled as she tried to turn the tiny screw under the knob. It was stuck tight.

"Is that an upgrade or a downgrade from arrogant jackass?"

Eloise shrieked, and her small screwdriver flew out of her hand, bouncing off the ceiling before clattering in the tub. Once again she hadn't heard him come in, but there he was, standing in the bathroom, his LA Phantoms shirt in his hand, water dripping from his hair onto his shoulders. Her eyes followed a bead of water as it slipped down his chest and over his flat stomach, where it settled in his belly button.

She gulped. All of the air had been sucked out of the room. She'd had some impression of fitness from the way his clothes fit, but her imagination was simply not good enough to come up with the reality of the man standing shirtless before her. Lean muscle stretched and bunched just under his skin as he ran a hand through his hair, more water falling to the floor and down his body.

"Do you want to tell me what you're doing in my shower?" he asked. "Or are DIY plumbing projects one of the services we offer?"

"I can explain," Eloise began, stepping out of the tub carefully. She glanced at the door.

"I was hoping you would."

"See, it's kind of like this..."

Eloise bolted for the door and heard Graham slip on the tile floor behind her. She ignored his muffled curse as she dashed across his room, tearing open the door that led into the hall.

"Eloise!"

She sprinted for the elevator and prayed it was there. She would go up to the next floor and hope that Graham would assume she had gone to the lobby instead.

"Come on, come on," Eloise begged as she jabbed the button repeatedly. Mercifully, the doors slid open, and she threw herself inside. She pressed the button for the next floor, and then rapidly hit the close button.

The door began to slide shut, but not quick enough. Graham jumped inside, slamming against the side of the car from the momentum of running down the hall.

"For fuck's sake," he panted.

The elevator began its slow ascent upward, and Eloise pressed her back against the opposite wall. Graham smelled like rain, sweat, and cold outside air, and the scent quickly filled up the small space. He looked ready to murder *her* for a change, glaring down at her like a vengeful underworld god. He opened his mouth to speak when the elevator shuddered to a stop.

"What...Did the elevator just stop?"

"It does that," Eloise answered sheepishly. "It usually gets moving again on its own."

"Usually." Graham didn't sound like he believed her. He reached across her body and pressed the illuminated third-floor button again. When the elevator did not so much as twitch, he began to push all of the buttons with increasing ferocity. "And what if it doesn't?"

"Then we do this." Eloise pressed the alarm button. "And we hope Rochelle doesn't have her headphones in."

"Shouldn't it connect to the fire department?" Graham's voice was half an octave higher than it normally was, and his skin was growing paler by the minute.

"It's a very old elevator," Eloise explained. "Don't worry. Rochelle will hear the alarm."

"Rochelle wasn't at the desk when I came back."

Eloise's heart and stomach raced to see which one could hit the floor first.

"Oh fuck."

"'Oh fuck' is right." Graham pursed his lips, putting his hands behind his head and threading his fingers together.

A long minute of silence stretched between them, filling the corners of the small elevator until it took up every available inch.

"Does Rochelle have a strong track record for being on time?" Graham finally asked.

"Not exactly," Eloise admitted, and sank to the floor, her pink polka-dotted skirt flaring around her. "This is a disaster."

"You don't say." Graham sat on the opposite side of the elevator, his long legs stretching across the car. Eloise focused on his kneecaps, which were pink from when he had fallen in the bathroom, otherwise she was going to drool over his naked chest.

It really had been too long.

"It could be worse." He looked up at the ceiling. "The power could have gone out, and it could be completely dark."

That might be an improvement. Eloise looked up at the lights, wishing they would blink out.

"I don't think I've ever seen anyone run so fast in heels."

Eloise looked back across the car to find Graham watching her, that hidden smirk playing with the corners of his mouth again. She felt a flutter quite a bit lower than her stomach.

"What?" she asked.

"If the one-hundred-yard dash was run in heels, you could probably take home Olympic gold," Graham said, and then covered his face with his hands and began to laugh hysterically.

Eloise frowned. "Are you okay?"

"No," he admitted, running his hands down his face, still laughing. "I hate being trapped in confined spaces."

Her heart clutched. Graham seemed so unflappable and confident every time they interacted. Never in a million years would she have guessed that being trapped would rattle him. She put her hand on his calf and gave it a gentle squeeze. Graham sucked in a sharp breath.

"It's going to be okay," she soothed. "We're not going to die in here. Rochelle will eventually show up for work. Or one of the guests will hear the alarm and call for help."

"That all sounds like quite a stretch," Graham mumbled.

"Worst case scenario, Kiki will be here at ten, and she'll call the fire department to come rescue us."

That made Graham smile a little. "At least we can count on Morticia... Why does Kiki work nights? Is she actually a vampire?"

Eloise rolled her eyes. At least Graham seemed a little more relaxed when he was talking.

"No, Kiki is not a vampire. But she would probably take it as a compliment." Eloise looked back up at the ceiling because her other options were Graham's gorgeous face or his gorgeous body, and she would need all of her willpower intact if they were going to be stuck for more than a few minutes.

"We needed someone to work the desk at night, and Kiki applied," Eloise explained, remembering how hesitant she had been to hire Kiki in the first place. "She had no experience, nothing on her résumé at all, but Edgar thought she was perfect. Thought she gave the place a certain flair."

Graham snorted. "That sounds exactly like Edgar. Aesthetics over everything."

The corners of Eloise's lips twitched as her heart squeezed at the rush of warmth and melancholy. "He had good instincts about people."

Edgar had taken a chance on her when she had no prior experience working in hotels. Her background was in corporate finance. He had barely glanced at her résumé during her interview, and instead spent nearly two hours talking to her about her hopes and dreams, coaxing wishes from her that she had never dared speak aloud to anyone. It was the least polished interview she had ever given, and he'd hired her anyway.

"Why don't we switch her with Rochelle?" Graham asked. "Kiki is very friendly and—"

Frustration spiked through her like a hot poker. "I thought you wanted to sell. Why do you care about the front desk schedule?"

Graham stiffened, his cheeks flushing pink. "It was just a suggestion."

"Yeah, well, unless you plan on contributing more than suggestions around here, keep them to yourself." Eloise clenched and released the fabric of her skirt a few times before she added, "And put on your shirt, for fuck's sake. Who sits around half naked while trying to have staffing discussions?"

"I can't." Graham held up the sodden ball of navy blue cotton. "It's all wet. The weather looked fine when I left, and then...downpour."

Eloise bit the inside of her cheek to keep from smiling. Thinking about how his face must have looked when the sky opened up in an unexpected Oregon downpour made her want to double over.

"Of course you find my misery hilarious. There was chafing, Eloise."

She gave in to the urge and laughed until her stomach ached.

"Am I really that obvious?" she finally managed, dabbing her eyes with her knuckles to try and catch the tears that had formed.

"You could make a fortune as a mime."

"That would be helpful," she mumbled ruefully, the stack of

bills and repair bids in her desk jumping to the forefront of her mind.

"Is it that bad?" Graham asked, and Eloise wasn't sure what look she gave him, but he held up his hands in surrender. "Fine. I won't ask. But if it's that bad, why don't you just sell and let it be someone else's problem?"

How many times had she asked herself that same question in the last few months? When she was sneaking back into the building after dark, or when she had foregone her own paycheck to make sure she could make payroll, she had wondered if this was all really worth it. Could she go back to the way her life had been before Crane Cove and this hotel?

That felt worse than being broke.

"You wouldn't understand."

"You're right. I don't understand why you are hanging on so tightly to the *Titanic* as it sinks beneath your feet. You have a lifeboat, so why aren't you jumping in it and rowing to safety?"

"Because people are depending on me," Eloise said, exasperation blending with desperation. "My employees, the town, the guests that have been coming here for years and love this place..." She let her head fall back against the wall with a thump. "What if I agree to sell, and the person who buys it decides to bulldoze it and build some soulless corporate family fun center?"

"You would be pretty rich at that point, so why would you care? You could start a cute little bed-and-breakfast with the money from the sale."

As far as suggestions went, it wasn't bad. There were numerous little bed-and-breakfasts up and down the coast that did quite well, even with the direct rental market in full swing. But Eloise didn't want a quaint bed-and-breakfast. She wanted the stained-glass ceilings and the carved banisters. She wanted the ballroom, the pool, and the glittering chandelier. Hell, she even wanted this stupid elevator that got stuck every few months.

She must have been quiet longer than she realized, because Graham spoke again, his tone gentle, like he was afraid of upsetting her.

"What would you do with this place if you got to keep it?"

Eloise had thought about this long and hard. She had data and spreadsheets on her computer downstairs. If Graham had shown any enthusiasm for the place before, she would have sent him all of her grand plans. That had been the plan before he had firmly shut her down via email. Edgar had seemed excited and supportive, but the money had never materialized.

"Well, first we'd need a remodel," Eloise began. Graham snorted. She shot him what she hoped was a withering glare. "What?"

"Nothing. Keep going."

"We need a remodel. This place is painfully out of date. And if we could bring it up to scratch, highlight the gorgeous original architecture while adding modern amenities, I think we could thrive as a bit of a luxury destination. Romantic getaways, weddings, anniversary parties, spa weekends..."

Eloise could see Graham turning the idea over in his head, chewing on it like a piece of sticky saltwater taffy. Hope buoyed in her chest and she continued.

"We could combine some of the smaller rooms into larger suites. We'd lose a little capacity, but we could charge more." She was on a roll now. "We could get an executive chef to make us a killer menu. We could reopen the dining room and source stuff locally—"

Graham held up a hand to stop her. "Look, this is an excellent fantasy, but we don't even have guests right now. We don't have anyone queuing up to hold events in this ballroom you're telling me we have. All I'm hearing is you asking me to sink a lot of money into a project that could easily fail."

Eloise felt like he had taken a pin to the happy little balloon she had just blown up. The worst part was that he had a point. She believed in her vision for the hotel and what it could be with the proper investment, but it could all amount to nothing.

But he was wrong about one thing.

____

CHAPTER TEN

"We do have an event coming up. In the ballroom."

"Prom doesn't count as an event," Graham told her. "Because I bet you donate the space for that. We have to make money."

The way her cheeks turned sunset pink told Graham he was right on the money—or lack of money. No one had a bad thing to say about Eloise. The McMahon twins and Kiki seemed to be on a mission to get her nominated for sainthood.

"We, um…" She fidgeted with the fabric of her skirt. "We hold a ball. The first weekend of November."

Eloise's blush deepened, and Graham's interest was officially piqued. What kind of ball was it that she would be embarrassed about it?

"Go on," he encouraged. When she hesitated, he tapped her knee with the toe of his running shoe. "Come on. It can't be that bad."

The way she sighed with her entire body was adorable.

"There's a fan group for this TV show, _Claymore Abbey_. Every November they hold a costume ball in our ballroom because it looks like the ones they use in the show. And I know you probably think that's stupid, but the costumes are actually really impressive."

Graham went still. Even his heart stopped momentarily, then took off like a car that had been filled with jet fuel instead of unleaded. It was a good thing he was already sitting down, because he felt a bit lightheaded.

There was a ball. A *Claymore Abbey* ball. There was a *Claymore Abbey* ball at this hotel that he owned, and there was a chance, even a slim one, that a certain internet mystery woman might be there.

"See. I knew you'd think it was stupid," Eloise said, drawing her legs under her skirt.

With a Herculean effort, Graham kept his tone neutral. "I didn't say it was stupid. It sounds...interesting. And it's the first weekend of November?"

Eloise nodded, but sadness flashed across her face. "I don't even know if it's possible to have it this year. I've been thinking about canceling."

It hadn't seemed possible, but Graham's pulse sped up in a rush of panic. "What would it take to make it happen?"

She raised a single, dubious eyebrow. "Money, mostly. Repairs."

Ideas flooded his mind, and Graham chewed on his lip while he weighed different pros and cons. The ball was about a month away. He could make all of this work to his advantage if he played his cards right.

"I have a compromise. Well, sort of a compromise. Thanks to Edgar's will, you hold most of the cards here." Time to try the carrot instead of the stick. "I will help you throw this event and get the hotel in some semblance of working order if after the ball you agree to look at some potential offers to sell."

Eloise tilted her head to the side and narrowed her eyes at him. "What are you getting out of this? I could read the offers and still refuse to sell. Then you're still stuck with me for the next four years until you're free to sell your half, *and* you'd have spent money you told me you weren't going to spend on the hotel."

Refusing to spend money on the hotel had been the main theme in most of his emails to her.

Graham ran a hand through his damp hair. "Well, in four years it will be easier to sell my half if this place isn't falling apart around our ears."

Eloise considered this for the longest minute of his life.

"Fine. I agree. But I'm not likely to change my mind."

"I can accept that." He held out his hand. Eloise looked at it like he was a cat presenting her with a dead mouse, then she took it. The warmth from the small contact ran up his arm and spread through his chilled body.

"Why do I feel like I just made a deal with the devil?"

"From what I understand, Lucifer was a beautiful angel."

Eloise's head fell back as she laughed, shoulders shaking, and it made Graham smile. Even if she was probably laughing at him instead of with him.

The last decade spent building his business had left his flirting skills rusty at best, since what little personal time he gave himself he chose to spend with his friends instead of dating. And, contrary to what most people believed, being friends with three famous people did not get him anywhere with women. Graham usually ended up with four different cell phones in his hands, taking pictures and getting feedback about how to get the best angle. Most of his nights out ended back at his house on the couch, watching a romantic comedy with Peter.

"I don't think I'll give you the satisfaction of asking you if it hurt when you fell from heaven," Eloise teased, stretching her legs out next to his. He sat on his hands so he wouldn't be tempted to run his hand from that cute little ankle strap up her calf.

"But I teed it up so nicely," Graham protested, the traces of his smile still lingering on his lips.

Eloise rolled her eyes, but her playful smirk remained. "Life is full of disappointments."

Graham didn't want the ease between them to end. He searched for something—anything—to talk about.

"So, we have a ballroom?"

Smooth.

Eloise nodded. "Mm-hmm. And a pool."

"A pool?"

"It's not huge, but it's good for laps."

"Ah, so no waterslide."

"No waterslide. And no, we will not be putting one in."

"Maybe you could give me a tour sometime," Graham suggested. "To get the lay of the land."

"Maybe." A small smirk played on Eloise's lips. "Or maybe I could just let you get lost."

Graham didn't know how long they were in the elevator because it felt like forever and no time at all. Eloise had a biting sense of humor the more comfortable she got, and he couldn't help but bait her, even if most of her jokes were aimed at him. Making her laugh was addictive, and he wanted more of the rush he got when she smiled at him.

Through the closed doors, a familiar voice called out, "Friendly neighborhood fire department!"

"Volunteer division," a second familiar voice clarified.

Eloise jumped to her feet, pressing her face into the seam where the doors met. "Chase and Cole, get us out of here right now!"

"We're working on it, angel," Chase shouted back.

When the twins finally got the doors open, Graham saw

that they had only traveled a few feet before getting stuck. Still, Chase held out his arms for Eloise, who jumped into them.

"You're the best ex-boyfriend ever," she said, her arms still wrapped tightly around Chase's neck.

He grinned. "Aww, thanks, angel."

Ex-boyfriend?

So, Chase was her type. Gigantic, gregarious, big muscles, and blond. Graham could not have picked a better foil for himself if he had tried. This new information colored all of his previous interactions with Eloise, and any hope Graham had that they'd been flirting in the elevator flew out the window. Eloise was just being the nice, friendly person everyone said she was.

"Hey there, beefcake."

Graham looked down at Chase's upturned, smiling face. It was hard to hate him, but it was easy to be jealous of how Eloise had flung herself at him. The only thing Eloise wanted to fling at him most days was a stapler.

"Were we interrupting something?" Cole asked with a conspiratorial grin. It took two beats for Graham to remember he didn't have his shirt on.

"Just got caught in the rain," he said. "Chafing."

The twins winced in sympathy.

Chase held his arms out like he had for Eloise. "Do you trust me?"

"Can Cole catch me? I don't trust that you won't twirl me at the end," Graham said, and he was a little too satisfied with himself when he heard Eloise's snort of laughter.

"See, I told you he liked me better," Cole said to Chase as he elbowed his brother out of the way. "So, did you want to try the *Dirty Dancing* lift?"

"I changed my mind. I'd rather fall down the elevator shaft."

Once Graham was safely back on solid ground—without

recreating any classic movie moments—he pulled his damp shirt over his head. It was cold and uncomfortable, but he couldn't stand next to the twins half naked. The comparison it invited was too cruel.

He needed a plan. In a month, Little_Teapot could be at his hotel. A few weeks to make this place something he could almost be proud to say he owned. It was better to focus on that than lusting over his business partner.

"Oh, you're a Phantoms fan?" Chase asked, pointing to his shirt.

Graham looked down at the logo. If he was being honest, he didn't care about football. He had a corporate box, but he only went to games to support Jordy.

"I guess you could say that."

"And on that note, I'm out. Today has been traumatic enough without listening to you guys blabber about football." Eloise gave Chase's enormous bicep a friendly squeeze.

All three men watched her leave. Once she was out of earshot, both twins turned back to Graham with wide grins on their faces.

"So, seriously, what was going on in that elevator?" Chase probed. "Did you pull the emergency stop? Should we have left you in there?"

"Nothing was going on," Graham insisted, hating that his voice went up at the end.

"He's blushing. Something is going on," Cole concluded with a nod. "Do you want any help there, or do you have it covered?"

"We can talk you up," Chase offered.

The tops of Graham's ears were on fire, and he could only imagine how red his face was. "There is nothing to help with because nothing is going on. We're just business partners. That's it."

"That's how it starts," Chase said, his grin widening. "The denial. Followed by the late nights working, unnecessary business lunches, sharing that tiny little closet Eloise calls her office..."

"Bringing each other coffee," Cole continued.

"By that standard, Eloise and I are in a relationship with Kiki," Graham countered.

The twins chuckled, and Chase gave him a friendly pat on the back. "You just wait and see."

CHAPTER ELEVEN

Eloise had not been able to get her time stuck with Graham in the elevator out of her head. She had lost more sleep over it, tossing and turning until she finally fell asleep in the small hours of the morning. Then the sound of his shower running as she got ready for work sent her into a spiral of sexual frustration like she had never known. She had seen too much for too long to not be able to picture in vivid detail how the water would slide down his chest and over his flat stomach.

"Have you ever been attracted to someone inconvenient?"

"Yes," Connor and Sybil answered at the same time. They looked at each other with deep suspicion.

"Who are you talking about?" Sybil asked, her eyes narrowing further.

"Who are you talking about?" Connor countered, and then they stared at each other for another long moment until Sybil finally broke and looked away.

"No one. It doesn't matter anyway," she said, stabbing her brisket with her fork like it had done her wrong.

Thursday nights were BBQ night at Cranberry Brothers Brewing. The twins, more specifically Cole, got in very early to start the smoker, and babied the meat all day long. The result was delicious. So, every Thursday night, Cranberry Brothers was packed.

Connor picked up his beer. "Who's inconvenient?"

Chase sat down next to Eloise before she could answer, his big arm looped casually around the back of her chair.

"Hey, I just wanted to check in and see if you're okay after yesterday."

Sybil sat up straighter, looking between the two of them. "What happened yesterday?"

Eloise wished the floor would open up and swallow her whole when she saw the way Chase's face lit up with mischievous glee.

"Cole and I got a call to go to the Crane Hotel because the elevator was stuck again. Guess who was inside. Guess."

"Eloise?" Connor ventured, entirely unamused with his youngest brother's storytelling style.

"And Graham. Shirtless."

"*He* was shirtless," Eloise quickly explained as Sybil's eyebrows shot up and Connor choked on his beer.

"That doesn't make it better," Sybil admonished. "You can't be attracted to a guy you've openly admitted you want to murder."

Chase's grin was so big that it made Eloise's cheeks hurt out of sympathy. "So you do think he's attractive. I *knew* it."

Eloise groaned and covered her face with her hands. "Do we have to talk about this so loudly? Half the town is here, and if Edith Nelson hears about this, the other half will know before lunch tomorrow."

"You're being dramatic. No one cares that much about your love life," Chase told her, giving her a friendly squeeze.

"When we broke up, people were stopping me in the grocery store to offer their condolences. People care!"

"People care about *my* love life," he corrected, stealing one of her shoestring fries. "You were just caught in the crossfire."

Eloise removed his arm from around her like it was hazardous waste. "In that case, I really don't need a reconciliation rumor getting started."

Chase laughed loudly. "Heaven forbid Graham gets the wrong idea about us. Want me to talk to him for you? Feel him out?"

"God, it's like listening to my homeroom kids talk." Connor rolled his eyes.

"Please don't," Eloise begged. "I'm just going through a dry spell. Nothing more than that."

"Well, if it's a dry spell and you need help with that..."

"And that is why we have vibrators," Sybil cut in. "So we don't end up having sex on Spider-Man sheets."

"I upgraded to Ninja Turtles, thank you very much." Chase stood, and picked up Sybil's empty beer glass. "And even though you're mean to me, I'm going to get you a refill. Eloise, think about Graham. There could be something there."

"There had better not be anything there," Sybil told her. Eloise shrank down in her chair and peeked at her friends through her fingers.

"It's her life, and she is allowed to fuck it up however she sees fit. Including sleeping with a coworker," Connor reminded her.

"Business partner."

"That does not help your case." Sybil glared at Connor instead of her, which Eloise was grateful for. "What does she do when he goes back to LA? Or when he turns out to not be who she thinks he is, hm?"

"Neither of those examples mean she can't scratch an itch with another consenting adult."

Eloise shuddered. "Do we have to talk about my hypothetical sex life over dinner? I didn't think this could get worse after Chase left, but I was wrong."

"You can't sleep with him, Eloise," Sybil insisted, crossing her arms. "He's your business partner. It would be awkward at best when things go south."

As much as Eloise's libido hated to admit it, Sybil was right. On the off chance that Graham was having the same kind of sexy, sweaty thoughts she'd been having, it couldn't go anywhere. She had never been good at separating sex from romantic emotions. She had learned that the hard way.

Besides, Graham had made it clear that he was looking to get out of their partnership as quickly as he possibly could. He was not looking to move to Crane Cove, and he was definitely not looking to be more than her business partner. The whole thing was a nonstarter.

"Yeah, I know," she agreed quietly, dunking her fry over and over again in the small mountain of ketchup she'd squeezed onto her plate.

Chase returned with Sybil's beer and sat next to Eloise again. "So where is Graham? I kind of thought he'd be here. Cole and I have been talking this up to him all week."

"Don't you have to work?" Connor asked.

"I own the place. I get to do what I want," Chase answered with a cheeky grin.

"Graham went back to LA this morning," Eloise told him. And it hadn't been a moment too soon. *Claymore Abbey* was on Thursday nights, and she could not be held accountable for the way this season made her scream at her TV. Or the way her vibrator—stuffed with new batteries—was going to make her scream after.

"Aw, man. Cole and I were going to see if he wanted to go apple picking at that place where you can make your own cider."

"See, he's unreliable," Sybil said, building her case against Graham.

"He said he had some meetings. He'll be back Monday." Eloise patted Chase's knee. "You and Cole can take him on a date next week."

Chase stuck his bottom lip out in an exaggerated pout. "I guess it's fine. It's supposed to rain this weekend anyway."

"It's Oregon. When is it not supposed to rain?" Connor nudged his empty glass towards his brother. "So, if he went back to LA and is coming back, what does that mean for your plans with the hotel?"

"We're going to try and pull off a mini refresh before the Claymore Abbey event."

Before he'd left that morning, Graham had stopped by the office and told her to get some bids together for the work she thought they could reasonably get done in the next few weeks. He had looked devastatingly handsome in a blue button-down shirt that had been tucked neatly into a pair of gray slacks that fit so well she had been happy to see him walk away. That man had an ass she could bounce a quarter off of, and she once again considered penning an adoring thank-you letter to whoever tailored his clothing. She had been so distracted by how delicious he was that it had taken her a full twenty minutes to remember to be annoyed that he had told her what to do like she couldn't figure it out on her own.

Sybil frowned. "What's the catch?"

How did she always know?

"I have to review offers to buy the hotel. But they'd have to offer millions for me to give that place up." Eloise shrugged. "I really think I'm getting the better end of the bargain."

Connor chuckled. "I'm looking forward to seeing what you're going to do with the place."

"Don't let him push you around. You let other people have

their own way too much," Sybil said and Connor raised an eyebrow at her.

"What Sybil means to say is," Connor began, and put his hand over Sybil's mouth when she opened it to protest, "if you need anything, let us know, and we'd be happy to help. But I can't hide a body on school nights, so if you decide to murder him, keep it to the weekends."

CHAPTER TWELVE

"Oh, you have got to be fucking kidding me," Graham cursed as he got out of the hired car.

It had been a day. After the long drive to Portland, his flight had been delayed enough to put him in the middle of Los Angeles rush-hour traffic. And now in his driveway were Jordy's motorcycle and Sam's Mercedes. Peter's car, he knew, was in the garage parked next to his own. It wasn't that he hadn't missed his friends, because he had, but all he wanted to do was open a bottle of wine and watch *Claymore Abbey* in his bathtub.

"You're home!" Peter exclaimed from the kitchen when Graham came inside.

The house smelled heavenly, which meant that Sam was cooking.

"What are you making?" Graham asked as he went into the kitchen and Peter handed him a glass of red wine.

"Butternut squash gnocchi with herbed brown butter. I can throw down a few more shrimp if you want," Sam offered, pointing to the shrimp he was deveining with the tip of his knife.

"Just give me some of Peter's. Nice beard. You grew that while I was gone?" Graham reached out and scratched the new growth of hair on Sam's jaw.

"I hate all of you!" Jordy shouted from the couch. Graham grinned. He was too easy to tease about his facial hair.

Graham wandered over to the living room. On the big-screen TV was the Thursday night football game between Green Bay and Atlanta. Jordy had his foot propped up on the coffee table, aided by a few pillows, and ice packs draped over his ankle and his knee.

"Are you going to be okay to play on Sunday?" Graham asked with a frown.

"Yeah, I'm fine," Jordy said, adjusting the ballerina-perfect bun Graham suspected Peter had given him. "I slipped at practice."

"I offered to give him a ride, but no, he insists on riding the death machine." Sam pointed his knife in Jordy's direction. "Your body is worth too much money for you to be riding that thing."

Jordy rolled his eyes, unmuting the TV as the game came back from commercial. "Nothing bad is going to happen."

"I'm not coming to the hospital after they scrape you off the freeway."

"Nice to know some things didn't change while I was gone," Graham said, walking back to the kitchen island and sitting on one of the stools.

Peter was putting together a salad in a big wooden bowl, which was probably the safest way for him to help.

"So, how is the hotel coming along?" he asked, not noticing as Sam removed half of the walnuts he had chopped from the cutting board.

"Wait! I want to hear this!" Jordy muted the TV before

limping into the kitchen to sit next to Graham. "Athena said something about a goth girl?"

"I will never understand how you and Athena are friends. She is way too cool for you," Graham said, shaking his head. "And Kiki is gay, so keep it in your pants."

"I had to ask." Jordy grinned. "It's always the ones you don't suspect. The goths, the nerds..."

"No one with an advanced degree would give you the time of day," Sam reminded him.

"Which one of us finished college? Hm?"

Somehow, between the four of them, Jordy was the only one with a college degree. Sam and Peter had never gone, and Graham had dropped out with a year left because the business was growing faster than anyone could have predicted. Graham wasn't sure what Jordy had gotten his degree in, but he trotted out his diploma to win petty arguments all the time.

"I graduated high school first," Sam pointed out.

"You were homeschooled! That doesn't count," Jordy sputtered.

The timer for the oven went off, and Graham was spared from having to talk about the hotel as he and Sam made the roasted butternut squash into gnocchi, and Peter set the table. It felt good to be cooking again after days of eating out for every single meal. When he got back, he was going to insist that Eloise show him where the kitchen was so he could cook for himself.

And maybe he'd make her dinner, too. With candles and wine and... Nope. He was not going down that road. That way lay danger.

"So, tell us all about the hotel," Peter tried again after they were all seated at the table for dinner.

Graham tried his best to describe it without catastrophizing, but he was still traumatized from the first room that Eloise had given him. And then there were the strange noises he was still hearing from the room next to his. Still, he told them about the hand carved front desk, the chandelier, and the stained-glass windows and ceiling in the lobby.

"The elevator is an absolute death trap, though. I got stuck in it yesterday with Eloise," he told them. He felt Peter perk up next to him. "No, we didn't kiss or anything. Calm down."

Peter sighed dramatically. "That was a golden opportunity. The way you just let these moments pass you by..."

"What moments?" Graham asked. "It's just Eloise."

Peter raised an eyebrow at him. "Just Eloise?"

"Yes! Just Eloise. There is nothing going on there, and there is never going to be anything going on there, so just get whatever romantic movie plot line you have going through your head out."

"I think thou doth protest too much."

"I'm with Peter on this," Jordy said around a mouthful of shrimp and gnocchi. "You are super defensive about this."

"Look, whether or not I'm attracted to Eloise is irrelevant because"—Graham began holding up fingers as he ticked off points— "she is my business partner, I don't want to move to a town with no cell phone service, I don't even want the hotel, and I'm not her type."

"How do you know you're not her type? Did she tell you that?" Sam asked from across the table.

Graham sighed and looked up at the skylight above his head, where he could see the last few streaks of pink and purple from the sunset coloring the clouds.

"I'm weirdly friends with her ex-boyfriend, and he is my exact opposite. He's like Jordy but bigger."

"Ah, so unbelievably handsome and charming. I can see why you're threatened. Ow! Sam, I need that foot for Sunday."

"You might be her type." Peter pointed his fork at Graham. "You should find out why they broke up. Maybe she doesn't like big, doofy blonds anymore. Maybe she wants to settle down with a mature man."

"Did you just call me old or Jordy doofy?"

Peter shrugged. "It works both ways."

After the dishes had been done and Sam had given Jordy the usual lecture with safety statistics about his motorcycle, Graham finally sank into his bathtub just in time for the opening credits of the new episode of *Claymore Abbey*. He opened the app he used to access the fan forum and saw he had messages from Little_Teapot.

> Little_Teapot: I know you're busy with your work trip, but I hope you're watching tonight because I've had a WEEK.

> Little_Teapot: Please don't be mad because I'm not ready to meet quite yet.

Graham felt guilty. She had told him that she wasn't ready to meet him yet, and he hadn't responded. It had happened right after finding out that Chase was Eloise's ex-boyfriend, and he didn't want to say anything that would make her feel bad. He understood her hesitation, even if he didn't like it.

> Foolproof42: I'm not mad. I've just been busy. Want to tell me about your week?

> Little_Teapot: Just a lot of work drama. And my living situation is kind of up in the air.

Graham's chest ached. He wished that she would confide in him more, or that he could do something to make it all better. Like buy her a house.

> Foolproof42: Is there anything I can do to help?

Little_Teapot: No, but thank you for offering.
I'm all snuggled up in my bed with a glass of
wine.

Foolproof42: Same, but in the bathtub.

Little_Teapot: Now that is quite the picture. Not
that I know what you look like, but the fantasy
is Grade-A Goodness.

Foolproof42: What do you want me to look
like?

Little_Teapot: Maybe like Lovingford. I'm into
tall, dark, and handsome lately.

Little_Teapot: WHERE IS ANNABELLE
GOING?!

They never got back to her little fantasy because the writers of *Claymore Abbey* continued to deliver on their promise to make this the most high-drama season yet. It was one thing after another and when the episode was over they stayed up past midnight trading theories about what was to come.

Foolproof42: Who is the American Heston
mentioned?! That can't just be something in
passing, right? Am I reading too far into this?

Little_Teapot: I'm more concerned about
Annabelle being out on the moors! How has no
one noticed she's gone yet?!

Foolproof42: It's a big house and her lady's
maid sucks?

Little_Teapot: I swear if they kill her off, I'm
boycotting next season.

Graham spent Friday in the office, trying to dig his way out from under the mountain of work that had piled up while he was gone. He was knee-deep in budget reports and cost projection analysis when the phone on his desk rang.

"Hello?" he answered, then growled as he highlighted an error. Or at least he hoped it was an error. If it wasn't, the marketing department was burning money.

"Well, grrr to you, too," came a female voice laced with a very familiar hint of exasperation.

Was he supposed to know who this was?

"Do you have any idea how hard you are to reach?" she continued as Graham tried to place her voice. "First, I had to look up the number, then I had to get through about a dozen gatekeepers. I got hung up on three times before I lied about who I was, so you either need to fire your assistant or give him a raise."

"Who is this?"

"It's Eloise. I'm trying to source bids, but I don't know what my budget is. Do I have a budget, or can I get a bronze statue of myself for the lobby?"

Graham pressed his knuckles to his lips to suppress the smile she couldn't see. She was adorable when she was grouchy. He took a steeling breath before he spoke, pushing down all the inconvenient butterflies that she had roused.

"We need to work on your negotiation skills. Always ask for gold first, knowing that you're okay with bronze."

"Are you saying I could have had a gold statue?"

"No, but it never hurts to try." Graham leaned back in his chair. His brain was already jumbled from all the reports he had been trying to power through, and it was impossible to come up with a number when he had no idea what a reasonable budget would be. "Can you just compile the bids into a spreadsheet and I can try and figure it out?"

There was a heavy sigh on the other end. "Yes, but only because you're going to be writing a very big check."

"How big?"

"Somewhere between Ouch and Holy Shit," Eloise answered. "There's definitely going to be a markup because of the quick turnaround. And when you see this, I want you to remember the linens I'm listing aren't even the ones I really wanted and have been lusting over for years."

"I will keep that in mind." Graham tried to stretch his back. Getting sore from sitting down was one of his least favorite things about being in his thirties. "How are things going?"

"Rochelle called out sick so I'm stuck at the desk until ten tonight."

"Can't we fire her?"

"Not unless you want to take her shift."

"Well, I hope you didn't have a hot date tonight," Graham said, and winced. Why had he said that? And why did he desperately want her answer to be no?

Eloise snorted. "Me? Hot date? Unlikely. I'm currently in a committed but loveless relationship with this spreadsheet."

"I will let you two have some privacy then. I'm dreading looking at it later."

"Coward."

Later that afternoon, he got an email from Eloise.

Subject: Budget Spreadsheet. Beware.

Mr. Thatcher,

Attached is the budgetary spreadsheet you asked for. I've outlined several different plans of action. Some of the timelines are very tight, so if you could get back to me quickly, that would be appreciated.

Thank you,

Eloise Price

P.S. Did you have Chase bring me lunch and dinner? He was being obnoxious about it. If so, thank you.

Graham rolled his eyes. If he knew Chase, he had said the food was from a secret admirer. He had been positively giddy when Graham had called Cranberry Brothers and told him that he wanted some food delivered to Eloise since she was going to be stuck at the front desk all day long.

He clicked on the attachment that Eloise had labeled 'spreadsheetofdoom.exl'.

Graham, being a sexually experienced adult, had thought he knew all of his preferences. But he had been wrong. Because he had just discovered a brand-new kink: a perfectly organized and color-coded budget spreadsheet.

The numbers were astonishing. He could not believe that bedsheets—and not even enough to outfit the entire hotel, according to Eloise's footnote—cost so much. But hell if he could remember the last time he had been so turned on. He typed out a quick response.

Re: Budget Spreadsheet. Beware.

Ms. Price,

All of this looks acceptable, even if my checkbook is shaking in terror. Out of curiosity, how expensive WERE those other sheets? Because the quote you sent me is staggering and caused me to have an out-of-body experience.

Godspeed,

Graham Thatcher

P.S. I might have. I couldn't have you dying of hunger. Can you imagine if Kiki got TWO ghosts?

P.P.S. Now that I'm giving you money, do I get the password to the computer?

Eloise must have been sitting near the computer because he had a response within minutes.

Re: Budget Spreadsheet. Beware.

Mr. Thatcher,

I've attached the quote. If the other quote I sent you gave you heart palpitations, I suggest you have an AED nearby for this one. Be glad I'm not angling for mattresses, too.

I now suspect the food was a bribe to get the password out of me.

Nice try,

Rumpelstiltskin

Graham's eyes widened when he saw the quote. Eloise had expensive tastes.

His phone rang. He hoped it was her. After her first call, he had sent an email to his assistant to let her through if she called again.

"Hello?"

"I was just checking to see if you were still breathing after that last email."

The sound of Eloise's voice further inflamed Graham's already hot blood, and his semi-hard cock twitched in acknowledgement. A thousand miles and plenty of good reasons were doing nothing to stifle his deepening attraction to this woman.

"I just picked myself up off the floor. You have very expensive tastes, Eloise."

Her throaty chuckle made his knees weak. "I know, but those are the best sheets on the market when you compare cost and quality."

"Why do I have a sneaking suspicion that you have a graph that compares sheets?" Graham asked, unable to keep the smile out of his voice.

"Stop judging me."

"I'm not judging. I'm going to be sending out your budget sheets to my underlings to shame them into doing better."

"An example instead of a warning. What a refreshing change of pace for me—Oh, someone's coming. Try not to make anyone cry."

Graham ran his hands through his hair after he put his phone down. What the hell was he going to do about this woman?

He had barely gone back to the work he was supposed to be doing, instead of lusting over Eloise's spreadsheets, when his phone rang again. The butterflies returned.

"That was fast. Miss me already?"

"Okay, first of all, who the hell are you talking to that you answer the phone like you're some kind of damn sex line operator?" Athena asked, and all of Graham's butterflies died.

"No one."

"Doesn't sound like no one."

Graham's cheeks burned. "Don't worry about it. Where are you? I called your office earlier and they said you were out."

"I decided to take some time for me. Long weekend. What good is all the money I charge you if I never spend it?...Hi, sweetie."

He heard her ordering a latte, and it kicked up a craving for Stardust. His usual coffee place wasn't cutting it anymore. Was everything else just going to taste like hot bean water now?

"I heard you're going back to Oregon. I thought this was supposed to be a quick trip."

Graham quit daydreaming about coffee and how he was going to get back in Sybil's good graces. "It got complicated."

"Uh-huh." Athena didn't believe him for a second. They had been friends long enough that she could see straight through him. Plus, she probably had the strongest bullshit meter in Los Angeles County. "I thought you'd want an update on our little side project."

Graham stilled. While he hadn't forgotten that he wanted to offload the hotel, he had forgotten that he'd asked Athena to look into Eloise's background. Things had changed so much in a matter of days.

"What did you find out?"

"Your girl—"

"Not my girl," he corrected.

He could hear her roll her eyes. "Do you want to hear what I have to tell you or not? Because if you're going to be interrupting me with those half-ass little side steps, I'll let you do your own dirty work."

"I'm sorry, I'm sorry." Graham pushed his glasses up and massaged the bridge of his nose. "We're just business partners, though. Seriously."

"Yeah, exactly why you're answering the phone with 'Did you miss me?'," Athena mocked. "I know you don't have anything else going on in that department."

Fucking Jordy and his big, gossipy mouth.

"So, your girl Eloise is something else. Good family. Real uppity east coast stuff. She went to Wharton, graduated with honors, had a good job in corporate finance, all that jazz. And then she just left."

Graham didn't understand. "She just left?"

"Yup. Up and quit one day. No one knew why, or they weren't saying. Even Chelsea couldn't get any dirt, and you know Chelsea makes Hercule Poirot look like an amateur."

This was true. Athena's assistant Chelsea could find out almost anything about anyone. She had missed her calling as a private detective, though working for Athena probably paid better and offered dental coverage and paid vacation.

"Moving on to the other thing I was calling you about,"

Athena continued. "My real estate friends have some potentially interested buyers. What's your timeline?"

Graham braced himself. "Um, remember how I said things got complicated? I kind of agreed to help her fix up the hotel—"

Graham held the phone away from his ear while Athena howled with laughter.

"It's not funny," he insisted.

"It's a little funny. You were acting all big and bad before you left, and now you're Mr. Fix-It. So, what does this mean for selling?"

"It means I'll be up in Oregon for a few weeks working on this." Graham ran a hand through his hair. "She agreed to hear offers in early November. I'll get back to you with an exact date. Thanks for handling all of this. I know I've been kind of scattered."

"Don't worry about it. Friends don't keep score," she reassured him. "But they do bill you."

Graham relaxed a little. His circle wasn't very wide, but it was deep.

"I know. You're the best, though. I mean it," he told her.

"Flattery will not get you a discount." She thanked the barista on the other end of the line. "I will see you in a few weeks, when you will hopefully be footloose, fancy-free, and signing some paperwork."

"I can't believe you're going back after the game," Peter pouted over his salmon at dinner.

Graham had changed his plane ticket from Monday afternoon to Sunday evening. It seemed wrong to leave all the work that needed to be done to Eloise. It had nothing to do with wanting to see her. Nothing at all.

"There's a lot to do," Graham reminded him.

To soften the blow that he was leaving earlier than planned, Graham decided to take Peter out to his favorite restaurant in Los Angeles, a cozy bistro with a weekly rotating menu. Fairy lights were strung into a canopy over the back patio where they were seated next to the privacy hedge.

On the other side of the patio, there was a loud gasp, followed by an ecstatic "Yes!"

Peter half stood to get a better look. "Oh. He just proposed. That's so sweet."

If there was a sappier, more hopeless romantic in the world than Peter, Graham had yet to meet them.

"I'm going to go say congratulations." Peter set his napkin on the table.

"Peter, no—"

But he was already walking away. Graham watched him cross the patio and touch the young woman's shoulder. She looked up and stared at him for a long moment, before bursting into a harder sob.

"Graham. I thought that was you."

An entire glacier formed in Graham's stomach at the sound of that voice. He had been so engrossed in watching Peter create a magical memory for the young couple that he had not noticed the man across from him take Peter's seat. His once-dark hair was almost completely grey now, but his green eyes were as sharp as they had always been.

"Are you sure you want to sit there? Someone might put it together," Graham said dryly.

"We do look a bit alike, don't we?" Russell Brooks studied Graham like a king looking at a portrait of his younger self.

"Was there a point to this visit?" Graham asked, doing his best to keep all but the barest hints of annoyance out of his voice. Showing emotion meant Russell won.

"A little birdy told me that you're looking to offload a property up in Oregon," Russell said. "A hotel?"

"Since when have you been interested in anything I do? If I remember right, you made it a point not to be interested."

The slight twitch of Russell's eye was the only hint Graham had that what he said had any impact at all.

"Tell me about the property, Graham."

Graham picked up his wine glass. He had no idea what to do with his hands. On the surface he was cool and unaffected, but underneath he was churning like a stormy sea.

"The building is roughly turn of the century, with much of the original character still intact." That was a nice way to put it. "The property includes several acres along the oceanfront. Nice town. Quaint. Could really be something with the right investor."

"So, you're in real estate now?" Russell asked.

Graham shrugged. "It's not like it isn't in my blood."

Russell's jaw tightened. "How much?"

He had no idea what the market was like for haunted hotels. But having something Russell might want made him feel good. Powerful. Any chance to even the score, even a little.

"You're just going to have to make us an offer we can't refuse. My business partner is reluctant to let go, but I think for the right price she could be persuaded."

"Most women can be persuaded for the right price," Russell said, and the slight raise of his eyebrow dared Graham to take the bait. He refused to give him the satisfaction of losing his temper.

"We've had some interest already, so if you can get the capital together, you should make an offer. I know things must be a little tight, what with Meredith's wedding and the Yoon deal falling through."

Paul Yoon was a friend of Graham's who had backed out of

a multi-million-dollar development deal with Russell's company about a year ago on Graham's advice. It had made the papers, and it had found its way back to Graham that Russell had thrown a heavy crystal award into a wall when he'd gotten the news.

"I'll think about it," he said. Russell stood and buttoned his sport coat as Peter made his way back to the table. "Say hello to your mother for me."

Peter sat back down in his seat and replaced his napkin on his lap. "Who was that?"

Graham watched his father walk back to his own table. Russell kissed wife number four on the cheek, while the daughter from wife number two drank her wine and looked incredibly bored. It was strange that they could be in the same place and she had no idea who he was.

"No one that matters."

CHAPTER THIRTEEN

By Sunday night, Eloise felt like she had run a marathon.

After a fourteen-hour day at the front desk on Friday, she had spent her Saturday standing in a dreary Oregon drizzle helping Connor run the high school cross-country meet. Her hands, feet, and nose had been numb by the time she was done helping pull out the stakes that made up the chute at the end of the race.

Then late Saturday night, one of the housekeepers had called out sick, so Eloise had spent her Sunday picking up the slack around the hotel. She vacuumed, changed sheets, dusted the million nooks and crannies all those gorgeous little details in the hotel created, and mopped the ballroom. The ballroom hadn't been necessary, but it was something to keep her busy so that maybe, just maybe, she would stop thinking about Graham.

Her conversation with Sybil, Connor, and Chase at barbecue night hadn't helped, and the borderline flirty emails they had exchanged about spreadsheets had only sent her deeper into a confused spiral.

She shouldn't want him. She had been over all of the very logical reasons why she should not want him over and over again until the list was tattooed on her brain. But she did want him. She wanted him so bad that her teeth hurt from clenching her jaw in frustration that she wanted him. The man looked like sin in a sweater, and then he went and did something thoughtful like send her food? How was a girl supposed to cope?

Graham wasn't the only reason for her confusion, though. After being largely silent after she had said she wasn't ready to meet him yet, Foolproof42 had resurfaced over the weekend, understanding and charming as ever. If he could handle her repeated rejections, big and small, with such grace, would it really be so bad to finally find out who the man behind the screen name was?

Foolproof42 was still an abstract of a person, though, and Graham was very real. And he was going to be back tomorrow, frustrating her and giving her brain scattering smiles in equal measures. It was a good thing he couldn't see her now. Her dark curls were a disaster after she had fallen asleep on Sybil's couch watching a movie, and her UPenn sweatshirt had a few bleach stains from cleaning. Eloise would perjure herself under oath if anyone asked if the idea of seeing Graham the next day gave her butterflies, but it did, and she wanted to look as devastating as humanly possible when he got back to the hotel.

That entire plan went straight to hell when she stepped into the hallway and saw Graham getting ready to open the door to his room.

Eloise froze like a deer staring down an eighteen-wheeler. Even if she had been able to make her legs work, it wouldn't have made one bit of difference because Graham had already seen her.

His eyes narrowed behind his glasses, and his lips parted slightly.

"It's ten o'clock, Eloise. What the hell are you doing here?"

He sounded confused instead of suspicious, and Eloise

thanked her lucky stars. For a moment, she had thought she was busted.

"Um, there's a leak," she said, surprised at how natural she sounded. "I was just coming to check on it. Weren't you coming back tomorrow?"

She could have sworn his cheeks grew pink, but it could have been the poor lighting. Graham ran a hand through his dark, thick hair, and then rubbed the back of his neck.

"Yeah. I, um, decided to come back early so we could get started first thing in the morning. We've got a lot to do in a short amount of time. Unless Crane Cove has an extreme hotel makeover team I don't know about."

"Sadly, no. I checked." Eloise took a few cautious steps toward him, drawn to him like the tide was drawn to the shore. "Is it a glasses day?"

Graham touched the edge of the frame. "My contacts were bothering me so I took them off on the plane. I don't recommend sticking your finger near your eye during intermittent turbulence."

Eloise tilted her head to one side, considering his face for a moment. "I think you could pull off an eye patch."

His chuckle was deep, and she felt the rumble of it in her core. Standing close to this man made it difficult to breathe properly, and her brain needed all the oxygen it could get before she did something stupid. Like touch him. Or offer to tuck him into bed.

"I should probably let you go to bed," she said. "You've had a long day, and you're probably tired. I'll see you in the morning."

Eloise was halfway to the stairwell door when Graham's voice stopped her.

"I know it's kind of late, but do you think I could get that tour now?"

Her stomach felt like a glass of champagne, all of the excited bubbles racing to the top.

She nodded, and then smiled. "Sure. Why not?"

Why not, indeed.

Eloise was going to have to start thinking with her brain instead of every other body part south of her neck. Her heart, stomach, even her vagina, had betrayed her into thinking spending more time with Graham was a good idea. And every time he smiled at her, or laughed at one of her terrible jokes, her brain stopped functioning altogether.

As they walked into the quiet dining room, Eloise was hit with a wave of nostalgia. Last year she and Edgar had been wrapping red and white garlands around the pillars that stood like sentries at the front of the room to make them look like candy canes just a few days before he had died. Bing Crosby had been crooning Christmas songs while they bickered about how many child-sized nutcrackers were too many nutcrackers.

Eloise blinked rapidly at the sudden onset of warm tears in her eyes. It was strange, the way grief rose up. How many times had she come into the dining room in the last year and not thought about Edgar at all? But now all she could remember was how Edgar had doubled the number of nutcrackers she had put out while she tried to figure out which bulb in the strand of lights was keeping the rest of them from turning on.

Graham's warm hand touched the space between her shoulder blades. "Are you okay?"

She nodded, trying to swallow around the rapidly growing lump in her throat.

"Yeah," Eloise answered, wincing at the way her voice cracked around the word. "Must be dust or something. We haven't used this room in weeks."

"Eloise..." His voice was low, half comfort, half warning. He didn't believe her and Eloise bit her lip to try and anchor herself, even as she felt all her edges rapidly fraying.

"It..." She sniffed. "Edgar and I decorated for Christmas. Right before..." She stopped to take a deep breath, blowing it out between pursed lips, then pointed at the columns. "We made those look like candy canes every year."

"Candy canes?" Graham asked, encouraging her to go on as his hand made small, soothing circles on her back.

"Yeah. And we would line the room with these, like, four-foot-high nutcrackers that Edgar thought were so cute. I swear we've got a million of them in storage because he kept buying them. God, he put them everywhere. From November to January, he would sneak them out, and then I'd put them away. Over and over again." Eloise sniffled and wiped her eyes on the cuff of her sweatshirt. "Sorry. I didn't mean to fall apart like that."

"If you call that falling apart, I'd hate to see what you'd say about my friend Peter when he watches *Moulin Rouge*. Full-body sobs, every single time." Graham gave her a small reassuring smile, then he frowned slightly. "Do you want a hug? I never really know what to do."

Eloise gave a watery laugh because he looked so earnestly concerned. "No, it's fine. I might really cry, and we would be stuck in some kind of awkward loop."

Graham relaxed and put his hands in his pockets. "If you ever want to talk about him, I don't mind. I know you two were close."

"I appreciate that." She worried her bottom lip with her teeth, then added, "He was really proud of you. I don't know what happened that made you not want to come to the funeral, but he was really, really proud of you."

Graham looked down at his shoes. "We had some disagreements over the last few years. Nothing that seems major now that he's gone, but at the time..." He shrugged. "He was such a stubborn old goat. It got to a point where we couldn't talk without fighting."

"What were you fighting about?"

"This place. What else?" He sighed. "I gave him money to retire. I was really excited I could do something big for him, and he bought this place instead. After that, it felt like every conversation we had was about money. I should have known better. He was always shit with money. The last conversation we had..." Graham took a breath, blinking hard a few times. "I didn't think he would have wanted me there, and—fuck, I didn't want to stand in the receiving line. Getting condolences from strangers...It felt like too much."

"It was a lot. I hid in a closet." Eloise gently touched his elbow. "Do you want a hug?"

"The awkward loop," Graham reminded her, swallowing hard.

"The offer stands if you ever change your mind," Eloise told him, and then stepped away from the dining room. It was easier for her to comfort than be comforted, and it felt like they could both use a laugh. She swept her hand down the hall like a game show model showing off a jet ski. "If you'll step this way, we're going to journey back in time, because no one has bothered to update this section of the hotel since the eighties."

"The 1880s or the 1980s?" Graham teased, and Eloise rolled her eyes. He began to head down the hallway ahead of her, and Eloise took a moment to admire the way the denim of his jeans cupped his ass.

It was a tragedy that no one had recruited him for a Levi's campaign yet.

"Are you coming, Rumple?"

Eloise was grateful for the dim light from the faux gas lamp sconces because at least there was a chance that Graham couldn't see how red her face felt.

"What is rumple supposed to mean?" she asked when she caught up with him and they fell into step.

"Rumpelstiltskin was getting to be a bit of a mouthful," Graham told her, and when she looked up at him, he was grinning at her. "Speaking of which, are you ever going to tell me that password?"

Her heart skipped a beat. "You're supposed to guess."

"Stubborn." Graham tilted his head to one side and wrinkled his nose. "Hmmm...Does it have to do with Chase?"

Eloise frowned at him and stopped in front of the doors to the lounge. "Why would it have to do with Chase?"

"Well, you two dated, and I've never seen a woman throw herself into her ex's arms—"

Eloise groaned in exasperation. "Oh my god." She pulled open the door. "I had been trapped in an elevator with you. I would have been happy to see my mother."

Graham stiffened. "I'm guessing you don't get along with your mom?"

"What gave it away?"

"You put her in the same category as me."

Eloise grimaced. That had come out awkwardly. It didn't take long for the guilt to follow. He hadn't deserved that. She turned the interaction over in her head as Graham explored behind the mahogany horseshoe-shaped bar, his head swiveling all around as he took in his surroundings.

The Crane Lounge was one of her favorite places in the hotel. The five-thousand-piece-stained-glass seascape set into the ceiling was a showpiece. Seeing guests marvel at it had always made her feel proud. The faux gas lamp sconces from the hall were used here, too, which kept the light to a warm glow and created inviting shadows in the corners.

She needed to replace a few lightbulbs.

Graham placed his hands on the bar top, and inclined his head to beckon her forward.

"Come here."

In the low light, he looked like the devil himself, master of all dark places. Cautiously, Eloise let go of the door and crossed the room. The door closed with a snick as she slid onto one of the bar stools, and a shiver slid down her spine. Graham's brow was furrowed, and she gripped the edge of the bar to stop herself from reaching up and smoothing his expression.

"I'm sorry," he said, reaching beneath the bar and plucking two rocks glasses from the stack. "I shouldn't have tried to pry like that. I just hate when I can't figure something out."

"Figure what out?" she asked as Graham selected their best bottle of whiskey from the high shelf. "What Chase was doing with me?"

"No." Graham poured some of the amber liquid into each glass, then picked one up, bringing it to his lips. "How he let you get away."

Heat from her cheeks spread through her body, pooling in all her most sensitive places, making her ache. The way the small muscles in his neck flexed as he swallowed made Eloise lightheaded, and she shifted on the stool, trying to find some of the friction she was craving. Clearly her session with her vibrator had not done its job if watching Graham drink whiskey was winding her up.

She took the other glass and gulped down the contents.

It *burned*.

Her throat, her chest, and finally her stomach were on fire as the liquid blazed through her body. Her eyes watered as she wheezed, and then coughed. Graham stretched across the bar and thumped her back.

"That wasn't supposed to be a shot," he told her gently,

amusement lacing the edges of his concern. Eloise wanted to die from mortification.

"Yeah," she rasped. "I figured that out."

"Do you want another one?" he asked, wrapping his long fingers around the neck of the bottle.

Eloise shuddered. Her stomach was still smoldering from the first one. "Are you trying to kill me now?"

Graham dropped his head as he chuckled, and the sound went straight to Eloise's panties. She pushed her empty glass to him for a refill.

"He gave me a pie," Eloise blurted.

Graham pushed the glass back, whiskey sloshing against the sides. "What?"

"When Chase broke up with me, he gave me a pie." This time Eloise took a small, careful sip, and while the liquor was warm, it didn't scorch when it went down. "He said I could either eat it or throw it at him."

"He bought you a pie to break up with you?" Graham's face was a combination of shock and horror, like he had been told the internet was going away.

"Actually, I think he got the pie from Connor. If I remember correctly, we broke up around the same time Connor basically turned into a one-man pie factory. I got three pies in one week. It was great."

Graham leaned on the bar, resting his weight on his forearms. "Are you going to compare me to your mother again if I ask what happened?"

Her face was going to be permanently red if she kept blushing. "Sorry about that." She thumbed the rim of her glass, trying to figure out how to best explain Chase and the aftermath. "We rebounded into each other. He was fun and a couple of years younger. He made me feel good about myself. After we broke up, I had people I had never even met coming up to me at the grocery store. It was a whole thing. Never date a McMahon if you don't want the whole town in your business."

"I will take that under advisement."

Eloise took another sip of her whiskey. "We just didn't really have any kind of spark. Good at being friends, but not a lot there after the initial infatuation had worn off. Does that make sense?"

Close proximity to her ex-boyfriend had never short-circuited her brain and set every one of her senses into overdrive. But being near Graham—hell, even when he was across the room—made her feel like she was lightning in a bottle, her blood crackling electricity in her veins.

He was looking at her thoughtfully, those gorgeous green eyes robbing her of any logical reasoning.

"Yeah, I think it does," he murmured, his eyes flicking down to her mouth. For a moment, Eloise thought he might kiss her, but Graham cleared his throat and pushed himself back upright instead. "We should reopen the bar."

Business as usual for her sex life.

"With what staff?" she asked, gesturing to the empty lounge. "Are you going to tend the bar?"

"I could until we find a couple of good bartenders," Graham said confidently. "Believe it or not, I used to be a bartender."

Eloise held up her glass. "Then why am I drinking straight whiskey?"

"Because if there is one thing I have figured out about you, it's that you are not the kind of person to half-ass shutting down a bar. I bet you turned off the ice maker and disconnected the soda gun."

"I don't know if I like that you have me figured out," Eloise said, and took another drink. "Why do you want to reopen the bar?"

"I was thinking on the plane." Graham began to take inventory behind the bar. "Assuming you don't sell, we need to get this place in some kind of working order again so no matter what I decide to do in a few years, it can be self-sustaining."

"And you think the bar is going to do that?" Eloise was skeptical. If people in Crane Cove wanted to drink, they had options in town, like Moonie's or Cranberry Brothers. No one was going to come out to the hotel for a beer.

"Alcohol has an excellent markup. And there have to be other ways for us to make money."

Everything that Eloise could think of cost her more money in payroll and overhead. Getting the restaurant going again—this time in a more upscale direction—might draw in people from town year-round, but the cost of hiring a quality chef, wait staff, and then paying for food that might not get eaten made her nauseous.

"Nothing that I can think of," she said, finishing her glass of whiskey.

"Maybe we need to think outside of the box," Graham said. "What's next on the tour?"

CHAPTER FOURTEEN

A tour.

Where had that come from? What could have possibly possessed him to ask Eloise to give him a tour after ten p.m.? He was acting like a teenage boy with his first crush, inventing reasons to be near her. What was next? Inviting her to a group activity and "forgetting" to invite anyone else? Having Kiki find out how she felt about him? Passing her a note asking her to check yes or no if she wanted to go to dinner with him?

What had happened to his resolve on the plane ride from LA to Portland to be professional with Eloise?

Well, he knew what had happened to that. Eloise had looked adorably disheveled, her ponytail pushed askew on her head, and he had lost all sense of reason when she had started walking away from him and he had gotten a good look at her ass in leggings. It occurred to Graham in that moment that he had only ever seen her in skirts or dresses, and while they had all been excellent, none of them really did her ass the justice it deserved.

And as the warm water rolled down his back, he relived

every glorious sway of those generous hips, every teasing smirk, and every time she had licked those tempting lips.

It was her mouth that had nearly gotten him in trouble. In the dim light, with the scantest bit of liquor in his system, Graham had nearly kissed Eloise. He had never wanted to kiss anyone so badly. He wanted to know if the good whiskey they had been drinking tasted better when sampled off her tongue.

Graham had been fighting an erection as Eloise pointed out which details were original and what had been remodeled at some point, but back in his room, he couldn't fight it anymore. He needed to take himself in hand before things got out of hand.

He wrapped his hand around his hard cock and hissed with satisfaction. It was relief and torture to finally be touching himself after being aroused for so long. The friction from his jeans had been too much and not enough, driving him slowly mad until they'd said goodnight and he'd stripped as soon as the door closed behind him.

He knew he shouldn't fantasize about Eloise, shouldn't imagine it was her hand stroking his shaft roughly, but he couldn't help it anymore. He had tried to be good for the last week and picture anyone else, but it was never quite enough. Those big blue eyes looking up at him, even if only in his mind, did more for him than his entire highlight reel ever had.

It was like someone had struck a match at the base of his spine and the fuse ran straight through his cock. His thighs shook, and then slowed to a quiver with the intensity of his orgasm, and he rested his head against the shower wall as he caught his breath.

He was so unbelievably, unmistakably screwed.

It was an uncharacteristically sunny Oregon October morning, and the early light was filtering through the colored panes of the stained glass, making a kaleidoscope across the carpet.

"Good morning, Morticia," Graham said as he walked behind the front desk. Kiki was reading a book, and he was afraid to ask her the title.

"Lucifer," Kiki replied, and they shared a friendly smirk. She placed her bookmark between the pages and closed her book. "You're up early."

After letting off some steam in the shower the night before, Graham had slept like a dead log. He had woken up early almost optimistic that he could sort out his feelings for Eloise.

Except Kiki was grinning at him like she knew something. Or she thought she knew something, which was possibly even more dangerous.

"I'm always up early," he said, trying to muster all the innocence he could. Not that he had a lot of innocence to muster after what he had done in the shower last night.

"Well," Kiki's grin widened, "I just thought since you and Eloise were up so late last night..."

She trailed off, and Graham turned his head to see Eloise come in the front door, balancing three coffees precariously.

If Graham had thought that seeing Eloise in the light of day would lessen his confusing feelings, he had been very, *very* wrong. She was wearing an outfit that made her look like she should be strolling through the streets of Paris nibbling on a chocolate croissant. Navy blue heels, a red skirt, a white-and-navy-blue striped shirt that sat just enough off her shoulders that it sent his overactive imagination into a tailspin. And then he got to her mouth.

Red lipstick.

Eloise had replaced her usual neutral pink with a bright, bold, fantasy-inducing shade of red.

Graham hadn't realized he was standing there gobsmacked until Eloise handed Kiki her morning coffee and said, "Did you break him?"

"No, but it's still early. You look adorable, by the way. Got a hot date?" Kiki looked at Graham as she said "date" and punctuated the question by taking a sip of her coffee.

"Me? Date?" Eloise laughed, and Graham wondered if he was imagining the nervous lilt. She shook her head and held out a cup of coffee to Graham. "Here. I don't think Sybil spit in it, but I had to endure a lecture about doing nice things for people who don't deserve it to get this."

He was touched, which only made his guilt about his shower activity grow exponentially. Not to mention the guilt about all the ways he had pictured them having sex in her office in the time it took her to cross the lobby.

And the way he was thinking about kissing her.

"Um, thanks," he said, and gulped down some of the contents. He gave her a tight smile even as he scalded his tongue.

Eloise frowned as she switched places with Kiki. "Are you okay? I thought you'd be more excited about the coffee after the way you went on and on about it in the elevator."

Graham edged around the desk until he was safely on the other side. "No, it's great. Super great. Super-dee-duper."

"Oooh-kay." Eloise drew out the word, and it would have been a mercy if the floor had opened up and swallowed him whole.

It did not help that Kiki looked positively smug as she gathered her things.

"I'll just leave you two alone," she said, and started to head for the door. "I'm sure you've got a lot to discuss."

"Actually—"

"I have some errands to run," Graham said quickly, and Eloise blinked rapidly. "I will, uh, see you later."

Like maybe tomorrow, when she would be wearing a shade of lipstick that didn't drive him to distraction. Tomorrow he might be able to look her in the eye without wanting to die of shame. Tomorrow he could be professional.

Today he was going to avoid his problems.

He caught up with Kiki just outside the front doors. "I don't know what you think is going on—"

"You and Eloise hooked up. It's cool." She shrugged, kicking a stray rock off the sidewalk as they walked toward the parking lot. "It's a bit like thinking about my parents having sex, but you both could use it."

"We did not hook up," Graham insisted, and his denial sounded over the top, even to him.

"Uh-huh. So why didn't I see Eloise go home last night after the two of you tried to sneak up the grand staircase? And why did she show up to work looking extra cute today?" Kiki took out her car keys, which had a little coffin keychain dangling down. "Plus you were so incredibly awkward. That was actually painful to watch. Was it bad?"

"We didn't have sex! Not that I would tell you if we did—"

"You're really bad at this denial stuff." Kiki unlocked her surprisingly sensible green Camry. Graham had expected her to drive something a little more unique, like a hearse.

"There's nothing to deny. Really." Graham ran a hand through his hair. "Eloise and I are just business partners. And speaking of the business, I wanted to ask you some questions."

"Me? What could I possibly know that Eloise wouldn't?"

"We're trying to brainstorm some ideas about how to bring in extra revenue—"

"Ghost tours!" Kiki blurted. "I've been telling Eloise for ages that we should do a ghost tour, but she doesn't want anyone thinking this place is haunted. I think we should just lean into it. Plus, it's October! What a great time to start."

Normally, Graham would have been on Eloise's side, but what Kiki had proposed made sense. It would cost them next to nothing and could bring in business to the bar before and after. The more he turned the idea over, the more he liked it.

"Draw up a proposal, maybe mock up some marketing for it, and I will absolutely consider it. I'm going to try and hunt down a chef today to get some kind of food service going again." Graham dug in his pocket for his key. "You wouldn't happen to know anyone, would you?"

"Actually, I do. Lemme go home and take a nap, and I'll take you to meet her. She's great. And as a bonus, I heard she's looking to move back to Crane Cove. It's perfect!"

"Move back? From where?"

"Portland," Kiki answered cheerfully. "You've met Gilda? She owns Coastal Cookie. It's her daughter."

Graham had met Gilda. The charming Black woman had a storefront in the historic district of Crane Cove, just a few doors down from Cranberry Brothers. She made all kinds of cookies, including jumbo cookies that were the size of a small plate. But her decorated sugar cookies were works of pure art. If her daughter was even half as talented in the kitchen as Gilda was with a piping bag, this could be amazing.

Kiki got in her car and dug around for a minute before scribbling something on a piece of scrap paper. "Pick me up around two." She handed him a receipt with an address scrawled on the back in a loopy script. "You know, it's kind of a shame you and Eloise aren't together. You could really be something."

———

Amara Walker was a revelation. Graham and Kiki arrived at the luxury hotel where she was currently a sous-chef just before the dinner rush started, and she brought them a small tasting menu with smoked scallop crudo, a grilled pork tenderloin with a sauce that made him moan, and a filet that he and Kiki fought over. Amara had grown up in Crane Cove and knew the hotel. She had a vision that Graham felt was in line with what Eloise wanted. She was familiar with many of the local farms, and even had ideas for bringing in products from the businesses in town.

After what had to be the shortest interview Graham had ever conducted, she was hired. He felt good about it. And it was one less thing that Eloise would need to worry about. It felt possible that the hotel would be on a path to either success or a successful sale in just a few weeks. While he was on a decision-making roll, he green-lit Kiki's idea to run ghost tours at the hotel. Given the amount of material she'd presented, he wondered just how long she had been planning this.

When Graham dropped Kiki off at her house, it was after dark, and the beautiful October day had turned into an epic downpour. His windshield wipers were going as fast as they could and it still looked like he was going through a car wash.

As he turned down Mulberry Street, his headlights caught a flash of red. The rest of the figure was swallowed up by the darkness, but he knew that red skirt. It had been in the back of his mind all day.

Careful not to splash her, Graham pulled up next to the sidewalk and rolled down the passenger window.

"Eloise?"

"Oh, for fuck's sake." Her hands went to her face to cover it. "This can't be happening."

He frowned. Why was she walking alone, in the dark, in the rain, without a jacket?

"Do you need a ride?" he asked, unlocking the doors. "Where are you going?"

"No, I'm fine. Really. I'm just walking home." Eloise wrapped her arms tightly around her midsection, glancing around the neighborhood. "It's not that far."

"Eloise, it's pouring. Let me give you a ride home."

"I'll get your car all wet," she protested.

"It's a rental."

"All the more reason for me to walk. I'll ruin the seat, and then you'll get hit with fees."

Graham rolled his eyes. "Am I really that bad that you'd rather catch pneumonia than let me give you a ride home?"

"It's not that..."

"Come on, Eloise. Seriously. It's not like I'm a stranger trying to lure you into my car. At least I won't murder you and dump the body in the woods." Graham turned on the passenger seat warmer and he saw her resolve waiver. "Who would call me an arrogant jackass if something happened to you, hm?"

"I'm sure there's a waiting list for the honor."

"But no one else would say it with such conviction."

That made Eloise grin, though she tried to hide it behind her fist. Warm satisfaction bloomed in Graham's chest.

"If you refuse a ride from a friend and something happens to you, you're absolutely going to get razzed on one of those murder podcasts."

She sighed heavily, but finally gave in. The dome light illuminated her appearance as she got in the car.

Eloise would have been dryer if she had jumped into the deep end of a pool. Her ponytail, which he remembered had been high and bouncy that morning, was limp, and loose tendrils were plastered to her face. Her shirt fit her like a second skin, and the white stripes were translucent. Small lines of pink gave away the color of her bra, and it took every ounce of willpower he had not to stare at her hard nipples.

Knights in shining armor did not ogle damsels in distress.

Eloise turned up the heat and held her hands up to the vents. "So, we're friends?"

"I was kind of hoping we were." Graham pulled back out onto the street. "And as your friend, I've got to ask, do you enjoy taking evening strolls in monsoons, or did something bad happen?"

All he got was silence from the passenger seat as they crawled down the street. After an entire song played on the radio—the lead single from Sam's latest album—Graham decided that she was probably not going to tell him.

"So, where am I going?"

More silence. He stopped at a stop sign and waited for her to answer. Eloise was looking out the window, her arms wrapped tightly around her midsection. Just as he was about to repeat the question, she finally said something.

"My car wouldn't start."

"And no one could come get you or give you a jump?" Graham was shocked. He couldn't imagine that Eloise, who everyone spoke so highly of, would have had a hard time finding help with her car.

When he looked over at her, she was worrying her bottom lip between her teeth.

"I, um, didn't ask."

"Why not?"

Eloise shifted in her seat. There was another long pause. "Because my check engine light has been on for a while and Sybil and Connor have been telling me to take my car in, but I never did, and I just didn't want to deal with the lecture."

"Why didn't you take your car in?" Graham asked.

Eloise was looking down at her lap, and right when Graham

thought she might answer, a car pulled up behind them and honked.

"Where am I going, Eloise?"

"The hotel," she answered quietly.

Graham took a right, though he was confused. Why did she want to go to the hotel? If her place was nearby like she'd said, then the hotel would be an even further walk.

"I can take you home. It's really not a big deal."

"I want you to remember you said that."

CHAPTER FIFTEEN

When Eloise's car would not start after she left Sybil's, she thought her bad day had reached its peak. It could not possibly get any worse.

She had been wrong.

The peak had not been that her shoes were not built for long walks, or when the sky opened up and dumped a bucket of water on her head. Nor had it been when the car that pulled up beside her had been Graham's.

He'd said they were friends.

A few days ago, it wouldn't have felt like he had taken a sharp tack and popped her balloon, but after last night and their crackling chemistry, Eloise had started to wonder if there was something there. She had even put in extra effort to look cute today, thinking there was no way her favorite lipstick could fail.

The way Graham had run the other way should have been her first clue that today had been doomed.

And as an encore, he was going to find out that she was a failure.

"I'm broke." Shame burned her cheeks. "I live at the hotel."

The silence while Graham absorbed that piece of information made Eloise want to jump from the moving car. Hitting the pavement at thirty-five miles per hour had to be less painful.

"I guess that explains why Kiki never saw you leave last night." He sounded calm, which she hadn't expected. She thought he would at least be a little shocked. "She thinks we're sleeping together, by the way."

"Oh god."

"Don't worry. I set her straight. No hanky-panky between business partners."

Eloise tried the door handle. It was locked.

"How did this happen? How are you so broke that you can't fix your car and you're living at the hotel?"

"It's kind of a long story." Eloise smoothed back her hair. "When Edgar hired me to the be the manager a few years ago, I didn't have any hotel experience. It didn't occur to me that it might be weird that he never let me look at the books, even though I had worked in finance. I got a monthly budget for operations, and it was always tight, but I made it work. After he died and I finally looked at things...It was bad. Really bad."

"So you moved into the hotel?"

"Not immediately." Eloise rested her head on the window. It felt so nice and cool. She had been tired all day, and telling this story was draining the last of her energy. "That happened a few months later when I got kicked out of my place. It was only supposed to be temporary, but then there were a lot of very expensive repairs, and bye-bye savings account."

"Why didn't you tell me?"

"Well, you'd been such a friendly, cooperative business partner." From the corner of her eye, Eloise saw Graham wince. She didn't feel bad. He *had* been a world-class asshole. "I don't know. Part of me didn't want you think poorly of Edgar. Or me. And I didn't want you to use our very red numbers against me to get me to sell the hotel."

"Is it too late to say I'm sorry? For everything I said and did—or didn't do, really." Graham rubbed the back of his neck. "I reacted poorly to the situation, and you didn't deserve it."

Eloise would have been less surprised if someone had told her that she was the princess of a small but prosperous country whose main export was pears. In her experience, powerful men did not apologize, no matter how wrong they were. And this was the second time in twenty-four hours that Graham had apologized.

"How bad is it?" he asked, turning down the road that led to the hotel.

"We sort of made payroll last month."

"So, now might not be the best time to tell you that I hired a chef today."

Eloise started to laugh. It was hollow, which echoed how she felt on the inside. More people to pay. The overhead. The restaurant had been a plan for down the road when they had their feet back under them. Not before the electrician had even had a chance to fix the wiring.

"Next you're going to tell me you've decided to let Kiki host ghost tours."

Silence.

"Graham, did you seriously tell Kiki she could host ghost tours at the hotel?"

"It's not a bad idea, really." Graham glanced over at her, and then quickly away. "She had a whole presentation ready, and it won't cost us anything to run—"

"Who watches the desk, Graham? Who? While Kiki is telling potential guests how many people have died at the hotel, who is watching the front desk?"

Graham pursed his lips, and she felt a little smug that she had backed him into a corner. Though the satisfaction was bittersweet because she had a whole new stack of problems to add to her mountain.

"I will figure it out," he promised. "And I will cover Amara's salary until the restaurant pays for itself. Which it will, by the way. She has some really great ideas. And Kiki said she would start marketing for the ghost tours tonight."

"I'm going to pretend those aren't happening." Eloise unbuckled her seatbelt as soon as he parked the car. Her entire body felt like it was weighed down with wet sand.

"It's going to be great."

She tried to glare at him, but he gave her one of his brain-scattering smiles, and all she could do was roll her eyes. The rain was still drumming steadily against the car, and Eloise braced herself to get soaked again.

"Hold on," Graham said as she reached for her door handle. He reached for something in the backseat, and then he got out, running around to her side of the car, and opening her door. One hand was holding an umbrella above his head, and the other he held out to her.

She took his outstretched hand, warmth traveling up her arm and down to her core. Underneath the umbrella was a tight squeeze, and she was pressed against his side as they walked around the puddles in the parking lot.

"So, which room is yours?" he asked as they reached the main doors. Eloise missed the contact the moment he stepped away to shake off the umbrella.

"Um..." She hugged herself to ward off the chilly October air, which made her clothes feel like a layer of ice against her skin. "We're kind of neighbors."

Graham had his back to her, so she didn't see his reaction to her confession, but after a beat of silence that felt like an eternity, his shoulders began to shake, and then he laughed. "I thought you were a ghost."

"Boo."

He wrapped up the umbrella and then held the door open for her. "So you fucking around with my shower wasn't a prank?"

Eloise shook her head. "I was trying to get you to switch rooms again. It was only a matter of time until I got caught."

"How has no one figured it out?"

At the front desk, Rochelle had her headphones on and was watching something on her laptop. She didn't even notice them as they walked through the lobby.

"I have a million and one reasons to hang around the hotel," Eloise explained as they climbed the stairs. She held onto the railing because it took an incredible amount of effort to put one foot in front of the other. "And I have keys to the exterior doors. I can sneak in and out pretty easily."

At the next landing, Eloise had to stop to catch her breath. Graham put a hand on her back as she swayed from a sudden bout of dizziness.

"Are you okay? Your cheeks are pretty flushed." He frowned and pressed the back of his hand against her forehead. "You're warm."

"I'm fine. I was freezing, and now my body is overcompensating. It's dramatic that way," Eloise told him, and pushed herself up the next flight of stairs, even though her body protested every single step.

Despite her insistence that she was fine, Graham hovered like he was her shadow. If she slowed, his hand was on her elbow or her back, like he was afraid she would stumble or fall backwards down the staircase. She didn't mind him touching her, but the reason he was touching her was embarrassing, and she moved away every time he tried to help.

"Roxanne loves birds," Eloise said as they reached their rooms.

"Are you sure you're not sick?" Graham asked, touching her forehead again. His hand slid down the side of her face to her cheek, and Eloise leaned into his touch like a cat. She was shocked she didn't purr.

"It's the password to the computer in my office," she explained, closing her eyes because keeping them open was more effort than it was worth. "Uppercase R, no spaces. Roxanne loves birds."

"What does that even mean?"

"Roxanne—Annie—is my favorite cousin. Actually, she's my favorite person." Eloise knew she was rambling, but she couldn't seem to stop. "And she loves birds. She's getting a whole PhD so she can justify traveling the world to go bird-watching."

"I didn't know you could get a PhD in birds," Graham commented as he took her key from between her fingers and opened her door.

"It's biology, I think. She's so smart. My whole family is smart. My sister is a doctor. My brother is going to be a lawyer. And what am I doing with my life?" Eloise fell down on her bed, her arms sprawled out on either side of her body. "No wonder my mom is so disappointed in me."

"I doubt your mom is disappointed in you," Graham soothed. Eloise felt his warm hand on her calf as he took off one of her shoes. Early that morning she would have loved to have had him kneeling beside her bed with his hands on her legs, but in that particular fantasy she didn't look like a drowned rat and his hands had been a lot higher. Like on her thighs, pushing them apart.

"She only calls to lecture me about my life choices and to brag about my younger siblings. I bet the only reason she wants me to come home for Thanksgiving is so she can use me as a cautionary tale. 'Beware, or you'll end up like Eloise.'" She sighed as his thumb pressed into the arch of her foot. It felt heavenly. "That feels good."

"Good." He removed her other shoe and did the same to her other foot. "Now to make up for all the shit you just said about yourself, I want you to tell me three nice things about you."

It was hard to concentrate with Graham's strong, warm hands rubbing out all the soreness from her feet, but Eloise tried.

"I make a killer spreadsheet."

She could have sworn Graham made a noise that was somewhere between a moan and a growl. The sound would have thrilled her if she wasn't so tired.

"I'm resourceful."

"Mm-hmm."

"And you might disagree, but I think I look really good in red lipstick."

His hands left her feet. "Why would I disagree?"

"It doesn't matter," she mumbled.

"I should let you get some rest," Graham said, standing and walking quickly to the door. "Knock on the wall if you need anything."

"Will do, buckaroo."

The door clicked shut, and Eloise could only pray to the universe that had been so cruel to her all day that he hadn't heard that.

Eloise woke up to someone pounding on her door in time with the pounding in her head. She groaned as she sat up. All her joints burned, and she felt like she needed to oil them.

"Eloise?"

Of course it was Graham. Why was he waking her up at...

Eloise looked at the clock by her bed, and then picked it up to look at the numbers closer because they couldn't be right. It was 7:15 a.m. She was late for work. In her entire adult life, she had never been late for work.

She scrambled out of bed and shivered as soon as she was free of her covers. Was her room always this cold? No time to think about it. No time to do anything. She didn't technically have time to brush her teeth. A shower could be skipped—hadn't Mother Nature taken care of that last night?—but morning breath was unforgivable.

The burst of adrenaline she had used to get ready wore off as she pulled open her door. Had it always been so heavy?

"I'm here. I'm fine. I just overslept." Eloise hoped her voice didn't sound as gravelly to him as it did to her. And she hoped he didn't want to have a long, drawn-out conversation because her throat hurt like she had swallowed rocks.

Graham looked her up and down, then down and up. He shook his head.

"No. Go get back in bed."

"I have to go to work," Eloise insisted, but he blocked her exit with his body. No matter how she tried to sidestep, he was there. "Graham, move."

"Do not take this the wrong way, but you look like shit."

"Just what every girl wants to hear first thing in the morning," she said dryly, pressing her forehead into his sternum. If she couldn't get around him, maybe through him was an option. But Graham was a brick wall that smelled divine and looked damn good in a blue sweater, and he would not be moved. A scorching finger traced her spine from her neck down to her mid back.

"You didn't even finish zipping your dress. You're sick, Eloise. Go back to bed." The brick wall moved them into her room, and all she could do was walk backward to avoid getting run over.

"Who is going to watch the front desk? And—" A cough rattled her chest, and she looked up at Graham after it had passed to see him look at her with concern.

"I will take care of it," he said, pushing her down gently onto her bed. "You can call me every fifteen minutes to check up on me if you want, but you can't work like this. Rest."

She wanted to argue, but the last few minutes had zapped her of her energy. When Graham handed her the pajamas she had tossed off in her whirlwind to get ready, she accepted her fate.

"Every fifteen minutes. You said so."

"Yes, I did. Do you need any help getting out of your dress?"

"You know, I didn't think the next time I'd hear a man say that was when he was moonlighting as Florence Nightingale." Eloise leaned forward to expose her back. This was already a mortifying experience, so she might as well go all in with it. "Do I get a sponge bath, too?"

"Those cost extra," he teased as he lowered her zipper in a business-like fashion. Eloise had never felt more sexless.

"Can you get me the box of tissues in the bathroom?"

While Graham went to look for the box of tissues that did not exist, Eloise stepped out of her dress and back into her pajamas. She was just laying back down when he came back with a roll of toilet paper.

"No tissues, but this should work in a pinch." Graham set it down on her nightstand and then drew the covers up around her body, tucking her snugly into bed. "Get some sleep. I'll be back to check on you later."

She narrowed her eyes at him. "You aren't supposed to be chivalrous, Lucifer."

"I know, Rumple. You can pretend it's all part of my dastardly plan." He smoothed her hair away from her face. It truly was fate getting in one last, cruel twist of the knife that he looked so gorgeous when she could have doubled as a corpse in a police procedural.

"Luring unsuspecting women with foot rubs and toilet paper. That's how the devil gets his due." Eloise yawned.

Before he left, Graham filled up her water bottle, gave her a stern command to stay hydrated that definitely made something wet, and made sure her curtains were shut tightly.

She was asleep before the door closed.

CHAPTER SIXTEEN

If he'd had any concept of everything Eloise dealt with in a day, Graham never would have volunteered to cover for her.

Kiki had offered to stay, but without her gigantic cold brew, Graham could see her start to wilt around the edges. After a crash course in the reservation system, she left him alone with a stack of administrative tasks that got interrupted just as he got into a groove by the phone or by a guest. Eloise must have been popular with the guests they did have because he had never had so many people so disappointed to see him.

He sent a passive aggressive email to a guest who couldn't seem to grasp the concept of "non-refundable." Then he was verbally harassed by a woman with a Pomeranian in her purse because it had rained during her walk and Spartacus had gotten wet. When Graham had suggested an umbrella, she had stomped off with a huff. The fact that she was still standing made him question a major plot point from *The Wizard of Oz*.

By the time Rochelle showed up late for her shift with an iced coffee, Graham had posted help wanted ads on every website he could think of and was going to ask around when he went into town. Someone had to be available. According to Eloise's detailed, perfectly organized records, she covered almost every missed shift. It wasn't surprising she was sick. She had worked herself into the ground. He would cover any overages in payroll to give her a break.

———

Graham knocked on Eloise's door that evening, balancing a covered tray on one arm as he waited for an answer. Through the door he heard some muffled cursing.

"Don't get up. I made a key," he shouted.

The lamp and the TV were the only sources of light inside the room. Eloise's bed had a small mountain of used toilet paper chunks she had repurposed into tissues, the empty roll sitting on the nightstand. Eloise was sitting up in bed, her mass of curly dark hair twisted into a messy bun. Her nose was red and her cheeks were flushed, but she had a little more color than she had that morning when he had seen her.

"I guess it's a good thing I went to the store," Graham joked as he handed her the tray. "You would have needed to use the sheets next."

"Ha ha," Eloise deadpanned, though the sound was comical with her stuffy nose. She looked down at the tray suspiciously. "What's this?"

With a dramatic flourish Peter would have been proud of, Graham lifted the cover. It had taken longer than it should have and a phone call to Sam, but he had made chicken noodle soup from scratch.

"Soup," he told her. "Free from poison, because I know that's where your mind went. I got the recipe from a friend of mine who believes if he hasn't made it from scratch it's worthless."

He unloaded the grocery bag next. "Tissues, the kind with

lotion, because your nose probably hurts by now... orange juice... cough drops..."

"Oh my god."

"What's wrong?" Graham looked up to see Eloise staring down at the bowl of soup with a combination of awe and confusion.

"This is amazing." She shook her head in disbelief. "Is your friend a chef?"

"A musician, actually. I didn't make the noodles, though. Don't tell on me."

"Your secret is safe with me." Eloise took a few more blissful bites of soup before asking, "How did today go?"

"Well, Rochelle told me that if I was going to get on her case about what time she chooses to show up for work that she just wasn't going to come anymore. So today was her last day." Graham held up a hand because he could see Eloise winding up for a freakout. "I'm figuring it out. I've got some interviews lined up for tomorrow—"

"Graham, you can't—"

"Kiki is helping out—"

"Oh god." Eloise sighed, her head falling against the head-board. "One day. I left you alone for one day."

"And nothing bad happened. We need more staff anyway. You cannot keep covering every single missed shift. And don't get wound up about payroll. I'm going to cover the overages." Graham cleared himself a spot on the bed and sat down. "I also did some ordering for the bar, met with the contractor, and was a stellar customer service professional." That last thing was a lie, but Eloise didn't need to know that.

"I would give the last few dollars in my bank account to watch you deal with guest complaints," Eloise said with a smirk that made him smile wide in return.

"Telling people to go to hell in a way that makes them look forward to the journey has never been a skill of mine," he joked.

"I never would have guessed from your emails," she teased.

As she ate, they fell into a comfortable conversation. Like parents out to dinner for the first time in a long while, their conversation naturally revolved around their very big child: the hotel. But Graham had to admit that for the first time in a long time, he was excited about what he was working on, and he couldn't help but wonder what his life would be like at this moment if he had bothered to visit sooner.

————

By Thursday, Graham was positive he had bitten off more than he could chew with all the projects at the hotel, but he was so damn happy he didn't care. Renovations had started that morning, a few new staff members had been hired and given a crash course, and on Friday night, he was opening the bar and Kiki was hosting her first ghost tour. When tickets sold out within thirty-six hours of being on sale, Eloise had been speechless. Graham knew she wasn't exactly happy and had her fair share of doubts, but she gave Kiki a big hug and told her she was proud of her.

Graham had been shocked when Eloise had invited him to go with her to barbecue night at Cranberry Brothers.

"And it's not just because I need a ride," she had said. "You've been a really big help this week. I think we deserve a little bit of a celebration."

They had been working together in her tiny office. After staying in bed all day Tuesday, Eloise was chomping at the bit to get back to work on Wednesday. Graham couldn't convince her to go back to bed, but he did confine her to the front desk and the office, with strict orders to sit still. They worked quietly in the office, and it was a miracle he got anything done because Eloise had chosen to wear a sweater dress that made it impossible for him to focus.

Sitting still only lasted one day. She had him stripping the linens from the rooms that were only getting redecorated, and then remaking beds in the rooms that guests had checked out of. Eloise had been surprised that he was competent at cleaning.

"I don't have a housekeeper back in LA," he explained. "I like cleaning my own house. It's soothing."

When they were done for the day, Graham thought he would pass the time by responding to outstanding emails. Instead, he spent a lot of time getting ready for something that was definitely not a date. Sybil and Connor were meeting them there, and the twins would be lurking in the background. Still, he pulled out every single shirt he had brought with him, weighing the implications of every choice. The button-down shirts he wore to work felt too formal, but his Phantoms T-shirt was too casual—and after a quick sniff, too stinky.

Five minutes before he was supposed to meet Eloise in the lobby, Graham settled on a forest-green long-sleeve Henley, pulled on some dark blue jeans, and checked his hair one more time before grabbing a jacket on his way out the door.

In the lobby, he looked around for Eloise. She was leaning over the front desk, explaining something to Fiona, one of their new employees. Graham stared.

From his position, he could spend his time appreciating the outfit she'd changed into. Her shapely legs were covered by black tights, which were more exposed than he'd ever seen them by the short, swishy black skirt she wore. With the way she was balancing on her toes to see what Fiona was pointing to on the computer, the skirt barely covered her ass. Her burgundy sweater matched the velvet headband keeping her hair out of her face. She was a heady combination of adorable and sexy.

Graham tried to think of non-sexual things, like balance sheets, but that just reminded him of her spreadsheets, so by the time she walked over to him, his hands were in his pockets to try and disguise his erection.

"I made Sybil promise to be nice," Eloise said as they walked out to his car. Her ankle boots gave her a few extra inches, but her head still barely cleared his shoulder.

"You had to make her promise? And here I thought we'd really made some progress while I've been doing the coffee run."

"You did make progress. She's decided you're not worth the jail time."

While Eloise's car was in the shop, Graham had been making the morning coffee run. Sybil now treated him with indifference instead of hostility, probably because he overpaid for the coffee.

Cranberry Brothers was packed. It was unrealistic to imagine every resident of Crane Cove was squeezed into the brewery, but it felt like it. People walked around from table to table, talking and laughing. Graham had no idea how the servers found who they were looking for, but they did. He had just started to look for Connor's head, figuring the tall blond would be easier to find than much shorter Sybil, when he felt Eloise's hand slip into his. It was small and soft, and her delicate fingers curled around his as she tugged him through the crowd. Graham felt like his feet were barely touching the ground.

Sybil and Connor were tucked away at a table near the back, and Sybil gave anyone who even glanced at the empty chairs at their table a look that made Graham want to hide. Pints of beer were already on the table waiting for them, and a bowl of popcorn sat in the middle.

"There you are," Sybil said, standing up to give Eloise a hug. Eloise dropped his hand, and Graham missed the small contact acutely. "If Thursdays get any more popular, we're going to need to eat in the kitchen."

"Chase said you'd like that one," Connor said, pointing to the beer as Graham sat down across from him. "How are things going up at the hotel?"

"Good. Busy," Graham answered, picking up his beer. He recognized it as one of the ones he had selected for the taps at the hotel bar. "It feels weird not to be there, though. Kind of like leaving your baby with a sitter for the first time."

"Right?" Eloise sat down next to him. "Logically I know Fiona will be okay, but I almost want to call and check up on her."

"You're both ridiculous," Sybil admonished, shaking her head as she drank her beer.

"Says the woman who hasn't taken a vacation in five years because she doesn't trust anyone with her coffee shop." Connor raised both eyebrows at Sybil, who rolled her eyes. "Pot, meet kettle."

Eloise leaned over and whispered, "I usually just zone out when they start bickering."

"So you spend a lot of time staring off into space?" Graham grinned at her, and she gave him a wide smile that felt like a sunny morning in the middle of winter.

"Basically." Eloise crossed her legs, and he got distracted by the way the hem of her skirt slid a little higher on her thigh.

"It's nice to know some things never change." Graham looked up at the sound of a new voice. A petite woman who could have doubled for Tinkerbell had come up to their table. From the look of surprise on Connor's face and annoyance on Sybil's, he figured they probably knew who she was. The newcomer grabbed an empty chair from behind her that had just been vacated and sat down next to Connor. She picked up his beer and drank from it. "Mmm. This is good. Is it new?"

"I was drinking that," Connor said, and the blond woman held out the glass, but he sighed instead. "I'll just go get a new one."

"I'll come with you," Graham offered, standing as Connor did. "I need to talk to your brothers, anyway." He waited until they were a few feet away from the table before asking, "Who was that?"

Connor sighed again, tugging a hand roughly through his hair. "Just Mallory."

"And why is Just Mallory stealing your beer?"

"Because she likes to mess with me," Connor answered, finding space at the end of the bar to stand. He caught Chase's eye, who brightened when he saw Graham. "She's Sybil's little sister."

"You came!" Chase leaned over the end of the bar and drew Graham into an awkward bear hug. It was like being squeezed by a tree. "Cole and I are going to drop off the kegs in the morning. If I had known you were a bartender, I would have hired you."

"Mallory's back," Connor told him, and Chase rose onto his tiptoes to look around.

"When did she get back?"

"I don't know. She just showed up like she always does. And I need a new beer because she stole mine."

Chase laughed. "Of course she did. You know you're bigger than her, right?"

"Shut up and get me a beer."

"This place is packed," Graham said when Chase came back with a fresh pint for Connor and a tasting flight they hadn't asked for. "What's your secret?"

"Cole's meat," he joked, then shrugged. "Mallory said we needed to give people a reason to come besides beer. This worked for us. In the summer we do a live music series on the back patio." He pushed the tasting flight towards Connor. "Can you give that to Mal? I want her opinion."

Connor narrowed his eyes at his youngest brother. "Do it yourself."

Too late Connor realized that he had played directly into Chase's hand, and the horror dawned on his face as soon as Chase smiled widely.

"With pleasure."

CHAPTER SEVENTEEN

The moment Graham and Connor were out of earshot, Mallory turned to Eloise, her green eyes bright with curiosity.

"Who is tall, dark, and yummy you're on a double date with?"

"It's not a double date," Eloise answered in unison with Sybil, who was glaring at her younger sister.

"Are you sure? Because you look hot as fuck, and I thought the poor guy was going to get a nosebleed the way he was looking at you." Mallory took another drink of Connor's pilfered beer. "There was definitely some heat there."

"There's no heat," Eloise protested weakly, and she could feel her face flush.

"He's her business partner," Sybil huffed.

"So? They can still bang like bunnies." Mallory reached across the table for the popcorn, and Sybil pulled the bowl out of her reach.

"Don't do it, Eloise. You'll end up regretting it."

"Eloise, do him. Hard. And then tell us all about it in excruciating detail because Sybil has clearly forgotten what it's like to be touched."

The gauntlet had been thrown, and smoke was practically coming out of Sybil's ears. Eloise loved the Morgan sisters separately, but together it was like throwing a match into a powder keg. And watching them bicker over her sex life felt a lot like having a devil on one shoulder and an angel on the other, except the angel was wondering if this could be considered justifiable homicide and the devil was making some very good points.

Eloise was attracted to Graham. So much so that watching him make beds was erotic. Who knew that a nicely tucked corner could be an aphrodisiac? But like Sybil had said, they were business partners, and she might regret it. Eloise knew from experience the perils of workplace romance.

She looked toward the bar and saw Graham and Chase headed back, with Connor following behind. Graham *was* tall, dark, and yummy. She was a dirty, rotten liar if she said she never thought about what he looked like half naked or imagined what he would look like fully naked. Naked, sweaty, and pushing into—

"Mallory! What the fuck. You don't call, you don't write." Chase set down the beer flight on the table and picked Mallory up into a bear hug, her feet dangling a few inches above the floor. Eloise sighed. So much for her little fantasy. Though the star was filling out his Henley nicely in the seat next to her.

"I was driving around New Zealand in a camper van." Mallory laughed, hugging Chase back. "I wasn't really stopping for postcards or shopping for souvenirs."

Connor frowned at them, folding his arms across his chest. "Put her down before you break her."

"How long are you back for?" Chase asked, setting Mallory down on the ground.

"I don't know. Depends on what there is to do around here." Mallory plopped down on Connor's lap when Chase took her chair. He rolled his eyes, but curled an arm around her waist to keep her from falling. Eloise felt Graham lean in.

"You're going to have to fill me in here," he murmured against her ear. His warm breath on her neck raised goosebumps all over her body.

Eloise leaned back, her shoulder blades brushing against his chest. "It's nothing, really. Mallory is Sybil's sister. The Morgans and the McMahons may as well be family. They're just comfortable." She tilted her head to look at him and got lost in the multitude of shades of green, like minuscule vines spreading out from his pupil. Her sweater felt too heavy, and her fingers itched to tear it off. In private. With Graham watching.

Cole came up to the table, his hands full with a tray.

"Alrighty, I've got a little bit of—Mallory!" Cole set down the large tray that was filled with barbecue, knocking over the bowl of popcorn, and it would have taken out Sybil's beer if her reflexes were even half a second slower. Mallory was lifted into another dangling bear hug, and Connor ran a hand over his face. "When did you get home?"

The interruption broke the spell between them. Eloise and Graham pushed apart like magnets with identical poles. Her cheeks burned, and she was grateful for the spectacle of Mallory catching up with the twins to distract everyone at the table. Her friends would have turned that small moment into something more than it was: Graham asking a question. He'd had opportunities to make moves, and he hadn't. Hell, he hadn't even said anything about the outfit she had agonized over for two days while she tried to think of an excuse to hang out with him outside of work.

"I'm just saying a basic itinerary would be nice," Eloise heard Sybil say. Mallory was back on Connor's lap, and Cole had produced a chair from thin air. Food was passed around the table, and when her heart jumped at a simple brush of Graham's hand, Eloise decided she needed to do something about this silly crush. She just didn't know what.

"If I had a basic itinerary, I'd give it to you. But that's just not how my life works." Mallory picked up one of the small beers Chase had brought over for her to try. She sniffed it. "Oh, that's interesting. You're getting creative, Chaser." There was a hum of approval after she took a sip. "Fuck, that's good."

Chase's chest puffed with pride, and Eloise snorted. Despite having four older brothers, she knew that he craved Mallory's approval the most.

"Do you want us to put you on the schedule?" Cole asked, making himself a sandwich with a roll and a few slices of brisket.

"Yes, please," Mallory said. "I need to go talk to Moonie after this."

"Actually, if you're looking for another job, Graham and Eloise are reopening the bar at the hotel." Chase pointed to Mallory with his fork, addressing Graham. "Mallory is a pretty kickass bartender."

"And she helped us launch this place," Cole added, heaping on the praise. "We probably wouldn't be where we are without her."

"Still living at home?" Sybil quipped.

"Connor lives at home, too," Chase whined. "How come you never give him shit about it?"

"Who says she doesn't?" Connor reached forward for his beer. "And I hopefully won't be at home too much longer. I put in an offer on a house today."

Mallory offered him a bite off her fork, which he took. "Which house?"

"Mrs. Whitman's old house."

"On Lilac Lane?" When Connor nodded, Mallory blushed a little, looked away, and let out a quiet "Oh."

"If you're looking for a job, Mallory, we could use the help," Graham said. "Especially from someone who comes so highly recommended. Could you start tomorrow night?"

Chase was practically vibrating with excitement. "Ooh, that's great! Kiki is starting ghost tours tomorrow night. We got tickets!"

"Of course you did," Eloise groaned, and she felt a warm hand on her knee. Heat flooded the pit of her stomach, making parts of her just a bit lower ache, as she stared at Graham's hand. She must have stared too long because he removed it, and she bit her lip to keep from demanding that he put it back. One meager, friendly touch, and she was so turned on she needed to squeeze her thighs together.

"It's going to be great," Graham said, half to her and half to the entire table. "Friday and Saturday nights, all October. We sold out this weekend, and next week is going quickly."

Eloise had had her doubts. It had surprised the hell out of her when the first weekend had sold out. There wasn't any real proof that the hotel was haunted, and she didn't want all the deaths that inevitably happened over a century dug up and put on display for the general public. It didn't fit the romantic, luxury hotel atmosphere she had dreamed about for the hotel. But she couldn't be upset about the revenue it could bring in, especially when Graham showed her the numbers. All her plans for the future hinged on the hotel eventually making money again, and if this was an easy way to keep the lights on, she could suck up her pride.

The conversation flowed around her, but Eloise couldn't concentrate enough to participate. Her thoughts bounced between the hotel and her inconvenient attraction to Graham like a tennis ball at Wimbledon. She needed to scratch this itch before she did something really irresponsible, like knock on his door at two a.m. wearing one of the new robes she had ordered for the hotel and nothing else. That would be an excellent way to humiliate herself, because when she zoned back in on the conversation, she saw Graham watching Mallory with keen interest as she told a story from her latest globetrotting adventure.

It felt like someone had tied her stomach to a cement block and dropped it into the ocean. Down, down, down it went. Mallory was gorgeous, with thick blond hair that had an enviable natural wave, a wide smile, and sea glass-green eyes that were always sparkling with humor, like she had a secret joke she wouldn't share. And she was interesting. When she talked, people listened. One summer night two years ago, Eloise had watched her charm an entire bachelor party at Moonie's until she had the rowdy group eating out of the palm of her hand. They'd bought a round for the entire bar, and then had tipped her generously for the pleasure of being in her presence. Of course Graham was interested in the petite bombshell.

The room felt too hot and crowded, and Eloise pushed back from the table. She needed to be somewhere else, anywhere else. As Graham loved to point out to her, her face broadcast her emotions, and jealousy wasn't a good look.

There was a short line for the bathroom, but she didn't want to make small talk with the women waiting. For once, she didn't think she was capable of being nice.

The back patio was empty, since the twins only kept it open during the summer. Chairs were stacked and pushed against the side of the building, and the tables were chained together so they wouldn't blow away. Eloise went to the railing and leaned against it, gripping the top to center herself. She tried to concentrate on the way the crisp night air bit at her cheeks instead of the burning in her stomach.

What was the matter with her?

The low roar from inside the brewery returned for just a moment before it was muffled by the door. Someone had followed her.

"Are you okay?" Graham's voice made her insides burn with desire, while her skin burned from embarrassment. Her grip on the railing tightened as she dropped her head, hoping to hide her flush.

"Yeah." The word came out hoarse, and Eloise swallowed to try and get some moisture back in the throat. "Yeah, I'm fine."

"The last time you tried to convince me you were fine, you were half dead on your feet and running a fever." Graham gently turned her around to face him, the back of his hand resting against her forehead. The contact was wonderful and mortifying. "You don't have a fever, so what's wrong?"

"Nothing," Eloise insisted, though her voice snagged on the second syllable as his fingertips traced the outline of her face, skimming her jawline until he firmly grasped her chin. How had he known she wanted to look away?

"You have an incredibly expressive face, Rumple." He hadn't used his nickname for her since she had given him the computer password on Monday, but the sound of it slid down her body like warm honey. "Why are you lying?"

"I'm not—" He raised an eyebrow, and Eloise sighed. "It's nothing. I'm being stupid."

"Of all the things you are, stupid is not one of them."

The sincerity in his voice and the intense way he was studying her made her toes curl.

"Why did you follow me out here?"

Graham released her chin. "You were flushed. I was worried you might be sick again," he said quickly, taking a half step back. He looked at the sky, which was changing from muted blue to velvet black, and ran both hands through his hair. He looked conflicted, and as Eloise opened her mouth to tell him she was fine again, Graham leaned forward and gripped the rail on either side of her hips so tightly, she could see the tension vibrating through his body as he rocked back on his heels. If he had been a string, she could have plucked a melody down his spine.

"I don't know what's wrong with me," he finally managed, shaking his head. "I didn't even think about following you, I just did it. You've got some kind of gravitational pull, and—"

"Me?" Eloise must be sick again because this was clearly a fever hallucination. "You were just ogling Mallory in there."

"I was not ogling Mallory. I was trying not to stare at you because every time I even glance your way, Sybil looks like she's trying to decide whether to make my death quick and painless or slow and agonizing."

Eloise frowned, trying to fit together the pieces of a puzzle she didn't have a reference photo for. "So, you're not interested in Mallory?"

Graham let out a humorless laugh. "No. And I think I'm going slowly insane from trying not to touch you." His eyes locked on the hem of her skirt. "I haven't been able to think rationally since I saw you in the lobby."

"Oh." It was all Eloise could manage when he looked at her like he wanted her for a snack. Her pulse had the same strength and cadence of a jackhammer.

"Oh?" Graham echoed, his eyebrows drawing together. His muscles loosened, like a panther who had been tensed for the kill, but had decided against pouncing. "Right. So, there's that."

He had accused her of having an expressive face, but right then, Eloise could see his thoughts play across his face like a movie screen. Distress, remorse, self-recrimination. It hit her like a fist to the gut when she realized that he thought her mono-syllabic reply had been some kind of rebuff.

"No, no, no—"

"Eloise, it's fine—"

Graham began to draw back, and panicked, Eloise seized the front of his shirt, pulled him to her, and kissed him. He stiffened, and then let out a low, satisfied hum that reverberated down to her core.

Eloise vaguely heard the noise from inside the brewery grow louder, but it was like her head was underwater. She was drowning in him, every sense focused on Graham like he was the air she needed to live.

"Elo—Ope!"

Eloise knew that voice instantly. Dale Swanson was the mechanic that Graham had sent her car to for repairs. Dale had moved to Crane Cove from Minnesota because he wanted to live somewhere that reminded him of *The Goonies*. Luckily for the cars in town, he had decided against actually living in Astoria, and the town was thrilled to have him, even if every conversation took a minimum of twenty minutes.

She uncurled her fingers from Graham's shirt, smoothing down the wrinkled fabric before stepping away. She plastered a bright smile on her face. Nothing to see here.

"Hi, Dale. How are you?"

"Oh, you know, can't complain."

Dale began to talk, and Eloise smiled and nodded, listening as well as she could when her heartbeat was located in her panties. Graham was leaning with his back against the railing and his legs casually stretched out in front of him. Somewhere in the middle of Dale's story about his sister's knee surgery, Graham finally interjected.

"Did you need something, Dale?"

The old man chuckled, adjusting his Minnesota Twins baseball cap on his almost bald head. "Oh, I just wanted to let

Eloise know her car is ready to be picked up. Sybil said you were out here, but I didn't know you had company."

"We were just talking," Eloise lied with a big, friendly smile. "I'll pick my car up tomorrow. Thanks for letting me know, Dale."

"Just talking?" Graham said when Dale had gone back inside, his voice taking on a low, husky timbre that made her shiver. He backed her up against the railing, his arms caging her in. "Is that what we were doing?"

She nuzzled the strong column of his neck before planting an open-mouthed kiss on his pulse. The way he shuddered made her feel powerful. "I'm a girl who appreciates a deep conversation," she purred, letting the innuendo hang heavy in the air. "But we should go back inside."

Graham groaned and rested his forehead against hers. "This is how you're going to kill me, isn't it?"

She couldn't help but grin. "Is it such a horrible way to die?"

He sighed, pressing his hips firmly against her belly so she could feel his arousal and Eloise started to reconsider her entire stance on exhibitionism.

"I'll go happily," he said, touching his nose to hers, "as long as I get to have you first."

"Should I put that on your headstone?" If she didn't make a joke, she was going to dissolve into a puddle of swoon. Graham rolled his eyes and stepped away.

Eloise fixed her headband and adjusted her sweater, then held out her hand to him. When he didn't take it, she frowned. "Aren't you coming inside?"

"I need to cool down a little first."

"Do you want me to wait with you?" she offered, moving closer, only to have Graham back away again.

"No. Because if you stay out here with me, looking like that..." He ran both his hands through his hair, then laced his fingers together behind his head. "You have no idea the amount of effort it is taking to keep my hands to myself."

"Is it the skirt?" She played with the hem, and Graham's needy groan made everything between her thighs throb. "I wore it for you."

"Go inside before I decide having a public indecency charge on my record wouldn't be so bad," he commanded, and a thrill shot through Eloise as she hurried to comply. She paused at the door, looking back to see Graham watching her with hungry eyes. With a wink, Eloise slipped back inside, hoping she could look calmer than she felt.

CHAPTER EIGHTEEN

Graham had no idea how long it would take for his aching, persistent erection to subside to a point where he could safely walk back inside and not have everyone in Crane Cove know that he and Eloise had kissed on the patio.

Well, sort of kissed.

The brief brush of her lips had not been enough. He wanted to devour her. But thinking about all the ways—and places—he wanted to kiss Eloise was not going to help the throbbing problem in his pants.

Graham took out his phone and opened the FanForum app. If things went the way he hoped they would, he was not going to be watching *Claymore Abbey* tonight. The episode would be posted online the next day, so he wasn't too worried about missing anything, but he didn't want Little_Teapot wondering what had happened to him. He had barely checked his messages all week, distracted by work and Eloise.

> Foolproof42: Something came up and I won't be watching tonight. Don't spoil it for me.

There. Done and dusted. But the message didn't do much to

ease the pang of guilt he felt abandoning his friend after being so absent to hopefully end up in Eloise's bed. Or his bed. He wasn't picky about the location.

His phone buzzed once in his hand.

> Little_Teapot: That actually works out great because I'm on a date. We can catch up about it another day. Hope everything is okay stranger.

A date?

Graham was relieved he wasn't breaking her heart, but it made him question their previous interactions. Who was she on a date with? She'd never mentioned anyone. But just last week they'd been a little flirty and that that hadn't stopped him from lusting after Eloise.

> Foolproof42: Everything is fine. Have a nice time. Be safe. Channel your inner Lady Amanda and punch him in the face if he gets too handsy.

Sitting next to Eloise without being able to touch her was another level of torture, especially with the way Sybil glared at him every time he broke some kind of invisible barrier of acceptable distance between them. A few test leans told him that six inches was the minimum amount of space required for the redhead.

Meanwhile, Eloise did absolutely nothing to help the constant simmering of his blood. At one point, she had licked some barbecue sauce off her fingers, and he had thought he was going to pass out. Then, just like she knew every filthy thing he wanted to do to her, she sucked the tip of her pointer finger while looking at him, and Graham had to drown his moan in his beer.

"We should get going. I have an early morning," Eloise said with perfect angelic innocence about a half hour after Graham was more than ready to leave. She hugged her friends, and as he waited, Chase came up and shook his hand, which was weird because normally the Viking tried to crush him in a hug. It was when he felt something square and plastic press into his palm that he knew what Chase was doing. There was no doubt in Graham's mind that he was blushing profusely as Eloise's ex-boyfriend palmed him a condom and winked.

"What did Chase do?" Eloise asked as they got into the car. "Because you look like you just walked in on your parents having an orgy."

"He passed me this." Graham handed her the condom with a resigned sigh. "Was I that obvious?"

Her head fell back and she laughed until she was wiping tears from her eyes. Graham put the car into reverse, shaking his head and trying not to smile. It was equal parts hysterical and mortifying.

"I thought I was being subtle," Eloise gasped, still trying to catch her breath from laughing as they drove back toward the hotel.

"I told you, Rumple, you have a very expressive face. You were giving me big, sexy bedroom eyes."

"I was not."

"The way you sucked on your finger says otherwise."

Even with just the passing light from the streetlights, Graham could see her deep blush. He wondered if she was always so bold, or if he brought something out in her. He hoped it was the latter. The idea that only he got to see this sexy, playful side of Eloise made him feel special.

She reached for the volume knob on the stereo, turning up

the radio before casually letting her hand drop onto his thigh. It felt hot as an iron through his jeans, and Graham wondered if he'd survive her touching his bare skin. God knew he wanted her hands all over him.

"I like this song," Eloise said, her hot hand sliding higher on his leg. His cock twitched like it wanted to try and reach her hand. "It sounds so sweet, but it's…"

"Absolutely filthy," Graham finished for her. He knew the story behind this song. He remembered Sam drumming out the beat with his fork and knife at a Michelin-starred restaurant in France when they had met up with him on his last big world tour five years ago. Apparently, he'd had a wild night with a girl he'd met in Barcelona a few days prior that had been incredibly inspiring. "Kind of reminds me of someone."

"Lower your expectations. It's been a while."

"How long is a while?"

"Long enough that I might need to check for cobwebs first," Eloise joked, but there was an edge of unease in her voice. As much as he was enjoying her hand creeping up his thigh, he took it in his own and squeezed gently.

"You know we don't have to do anything, right? We could just make out and cuddle."

"I know, but—" Her phone began buzzing loudly in her purse, distracting her as Graham parked the car at the hotel. She didn't reach for it and looked ready to finish her thought, but it began buzzing for a second time. "I'm sorry. I need to check that."

"Take your time," Graham said, releasing her hand so she could dig in her purse. When she frowned, his heart sank. "What is it?"

"It's Annie. My cousin." She tacked on the second part, like he had forgotten that her favorite cousin was the password to the office computer. "One call means she's bored and just wants to chat, two calls means something is up." Eloise bit her bottom lip, and Graham's heart clutched. His cock was going to be angry, but he couldn't do anything when she looked so conflicted.

"I'm going to leave the car on," he said, taking her chin in his hand so she would look at him with those big, beautiful blue eyes. "Take all the time you need. I'll just...go for a swim so I don't climb the walls."

"Thank you," Eloise mouthed as she answered her phone. "Hey, Annie. What's going on? Are you okay?"

His arms, legs, and lungs burned as pushed off the pool wall, turning into another lap. Graham didn't know how long he had been swimming, or which lap he was on, but it was doing next to nothing to take the edge off. Even if his cock wasn't painfully hard anymore, he needed the sweet relief of release so badly he wanted to crawl out of his own skin. His hand wasn't going to cut it tonight, but the longer Eloise took talking to her cousin, the more he thought it might have to do.

When his hands touched the tiles on the other side of the pool, Graham surfaced, clinging to the edge of the pool while he sucked in air, his chest expanding with the effort to get in as much as possible as quickly as possible. The click of the door closing echoed through the space, and he lifted his head to watch Eloise walk across the pool deck. Blood immediately rushed back to his cock, and he pressed against the wall.

"Is everything okay?" Graham asked as Eloise put her purse down and then took off her headband, tossing it down on her bag.

"Annie's boyfriend is a jackass," she seethed, planting her hands on her hips. "She's too good for him, but she puts up with his shit because he ticks the boxes on what she thinks she wants." She began to pace in short circuits. "She wants mail addressed to Dr. and Dr. Price-Booth, so she'll give up orgasms to get there. And I can't even say, 'Honey, if he's not going to go down on you, I don't think he's going to hyphenate his last name.'"

Graham couldn't believe what he was hearing. He wanted to shove his face between Eloise's thighs so badly he would have let her tattoo Lucifer on his lower back to make it happen. And Annie's boyfriend had just made it a million times harder for him to pick up where they had left off on the brewery patio. Jackass, indeed.

"And we were getting somewhere," Eloise continued, tossing her hands up in frustration. "You were being sweet, and fucking hell, that was sexy, but you know what I realized on the way in here? There is no sexy way to take these tights off. And I didn't wear cute underwear because I didn't want to get my hopes up. So, thanks a fucking lot, Jake, you killed the moment."

Even though his arms felt like Jell-O, Graham lifted himself out of the pool while Eloise ranted. At the close of her tirade, she looked up at him in surprise, like she hadn't noticed him approach. Graham took her face in his hands, his entire existence centering on the woman in front of him who was watching him with wide, impossibly blue eyes.

"He did not kill the moment," Graham said, his voice coming out in a low, husky rumble. Then, he bent down and kissed Eloise the way he wished he had back at the brewery.

Dear god, Graham could kiss.

His lips were somehow both firm and soft, and at the first hint that he wanted to deepen the kiss, Eloise parted her lips to give him entry. Her legs became about as useful as tissue paper in a rainstorm as his tongue slid against hers, and she clung to his shoulders, reveling in the way his muscles tensed under her hands. Water seeped through the front of her sweater as they pressed together, and Eloise wondered if she'd ever be able to smell chlorine again without getting faintly aroused.

Graham was more than faintly aroused.

"Mmm...we should go back to my room," Eloise suggested, her breath catching as Graham's teeth grazed her throat. His hands were everywhere, making her dizzy with raw, greedy need. Well, almost everywhere. Not where she needed them most.

"Does your cell phone work in here?" His voice was dark and ragged, but the question was so strange, it pulled Eloise out of her haze for a moment.

"No," she answered, and the wicked smile that spread across his face sparked a fresh wave of heat. The look in his eye was probably illegal in the Bible Belt.

"Good." Graham guided her backwards, his hands on her hips and his mouth devouring hers in hungry kisses that tasted faintly of beer, until they tumbled onto one of the chaises that lined the side of the pool. It was so perfectly awkward that Eloise started to giggle, and Graham joined her, his forehead resting on her chest as his shoulders shook. "That was smoother in my head."

"You've got to stick the landing," she teased, combing her fingers through his wet hair. "How was that supposed to go in your head?"

"I was going to lay you down gracefully, say something clever like, 'I'll show you a sexy way to take off those tights,' and then I was going to ask if I could go down on you."

Eloise was positive that her panties hadn't just melted, they had disintegrated. Visions of those green eyes looking up at her

from between her thighs made her pussy clench with anticipation.

"Yes."

"What?"

"Yes, you can absolutely go down on me." When his hands
slid under her skirt, Eloise remembered why she had worn tights
in the first place. "But you need to know that I didn't have time
to shave."

Graham cocked an eyebrow. "Why the fuck would I care
about that?"

Eloise gave a small shrug. "Some guys care."

"You have been having sex with the wrong guys, Rumple."
His fingers bunched around the material at her hips and began
to drag it down, and the heat in his gaze stole Eloise's breath. It
had been years since a man had looked at her with such
reverence.

"What are you thinking about?" Graham asked, planting
kisses on her skin as he rolled her tights down her legs. He was
right. It was sexy watching him take them off.

"That this is most definitely a dream, and if anyone wakes
me up, no jury in the world would convict me."

Graham's husky chuckle fanned the flames in her blood into
a wildfire. His teeth found a sensitive spot behind her knee she
hadn't known existed, and she bit down on a moan. Eloise lay
back in the lounge chair, because if she kept watching him, she
would actually combust. Not watching, though, meant she was
more acutely aware of the way his knuckles brushed against her
calves, and how the end-of-the-day stubble on his jaw scratched
her skin. Could he hear the way her heart was beating?

"Fuck, you're soaked," he said as he pushed her skirt higher
up on her hips.

"Well, if someone hadn't been edg—*ohmygod*." Eloise's hips
arched off the chair as Graham licked her through her purple

cotton underwear, so sensitive that even the muted sensation set off little fireworks.

"So good." Another lick. A suckle. A playful nip that made her whimper. By the time he tugged her panties off—mercifully swift this time—Eloise was a gasping, needy wreck. Her nipples were painfully taut, and her hands slid under her sweater and into the cups of her bra. The relief that washed over her as she touched them made her moan, the sound echoed from between her thighs. "That's it. Now let me know what feels good."

His tongue slid through her aching folds, and Eloise shuddered. "It already feels like heaven."

And then his tongue circled her clit and Eloise saw stars. She must have made some kind of noise, because she felt Graham's chuckle. He continued to taste her, making his own happy little noises, until she truly thought she couldn't take another moment of sweet torture.

"Graham," she whined, pushing her cunt harder against his mouth. She was so close. "Please."

"Tell me what you want."

"I....I don't know. Please."

"Do you want me to fuck you with my fingers?"

A new rush of wetness flooded Eloise. "Yes."

It was almost embarrassing how easily his finger slid into her. Almost. But it felt too good for Eloise to be self-conscious about the sound her wetness made as his fingers moved in and out, like he was searching for something. And then he found that something inside of her that made her cry out.

"Holy fuck!" A strong arm held her hips down as Graham added another finger, and Eloise bucked against him. "Oh god...don't stop...don't...Oh my god..."

Pleasure twisted tighter and tighter in her core, until a slight, ghosting nip of her clit sent Eloise careening over the edge. It was a good thing that he was holding her down, or she would have thrown both of them off the chair as her orgasm tore through her in quaking, clenching waves. Graham stayed with her, wringing every last ounce of pleasure he could from her, and then she finally relaxed, boneless, into the chair.

"That good, huh?" Graham teased, helping her back into her underwear as the last remnants of pleasure crackled in her blood like sparklers. Eloise rolled her eyes, but couldn't stop the contented smile that stretched across her face.

"If you have to ask..."

Graham pulled Eloise into his arms, and she snuggled against him, her fingers going to the light dusting of hair on his chest. His glorious, solid, perfectly muscled chest. And while she was sated, there was something hard and insistent prodding her hip.

"We don't have to do anything else," he said. "I can easily get myself off to the memory of you coming around my fingers."

And just like that, Eloise was aroused again.

"What if I wanted to watch?" She reached between them and grasped his hard length, relishing his sharp intake of breath. "Or maybe help?"

"Have you been reading my journal?" he rasped, biting her shoulder as she gave him an exploratory stroke through his swim trunks. "Jesus, fuck..."

"That good, huh?"

"If you have to ask..."

CHAPTER NINETEEN

Graham stepped under the lukewarm spray. He was a man on a mission, and that mission did not require a completely hot shower. Eloise had told him he had five minutes to wash the chlorine off his body while she slipped into something more comfortable. He really hoped that was code for "naked."

He brought his fingers to his nose and inhaled. They still smelled like her, sweet and musky, and his balls throbbed painfully. If he didn't get off soon, he worried they were going to explode. Or fall off. The possibilities were limitless and all equally terrifying. There were commercials about the dangers of prolonged erections.

Soap was quickly and liberally applied to his body, with tender care given to the aching parts of his anatomy. It was tempting to stroke himself to relieve the pressure. The memory of her coming was burned into his memory, and he could still feel her walls clenching around his fingers. It would take no effort at all.

The metallic scrape of the shower curtain being opened made him jump, and Graham caught himself on the wall.

Which was for the best, because if he hadn't been holding on to something, he probably would have fallen.

Eloise was naked. Gloriously, gorgeously naked.

It was strange that he had been up close and personal with her pussy less than twenty minutes ago, but this was the first time he was seeing her breasts. They were large, tipped with dusky pink nipples, and he wanted to drown himself between them. Her waist flared into generous hips, and he could see her ass in the mirror.

"Are my five minutes up already?"

Eloise stepped into the shower with him, pulling the curtain closed behind her. "I got impatient."

Graham wasn't sure who reached for whom, but they met in a slippery, hungry kiss that lasted only until the water touched Eloise's skin. She jumped.

"Oh my god! Why is this so cold?"

"I was in a hurry!"

His hands explored her curves as she adjusted the temperature, unable to resist touching her. The water warmed, and Eloise stepped back into his arms, their kisses less frantic, but still bone-meltingly deep.

"So, I was thinking," she began, one hand sliding down his torso to grasp his stiff cock. "I'd like to repay that little favor you did for me by the pool."

"Was it little?" If he didn't joke, he was going to end up begging.

"Fine." A bemused smirk tugged at the corner of Eloise's mouth, and Graham couldn't help but kiss that tempting corner. "I'd like to repay that earth-shattering orgasm you gave me. Can I give you head?"

The sound he made was not at all dignified, and Eloise chuckled as she sank to her knees in front of him. How many times had he jerked off to this very scene? More than he could count. And it was infinitely better in person. She studied him, running her hands up his thighs, and Graham felt some precum leak from the tip.

"You are so sexy it isn't even fair." Eloise wrapped her hand around his cock and gave it an exploratory pump. His entire body shuddered.

"Oh, fuck," Graham whimpered.

"Maybe later, if you're lucky." And then she flicked her tongue over the head.

Pleasure shot through Graham like he'd been hit by a lightning bolt. It obliterated his knees, and his hands hit the shower wall with a loud smack as he struggled to stand. Eloise had the audacity to wink, but it was impossible to admonish the woman who was licking his cock like it was an ice cream cone on a summer afternoon.

God, she had barely begun and he felt like he was going to blow.

All those times he'd taken himself in hand, picturing this moment, he had promised himself that if it ever happened for real, he wouldn't miss a single second. So, instead of closing his eyes and sinking into the feeling of her hot mouth sliding up and down his cock, Graham looked down and saw big, blue eyes looking up at him. His heart clenched with something that went beyond desire, and longing opened a canyon in his chest as he ran a hand over her hair, sinking his fingers into the thickness.

Then he hit the back of her throat and she hummed, and Graham lost most of his higher brain function. The fingers in her hair tightened, and by the way her eyelids drooped, he had a feeling she liked that.

"Do you want me to fuck your mouth?" he asked, his voice sounding like gravel to his ears. Her little nod was the final nail in his coffin. Thought ceased, and he just moved, his hips pistoning until he felt his release building to a point where he wouldn't be able to hold it back much longer. It took effort, but he released his grip on her hair to give her the opportunity to back off as he gasped that he was close, but Eloise just sucked harder, her hands grasping his ass and pulling him closer. His orgasm ripped through him, his abs clenching so hard with the force of it that he bent over double. Wave after wave rushed over him, dragging him under into a deep, tumultuous ocean of pleasure. Vaguely, he felt Eloise release his cock, one of her hands stroking him as he shuddered, every nerve in his body as sensitive as a live, exposed wire.

"Holy...shit..." Graham panted, trying to gather the scattered piece of his consciousness. Was it normal to feel like he was floating after an orgasm? He looked down to check, and yes, his feet were still planted firmly on the shower floor.

Eloise gently cleaned him off, and then washed her chest, which had taken the second half of his orgasm. "I was not expecting that much," she joked, rising on equally unsteady legs. "Is it always like that?"

Graham shook his head, still not able to form a coherent thought, let alone a full sentence. The answer seemed to satisfy Eloise, and a smug smile spread over her lovely face. The canyon opened up again, and Graham wrapped his arms around her, resting his forehead against hers. A soft, content sigh escaped from him as her arms twined around his neck, all of her glorious softness pressed against him. There was no way to describe the feeling of completeness that permeated his being as they stood there, not talking, just holding each other.

For years, Graham had felt unsettled, restless, that if he stood still for too long he would fall behind. There had been a business to build, maintain, and further. Even if there had been time for a love life, he hadn't met a woman who interested him—who challenged him—the way that Eloise did. She was one of a kind, his Eloise. Smart, stubborn, and the perfect balance of fiery and sweet. Though there was nothing sweet about the way she had sucked his cock...

Eloise placed soft kisses along the line of his collarbone that Graham felt down in his groin. She was going to be the death of him. It had been minutes, and already she was getting another rise out of him.

"We should probably get out before the water gets cold," he said, his hands sliding down her back and over the curve of her ass, giving her a firm squeeze so she couldn't misinterpret his intentions.

"Mmm...Now you care about cold water." Eloise turned in his arms, bending over to turn off the shower. The view made his head spin.

———

Hungry kisses and groping hands hindered their futile attempts to dry off, and when Eloise and Graham finally managed to make it to the bed, they were still dripping.

"I brought...oh god...some condoms over," Eloise gasped as Graham's tongue slid across her nipple, her hips arching as he drew it into his mouth. Her fingers tangled in his wet hair, as if drawing him closer would somehow relieve the empty ache that had been building in her since she stepped into the shower with him.

"Eager?" he teased, switching his attention to her other breast, his hand filling with the one he had just lavished. The whimper Graham drew from her when his teeth scraped the sensitive tip sounded only a fraction as desperate as she felt. No amount of writhing or incoherent pleading seemed to speed Graham's pace; he was content to torture her slowly. Wetness she knew was not from their shower slicked her thighs as she squeezed them together, and she moaned in frustration when it did nothing to ease the ache there.

"You're such a fucking tease," Eloise groaned, and Graham had the audacity to chuckle. The amount of wetness she found when her fingers slipped between her folds was shocking, and she arched again as she circled her clit, so close to the edge with that small touch.

Graham grabbed her wrist, pulling her hand away. Before she could protest, he was sucking her fingers clean, and somehow she got even wetter. His green eyes were heated and possessive, like she'd done something forbidden by touching herself.

"Graham," she pleaded as he swirled his tongue around the tip of her index finger. "I need to come soon."

A satisfied smirk quirked the corners of his lips, and in that moment, he truly looked like the devil, ready to give her any pleasure she could dream of, if she only gave him her very soul. And if what he'd given her at the pool had only been a preview of his skills, she would give him anything he wanted without a second thought.

He stroked his cock a few times, and Eloise felt her cunt clench in response. She wanted him—no, *needed* him—inside of her. Mercifully, he grabbed a condom from the nightstand, and rolled it down his length. His eyes devoured her as they slid down her naked body. Normally, Eloise would have been a little self-conscious, wondering if he was judging her shape and size, but with Graham, she felt like the sexiest woman on the planet. She hooked her legs around his hips, digging her heels into his perfect, hard ass, pulling him to her.

"I was admiring the view," he said as he hovered over her again, the head of his cock teasing her entrance.

"You can look all you want later," Eloise promised, running her hands up his chest. "Right now, I need you to fuck me."

In a single commanding stroke, Graham filled her. If she hadn't been dripping, it might have been painful, but instead her body lit up like the Rockefeller Center Christmas tree. The fullness and the way he stretched her was divine. And just like he knew exactly what she needed, Graham threaded his fingers into her hair, tugging it hard enough that it only bordered on pain, all his weight balanced on his other arm. Eloise slipped into the sensations, losing herself in the way his teeth scraped her neck, how she immediately missed him deep inside of her when he slid back, and the surge of pleasure when their hips came together roughly. Tension built and twisted, too much and not nearly enough. The end was in sight, but perpetually out of reach. But, if sex with Graham was going to be her Sisyphean feat, she'd push this boulder up the hill all night long.

"Fuck, you feel good," he rasped, nipping at her earlobe. "So wet and tight..."

Those words, and his tongue tracing the shell of her ear, sent shivers down her body, and she moaned loudly in response. She dragged her fingernails across his back, which drew a coarse curse from him, and then he grasped her hips, tilting her pelvis slightly, and the next thrust caused pleasure to ricochet through her like a pinball. All Eloise could do was hold on as Graham's pace reached a furious pitch, the sound of the headboard smacking into the wall and her own drumming pulse filling her ears.

There was no gradual build to her orgasm. It roared up on her like a tidal wave, smacking her down and pulling her under. It consumed her, churned her over, and when she finally surfaced, gasping for breath, Graham had slumped on top of her, panting and still. Her hands soothed his sweaty back, vaguely aware of the welts from her nails through the tingly sensation in her hands.

"That was..."

"Yeah, I know," she finished for him. How could they possibly be expected to put words to what had just happened? "Transcendental" was the only word that came to mind, and it made Eloise giggle.

Graham trailed kisses down her neck. "What's so funny?"

"I feel like I'm floating," Eloise told him, because it was true. She felt lighter than a feather drifting lazily on the breeze. They lay there kissing and touching until the sheets grew cold from the water that hadn't bothered to towel off before jumping into bed.

"Do you want to go to my room?" she asked, kissing his jawline and enjoying the way his stubble scratched her nose. "The bed isn't wet."

"Yes, please." They untangled, and Eloise felt a pang of loss when Graham pulled away. "I've been trying to figure out what I was going to say when Kiki inevitably caught me stealing new sheets."

"Ice cream accident," she answered easily, picking up the silky robe she had intended on surprising him with before she had decided on jumping him in the shower instead. A delicious thrill zipped through her body when she saw how Graham watched her with hungry appreciation.

"Do we have any ice cream?" Graham asked as he fished a fresh pair of underwear from his suitcase, and then pulled a Sam Shoop concert T-shirt over his head, leaving his hair adorably rumpled.

"I might have some in my mini-fridge."

With a flourish that made her laugh, Graham gestured toward the door. "After you."

CHAPTER TWENTY

Eloise woke up to the familiar trilling of her alarm, though her limbs felt like they were made of rubber and it hurt to open her eyes. With a groan, she reached over to turn it off and a warm arm curled around her middle, drawing her back against a solid body. The brief flash of panic dissolved into warm memories of sharing her pint of freezer-burned cookie dough ice cream while sitting cross-legged on her bed. After finding out they were her favorite, Graham dug out the chunks of cookie dough for her as they talked—about the hotel, the town, their favorite movies, and which songs made the best shower ballads—idly touching each other in small, sweet ways, until they couldn't keep their eyes open anymore. Graham hadn't offered to go back to his own bed, and Eloise hadn't suggested it.

"Why did you even set that thing?" Graham grumbled, his voice still gravely, and he pressed a sleepy kiss to her bare shoulder. "We're in charge. Can't we sleep in?"

"If neither of us shows up with her coffee, Kiki is going to get suspicious," Eloise pointed out, snuggling back against him even though she knew it was going to make it harder to get out of bed. No man had the right to feel so good.

Another rumbly grumble from behind her made her giggle. "She already thinks we're sleeping together. We should just lean into it and take the morning off."

"How did you ever get to be so rich when you're so lazy?" she teased, and then moaned as he cupped her breasts, teasing the nipples into needy points. "Playing dirty now?"

"God, I hope so."

As much as she wanted to spend the day exploring his body —and it was very, very tempting—too many people had seen her leave Cranberry Brothers with Graham the night before. If she didn't follow her usual routine, there would be questions. Questions about their relationship and where it was going. Questions that Eloise wasn't prepared to answer after one night, but that wouldn't stop the Spanish Inquisition.

"I will go get Kiki's coffee." She wiggled out of his grasp, wrapping her robe tightly around her body as she got out of bed. "And you can laze about in bed all morning while I get some work done around here."

But what a sight he made in her bed. Still on his side, Graham had propped himself up on his forearm, the curve of his bicep pushing against the worn cotton of his T-shirt. His dark hair was adorably mussed from sleep, and Eloise's hands itched to comb through it. Dark stubble shadowed his jawline, and she briefly wondered what he'd look like with a beard. Devastating, probably. Which wasn't fair because he already looked good enough to tempt her back into bed, gossip and work be damned. Before she could cave like the weak-willed hussy she was, he rolled out of bed.

"Counteroffer. I take you to get coffee, we pick up your car, and then we make out in your office while we pretend to work."

A fresh wave of lust nearly liquified her knees, and Eloise almost didn't trust her voice when she found it to respond. Images of grinding against Graham while he occupied her office chair were making it difficult to form a coherent sentence. "W-won't it be kind of weird if we show up together?"

He shrugged casually as he pulled her against him, his hands exploring the curve of her ass. Again. Eloise was starting to suspect he was obsessed with it. "We work together. It's perfectly innocent for us to be grabbing coffee before we start our day."

Eloise was doubtful and tempted to tell him no, but then he curled a hand around the back of her neck and kissed her until she was breathless and gripping his shirt to keep upright.

"Okay. You win."

Eloise decided that almost nothing could ruin her good mood that morning. They'd had great sex the night before, had snuggled all night, and in the light of day, he still wanted to be around her. There may have been a bit of shyness between them, but it was colored with happiness instead of awkwardness. On the drive into town, their eyes had met several times, and they'd laughed, blushed, and looked away, only to repeat the process a few moments later. They were too old for schoolyard crushes, but it was the closest thing Eloise could relate it to.

Nothing but the deafening sound of a conversation ending mid-sentence and the heavy looks of nearly everyone she was close to in town staring at them.

Connor, Cole, and Chase were slack-jawed. Sybil had her mouth pressed into a hard line, radiating disapproval from behind the counter.

"Good morning," Eloise said brightly, taking a few long strides away from Graham. She smiled warmly at the twins, who were dressed in identical Cranberry Brothers Brewing shirts. "I didn't know you boys got up this early."

"As a rule I try not to, but apparently the most interesting things happen before eight in the morning." Chase wiggled his eyebrows, a knowing smirk curling the corners of his mouth.

Sybil huffed, pushing up the sleeves of her oversized red sweater. "There's nothing interesting happening here, you overgrown toddler." She moved through the familiar dance of preparing coffee, though her agitation was clear in the way she manhandled the espresso machine.

"Really? You don't think it's *interesting* that they showed up together?" Chase tilted his head, his smirk widening into a grin as Eloise felt Graham come up behind her. The warmth from her cheeks spread down her body, pooling between her thighs. She took a big step closer to the counter.

"What's so interesting about it?" Her voice was too high-pitched. She was a garbage liar when she didn't have time to prepare. "We work together. Can't we grab coffee before work?"

"And I was going to drop her off to get her car," Graham added. "It's innocent."

Apparently Graham was a bad liar, too.

"You doth protestest so much," Chase tsked.

Connor rolled his eyes. "That's not how that goes."

Cole barreled in. "I don't know about you, but I always blush when I innocently get coffee with my coworkers."

Eloise touched her cheek, wondering if she looked as warm as she felt. But Cole wasn't looking at her. A quick glance over her shoulder showed that Graham was crimson from his hairline to his neckline and studying the menu like his life depended on it.

"Oh, Graham, we wanted to confirm some things about your delivery later." Before he could protest, the twins pulled him away, and he looked helplessly over his shoulder. Eloise bit her lip to keep the laugh bubbling up inside of her contained.

"Didn't get a lot of sleep last night?" Connor asked. She

looked up at him, and he was losing a battle with his own smirk. His blue eyes glittered with barely repressed amusement.

"What makes you say that?"

"The hickey on your neck."

Eloise's hand flew to her neck, like she'd be able to retroactively hide the bruise. And then Connor snorted.

There was no hickey.

Where was a rogue asteroid when a girl needed one to end her existence?

On the other side of the shop, Graham wasn't faring much better. He rubbed the back of his neck, and Eloise got briefly distracted by the gentle bulge of his bicep, until the hiss of the steamer broke her out of what would have been a very spicy daydream.

"How was it?" Sybil asked, securing a lid on one of the special Stardust Coffee travel mugs she gave to customers after their one-hundredth visit. This one had Cole's name engraved on the side.

"It was fine." Eloise looked over at Graham as Chase slapped his back so hard the sound reverberated around the room. It was surreal seeing her ex congratulating the guy she'd nailed last night, but what about the last twelve hours had felt plausible? If anyone had asked her two weeks ago if she would ever count down the minutes until she could get Graham Thatcher alone again, she would have laughed until she peed her pants.

Connor winced. "Shoot me if a woman ever says 'It was fine' after we sleep together the first time."

"You'd need to have a sex life first," Sybil jabbed, filling Chase's mug next. "Tweedle Dum! Tweedle Dee! Come get your shit!"

"I have a sex life," Connor countered. "I just keep it out of town."

"It was better than fine," Eloise amended. "It was great."

Sybil shook her head. "You already said fine. No take-backs."

Eloise groaned, and then a warm, strong hand pressed against her lower back. "I think they're on to us," Graham whispered in her ear, and she shivered as his breath trickled down her neck. Whatever delicious, expensive scent he used—she needed to look again the next time she was in his room—washed over her, and her toes curled in her heels.

"What gave you that idea?" she teased, smiling up at him. When he smiled back, her heart did a giddy somersault.

"I got suspicious right around the time your ex-boyfriend fist-bumped me."

The ex-boyfriend in question slid in next to them, wrapping a gigantic arm around her shoulders. "Aren't you two just the cutest?" Eloise looked up at him, beaming like he had personally orchestrated their entire relationship. Whatever their relationship was. "I called it after the elevator. Though if you could have hooked up last week, I wouldn't owe Connor twenty bucks."

"You bet on us?" Eloise was aghast, and also not exactly surprised. The McMahon brothers—at least the three she knew well—were competitive down to their bones.

"Why do you think Sybil is being such a grouch? She had money on Halloween."

"I did not have money on Halloween. I said *if* I was going to join in your juvenile betting, my money would be on Halloween." Sybil shot an accusatory glare at Graham from around the espresso machine. "And *you* couldn't keep it in your pants and I lost a hypothetical bet. Maybe I'll make your coffee decaf today."

"I didn't even do anything. The punishment does not fit the crime."

"Decaf or regular. You'll never know."

Watching Sybil and Graham lob darts at each other, with Connor occasionally playing both sides to egg them on, Eloise's chest felt warm. It was a weird thing to feel content about, but it felt so incredibly natural for him to be there, going toe to toe with her friends, like they did this every morning. And when the corner of Sybil's mouth twitched with amusement, she felt a possessive surge of pride.

Developing feelings for Graham beyond a simple, lusty crush was a bad idea. If she repeated it enough to herself, she might remember that. His life was in Los Angeles, and he hadn't even hinted at wanting to leave city life behind. Crane Cove didn't even have a McDonald's. And, with a note of sourness, she reminded herself that he wanted to sell the hotel. All the improvements he was funding were to make the hotel more appealing to potential buyers, not because he bought into her grand vision of the future.

Still, she couldn't help but wonder how easily he would slot into Wine and Whining.

CHAPTER TWENTY-ONE

"So, I heard you slept with Eloise."

Olives spilled across the bar, a couple rolling over the edge. Graham righted the half-empty container he'd just finished filling, shooting what he hoped was a withering glare at Mallory. She just grinned at him, looking even more like Tinkerbell with her blond hair twisted into a bun. Hadn't people been scared of him once? At least a little? A few months ago he had commanded something that resembled respect, and now a pint-sized pixie of an employee was harassing him about his love life. Sex life. Whatever.

"How did you know?" he asked, trying to sound casual even though he could feel the back of his neck growing hot.

Mallory helped him herd olives into the trash, and then refilled the garnish container. "I didn't for sure. But thanks for confirming it." She gave him a dazzling smile. "Did you get coffee together this morning?"

"Yes. Why?"

"I had a side bet with Connor. They wouldn't let me into the pool, so I bet Connor that the two of you would get coffee together the morning after. He thought you two would be more...discreet."

"I didn't really even think about it."

"Of course you didn't. You're smitten."

Graham ran a hand down his face. This conversation was rapidly getting out of control.

"I'm not smitten. I—" From the corner of his eye, he saw the door to the bar open and Eloise slip in. His train of thought evaporated as his eyes swept from her feet to her head, and then down again much slower so he could imprint this moment in his memory. She was wearing an off-the-shoulder green velvet dress, with a neckline that dipped just enough into her cleavage to make him dizzy, and it hugged the curves he was obsessed with in a way that made his mouth water. When had he last touched her? That afternoon? Too long.

A sharp elbow dug into his side, and when he was able to pry his eyes away from the sway of Eloise's hips, Mallory had a smug smile stretched across her face.

He was not smitten. This was a normal, healthy hunger for a new partner after a long sexual drought. It was normal to daydream about breathy laughs turning into moans in the small supply closet on the second floor of the west wing. Or to drop off dinner before taking a pre-work nap. Absolutely nothing out of the ordinary about the fluttery beat of his heart.

Definitely not smitten.

"Is everything okay?" he asked. Eloise had that pinched look he was becoming disturbingly familiar with. Something was wrong.

She sat on one of the stools, her frown deepening. "I was just looking for Kiki. This whole thing kicks off in"—her eyes flicked up to the antique clock on the wall, and her deliciously red lips pursed—"a little more than an hour, and I haven't seen her yet." Mallory pushed a drink into her hand. "What's this?"

"A blackberry Dark and Stormy," she answered. "I also cooked up a little gin cocktail to make tonight extra special."

"I don't see how this helps with my missing Kiki problem."

"Drink it," Mallory insisted.

Eloise took a tentative sip, and her satisfied moan stirred up a lot of excellent memories.

"Oh, that's amazing," she said, taking another drink. "How did Moonie take it when you told him you were working here instead?"

"I'm still doing some shifts over there, so he wasn't too pissed. With three jobs, I might even be able to leave sooner."

That caught Graham's attention. "Leave? Why leave?"

"This is what I do. I come home, I work, I leave. Kind of like a bartending Mary Poppins." She pulled out a small chalkboard, a miniature easel, and a fitful of colorful pens from her bag that she had stashed under the bar.

"If you pull out a hat stand, I'm out." Graham leaned across the bar, resting his weight on his forearms. He skimmed his thumb over the inside of Eloise's wrist, getting buzzed from her shiver. "You know it's going to be okay, right?" he said quietly, and she bit her lower lip. "Kiki will be here soon. It's her big night, and she wouldn't miss proving you wrong for the world."

Eloise snorted but didn't relax. She stared into her cocktail. "I feel like I've been wrong a lot lately."

"Nah. Not about anything really important." He put a finger under her chin and tilted her face upward so she'd have to look at him. "Well, most important things. You did pick Captain America over Iron Man, but I can forgive you for that."

She gave him a shadow of a smile. "You're just mad I picked the poor kid from Brooklyn instead of the billionaire."

"I *was* the poor kid from Brooklyn, except not Brooklyn."

"Oh?"

"I'll tell you about it later," he promised. "And come on,

Tony's got an arc. Cap's a Boy Scout. He went from scrawny good guy to buff good guy who'd been injected with steroids. The only character growth was in his muscles."

"It wasn't steroids. It was Super Soldier Serum."

He gave her a dubious look, arching one brow slightly. "Which is a steroid on steroids." Graham grew thoughtful. "You know, steroids have been known to inhibit performance. Do you think that's why he doesn't date in any of the movies? Can't get it up?"

Eloise's posture had relaxed. If having a ridiculous conversation about superheroes relaxed her, Graham would spend the whole night trotting out his entire breadth of comic book knowledge.

"Maybe I like a Boy Scout," she said saucily.

"No, you don't." Graham leaned in closer, dropping his voice so Mallory wouldn't hear him, though she was doing a remarkable job pretending not to eavesdrop. "Because the morally upstanding, straight-laced guy wouldn't have pulled you into the supply closet this afternoon so he could—"

"Why'd you stop? You were just getting to the good part." Eloise twisted to see what Graham had seen. He could hear the color drain from her face as she said, "Oh. My. God."

Kiki's long, black hair was straight and parted down the middle, and her blood red lips stood out in stark contrast from the pallor of her face, which was somehow paler. But the coup de grâce was the form-hugging, floor-length black gown she wore that made her look taller, willowier. She crossed her arms and subtly lifted one eyebrow.

"You went full Morticia," Eloise squeaked, and then tossed back the remainder of her drink in one swallow. "I'm going to need more of these."

"Here." Mallory replaced her empty glass with a burgundy drink. "Try the Pomegranate Poison."

Eloise wobbled a little on her stool. "The what?"

"Pomegranate Poison. It's what I named the drink."

"But *why?*"

"It's a little morbid," Graham pointed out.

"Elias Crane was poisoned by his wife. It's on theme," Mallory explained with a shrug, then beamed at Kiki, who was sliding onto the stool next to Eloise. "You look absolutely phenomenal, Keeks. Spectacularly spooky."

Kiki flushed with pleasure. She either hadn't picked up on Eloise's palpable distress or was pretending not to notice. "I wanted to be atmospheric."

Graham snorted. Atmospheric was one word for it. Kiki did look spectacularly spooky. He half expected bats to swoop down from the ceiling, or for there to be a flash of lightning followed by a rumble of thunder. But the lights didn't so much as flicker as she switched into her role as tour guide, going over her script with Mallory. Her voice was pitched lower than normal to give it an air of mystery. If her job at the hotel didn't pan out, Kiki could make a killing as a very specific type of phone sex operator.

Across from him, Eloise had her hands wrapped so tightly around her drink he worried the glass would shatter in her hands. She would vibrate like a tuning fork if he tapped her shoulder.

"You need to relax," Graham soothed, wresting the glass from Eloise's iron grip. She narrowed her eyes at him, then dropped her gaze to the bar, becoming engrossed in the stack of coasters for a moment before quietly answering him through clenched teeth.

"Easy for you to say. Your entire future doesn't depend on this going well."

"No, it doesn't." Eloise's head snapped up, and he rushed

ahead before she could cut in. "And neither does yours. You have options."

"Like selling?"

"Exactly."

The look Eloise gave him made the icy glares she had given him his first few days in town look positively warm by comparison. She picked up her drink and swallowed it in one impressive gulp, then grabbed Kiki's hand and pulled her off her stool.

"Come on, Kiki. We should get you in position before people start showing up. Don't want to ruin your grand entrance," Eloise said, her tone so flat that it sent uncomfortable shivers down Graham's spine. Kiki threw a helpless glance over her shoulder at Mallory, but followed her boss out of the bar.

Graham and Mallory watched the door close slowly behind them, and there was a beat of heavy silence before Mallory let out a low whistle.

"Wow. I thought you were smarter than that."

"What's that supposed to mean?"

"You walked right into that very obvious trap." She shook her head, putting the garnish containers in their proper place. "Never thought I'd see a man tap-dance on his own grave."

Graham frowned, crossing his arms. "I don't even understand what I did wrong."

Mallory looked up at him with a slightly dubious expression on her face. "Really? You can't see a single thing wrong with that little conversation?" When Graham shrugged, she sighed and rolled her eyes. "You just think about it and let me know when you come up with something. Because that was like watching a high-speed crash happen in slow motion."

Graham couldn't concentrate. They were slammed from the moment they opened until the first tour group left on their journey through the hotel's twisted history. He dropped two glasses within the first twenty minutes, couldn't remember drink orders, and came very close to spilling the olives again. Mallory caught them right before they tumbled all over the floor.

"Pull it together," she hissed at him, before turning to smile brightly at the next person who bellied up to the bar.

He wanted to blame it on not having tended bar in about ten years. His muscle memory was gone. Most of the recipes he'd once made without a thought had disappeared from his brain without a trace. He should have practiced, but he'd assumed that it would be like riding a bike. Too bad he was terrible at riding a bike.

But in the half second he allowed himself to be honest, Graham knew that the reason he couldn't focus was because he had no idea where he had gone wrong with Eloise. All he had done was reminded her that she had options. She was stressed, and he had just tried to help. She couldn't be mad at him for that...could she?

As the first wave ebbed, Connor slid onto the corner stool, and Sybil boosted herself up next to him. At the other end of the bar, Mallory was chatting to a trio of local men while she poured them beers. When she caught sight of her sister and friend, she gave them a small nod of acknowledgement, and extracted herself from her conversation. Graham noticed she didn't give the guy who paid his change, and he didn't complain about the large tip he had given Mallory.

"Where's Eloise?" Sybil asked as she readjusted her messy bun.

"Yeah," Connor chimed in, looking around the bar. "I thought for sure she'd be in here hovering."

"They had a little spat before opening," Mallory explained, and Graham wished she was taller—or he was much shorter—so he could hide behind her. Sybil's glare had to be taking years off his life. "He put his foot so far in his mouth it came out his ass."

"It was not that bad."

Mallory put down a few bills on the bar in front of Connor. "Double or nothing he can't figure out where he went wrong in the next fifteen minutes."

Cautiously, Connor extracted a few dollars from his wallet. "Are you going to tell me what he did?"

"So you can help him? No."

"How will I know if you're cheating?"

Sybil rolled her eyes, snatching the money from the bar and the money from Connor's hand, and she folded it neatly before tucking it into her pocket. "I'll be the judge, though God fucking knows why I try and referee your little games." She crooked her finger at her sister, and Mallory got on her tiptoes to lean across the bar and whisper into Sybil's ear. Her eyebrows shot up, and the full hurricane force of her glare fell on Graham again. "Wow. You are not as smart as I thought you were."

"I didn't do anything wrong!"

Mallory held out her hand to Sybil. "You might as well hand me the money now."

Graham pursed his lips. There was nothing wrong with trying to help. And if Eloise had a problem with what he had said, she should have said something instead of marching off.

With a low growl, he picked up a tray of used glasses to take them to the dishwasher. Mallory reached for them, prying the heavy tray from his hands.

"I'll take these. Connor, come on."

His brow knitted together, a mixture of confusion and suspicion. "Why do I have to go with you?"

"Because," she began, circling around the bar to deposit the tray into his hands, "I don't trust that you won't try and cheat while I'm gone."

"As if you're a paragon of fair play and honesty."

"I'll forgive that because I know you're still bitter about Scrabble."

"I am not still bitter. You cheated. 'Yolo' is not a word," Connor insisted. "You cannot cite the Urban Dictionary."

"Says who?" she asked, tilting her head to look up at Connor, her hands firmly on her hips.

"The rules!"

Mallory rolled her eyes, and Connor raised an eyebrow in response. The look probably would have intimidated someone else, but Graham was starting to think Mallory was impervious to intimidation.

"It only says dictionary, it never specifies that it needs to be Merriam-Webster. If you have a problem with how that was judged, you need to take it up with your grandpa."

"I never should have agreed to let Grandpa Beau referee. You're his favorite." Connor inclined his head in Sybil's direction. "Aren't you worried Sybil's going to help him?"

Mallory scoffed. "Absolutely not. Sybil doesn't care if he fails."

Connor trailed after Mallory, their argument about what could and could not be used as words in Scrabble fading as they left the bar. Graham glowered, his retreat not only having been cut off, but he'd been left—alone—with Sybil. He just wanted to be by himself for a few minutes.

"If they ever ask you to play a game, don't do it." Sybil warned him, studying the drink specials Mallory had written on the small board. "Connor's brother Chris has a scar from a game of Candyland."

"I will take that under advisement. Did you want a drink or...?"

"Mallory's wrong, by the way," she said, tapping the Spooky

Stormy. "I do care. Not about you, really, but about Eloise. Which is why I'm going to attempt to help you."

"How magnanimous of you," Graham responded dryly as he began to muddle the lime and mint in the bottom of the shaker. It felt good to squish something.

"When was the last time you were in a relationship?" The glare he flicked her way must not have been sufficiently withering, because Sybil merely crossed her arms on the bar top with a put-upon sigh. "Look, I get it. Dating sucks, and relationships are rarely worth it. I'm considering getting a cat so I can really commit to the whole spinster thing."

"You mean you don't have suitors beating down your door with your warm, nurturing personality?"

The corner of her mouth twitched. "Do *not* make me like you."

Graham poured rum over the freshly smashed blackberries, then smacked the top on the shaker a little harder than was necessary. "Why does it matter when my last relationship was?"

"Because you've either forgotten everything you ever knew about women, or you didn't know much to start with."

"Probably the second one," he muttered through gritted teeth.

"Shocking." Sybil sniffed her drink when he handed it to her, and took a small, cautious sip. Her eyes widened ever so slightly. "This is actually pretty good. You're not as useless as I thought you were."

Graham's patience had grown brittle. "Are you going to help me, or give me shit? Because I've got other things I can be doing."

The silence between them lengthened until a 737 could have landed on it. Sybil seemed unperturbed, taking a long drink while she stared him down. Just as Graham's temper was prickling, she spoke.

"It's like this," she began. "The second greatest mistake a man can make is starting a land war in Asia. The first is telling a woman how to fix her problems when she didn't ask for your help."

"So I'm an ass because I tried to help? That's bullshit."

"No, what's bullshit is that instead of being supportive and validating Eloise's very valid feelings, you tried to twist the situation to your advantage."

"I wasn't twisting anything."

"She expressed that she was stressed, and your response was to remind her that she can sell the hotel, which is what *you* want."

"It's—" Graham cut himself off, because he wasn't sure how to finish his thought. He had been dangerously close to saying that selling the hotel wasn't what he wanted. Was that true? Had he changed his mind? "It's complicated, okay? I don't want Eloise to feel like she's trapped. She has options, and she forgets that."

"Was tonight the time to tell her?"

He opened his mouth, and then shut it. Fuck.

"I don't think I like you very much," Graham said weakly.

Sybil snorted. "I'll put you on the list."

CHAPTER TWENTY-TWO

By the time Graham got back to his room, he was dead on his feet. He hadn't considered himself a particularly sedentary person, but there was a different kind of stamina to standing for six hours as opposed to running four miles or even going on a long hike. He knew he'd ache in the morning, and it didn't take much of an imagination to picture how miserable he would be working brunch service.

He was renewing his search for another bartender in earnest on Monday. But his sore feet and staffing issues paled in comparison to the problem he'd created with Eloise.

Sybil was right, even though it pained him to admit it. It hadn't been his intention, but he had been unsupportive and dismissive of Eloise's feelings. The cold shoulder she'd given him the rest of the night had sent the very clear signal that she wasn't ready to forgive him, much less talk to him. And if her intention had been to torture him with her nearness and that green dress, she had succeeded in spades.

He wanted to knock on her door, but it was late. In the morning, he'd apologize. Tonight, he needed to come up with a plan.

"Isn't it past your bedtime?" Peter teased when he picked up the phone. If there was anyone in Graham's life who could come up with a decent way to grovel, it would be Peter, who could teach a master class on romantic film.

Graham didn't see any point in beating around the bush. "Have you ever fucked up really bad with a woman?"

"Once, but it's not really an experience that translates to a broader audience. What did you do? Wait! Let me put you on speakerphone."

"Speakerphone?"

"Hi!" chimed Jordy and Sam in unison. At least he hoped it was Jordy and Sam. Graham wasn't thrilled about opening up to strangers.

Graham stretched out on his bed. "What are you guys doing?"

"Having movie night at your house," Jordy said. "It's not as much fun without you trying to smother Peter with a pillow when he quotes along with *Legally Blonde*."

"What, like it's hard?" Peter quipped, and then there was the sound of pillows hitting his body and a muffled groan.

"When are you coming home to watch him? Dempsey is on vacation so there's no one to monitor him," Sam said dryly. Dempsey, Peter's assistant, got six weeks' paid vacation, and they used every single day every single year. "It's an apocalypse-level event to have you both gone at the same time."

Graham sighed, running his hand over his face. "Things got a little complicated in the last twenty-four hours."

His friends listened attentively as he recapped the last day, from the kiss at barbecue night through their argument at the bar. Jordy only interrupted once to ask him how the sex had been, and then there was a muffled scuffle, which he could only assume meant Sam had thrown a pillow at him and Jordy had retaliated. They were as predictable as middle school boys.

"Ah, I see you've fallen for one of the great classic blunders," Peter said when he was finished. "The first, of course, being never start a land war in Asia. And then this."

"Why is everyone so obsessed with land wars in Asia? That's the second time I've heard that tonight."

"It's from *The Princess Bride*, the greatest film ever made," Peter explained. How could Graham have forgotten? They'd watched it enough that sometimes he wished someone would toss him into the Pit of Despair. "Whoever said that must be absolutely delightful."

Graham tried to imagine anyone describing Sybil as "delightful." It was too far-fetched. And if she ever met Peter, she would eat him for breakfast and use his bones as a toothpick.

"Not exactly." He pinched the bridge of his nose. "But she had a point."

"Yeah, you do try and fix things no one asked you to fix," Sam agreed, and Graham hoped he could feel the weight of his glare through the phone. He needed to get around to upgrading the Wi-Fi network in the hotel so they could video chat without it freezing. Not that he was going to be around long enough for it to be a problem.

Because it was becoming a habit, he realized, to imagine himself living in Crane Cove and running the hotel. His mental to-do list was a mile long with little things he could do to make the place more to his liking. Which was irrational, because he already had a life in Los Angeles that he had worked very hard for and had spent years perfecting.

"So why don't you just apologize?" Jordy asked. "It wasn't that bad."

There was a snort of derision from either Sam or Peter.

"Have you tried going down on her?" Jordy continued.

"Women have a hard time staying mad when you've got your face between their—"

Peter cut him off. "Is everything about sex with you?"

"Generally, yes."

Graham couldn't tell what was being said because they were all talking over each other, and he watched the minutes pass on the nightstand clock, each one bringing him closer to when he needed to get up in the morning.

"Guys," he finally cut in. "This really isn't helpful. Can you just tell me what to do so I can go to bed?"

"You apologize," Sam told him plainly.

"Thank you. I hadn't thought of that."

"Don't get smarmy. You asked. But I don't get why you're getting so worked up about this. If you're only having sex, how she feels about you long term is irrelevant. You're out of there forever in a few weeks."

Leave it to Sam to cut to the chase with surgical precision. There was no good reason for him to feel like his stomach had been twisted up into more knots than a balloon animal, but the marrow deep need to go find Eloise, hold her close, and make this all better was nearly overwhelming.

"Take a peace offering," Jordy suggested. "A coffee, or a cookie. Maybe a pony."

"Peter, I thought you'd have more of an opinion."

"Personally, I'm a fan of the boombox over the head, but I guess a cookie and an apology works, too."

Graham spent a few more minutes on the phone catching up with his friends, a pang of guilt hitting him in the chest as Peter detailed some last-minute projects that were making his usual travel schedule even crazier for the next eight months. Even though Peter was working and not just hanging around the house all day, it was hard not to feel bad about missing out on the little time they all might have to spend together for a while.

After confirming that he would be at the next Phantoms home game, Graham hung up and looked at the time. If he went to sleep right now, he would not be getting enough sleep before he needed to work in the morning. And with the way his mind was buzzing, there was no way he was going to be getting any sleep any time soon. He lay still, listening for any movement on the other side of the wall that would tell him Eloise was awake, but all he heard was the groan of the heating system as it turned on.

Tomorrow. He would apologize tomorrow. Somehow.

A shower didn't settle him down, and after twenty minutes of tossing and turning, he finally gave in and picked up his phone. It had been a while since he had mindlessly scrolled the general *Claymore Abbey* forum, and it was quickly clear from the different threads that he had missed a lot on this week's episode.

> Foolproof42: I haven't had a chance to watch yet, but WHO IS CAPTAIN GODDARD?!

> Little_Teapot: I just finished watching the episode. How have you not watched yet?! Do you care about spoilers because I'm dying right now.

> Foolproof42: TELL ME

> Little_Teapot: He rescues Annabelle! Scoops her up out of the marsh and she rides in front of him back to the Abbey. I swooned. And guess what? He was already on his way there! I guess he's the son of a friend and was invited as a potential match for Amanda. Oops.

Foolproof42: Annabelle isn't even out yet! Lady Amanda is NEVER going to catch a break. Ever. Speaking of catching a break, how was your date?

Little_Teapot: Great. But we kind of had a fight today and now I don't really know what to think.

Foolproof42: It's been brought to my attention I kind of suck at relationships, but if you want to talk, I'm here.

Little_Teapot: I was really stressed about work and instead of just listening, he tried to fix my problem and it felt invalidating.

Foolproof42: Yeah, I just found out we're not supposed to "fix" problems. How do you wish he'd handled it? For science.

Little_Teapot: I wanted him to listen and tell me it's going to be okay. The support would have been great. I'm a big girl. If I need help, I'll ask for it.

And that, Graham decided, was the difference between Teapot and Eloise. Eloise would rather work herself into the ground than ask for help. If he didn't remind her that she had options, she would hold onto the hotel until it drove her right into bankruptcy. Still, he didn't like that he had upset her, even if he stood by what he said.

His conversation with Teapot veered back into the safe harbor of *Claymore Abbey*, and they chatted back and forth for another fifteen minutes about where they thought the rest of the season was headed and reignited their feud about who they thought Lady Meryl would end up with, Ryston or Heston.

Foolproof42: I'm just saying that if Ryston doesn't come up to scratch soon, Meryl needs to cut her losses. If I was her, I'd give him this house party to figure his shit out and then move on.

Little_Teapot: To who? Heston? I know you root for anyone who glares at each other to get together, but those two would be a BAD match. All they would do is fight.

Foolproof42: Or fall hopelessly in love.

CHAPTER TWENTY-THREE

The mornings were getting colder as the calendar edged closer to November.

Eloise had been grateful for the newly repaired heater in her car as she drove into town to get some coffee. Sleep had been elusive as she turned her argument with Graham over in her head, like trying to solve a Rubik's cube that had a few stickers rearranged. No matter which way she twisted it, it didn't quite make sense.

Was it her fault? Or was it his?

Should she have walked away when she felt her frustration and anger gathering steam? Instead of waiting for him to come and talk to her—and glancing at him every few minutes wondering why he wasn't coming over—should she have gone and talked to him? Her pride told her she was right, but her bruised heart was whispering something different.

The questions had gnawed at her long after she went to bed. Determined not to go to him when he got back to his room, Eloise had watched the newest episode of *Claymore Abbey* on her laptop with her headphones in and the volume all the way up.

Eloise yawned as she pulled open the door to Stardust.

"I saw that," Sybil said from behind the counter as she finished twisting her thick auburn hair into a bun. "Late night?"

Eloise nodded, rubbing her arms to try and dispel the chill that had settled into the wool of her sweater in the walk from her car to the coffee shop. "That obvious?"

"Your under eye concealer is doing some heavy lifting today." She plucked a large coffee cup from the stack. "So, did Graham apologize yet?"

"No." Her mood sank lower. "I don't really know what to think right now."

"That he's a man," Sybil began, pausing briefly as the front door opened, and then continued as if nothing had happened, "and all men are useless?"

"Oh good, I caught an early performance. And here I thought I'd miss the Saturday showing of Sybil's one-woman show," Connor quipped. Eloise looked up at him as he put a plate heaped with cookies and secured with an abundance of saran wrap on the counter. "The opening monologue is always so riveting."

Sybil rolled her eyes, dumping two shots into the coffee cup before starting two more. "I wouldn't have enough material for a marquee performance if men weren't so disappointing."

"Present company excluded?"

"Never."

"Who hurt you?" Connor asked curiously as he leaned against the counter, running a hand over his face. He looked as tired as Eloise felt, and she wondered when exactly he had made all of those cookies. "Please tell me Graham apologized. I can't lose to Mallory again."

"If you want to stop losing money to Mallory, stop betting on my love life."

Sybil cackled. "Kitten has claws this morning. I love it." She handed Eloise the large cup of coffee, then began making Connor's usual order. "And unless you want to hand my sister your paycheck, stop agreeing to double or nothing."

"It seemed like a safe bet."

"Not as safe as you'd think." Eloise leaned back against the counter, the heat from the coffee cup seeping into her skin as the comforting aroma of coffee drifted up to her nose. Why hadn't Graham said anything to her the night before? There had been ample opportunity. And it wasn't like his room wasn't right next to her own. The idea that, once again, she was more invested than the other party made her chest ache.

"Eloise, I don't give two shits what happens to Graham, but I care about you, and I don't want you to get hurt." Sybil secured the lid on Connor's cup and handed it to him. "I think you need to think about what you want here. Is he worth losing sleep over? Because in a few weeks, he goes back to LA and whatever kind of life billionaires lead, and you'll still be here."

"Not a billionaire," Eloise murmured into her coffee as she took her first sip. The caffeine hit her like a wrecking ball, and she coughed in surprise. "How many shots did you put in this?"

"Four. Don't change the subject." She peeled back the saran wrap on the plate of cookies and picked one up, eyeing it suspiciously. She sniffed it, took a cautious bite, then let out a soft, satisfied sigh. "Oatmeal raisin. This counts a breakfast food." She stashed two more in her sweater pocket.

Eloise took the cookie Connor offered her, letting the rich blend of spices settle on her tongue with the bursts of sweetness from the raisins. It was soft yet chewy, and she took advantage of the time it took her to finish it to wrangle her thoughts.

"I don't know if he's worth losing sleep over," she said after another sip of her strong coffee that was destined to give her heart palpitations. "But I didn't feel this way when I was dating

Chase. Graham and I barely had an argument, and I feel...awful."

"That's because your relationship with Chase didn't mean anything," Connor said. She looked up at him, surprised by the bluntness of the answer. "What? It didn't. You both had a little fun for a few months and settled into your rightful path as friends. Graham is different."

Sybil crossed her arms over her chest and raised a skeptical eyebrow. "Elaborate, and remember that I can cut off your coffee privileges."

Connor didn't even seem fazed. "First of all, he's an adult. Chase is an overgrown Golden Retriever masquerading as a person." He looked to Sybil to disagree with him, but she waved him on. "You need someone who is going to challenge you but support you at the same time. I think that's what he was trying to do. Did he maybe do it wrong? Yeah. But sometimes us useless men need a map. Preferably one that's been highlighted and has the important landmarks circled."

"So, you think I need to be the one to crack first?"

"Do you want to be right, or do you want Graham?" He wrapped a strong arm around her shoulders and gave her a comforting squeeze. "I'm going to go freeze my ass off watching teenagers run through the woods. Talk to him, okay?"

Eloise was vibrating by the time she got to work. She had stayed to talk to Sybil until a group of walkers had come in for their morning caffeine fix, and then she had stayed to talk to them too. It didn't take an advanced degree to see that she was stalling going back to the hotel.

Avoidance was the name of the game. If she never asked Graham how he was feeling, they could keep going in Schrodinger's relationship—neither here nor there, both existing and not existing. Living in limbo had to be better than rejection, right?

Except it wasn't. It had stolen her sleep and turned her into a jittery, over-caffeinated mess. If she hadn't been too proud and too scared the night before to talk to Graham about her feelings —all of her messy, complicated feelings—she might have been sad, but at least she wouldn't have that awful, top-of-the-roller-coaster feeling in the pit of her stomach.

The manager's office was empty. She didn't know why she had been expecting Graham to be waiting for her there, but the way her heart shriveled up like a raisin left no room for interpretation: she was disappointed.

Eloise pulled out her chair, and was surprised to find a plate of golden, chocolate chip blondie bars with a generous amount of flaky salt on the top, just like she liked them. There was a folded note on top, with an E scrawled on the paper.

I couldn't sleep last night, so I made these. Can we talk today? – G

The unsettled feeling in her stomach was replaced by timid butterflies, and her hope reinflated. At least she hadn't been the only one losing sleep.

"Oh...hi."

Eloise turned. Graham was standing in the doorway, a few orange and red dahlias clutched in his hand. He quickly hid them behind his back, his cold-kissed cheeks growing redder by the second.

"Stealing flowers from the landscaping?" Eloise teased, and he let out a short sigh, extending the flowers to her.

"The florist doesn't open until noon on Saturdays," he explained, shoving his hands into the pockets of his slacks as soon as she took the flowers from him. "I don't know how to do this."

"Do what?" When Graham waved a hand in the space between them, she raised an eyebrow. "Use your words."

"This. Us. Whatever this is." He let out a rough sigh and closed the door behind him. "Our fight wasn't that bad. I mean, can we even call it a fight? And it just felt..."

"Big?" Eloise offered, and he nodded, pushing a hand through his thick, dark hair.

"I'm not sorry about what I said, because I think you needed to hear it, but I'm sorry about how I said it. I'm sorry that I hurt you. I'm sorry that you didn't feel supported, because I wanted you to feel supported. And I don't know how to make things okay again, so I made brownie things and tried to get you flowers and it all feels wrong now...I'm really sorry. I didn't sleep and I'm rambling, but I'm sorry."

Eloise brought the dahlias to her nose, pretending to smell the sweet flowers, but she needed the blooms to hide the small, wistful smile that blossomed on her face. Her heart tugged, twisted, and grew at the painfully earnest, tortured way Graham waited for her to answer.

"You look really tired."

Graham snorted. The tension in the room slid away, and in two steps, Eloise was in his arms, her cheek pressed against his chest and his nose in her hair. They stood wrapped up in each other for minutes that felt infinite, and with every passing second, she relaxed more until she wasn't sure where either of them began or ended.

"I really needed this," she murmured into his sternum, taking a deep breath and inhaling every wonderful scent that made up Graham. "I shouldn't have walked away last night. I'm sorry. Conflict can make me feel very uncomfortable."

"I didn't want to cause a problem, but I worry that you forget that you do have options. You are possibly the most stubborn, determined person I've ever known, not to mention loyal and kind, and I would hate for you to lose sight of what's best for you while you're taking care of everyone else."

Eloise tilted her head up to meet his eyes, and saw his brow creased with concern. She reached up to try and smooth it out with her fingers, and then stroked the stubble on his jaw. Graham pressed his face into her palm, like he couldn't get close enough to her, his eyes drifting closed for a moment.

He wasn't wrong. She was all of those things. But the hotel was what she wanted, even with all of its problems.

"I can decide what's best for me," she reminded him.

"I know. But that doesn't mean I'm not going to worry." Graham kissed her palm, and her stomach did a giddy flip.

"I guess you can worry." On impulse, Eloise stretched upward on her tiptoes and pressed a kiss to Graham's lips. Tender affection spread through her chest like warm honey, slow, soft, and sweet. His mouth followed hers as she lowered herself back to her regular height, but neither of them pressed to make the kiss deeper.

When he finally did pull away, Graham rested his forehead on hers. "Whose bright idea was it to serve brunch at the hotel?"

"Yours," she reminded him, rubbing their noses together, which earned a small smile from him. "Are you going to make it through service?"

"If I don't drop anything, it will be a miracle. I might even give myself a raise." His arms tightened around her waist. "Do you, by any chance, want to come to my room between shifts and take a nap?"

Eloise relaxed. She had thought he was going to suggest makeup sex, and she was too tired. Supercharged with caffeine, but tired. A middle-of-the-day nap sounded decadent, the kind of indulgence she never gave herself. And snuggling with

Graham? The bourbon-soaked, chocolate-covered cherry on top.

"I would love to take a nap with you."

CHAPTER TWENTY-FOUR

Somehow, they had limped through the weekend.

Brunch service had teetered on the edge of disaster when their pseudo-soft open had become a very hard open very, very quickly. The community had shown up—out of boredom, support, or morbid curiosity, she didn't know—in a big way, all lined up, waiting for the dining room doors to open.

And who was at the front of the line, grinning so wide Eloise thought their faces would break?

Chase and Cole.

It was hard to be annoyed with the giant Viking-like twins when they were so genuinely proud and supportive. Even if they did quiz the poor teenage waitress about every menu item.

Eloise had helped run food and drinks, so by the time she and Graham got back to his room, sex had been the furthest thing from either of their minds. They kicked off their shoes and collapsed onto the mattress, moving just enough to touch each other before slipping into a deep, dreamless sleep. When she woke up, they had gravitated toward each other in their sleep, her leg twined between his, and his arms around her body.

It was the best nap of her life.

The second night of bar service went better now that Graham had his sea legs back. Nothing broke, and he was more charming than Eloise had ever seen him. Making little old ladies blush with his single-dimpled smiles seemed to be his specialty.

A date had been Graham's idea. Pitched as a celebratory dinner when they were getting coffee that morning, Sybil had glared at him from behind the espresso machine.

"Work dinner or date?"

Graham had blushed, stammered, and then clarified, "Date."

Which was how they had ended up driving up the Oregon Coast Highway after Eloise was done with work. Going out to dinner in Crane Cove seemed like an engraved invitation to gossip about their fledgling relationship, so Graham had made reservations at a nice restaurant in Salty, which was even smaller than Crane Cove.

Mondays had never screamed "romantic date night" to Eloise, but as she hid her smile behind her hand while Graham cursed the entire time he parallel parked the car, it could not have felt more perfect.

"I hate parallel parking," Graham grumbled as he opened Eloise's door for her. She bit the inside of her cheek to keep from laughing. Poor guy looked genuinely bothered.

"I didn't have to marshal you in with those little light-up sticks, so I think you did a great job," she reassured him, curling a hand around the back of his neck and drawing him down for a long, tender kiss that sent a sizzle of promise down her spine.

"I'm surprised this place is so busy on a Monday," Eloise commented as she glanced inside of the restaurant. "During low season, too."

"Apparently they just got an excellent write up in a fancy food publication," Graham told her. "Sometimes I think Kiki is trying to set me up for failure when I ask her for suggestions."

"Why would you say that?"

"She sent me to Sybil for coffee."

Eloise snickered as they entered the restaurant. The Tidewater was a small bistro with rich, dark blue walls, accented with gold leaf and white paint meant to look like the tide receding from the shore. The lights overhead were globes, crafted from sea glass, casting a soft, warm glow over the twenty or so tables.

One strange interaction with the guy working the host stand later, Eloise and Graham were tucked into a table in the corner.

"Graham, what did he mean when he asked if you had 'it'?"

Graham was studying the wine list like he was going to step in as the sommelier. He glanced up quickly, and then refocused on his task. "Nothing."

"Graham."

He sighed. "I may have resorted to some bribery to get a reservation at the last minute."

"What kind of bribery?"

"A signed Jordy Taylor jersey."

"Must be nice to be rich," Eloise joked, though the teasing sounded a little hollow when it came out. It would be nice to have the kind of wealth Graham had. To be able to snap her fingers and get whatever she wanted, to solve any problem, would be a dream after the last year.

"Sometimes yes, sometimes no," he said, pausing to order a bottle of white wine for them from the waiter who appeared at the table. They filled in the time waiting for the bottle to come with small talk, catching up about the day and the upcoming week. After they got their wine and a basket of bread, Eloise couldn't help but pry.

"What did you mean 'sometimes yes, sometimes no'?" She tore a slice of warm sourdough in half. "You can buy anything you want. Problems just evaporate in the face of your bank account."

"Not necessarily." Graham picked up his wine glass, sniffed the contents, and then took a measured sip. "It's hard to know who only wants to be your friend—or more—because of your money. Especially in LA. At least here I know Chase and Cole enjoy hanging out with me because I pick up the tab."

"That's not true."

"It's a little true." He did an impression of the twins pretending to reach for their wallets when it was time to pay, or conveniently needing to use the bathroom when the check came. "But they also never charge me at the brewery and gave me a discount on the kegs for the bar, so..."

"They'll keep you young."

"There has to be an easier way."

Eloise's pulse jumped as his foot brushed her ankle under the table. They'd slept together since their nap date, but only in the purest sense of the word. Kissing, yes, a little groping, but the weekend had zapped any energy they had to do anything but cuddle and watch *Golden Girls* reruns. Which was nice, but she wanted more. She could feel herself flush as she thought about the lingerie she'd worn under her black dress. They wouldn't be too tired tonight.

"I want to know about your life in LA," she declared, needing to distract herself before she told him that the fancy restaurant with the prix fixe menu he had literally bribed his way into wasn't necessary, he could just have her in the backseat of his rental car. "Your friends, what you do for fun. I feel like you know a lot more about me than I know about you."

"That is very untrue. You have plenty of secrets." Graham thanked the waiter as he set down their first course, which had been plated to look like a tide pool at low tide. There was even some kind of foam to mimic the surf. He pierced a gelatinous glob with his fork, and a sauce ran out, filling the little faux pool with "water."

"Oh, wow," Eloise breathed, touching the tines of her fork delicately into the sauce. Gingerly, she brought the fork to her mouth and tasted it. Salty, tangy, and though she couldn't quite place the flavor, it was undeniably exquisite. "This is officially the nicest date I've ever been on."

"That is a tragedy. How has no one ever whisked you away in their private jet for a night at the opera?"

She frowned as a few dusty memories pinged like a cross country telegraph. "Isn't that a scene from *Pretty Woman*?"

"It's one of Peter's favorites."

"See, this is what I want to know. How did you become friends with someone who can't cook, can't drive, and watches *Pretty Woman*?"

"I met Peter through Sam, who I met at a charity thing. Jordy I met while I was still bartending. We sort of cemented our little group after a rather disastrous golf tournament. I think it was for cancer research."

"You can't throw out 'disastrous charity golf tournament' and not elaborate."

"We had to let two groups play through while Jordy was stuck in a sand trap, Sam got chased by a goose, and Peter accidentally drove the golf cart into a pond."

Her eyes widened. "How did he accidentally drive a golf cart into a pond?"

"First, he drove us into a—it wasn't quite a ditch, but it wasn't far off." He made a curve with his hand to demonstrate. "Then, he thought it was in reverse and stepped really hard on the gas." Graham sipped his wine. "The best part was this all happened while he was telling the caddy about this racing movie he'd done. How he'd done some stunt driving, learned to drift, then ka-thump." He shook his head, barely suppressing a laugh. "Sam was laying on the ground laughing so hard I thought he was going to pass out, Jordy was filming the whole thing, and the poor caddy looked like he was going to throw up because he was convinced he'd just lost his job."

"Did he lose his job?"

"Oh god no. Peter paid for the golf cart and signed an autograph for the owner's daughter. Smoothed the whole thing right over. No one stays mad at America's Sweetheart."

Again, the telegraph wires in Eloise's brain hummed as connections were made, and little details slid into place.

"Is your Peter, by any chance, Peter Green?" she asked and braced herself to be laughed at.

He dipped his bread in what was left of the sauce and the foam on the plate and nodded. Casually. Like it was an everyday thing to basically be roommates with someone whose face was regularly on the front of magazines.

"And let me guess," Eloise continued, "Jordy is Jordy Taylor, and Sam is..." She searched her brain for things he'd said about Sam. Graham's Sam was a musician, and she'd worn a certain artist's tour T-shirt to bed last night. "Sam is Sam Shoop."

Again, he nodded.

"What's it like? Being friends with famous people?"

Graham sighed, and picked up his wine glass. After a long drink of his wine, and their waiter clearing away their starter and placing salads in front of them, he answered her question.

"Utterly chaotic and surreal."

With a little prompting, he told her about his friends. And while he tried to keep an exasperated tone, there was an achingly affectionate note threaded through every story. Graham loved his friends. And it sounded like they loved him back. She was impressed by how hard they worked to line up their schedules so they could spend time together, even if it was just to get brunch.

"Peter has been pushing to name our little group the Brunch Bros, and while I've been up here, he convinced Sam and Jordy that we needed club jackets. He emailed me a few mockups today."

"Are these jackets going to be licensed so us common folk can buy them?" The scowl he shot her made her giggle. It was impossible to believe that he was cross with her when their legs were tangled beneath the table. Eloise fended off a play for one of her candied pecans with her fork. "You're a very good friend for humoring him."

"I learned a long time ago that once Peter gets an idea in his head, he cannot simply let go of it. And the jackets are nothing compared to my thirtieth birthday party."

"What happened at your birthday party?" Eloise was intrigued, especially when Graham flushed, and ran a hand down his face.

"Oh god. So, Peter loves to travel and wanted to take me on this crazy, globe-trotting trip because he couldn't believe I hadn't seen the northern lights in Iceland or something like that. I talked him down to what I thought was a simple house party." He shook his head. "It was an Around The World in 80 Days themed party. There was a hot air balloon in my backyard. And a camel. The sushi chef was great. The can-can dancers may have been a bit over the top."

"There was a hot air balloon, and the can-can dancers were a bit much?"

"I'm just glad he didn't get the permit for the fireworks. Or the elephant."

Eloise felt the laugh building, and she tried to tamp it down. She really did. It was clear that Graham wasn't as amused by his friend's antics as she was. But the sound couldn't be repressed.

The laugh started deep in her belly, and her last-ditch effort to smother it by taking a drink of wine only resulted in the most awkward swallow of her life. She laughed until her sides ached and tears stuck to her eyelashes. When she finally caught her breath and dabbed away any dampness that threatened to make her mascara run, she glanced across at Graham, who was looking back at her with a barely suppressed smile.

"Are you done laughing at my pain?"

"Yes, you poor, abused rich man." Eloise gave his leg a playful squeeze. "How terrible it must be to have a friend who loves you that much."

"How would you feel if Sybil threw you an elaborate surprise theme party?" He raised an eyebrow, like he had just thrown down a full house in a high stakes poker game.

"I would love it." She stole a pecan from his plate, popping it into her mouth a triumphant smirk. "But that will never happen. Sybil hates giant spectacles. She harrumphs at the town Christmas tree lighting every year."

He laid his hand on the table, palm up, and she accepted the silent invitation. His hand was big and comfortably warm, and the slight dampness on his palm was the first indication she'd had that he was nervous.

"You're going to have to explain the appeal to me, because I'm currently on Sybil's side, and that's something I never thought I'd say." Graham turned their hands over, and traced the lines in the palm of her hand, following each one to its end, and then back to the center.

"It's just..." Eloise shivered as his fingers stroked her palm, heat simmering low in her belly. How was a woman supposed to think about anything other than having those fingers stroking other places on her body? "It's having someone care enough to make that kind of effort. The planning, the coordinating—that they see you and want to make you happy." She caught his fingers, trapping them with her thumb. "And maybe your friend Peter massively overshot the mark, but it's pretty clear to me that he loves you a lot. The last time someone threw me a party, I was six. And there definitely weren't can-can dancers or a hot air balloon."

He frowned, and she wanted to kiss the downturned corners until they lifted again. "I guess I never thought about it like that before. I kind of sound like an ungrateful jackass, don't I?"

"If Peter ever decides to give up acting and wants a job as an event planner, you can tell him we're hiring," she teased. That got an eye roll and a small chuckle. "I like to think I'm a pretty decent boss, and the town is charming. And no traffic, which definitely gives us a leg up on LA."

"You're forgetting about the terrible cell phone service. He'd shrivel up and die within a week."

"You get used to it."

"You don't get used to it, you just learn the different spots in town where you get a signal."

"If you don't like it, why are you sticking around?"

"The scenery is fantastic," he answered easily, giving her a heated, languid smile that made her think he was not thinking about the ocean views. "The food is good. The people are nice. And like you said, no traffic." He paused, then added thoughtfully, "The hotel could use some work."

Eloise rolled her eyes. "Someone should say that to the wealthy man who owns it."

"Nah." Graham shook his head. "I heard he's useless."

CHAPTER TWENTY-FIVE

As first dates went, Graham thought that had gone very well. It had gone so well that he wasn't sure how he was going to cope the next time he went back to Los Angeles.

Somewhere between the starter and dessert, Eloise had cracked him open like a lobster claw and found all his soft, squishy bits. They had spent time together, sent business emails that bordered on flirtation—he lusted after her spreadsheets, for God's sake—but he hadn't been fully prepared for how disarmingly charming she could be. Graham was enchanted by the tiny smile that formed in the corner of her mouth when she found something amusing. He had never wanted to bottle up a moment more, just to keep it in his pocket and carry it around, than when they'd barely held hands across the table, only their fingertips touching.

He could spend the rest of his life caught in a time loop that revolved specifically around that dinner, and he'd never complain.

The road back to Crane Cove was dark, illuminated by his headlights and the waning half-moon that played peekaboo as clouds drifted by in a sleepy daze. Eloise held his hand in her lap, their fingers laced together, and he kept looking over to see what she was doing. Sometimes she studied his fingers, measuring the length between each knuckle with her free index finger, and then other times, when the trees stopped for a while, she looked out at the ocean.

"What are you thinking about?"

"Hm?" Eloise turned her head, and he could see the faintest hint of a blush in the scant light of the dashboard. "Oh, nothing."

"You're never not thinking, Eloise." It was one of his favorite things about her. Her mind was always in motion. Sometimes she started a conversation with him that she'd already half-finished in her head.

"I'm just trying to figure you out."

"I could probably help with that," Graham teased, squeezing her hand. Her blush wasn't faint this time, and he smiled. "What do you want to know?"

Eloise pursed her lips, her brow creasing while she picked out her words. "How did you become so successful?"

Graham thought about giving her the answer he'd used at parties, about how it was a combination of timing, luck, drive, and skill. And that was a true answer. But it wasn't the truth. The truth was dark and uncomfortable, something he had never told even his closest friends.

But Eloise had already experienced some of the worst parts of his personality, and she was holding his hand and stroking the inner part of his wrist in a way that was comforting and erotic.

"My father," he finally said.

"You wanted to make him proud?" she ventured, and Graham's grip on the steering wheel tightened. The urge to lie was strong. Eloise would understand if he had wanted to make his parents proud; she had admitted that about herself. But pride wasn't what he had been aiming for when he had worked ninety-hour weeks during the startup phase.

"No." He worked hard to keep his tone even, but it was impossible to keep the icy hatred out of his voice. "I wanted to make him sorry."

The words tumbled out of him in awkward batches as he tried to piece together the story.

"I don't tell people this. I don't want the pity or the judgment." Graham licked his lips, his mouth suddenly dry. "Edgar told you that we lived with him until I was about six?" She nodded. "Did he tell you why?" She shook her head.

He took a breath, his stomach pitching like he was on a boat. "I'm a bastard, in the most traditional sense of the word. When my mom found out she was pregnant, she wanted to go home, but my grandparents are very conservative. Traditional family values." He rolled his eyes. What an oxymoron. "They told her not to bother."

"That's terrible."

"I wouldn't say their absence in my life has been a loss."

"So, your mom moved in with Edgar?"

Graham nodded. "They didn't approve of his 'lifestyle' either. So, my mom moved in with the uncle she hadn't seen in years. And my father—fuck, I hate calling him that—he sent a lawyer with a contract and a checkbook. He paid her fifty grand to not put his name on the birth certificate, and to never contact him again. And that was a lot of money back then, especially to a girl who had lost her internship and dropped out of college."

"How did they even meet?"

Graham remembered his mother's story. She'd sat him down at the kitchen table to tell him, the oak dining set acting like a shield between them. She hadn't been able to meet his eyes when she told it, looking at her hands, which twisted and fidgeted in her lap, or at the wall behind his head, but never at him.

"He was her boss. She wanted to get into project management, and she got this internship at a real estate development firm. It was mostly running for coffee and delivering the mail. Which is how she met him." Graham's shoulders tensed. "The CEO. Said he wanted to help her get ahead. Found reasons to keep her late or have her show up early. Special projects. And that's how their affair started. He was married, but he fed her the same tired lines about wanting to leave his wife, how she was so different from any woman he'd ever known, how if she could just be patient he would find a way to leave his wife. But my mom was a middle-class kid from the middle of nowhere special. He was never going to leave his wealthy, high-society wife for her."

"How did you find out? Did she tell you?"

That made him laugh, though the sound was weak and hollow.

"I was trying to find my birth certificate and social security card for my financial aid applications. Mom said she'd take care of it when she got home, but she worked a lot, so I wanted to take something off her plate. I was digging through her box of important papers and surprise, surprise, I found the contract." He shook his head. "Seems like every time I try to be proactive and helpful, it bites me in the ass."

"I don't think there's a right time to tell your kid that their dad is a world-class asshole, but you shouldn't have found out like that." She squeezed his hand. "Did you ever meet him?"

The car felt too small for that memory. It had fueled and sustained him when things were hard, it had inspired him to make big, bold decisions, but he still wanted to hide from it. Because when it wasn't driving him, it hurt him.

"Yeah, I did." He untangled his fingers from hers, pulling

away before she could pull away from him. "I was twenty. I had this idea that I thought could be something, but I needed money to work on it. I didn't have any credit, so I couldn't go to a bank, I wasn't going to ask my mom for money, and I wasn't well-connected. But I knew my dad's name from my mom's copy of the contract. When I called to set up the meeting, his secretary brushed me off, but she called me back within the hour to set something up."

He swallowed several times, trying to work down the painful lump in his throat. He refused to get emotional about this. "I thought maybe he wanted to meet me. That he had regrets about not being around to watch me grow up. By the time I got there, I had this entire reunion built up in my head. We'd hug, he'd apologize, and then he'd ask me over to dinner so I could meet my siblings." Graham shifted in his seat, unable to get comfortable. He'd squirmed less when Russell had stared him down from behind his massive mahogany desk.

"It's eerie how much we look alike. Like looking into a time machine." The moon disappeared behind the clouds again, and Graham flicked on the car's brights. "I didn't even get to start my presentation before he told me that I would never amount to anything."

He wouldn't tell her everything his father had said to him that day, though those words were carved into his brain. "So I decided to prove him wrong. I worked my ass off. I dropped out of school to focus on the business. And I built it so big he would never be able to pretend I didn't exist again."

It felt like a small eternity where the only sound in the car was the hum of the engine and the radio turned down low. Graham imagined a hundred different reactions to his story in the infinite span of time, each one a little worse than the last. He had worked his way up to her never speaking to him again, when he felt her hand cup his neck, her fingers sliding into the hair at the base of his skull, her thumb gently stroking his jaw.

"It's his loss," she said softly. "Even if you never achieved anything, he missed out on knowing you. It takes a small, terrible man to need to make his own child feel worthless to justify his neglect." Her grip tightened slightly. "You're a good man, Graham."

"No, I'm not," he rasped, the words sticking in his throat. He didn't feel like a good man most of the time.

"Yes, you are," Eloise insisted. "You're loyal, and thoughtful, and you care about people."

Graham's heart hurt, it was so close to bursting. He took her hand off his neck and brought it to his lips, kissing her wrist, then the back of her hand, and then her palm. Everyone in town had been right. Eloise was all that was good and sweet in the world. She was strong and steady when he felt weak, unwavering in the support he didn't think deserved. In that moment, he wanted to be exactly who she thought he was.

CHAPTER TWENTY-SIX

"We have to go inside," It was a weak protest, said between hungry, probing kisses that made her blood simmer and her nipples harden into sensitive peaks. No amount of squirming gave her the relief she wanted, and Graham's hands were everywhere but where she wanted them most.

Her eyes opened as he pulled back just enough so their lips were no longer touching. The windows were covered in fog, which meant they had been making out a lot longer than she thought they had.

"We really don't," he murmured, the drag of his lips giving her goosebumps.

Eloise tilted her head, giving Graham easier access to her neck, unable and unwilling to pull away as he nibbled his way along her jaw. His teeth scraped the sensitive curve near her pulse, and she shuddered, squeezing her thighs together. So much for a quick, tender kiss after they parked.

A little emotional intimacy, and she was ready to hitch up her skirts and ride him in the front seat like she was a horny high schooler sneaking around. They had two perfectly nice beds inside, but when he palmed her breast, all reasonable thoughts deserted her.

"Are you worried Kiki is going to see your erection?" She squeezed the undeniable ridge against his thigh. Nope. No missing that without some serious rearranging.

"Well, now I am."

"I will help you take care of that"—Graham's cock twitched against her palm—"if we go inside."

He groaned, then nipped her neck before settling back into his seat. He looked at his lap, assessing his options, then he unbuckled his belt, undid his pants, and reached inside.

"We are walking quickly, Rumple," he told her sternly, adjusting himself beneath the fabric. "We are not getting side-tracked by Kiki. There is no emergency that can't wait until after I've bent you over the bed, pushed up your dress, and fucked you hard enough to make up for the last three days."

"I'm not getting undressed?"

"No." The way Graham's eyes raked down her body made Eloise hot all over, and she once again reconsidered her stance on sex in public places. Only the threat of someone seeing and alerting Willis, the local cop who usually worked nights, kept her from telling him she'd changed her mind and he could have her wherever and whenever he wanted.

"So, the lingerie I wore in anticipation of roughly this exact scenario..."

The low, menacing growl she got in response sent an electric thrill through her. She wanted that noise again.

The last time Eloise had moved that quickly through the parking lot, it had been a torrential downpour and she had been wearing white. Graham all but dragged her toward the building, and she was half surprised he hadn't thrown her over his shoulder like a caveman.

"Graham! Eloise!" Kiki called across the lobby as soon as they crossed the threshold. Graham groaned, and Eloise had to purse her lips so he wouldn't see her smile.

"Don't do it," he warned, but Eloise was already crossing the lobby to the front desk.

"You look fancy," Kiki cooed, beaming at them. "Hot date?" She gave Graham an exaggerated wink, and he rolled his eyes.

"Did you need something?" Eloise asked, trying her hardest not to laugh at all the aggravated tension vibrating off Graham.

She held up a few slips of folded paper. "Messages. For both of you. Let's see...Eloise—"

Graham reached across the desk and snatched them from her, stuffing them into his back pocket. "We'll sort it out later. Thank you, Kiki."

A firm hand on her lower back propelled Eloise to the elevator. For once, the doors slid open the moment it was called, and she was nudged inside.

"I didn't think you rode the elevator anymore," Eloise said, leaning against the back wall of the car. Ever since they had gotten stuck, Graham used the stairs exclusively.

"I don't," he answered, hitting the button for their floor, and then he was in front of her in two commanding steps. He caught the back of her neck, holding her firmly in place while he kissed her until she was whimpering and pressed desperately against him.

Still not enough.

Eloise clung to him, her arms wrapped around his neck, her fingers tugging at his hair. Strong hands cupped her ass, and then her feet were off the floor, her legs automatically circling his hips. They moaned into each other's mouths when Graham rocked against her, the friction wonderfully torturous against her swollen cunt.

"I can't touch you like this on the stairs," he panted, using his hips to keep her in place as he pushed her dress up her thighs. Eloise had never been so grateful for the slow, halting pace of the elevator than when Graham's fingers found her clit through her soaked lace panties.

"Oh fuck...yes..." Eloise's head tipped back as she shamelessly rubbed herself against his hand.

"I could already be inside you if you hadn't stopped at the front desk."

"You can spank me for it later." That comment earned her another growl, but before she could think of something else naughty to say, the doors opened onto their floor. Eloise whined.

Graham lowered her onto unsteady legs, and she smoothed the skirt of her dress. A smarting swat to her ass made her jump.

"Quickly, Rumple."

The door to her room had barely shut before Graham was on her again, pressing her against the wall, cupping and squeezing her breasts through her dress while he kissed her neck, finding every sensitive spot she had. Her head lolled to the side and from around Graham's shoulder, she noticed they were across from the full-length mirror. When Graham grabbed her leg and hitched it around his hip, she gasped. Watching him rock against her took her breath away.

In the mirror, she saw Graham look over his shoulder, and their eyes locked in their reflection.

"Do you want to watch me fuck you?"

Her heartbeat could have outpaced a hummingbird's wings, and all she could do was nod.

She watched him pull a condom from his pocket, and then she felt his hand undo his belt, then his pants, his knuckles brushing against her inner thigh.

"Hurry," she whined, and took his earlobe between her

teeth. Feeling him tense, then shudder, as she ran her tongue along the edge was intoxicating. She felt powerful.

"Goddammit, I can't think when you do that." His voice trembled a little, and the powerful feeling intensified.

Mirror Graham pushed down his pants, and Eloise marveled at the glory of his ass. He might as well have been carved from stone for all his perfection. Lean, but rock solid. She knew she wasn't light, but he didn't act like it was much of a burden to lift her up enough so that she could lock her legs around him again.

The head of his cock bumped against her opening, and Eloise rolled her hips, trying to bring him inside her. Graham reached between them, pulling her underwear to the side.

"Guide me in," he instructed. With a bit of adjusting, she was able to grasp his length, hot and hard in her hand, and maneuver him so the tip slipped inside. That small relief made her eyes flutter closed, and his hand tapped her ass in response. "Eyes open. Watch yourself."

She forced her eyes open. Who was the woman looking back at her? Her hair was disheveled, her cheeks were flushed, and her lips were swollen from demanding kisses. She watched her mouth fall open in an O as his hard cock slid into her by sweet, stretching degrees. The combination of touch and sight had her entire body singing with each short thrust. Her shoulder blades digging into the wall, the scrape of Graham's five-o'clock shadow against her neck, balanced with the sight of his ass and thighs flexing and bunching with each movement.

And then there was the way her best pair of black heels looked hooked around his lower back. That was a visual that would be burned into her mind for eternity.

"Oh fuck," Eloise moaned as Graham adjusted the angle of her hips and her clit rubbed against his pelvis.

"There we go," he rasped, and thrust up into her again. "I love making you curse."

She thought about making a smartass remark, but the next roll of his hips made him hit something inside of her that felt amazing, and within a few minutes, Eloise was stringing together incoherent swear words as encouragement, meeting his thrusts as she chased her bliss.

"Shit!" she shouted as Graham bit her neck and the orgasm that had been building inside her exploded. Her muscles clenched tightly, and from far away, she thought she heard Graham grunt and then moan, his body finally slowing to a stop. He held her until she relaxed, her bones feeling like warm Jell-O.

"I need to send my trainer a thank-you note for never letting me skip leg day," he panted, carefully lowering Eloise to the ground, and then laying down on the carpet, arms crossed over his forehead.

"Are you going to be able to walk tomorrow?" she teased, a satisfied, giddy smile stretched across her face.

He shook his head, smiling the same way. "Nope. Absolutely worth it."

It took time, but Graham eventually found the strength to get up and clean up. In the intermission, he went to his room to change into comfortable clothes, and Eloise stripped off her dress, shook out her hair in a vain attempt to make it sexier, and then got caught trying different seductive positions on the bed.

"I didn't want the lingerie to go to waste," she explained, conjuring innocence from thin air.

"I want it written on my tombstone that I died from having too much sex." He tugged his T-shirt over his head, tossing it to the side and joining her in bed. His bare skin felt hot under her hands as she pushed him onto his back, straddling his hips and grinding against his growing erection. "You looked so sweet and innocent when I met you."

"I was sweet and innocent when I met you. You corrupted me. It won't be long before I'm begging you to fuck me in the office."

His cock throbbed against her thigh. "Can I fuck you in the office?"

And because she loved it when he laid out his dirty plans for her, Eloise bent forward, the lace cups of her bra scratching against her nipples, and whispered all of the possible ways he could fuck her in her small office and have no one be the wiser. She kept talking until Graham's cock was straining against his flannel pajama pants, and her own body was zinging with anticipation.

Eloise had meant to ride him hard and fast, to see just how many orgasms she could wring out of her body. But after she took him inside of her in one slick stroke, he pulled her down for a kiss. Not one of their usual, desperate kisses, but one that was slow and soft, like they had all the time in the world.

The minutes melted together as she rolled her hips, unhurried, and he matched her languid pace, rocking beneath her. The tension built slowly, plateauing before rising again, and Eloise let herself float along the current of sensations. Her only anchor was Graham's green eyes, which never left her, watching her with tender emotion that she couldn't quite put her finger on, but she felt deep in her chest.

She slid her hands from his chest up the length of his arms, her palms learning every dip and swelling of lean muscle, and found his hands, lacing their fingers together. Gently, he squeezed her hands, and then caught her mouth for another warm kiss.

Eloise came undone with a soft shudder, contentment washing over her like slipping into a perfectly warm bath. She relaxed on top of him with a sigh, and wished she could purr when he stroked her back.

"I'm never going to move," she warned him, snuggling deeper into his arms, her face tucked against his neck.

He kissed her forehead. "That's okay. I like you here."

CHAPTER TWENTY-SEVEN

"Mmmm...these are so good, but I'm starting to get concerned Connor might be a Keebler elf," Graham said as he bit into another spicy, sweet ginger molasses cookie. "He's made a lot of cookies."

Eloise had produced a gallon-sized plastic bag stuffed with the cookies after they'd cleaned up, saying that Connor had given them to her that morning at the coffee shop. Graham had a bag of chocolate chip cookies in his room that Connor had given him at brunch on Sunday, but he was hoarding those like a dragon with a pile of gold.

"I don't think he'd fit in the tree," she said, reaching across him for another cookie.

They were snuggled in her bed, trying to find something to watch on TV. So many channels, and nothing to watch. The scene was domestic to its core. They stalled on a cooking competition until it went to commercial, then began flipping through channels again.

Graham couldn't remember ever feeling so at home.

His life was better with Eloise in it. But could they make this work outside of this little bubble of time they had together?

When their days were long, when they were both swamped with work or other personal commitments, would this feel like it was worth the effort?

People made long-distance relationships work all the time. He'd seen it happen. He had also seen relationships fall apart at their hastily sewn-together seams when the couple couldn't devote the time needed to maintain the relationship.

They'd survived a hectic weekend where they had run on different schedules, but that was different. At the end of those long days, they had been able to reconnect, if only briefly before they both succumbed to exhaustion, by being near each other. Holding Eloise calmed and centered him, and all the worries of the day faded away. Would it be the same when all they had was the phone?

Eloise flicked cookie crumbs off his stomach, and Graham tried to stop worrying about the future long enough to enjoy the present where her body was half draped over his.

"I wonder if he'd take requests," she said. "My grandma makes these chocolate sugar cookies for my Christmas box every year, and I've had a craving."

"Your grandma makes you a Christmas box?"

She nodded, slipping her hand under his T-shirt, goosebumps springing up on his arms as she casually stroked his bare stomach.

"Every year she sends me a box filled with cookies—chocolate sugar cookies, gingerbread, snickerdoodles, peanut butter cookies."

"That's cute." Graham paused on a home renovation show. Eloise's Christmas cookie box reminded him of Teapot. Were cookie boxes a universal grandma thing he had missed out on? Maybe not. He couldn't imagine Peter's grandma, who had been a Hollywood star when films were still black and white, using her kitchen, let alone baking enough cookies to fill a postal box.

"Mmm. Last year, my cousin Annie came down to stay with me after Edgar—" She paused and looked up at him for confirmation it was okay to continue. Graham kissed her forehead, and the small tension he'd felt in her back eased. "Annie came to stay with me during her school break, and we bartered cookies. Did you know one chocolate sugar cookie is worth two peanut butter cookies?"

"That sounds like highway robbery."

"Basically extortion," she agreed. "She did buy me a teapot at a thrift store, so I had to forgive her." Eloise pointed across the room to the desk in the corner. His room had the same desk, but it wasn't covered in personal items like hers was. He had never noticed the forest green teapot, painted with pink and white flowers, before. "I have a whole collection at home, just boxed up in my parents' garage."

A chill spread down his spine. Teapot had a collection of teapots boxed up in her parents' garage. And she got a box of Christmas cookies from her grandma every year. But that could just be a coincidence, right?

"Why didn't you bring them with you?" he asked.

"I didn't know how much space I was going to have. The entire move was impulsive. I've been meaning to go back and get them, but this place sucks up a lot of time, and I've found that I really enjoy having a few time zones between me and my mother."

"You're making me really scared to meet your mom," he said, and realized two beats later, when he saw Eloise staring at him, her blue eyes slightly wide, what he had said. That he wanted to meet her mom. Heat flooded his face, and he tried to walk back the statement in halting, stuttering retractions, but only nonsense came out of mouth.

She kissed him to silence him, putting him out of his

awkward misery. "I like you enough that you do not have to meet my mother."

"What if I wanted to meet your mom?"

That surprised both of them. They stared at each other for what felt like forever, until Eloise pressed the back of her hand to his forehead.

"You don't feel sick..."

Graham rolled his eyes, pushing her hand away. "I'm not sick. Forget I said anything."

"It's just...My mom, Graham. We've talked about her."

They had talked about her mom briefly after Graham had walked into the office at the tail end of a tense conversation. It frustrated him that her mom couldn't see how wonderful Eloise was. How much she meant to her community.

"Is she why you left home?"

"No... Yes, a little, but mostly no."

"Are you ever going to tell me why you moved across the country to a small town with no cell phone service to work at a hotel with leaky pipes and a shitty heating system?"

"Can I get a new heating system?"

"You're avoiding the question, Rumple. You don't have to answer, but don't deflect."

"Do you promise not to think less of me?"

"I promise."

———

Eloise took a deep breath, held it, and then let it out slowly in a futile attempt to calm herself. If Graham could talk about the walking piece of shit he got half his DNA from, she could talk about the events that had brought her to Crane Cove three years ago.

"Well," she began, resting her head on his firm chest so she wouldn't have to look him in the eye while she told her story. She was a coward, and she didn't care. If Graham lost respect for her, she didn't want to see it happen on his face.

"After I graduated, I was working as a financial analyst for a big corporation. I didn't love the job, but it paid well and I was good at it." Eloise remembered the long hours sitting in front of her computer, creating spreadsheets and reviewing data to send reports. It hadn't been hard for her, but it had brought her no joy. "There was this guy on my floor, Don. He was handsome, and popular, and I had this silly crush on him. I was convinced that he didn't know I existed until he stopped by my desk when I was working late to help someone get a project done."

In hindsight, it should have been so obvious. Why would Don, who had never spoken to her in an entire year of working there, seek her out? But she had been young, and he had smiled at her like she was the answer to every question he'd ever had, and she had fallen for every line.

"He was just a little stuck on something, and would I mind taking a look at it over dinner?" She scoffed at her younger self. "A few glasses of wine and a salad...Long story short, we started having an affair. Well, I thought we were dating, but he said we needed to keep things quiet because office gossip is brutal."

Eloise reached for another cookie. Shoving some more sugar in her face would make her feel better. "I didn't really even notice he was passing his work off to me. 'Hey, babe, can you get this report done for me? I'm super swamped.' 'I really wanted to take you out tonight, but I'm so behind.' And like an idiot, I volunteered to do it for him."

"Hey." Graham cupped her jaw and tilted her head back to look at him. "You're not an idiot. You are the furthest thing from an idiot. Don the dickhead taking advantage of your kind heart doesn't make you stupid."

Her heart and her stomach did a synchronized backflip. He

looked so earnest and serious, and his thumb making slow circles on her cheek was going to turn her into a useless puddle of goo.

"I haven't even gotten to the worst part yet," she whispered.

"I'm never going to think less of you, Eloise."

Eloise turned her face into his hand and kissed his palm, and then resettled herself. "This went on for about a year. And then the holiday party rolls around, and I ask Don if we're going to go together, and he said it wasn't a good idea. I assumed it was the office gossip, but it wasn't. Because that night, two things happened. First, Don got promoted because of his excellent work over the past year, and then he proposed to his long-distance girlfriend."

"What?!"

She jumped, sitting bolt upright. His hands were fisting the sheets, and she'd seen that thunderous look on his face before. He'd been on the phone with his office down in Los Angeles, and the words that had come out of his mouth probably could have been used against him in a court of law.

"I didn't know—"

"Of course you didn't know. But he knew. He—" Graham growled, and it wasn't the kind of growl that sent delightful shivers down her spine. "I could probably have him murdered, you know. I've got enough money."

Eloise snorted. "Sybil would do it for free. And she probably has a good spot to hide the body." Graham glowered at her, unamused by her attempt to lighten his murderous mood. "Graham, it was years ago, it's not that big of a—"

"Don't. Don't minimize what that asshole did. He used you. You quit your job and moved because of him."

"Yeah, and I found this place, and my friends, and you because of it." She snuggled up against him again, dragging her fingers through his dark hair. "Maybe we should send him some flowers. With poison ivy as greenery."

"That's slightly better," Graham conceded, his body relaxing in small degrees as she combed through his hair. He sighed, wrapping his arms around her again. "I wouldn't look great in orange, anyway. Did you at least confront him?"

"No. I went home, drank several bottles of wine, and applied for jobs. Any job. I applied to be an online dating ghostwriter."

"What is that?"

"People pay you to write their dating profiles for them. Maybe even some of the early, awkward interactions."

"Ah. A modern-day Cyrano de Bergerac."

She was tickled that his brain immediately jumped to the play, and not any of the modern adaptations. Not that she wasn't a fan of *Roxanne* or *The Truth About Cats and Dogs*, but there was something sexy about a man who knew the classics.

"I thought I would have been great at it, but six-glasses-of-cabernet Eloise is not eloquent. Or funny."

He grinned. "I doubt that."

"You're incredibly biased." Eloise picked up the remote and began to change the channels again. "Luckily, drunk Eloise applied to be the manager here, a job sober Eloise never would have applied for, and the rest is history."

She stopped on the channel that played *Claymore Abbey* reruns. The show that always preceded it was an early 1990s comedy whose exact storyline she'd never been able to puzzle out because she only caught portions of episodes, and at this point, it was more fun to guess what was going on. Since the principal cast was seated on the bus, she knew the episode was nearly over.

"Don't judge me, but *Claymore Abbey* is on next, and it's my comfort show."

"Why would I judge you for that?" he asked, and when she

tilted her head back to look at him, he had an amused frown on his face. "Addictive television is for everyone."

A needling thought prickled the back of her mind. She had heard that exact phrase before from Foolproof42 when they had first started talking.

> Foolproof42: Why are you always up so late? It's 2:30 where I am.

> Little_Teapot: Me, too. I'm covering a night shift. There's a stretch of Claymore Abbey reruns right now. Are you watching?

> Foolproof42: I am now. What kind of job do you have that you can watch TV at work?

> Little_Teapot: Not going there. Those kinds of details get a girl stalked and killed.

> Foolproof42: So you're a girl?

> Little_Teapot: Aren't you?

> Foolproof42: Nope. Addictive television is for everyone.

It was a giant leap based on circumstantial evidence, but there were similarities. He was a man. He was visiting Oregon on business. And Foolproof42 had once said that he looked a bit like Lovingford, which had been Eloise's first impression of Graham.

"Are you a fan?" she ventured, curious to see what he would say.

Graham blushed. "I've, um, seen a couple of episodes. Reruns and stuff."

"So, you have absolutely no opinion on who Lady Meryl should end up with?"

Foolproof42 definitely had an opinion about that. It was one of her favorite things to tease him about.

He opened his mouth, then shut it, his blush growing deeper.

"I mean, Ryston declared his intentions two seasons ago. That has to count for something," Eloise continued. A muscle in Graham's jaw twitched. "Once he gets his finances in order—"

"If he hasn't proposed yet, he's not going to do it!" Graham erupted, tossing his hands up in the air. "Ryston is a wastrel and will never stop gambling long enough to get his finances in order. And if he ever finds out that all the family has left is their good name, he'll toss Meryl over for an heiress. Why can't anyone let go of the version of Ryston we met?

Eloise schooled her face into a semi-serious expression. "He was so sweet, though."

"Yeah, and I think we were all a little jumpy because of everything the writers have put Amanda through that none of us were nearly suspicious enough when Ryston declared his intentions so quickly. How many London seasons is a girl supposed to sit through waiting for a man-child to come up to scratch? She may as well be a potted plant at balls these days."

"A wallflower," Eloise corrected, biting her lip to keep from laughing. She could almost see the smoke coming out of his ears on a fictional character's behalf. "And she hasn't had any other offers. Who is she supposed to end up with? Heston?"

"At least she has chemistry with Heston."

"They can't get through a conversation without arguing!"

"We can't get through a conversation without arguing," he pointed out, tapping her nose affectionately. "And I like to think that you've at least got a crush on me."

"Only a little one." She held up her thumb and forefinger, then brought them close together so that there was only a sliver of space between them. "Maybe about this much."

That bit of smartassery earned her a dimpled smile as Graham leaned into her, easing her onto her back. "I can't believe I put up with you, Rumple. You're terrible."

"I'm an angel," she countered, trying to act like her pulse wasn't beating between her legs, slightly north of where his strong thigh was tucked between hers. Her hands roamed over his back, feeling muscle through cotton, and she wished he hadn't put his shirt back on.

"Lies." He kissed her, toeing the line between tender and playful when he nipped her bottom lip, and Eloise's entire body hummed with happiness. He tasted like sugar, ginger, and wine, and she wanted more. She wrapped a hand around the back of his neck, trying to draw him back down to kiss her again, but he wouldn't budge.

"I have references," she said.

"You have this entire town fooled." He shook his head with mock reproach. "But I know the truth."

Eloise raised an eyebrow. "And what's that?"

"Underneath that sugary sweet, angelic exterior"—Graham brushed their lips together—"you're a brat."

She laughed against his mouth. "I am not!"

"Mmm." He gave her a short kiss, then punctuated each item on his list with another peck. "You're sassy, opinionated, stubborn, a little scary when you're mad, and you have the filthiest fucking mouth when I'm inside you."

She gasped, and then moaned as he seized the opportunity to kiss her, his tongue sliding over hers in a way that reminded her of all the wonderful things that tongue had done to her body. Particularly the place that was currently making her fresh pair of underwear wet.

It wasn't until she was squirming beneath him and trying to take his clothes off with no cooperation whatsoever that Graham finally pulled back.

"I guess what I'm trying to say is that I like that you're comfortable enough around me to show me all the sides that make up who you are. Every wonderful one."

A mess of emotion hit Eloise in the chest like a wave. It was overwhelmingly close to love, but she wasn't ready to tack that label on to it yet. But it was sweet and yearning, warm like a cup of cinnamon tea on a dreary winter morning. This was a feeling she wanted to curl up into for the rest of her life.

Graham saw her. He really saw her.

He didn't back down or run away when she got mad. He never demanded or suggested that she make herself smaller to make him more comfortable. In fact, he encouraged her to be braver and bolder.

The realization left her, for what felt like the first time in her life, without the use of her very expensive education, and only one word came to mind.

"Fuck."

CHAPTER TWENTY-EIGHT

It had taken some convincing, but Eloise had agreed to decorate the hotel for Halloween. After one very rainy, muddy trip to the pumpkin patch—assisted by Chase and Cole, who invited themselves along—and a visit to the holiday supply closet, the lobby looked sufficiently spooky.

Fake spider webs were placed on every prominent surface in the lobby, a plastic severed hand covered the bell on the front desk, and they'd managed to make it look like bats were flying out of the fireplace. Kiki had produced, a little too easily, a full-sized skeleton wearing a bellhop uniform.

"Clarence" was quite a hit with their guests.

Life in Crane Cove moved slower than in LA, but Graham didn't mind. There was no traffic. People who stopped by the hotel for a drink or brunch on the weekends had learned his name and said hi to him in town. He hadn't been home in nearly two weeks, and besides his friends, he didn't miss it. Days passed where he didn't check his work email, and sometimes he even left the hotel without his cell phone. Nothing had burned down yet, and he felt freer.

His day-to-day challenges were different now. He fixed slow

drains and toilets that wouldn't stop running. Instead of directing large departments, he tried to manage Kiki and Mallory, who smiled to his face and then did whatever they wanted behind his back. Sometimes not even behind his back. And they both paled in comparison to Eloise, who needed to be bribed and badgered into working more reasonable hours. Luckily, Graham wasn't above extortion when it came to her.

When he wasn't paying very much attention one morning at the coffee shop, Sybil and Connor got him to agree to volunteer at the elementary school fall carnival. In Los Angeles he attended swanky fundraisers that cost thousands of dollars per plate. In Crane Cove, he ran the bean bag toss and tried not to turn into a puddle watching Eloise paint the faces of six- and seven-year-olds from across the gym.

It was easy to forget that he had another life in another city.

He knew he had to go back eventually. He had a life and a business in Los Angeles, but Graham was starting to wonder if he could split his time between the two places. A few days, maybe a week, in LA, and then back to the near perpetual drizzle of the Oregon coast. The only people who would miss him were his friends, but they were so busy with their own careers he didn't think it would change much. It was something he needed to discuss with Eloise, whenever he found the time and the courage.

———

"Kiki, if you do not stop humming 'This Is Halloween', I'm going to fire you," Graham warned.

Across the table, Kiki casually scratched her nose with her middle finger. Next to him, Eloise started to laugh, and covered the noise with a cough when he gave her a stern look.

"Tickle in my throat," she said innocently. The urge to kiss her was overwhelming, but his hands were covered in pumpkin guts and they were surrounded by friends.

Getting invited to Sybil's pumpkin carving party felt like a big deal. Sitting at her dining table, bumping elbows with Connor on one side, and trying not to jostle Eloise as she painstakingly shaved off layers of pumpkin shell to make one of those fancy pumpkins with a full picture on them, he felt like he belonged.

"Graham, can you help me in the kitchen?" Sybil asked, peeking her head around the corner.

"It was nice knowing you, boss," Kiki teased, and squealed when he swiped a dirty finger down her nose as he passed.

Sybil's kitchen was cozy. Soup simmered on the stove, and fresh rolls Connor had made were heating in the oven. His stomach growled as he washed his hands in the farmhouse sink. "What can I help with?"

"I just thought it was time we had a talk," she said, selecting a chef's knife from the block. The hair on the back of his neck and his arms rose. When she plunged the knife into a head of lettuce instead of his heart, he relaxed.

But only a little.

"If you were wondering if I had any friends or family that would miss me if you killed me, the answer is yes." Graham started to open cupboards, looking for a salad bowl. "My mother thinks I'm pretty okay. Might take her a few weeks to notice I haven't called..."

"I'm not going to murder you. Yet." She gave him a small nod of thanks as he placed a bowl on the counter next to her. "But Eloise tells me things, and you need to know where I stand."

"Do we have to have this talk while you're holding a knife?"

"Why do you assume this is a bad thing, Graham? Is there something you need to tell me?"

He shook his head. "No."

Sybil went back to chopping. "Besides Connor, Eloise is the best friend I have. She is kind, generous to a fault, and gives people too many chances. She is the best thing that will ever happen to you, and you need to know that you do not deserve her."

Graham opened his mouth and got out a single syllable in protest before Sybil pointed the knife at him like it was her finger.

"I'm not done. Don't interrupt."

He sighed and crossed his arms, trying to protect at least some of his vital organs. She narrowed his eyes at him, but put down the knife long enough to put the chopped lettuce into the bowl, and then she grabbed a small carton of cherry tomatoes.

"No one deserves someone as good as Eloise," Sybil continued. "I don't deserve Eloise, either. So, if she gives you her heart, don't you fucking break it. If you make her cry, I will make you cry. I will come for you in the night and—"

"Murder me and bury the body where no one will ever find it, I know."

It was sweet how much Sybil loved her. Eloise needed people in her life that protected her and championed her. To remind her that she was special and capable on the days when she forgot. And Sybil was right. He didn't deserve Eloise, but he wanted to try.

"I want to take her to LA with me," he confessed, and the tomato Sybil was slicing shot across the counter and bounced off the backsplash. "The next time I go," he clarified when she glared up at him with an intensity that threatened to turn him to stone. "Not permanently."

Her face relaxed, but only marginally. And when she didn't say anything, Graham felt compelled to fill the silence with reassurances. "I'm not going to hurt her. I promise."

"Yeah, I've heard that before. But guys like you just can't seem to help it."

He wanted to know what she meant by that, but Connor and Eloise came into the kitchen, a paper towel wrapped around her hand, with Connor holding her arm above her head.

"Pumpkin carving injury," he explained, turning on the kitchen sink with a nudge of his elbow.

"I'm fine," Eloise insisted, but her voice was wobbly and all of the color drained from her face when Connor removed the paper towel. The cut on her finger didn't look bad, but it was bleeding steadily. And as she watched the water wash her blood down the drain, Graham saw perspiration form on her forehead.

When her eyelids fluttered, he moved behind her, wrapping his arms around her waist. "Look at me," he instructed, kissing her cheek to get her attention. She looked up at him in slow motion, her big blue eyes unfocused. "There you go, Rumple. How are you feeling?"

"Like I'm going to throw up," she admitted weakly.

"In the sink, please," Sybil said, handing Graham an ice pack that he pressed against the nape of her neck. "Or on him. Just not on my floor."

Eloise swallowed, and then leaned against him, her cheek resting against his chest. "I hate this."

"Sam hates blood too," Graham told her, kissing her clammy forehead as Chase entered the kitchen with an intense-looking first aid kit. "He cut himself slicing an avocado and dropped like a rock. He had to get stitches in his hand and his forehead." She groaned, and he ached that he couldn't do more for her. "You're doing great."

"Let's lay her down before she falls down," Chase suggested. He helped Graham ease Eloise to the floor, and then had Connor elevate her feet while Graham held her noninjured hand. It was strange seeing Chase go from his normal, goofy self into EMT mode. He was calm, collected, and direct. While he bandaged her finger, he had Graham talk to her so she wouldn't look.

"All done," Chase announced just a few minutes later, taking off his blue nitrile gloves. "You can look now."

Her finger was wrapped in gauze and finished with a Spider-man Band-Aid.

"You keep those in your kit?" Connor asked, raising an eyebrow at his youngest brother.

Chase grinned in response. "Everyone loves Spider-man. It's the universal feel-good Band-Aid."

"Thank you, Chase." Eloise squeezed his knee, and he gave her an affectionate pat in return.

"Anytime, angel."

A few weeks ago, Graham might have been jealous that Eloise had a friendly relationship with her ex-boyfriend, but now that he knew them both better, it was easy to see there weren't any lingering romantic feelings between them. Just friendship. And Graham was grateful Eloise had him in her corner, ready to swoop in with a joke or a Band-Aid to fix her hurts.

"Oh god. Did you all have to come watch me almost faint?" Eloise asked as she sat up. He'd been so focused on her that he hadn't noticed that the rest of the party had filled the kitchen and were watching anxiously, waiting to help.

"Out," Cole barked, herding the assembled mass out of the room. "Pumpkins won't carve themselves."

"You, too," Connor said, taking Sybil by the elbow and steering her toward the dining room.

When they were finally alone, Graham sat with his back against the cabinets and drew Eloise to him, so her back was against his chest and her head lay back on his shoulder.

She gave a weak laugh. "That was embarrassing."

"Nah." He kissed the sensitive curve where her shoulder met her neck.

"Everyone was here to watch me freak out."

"You did not freak out. You held it together quite well." She rolled her eyes, and he chuckled. "I guess this explains why you didn't want Kiki to buy that zombie eating the brain."

"That was about the potential for mess. Do you want to try and get fake blood out of the carpet? Because I don't."

Graham grinned. "There's my girl." She flushed, and he felt better seeing the color return to her cheeks. Cranky and pink was better than shaky and pale.

"It's just my own blood. It's supposed to stay inside."

He chuckled. Sam had said the same thing when they had been huddled inside of the small, curtained room in the emergency room waiting for him to get stitches.

"Do you want to go to LA with me?" Graham blurted, and Eloise tensed slightly in his arms. "Just for two days," he continued. "The next time I go. We'd leave Wednesday and be back Friday."

"But what about the hotel? And the ball. I've got to do so much for the ball still." She worried her bottom lip between her teeth. "I don't know if I can leave."

"The hotel will be fine. And anything you need to do for the ball can be done remotely or when you get back." He placed gentle, lingering kisses on her skin, starting at her shoulder and following that tempting curve up to the sensitive place behind her ear. "I have fast Wi-Fi and cell phone service. You'll be amazed at how much you can get done."

"Graham..." Her resolve was crumbling like a sandcastle in the face of the incoming tide. He went in for the kill.

"I want you to meet my friends. And my friends want to meet you."

Eloise twisted in his arms, her blue eyes wide. "Really?"

"Yeah. They want to know why I never come home."

"Okay," she finally agreed, but quickly added, "But we have to be back for work on Friday night. I let Kiki add an earlier ghost tour for Halloween."

Graham smiled so wide that his cheeks hurt, and he suppressed the urge to cover her face in excited kisses. Plans began zipping through his brain, more chaotic than dropping a match into a box of fireworks. There was so much to do and plan and no time to do it. But he was going to show Eloise his home, and she was going to meet his friends, and it was hard to be anything but happy.

CHAPTER TWENTY-NINE

Even though Graham had all but moved into her room over the last few weeks, spending every night in her bed and getting ready in her bathroom, his suitcase and clothes had stayed in his room. So when they met in the hallway Wednesday morning to go to the airport, Eloise was surprised to see that Graham was wearing gray slacks and a black button-down shirt. With his coat tossed over his arm and his suitcase in hand, he looked like he had just finished shooting a travel spread for an expensive life-style magazine. She felt out of place in her own travel outfit: leggings, her Cranberry Festival volunteer shirt from two years ago, a long cardigan, and slip-on shoes. She hadn't bothered to do her hair besides gathering it into a hasty bun.

They didn't look like they belonged together. It shouldn't have bothered her—it was just clothes—but it did. They were going to LA to meet his friends. What if they didn't like her? What if they judged her for showing up looking like she had rolled out of bed?

She turned around and went back into her room to change.

The drive to Portland was quiet. Normally they could easily fill a silence, but Graham seemed distracted. As soon as they hit cell phone service, his phone began to buzz. It didn't stop. Every time she would try to speak, his phone would buzz in the cup holder. It was easier to stay silent.

Returning his rental car made her more uneasy. Why return it? They would only be gone two days, and picking up a new car added an unknown time element to their return trip. She hadn't said that, though. Even though the money wasn't a problem for Graham, she'd learned that he hated spending unnecessarily. It was why he flew primarily commercial instead of private. Paying the rental car fees and paying for parking would have grated on him.

Airport security wasn't busy, but Graham still walked them over to the lane designated for first class and elite frequent flyers.

"I usually use pre-check," he told her as they loaded their belongings into bins and onto the belt. It was just a comment, but something about it plucked a sour note inside of her.

"Shoes," the TSA agent reminded Graham when he stepped up to the scanner.

"Right. I forgot."

The best part about the airline lounge, Eloise decided, was the pancake machine. It would offend Amara's culinary sensibilities, but she wanted one for the hotel. All she had to do was press a button and a few minutes later, out popped a piping hot pancake.

She turned to tell Graham, but he was by the coffee bar talking to the kind of man that looked like he would have worked at her old job. The little bubble of excitement she had felt over the pancake machine popped, and she went and found a seat by the wall of windows. A jet was pulling into a gate, and she took out her phone and took a picture of all the airplanes.

> Little_Teapot: Leaving on a jet plane. Hope
> you're having a good day, friend.

Eloise sent the message to Foolproof42, the picture of the plane attached. He had been quiet lately, but so had she. Graham and the hotel took up most of her time. Graham was even watching *Claymore Abbey* with her, which was fun because he got invested in each episode and freely shared his strong opinions on characters and storylines. But she missed her friend and wondered if he had forgotten about her. She wondered if he was still in Oregon on business, and if he knew about the *Claymore Abbey* ball.

Graham worked the entire flight to Los Angeles. As soon as the airplane took off, he brought out his laptop, hooked up to the Wi-Fi, and started typing out emails at a blistering pace. Eloise tried not to take it personally. She sipped champagne and watched Peter's latest movie on her phone so, if nothing else, she could at least talk to him about that.

A sleek black sedan picked them up at the airport in Los Angeles. Eloise let herself into the backseat while the driver loaded their bags into the trunk, sliding across the leather seats to let Graham in behind her, but he was standing on the curb, talking on his phone. Again. Never in her life did Eloise think she would miss the terrible reception in Crane Cove, but she would have given her favorite teapot to have the same problem right now. It was selfish, but she missed being important to him. Competing with an incessantly buzzing phone was not the kind of trip she had signed up for. Friday could not come soon enough.

"You've been quiet," Graham commented as their driver turned up a winding hill. Gated, mostly modern houses lined the road, all a lot closer together than she had expected.

Somehow her vision of rich people in Los Angeles had included more space.

Eloise shrugged. "I've just been taking in the sights."

She didn't want to be difficult, so she didn't say what she was really thinking. That it was amazing that he had noticed her being quiet at all with as much as he'd been on his phone. All of her emails had been answered in the first hour of LA traffic. It was amazing what she could get accomplished without anyone interrupting her. Or trying to talk to her.

"We're almost there." The end of his sentence was drowned out by a motorcycle revving its engine as it passed them. "And I bet that was Jordy."

"Should he be riding a motorcycle when he has a game tomorrow?" She frowned, leaning towards the middle to see where the motorcycle was headed.

"No, but that's not going to stop him."

Eloise looked at Graham to make a joke, but he was typing away on his phone, a small frown on his face. A strange heaviness settled over her like a thick morning fog, and she looked back out the window.

His house reminded her of him when they'd first met: dark, expensive, precise. The modern home was a shade somewhere between black and gray, made up of straight, sharp lines, and she wondered if the interior had the same foreboding presence.

The motorcycle that had passed them going up the hill sat in the driveway, its rider shrugging out of his heavy leather coat. He gave them a short wave, and it took Eloise a moment to realize that it was, in fact, Jordy Taylor. She'd never seen him without his football pads on before, and even then, only briefly during a game she wasn't paying a lot of attention to anyway.

He was taller than she would have expected, and built in the same solid way the McMahon men were. With his shaggy blond hair, which was kept out of his face by an elastic headband, he could have easily slipped into their family photo unnoticed. The broad, friendly smile he gave her, which crinkled the corners of his eyes, eased the knot in her chest.

"Ho-*ly* shit!" Jordy whooped, meeting them halfway between his bike and the car. "You actually did it! You brought her."

"Don't be weird," Graham warned him from behind her.

"Hi." Eloise held out her hand. "I'm Eloise. It's nice to finally meet you."

"I don't do handshakes," he told her, and her heart gave a stuttering beat, convinced she had done something wrong and offended him—did athletes not give handshakes?—before he enveloped her in a bear hug. Jordy smelled faintly like gasoline and pine, which wasn't an unpleasant combination, and the strong squeeze was like a human-sized weighted blanket. "It's nice to meet you, too."

"Be gentle with her," Graham growled, and she heard the car ease out of the drive while Jordy rocked her back and forth.

"I can't help it. I'm excited." He didn't fully release her, keeping an arm looped around her shoulders as he walked towards the house, leaving Graham to grab their bags. "He doesn't bring girls home. Or date, really. I was about to start leaving brochures for monasteries since he insisted on living like a monk."

"Jordy! Shut up!"

"And definitely not pretty girls." Eloise blushed so hard that she felt like she'd opened an oven and stuck her face inside. "Are you sure about him? Because if not—"

"Jordan, I swear to God—"

"Calm down. I'm not going to steal your girl." Jordy smiled down at Eloise and winked. "Unless you want to be stolen."

Everything Graham had told her about Jordy was true. He was an unrepentant flirt. Well, Graham had used more colorful language to describe him, but Eloise doubted she would ever get the full Jordy Taylor Experience.

She touched his cheek, frowning a little. "Did you start growing your beard over?"

Jordy tossed his hands up in the air, and Graham laughed. "That was a low blow. See if I help you with the two scary ones now," he warned, opening the front door for her.

Not even two steps inside, and the smoke detector went off.

"Peter! The towel!"

"Isn't it nice to be home?" Jordy asked Graham, who had dropped their bags and was hightailing it to the kitchen. There was some masculine cursing further inside the house, and Eloise followed Jordy into the kitchen, where Sam Shoop was using a set of tongs to drop a smoldering dish towel into the sink.

And this was the surreal moment. Jordy could almost be a fully regular person to her, because she didn't follow football and wouldn't have noticed him on the street. But Sam Shoop and Peter Green? That was another level entirely.

She had grown up with Sam Shoop's music—literally, because they were roughly the same age—and she'd even had a poster of him on her wall in high school. His moody, heartbroken third album had propelled her through her own intense breakup in college.

And it was impossible to turn around and not see Peter Green's face somewhere. Tabloids, movie posters, advertisements. He was everywhere. Once, Sybil had turned over every magazine with a picture or mention of him on the cover while they were in line at Hudson's Grocery, and that had taken away over half of the options.

"It was just a little fire." Peter held his hands up. "No one got hurt."

"I think the dish towel would disagree," Sam said, waving a

baking sheet around the stove to try and clear the smoke while Graham opened the kitchen window.

"Did you have to let him help you?"

"Who said I let him? He's worse than a toddler."

"I was trying to clean up. Then I heard the door open and–"

"The towel caught on fire. I was here for that part." Graham pinched the bridge of his nose, shaking his head. "Do I have any towels left?"

"Umm..." Peter put his hands into the pockets of jeans, and in avoiding Graham's glare he caught sight of Eloise. He went from chagrined to delighted in a snap and came to where she was hovering at the edge of the kitchen. He smiled at her.

It was like staring into the sun.

No one should be that beautiful. It wasn't fair to the rest of the human race that he was allowed to walk around, not to mention be on billboards.

"You are absolutely perfect," he said, leaning in so they were eye-level. "And your babies are going to have the most incredible eyes. They'll be able to conquer the world with a single look."

Eloise was sure she was going to melt into the floor. Partly from mortification that he may have implied she was going to have Graham's babies when she wasn't even certain of their relationship status, and because Peter Green, annual fixture of *People Magazine*'s Sexiest Man Alive list, had just told her that she was perfect.

"I'm Eloise," she squeaked, and held out her hand. Peter took it in both of his hands, giving her a friendly, whole-hearted squeeze.

"Peter. Is it true that you called Graham Lucifer to his face?"

"That's what one of our employees calls him. I called him an arrogant jackass."

Peter blinked twice, and then began to shake with laughter. Soon he was doubled over, his hands on his knees for support as his shoulders shook and he struggled to get a full breath. When he straightened, he wiped his teary eyes and then took Eloise's hands in his again. He looked over his shoulder and announced, "I love her. Can we keep her?"

"Please don't scare her off," Graham begged, bent over the freezer getting ice. "I like her."

"I'm not going to scare her off. I'm not going to scare you off, right?" Eloise shook her head quickly, and that satisfied him. Peter set her up on one of the barstools at the island and clapped his hands together. "Can I get you something to drink? We've got still water, sparkling water, flavored sparkling water, wine, various alcohols, I think there's some soda in the garage..."

Graham set a martini glass down in front of her and poured a slightly cloudy drink from a cocktail shaker. When he finished it with a lemon twist, her stomach gave a pleasant flutter.

"What is that?" Peter asked.

"A vesper. My favorite."

Graham placed a reassuring hand between her shoulder blades and kissed her temple. "Remember, you don't have to answer every question he asks you."

The rush of heat through her entire body was a normal response, but it was sharper after a day of longing for his attention. She leaned toward him, and kept leaning, because he was walking toward the living room, his phone going to his ear.

"A vesper. Just like in Bond," Peter commented, drawing her attention back to him. "My father was actually in the running to play Bond. After Roger Moore. The role went to Timothy Dalton, but it's something he likes to bring up anytime someone has a martini."

"So it comes up a lot?"

"More than anyone wants it to." He shook his head ruefully,

but he was smiling. Peter patted the counter. "Tell me about you. I want to know everything. Nothing keeps our Graham Cracker away from work like you have."

"I mean, it's not just me. There's a lot of work—"

At the stove, Sam snorted. Eloise had forgotten he was there. The dark-haired musician tipped the pan he was holding slightly forward, catching the flame, and lighting whatever he was cooking on fire. Her eyes widened.

"He knows what he's doing," Jordy said, sitting down on her other side, beer in hand. "Graham doesn't get mad at *him* for starting fires."

"That's because mine are on purpose and the fire department has never shown up when I'm cooking."

"Yet," Peter corrected. "The fire department hasn't shown up yet."

The flames died down in the pan within minutes, but it was hard for Eloise to take her eyes off him while he cooked. Every move seemed choreographed and sure. A little of this to the pan, a little of that, check whatever smelled delicious in the oven, and back to the pan.

"What are you making?" Eloise asked, sipping her drink.

"Chicken Suprême. And it's almost done, so if someone could get Graham..."

"I'm back, I'm back," Graham said, stepping into the kitchen.

"It's nice to know some things never change," Jordy commented. "You're back to wandering out of rooms and glaring at your phone."

Well, at least it wasn't just her.

Graham helped Sam plate, and then they all sat around the dining table, Eloise sandwiched between Peter and Graham. There was sliced chicken with crispy skin and a simple sauce drizzled on top, rice pilaf, and a harvest salad with roasted root vegetables, goat cheese, and a tangy dressing. Saying that Sam was a good cook was like saying Serena Williams was good at tennis: technically true, but a massive understatement.

Layers of tension seemed to peel off Graham as they ate and talked. He was morphing back into the man she knew, joking and teasing, and occasionally touching her leg, like he was reassuring himself that she was there.

It had been a long day, and she decided to let it go. He was only back for two days and he wasn't even going into the office. A few calls and emails on their traveling day wasn't hurting anyone. She could have his attention tomorrow. Still, she couldn't shake the nagging feeling that when he inevitably came back to LA that he would be too busy for her. Out of sight, out of mind.

CHAPTER THIRTY

Jordy left with just enough time to make it to the team hotel before curfew, cursing the league the entire time for making them stay at a hotel the night before a game, even when it was at home. Sam used Jordy's exit as an excuse to leave, and Peter gave an exaggerated yawn and said he had an early call time in the morning, retreating to his bedroom.

Eloise stood at the sink, handwashing all the dishes, even though the dishwasher was right there. The sleeves of her black sweater were pushed up to her elbows, and a few curls had escaped her twist. His friends had offered to help, but she had shooed them off, insisting that it was the least she could do.

They liked her, he thought. It was hard to tell with Sam, but he hadn't been outright rude, so Graham was counting that as a win. Jordy had flirted with her mercilessly, and Peter had asked her so many questions that Graham had offered to print him off an application for the FBI academy. That gave Eloise a five-minute reprieve before he launched into the "Who do you think you were in a past life?"-type questions.

It had been a long day where he'd felt pulled in every direction at once. In the past few weeks he had forgotten just how much his phone rang all the time. He was behind at work, and working at the airport and on the plane had barely made a dent in the mountain of emails he had been putting off. A day at the office where he could put his head down and work was needed, but he felt guilty enough about the day Eloise had probably had. Leaving her to fend for herself was not the trip she had signed up for. He couldn't tell if she was mad at him, tired, or over-whelmed by his friends. She had been off in another world during the moments he'd come up for air.

He missed her, and he'd been sitting next to her all day.

"So, did you like them?" Graham asked, wrapping his arms around her waist and nuzzling her neck. She sighed softly, and leaned back against him.

"Mmm, I think a better question is did they like me?"

"They loved you. Peter asked to keep you five times. Jordy offered to be next in line when I inevitably screw this up."

Eloise giggled, an adorable pink blush rising on her cheeks. "I want Peter and Jordy to follow me around all day. They'd do wonders for my self-esteem." She rinsed off the dish she had been wiping with the sponge, and frowned. "I don't think Sam likes me very much."

"Sam doesn't like anyone."

"He likes you," she pointed out, stacking the clean plate on top of the others.

Graham kissed her cheek. "He tolerates me. Sam is basically a feral cat that occasionally comes inside."

"Kind of like Sybil. Can you imagine if they ever met?"

"Lord protect us. That much hostile energy in one place would probably cause a rift in the space-time continuum."

"I hope it would take more than that." Eloise tilted her head backward to look at him. "I like them. They were different from what I was expecting. Very...normal."

"No one has ever called Peter normal."

That earned him a full laugh, and he felt the last vestiges of tension his body had been holding slip away. She wasn't mad at him. He'd been imagining that. Eloise had never had a problem telling him off before. If something was wrong now, she would say something.

"You know, I have this extra-large shower with a bench…" He pressed her against the counter, letting her feel his burgeoning erection against her lower back. Being near her did things to him. "We could wash the airplane off…"

Eloise contemplated his offer. "Does it have more than one head? Because we've established that we're too old for alternating who gets to stand under the hot water."

"It's about a step below a car wash. Water coming from every angle."

"Well, if there's water coming from every angle, do I even need you in there?"

"It would be quicker with me in there."

"That depends. How good is your water pressure?"

"Excellent, unfortunately." Graham eased back, and put his hands on her shoulders, giving her a gentle squeeze. "We've had a long day. It's okay to tell me if you're tired."

She nodded, drying her hands on what was possibly the last dish towel in Graham's house, and then turned to face him, resting her cheek on his chest. "It's been a really long day."

"Then we can just take a shower and snuggle."

"Sometimes you're really sweet." Eloise rose up on her tiptoes and gave him a short, sweet kiss.

His stomach fluttered. Had he kissed her at all that day? He didn't like that it was the end of the day and he couldn't remember.

"Don't tell anyone. You'll ruin my reputation."

———

Graham woke, as he usually did, with Eloise's leg hitched over his own, her entire lower half exposed to the world. She was probably seeking heat, since she always kicked the covers off in the middle of the night. The first few times they had shared a bed, the way she moved around had woken him up. But now he slept through it unless she kicked him particularly hard. Still, he wouldn't trade the random Eloise-induced bruises for a more peaceful night's sleep because then he wouldn't get to wake up with her. And he loved waking up with her.

In all the mornings he had woken up with her, he had never noticed her hair before. Not really. Probably because Eloise kept their room back at the hotel as dark as a cave, and at home he had automatic window shades that went up with the sun. It was a more peaceful way to wake up, though he did enjoy how she groaned every time her alarm went off. But this morning, the California sun was streaming in through the window, finding all the brilliant shades of brown in her hair and illuminating them. It was fascinating.

His fingers hovered over her hair, afraid that if he touched her, it would break the spell. She was a magical thing like this, her lips slightly parted, her breaths coming as soft sighs. Gently, he passed his hand over her hair. It was sun-warmed and soft.

"You're staring at me again," she mumbled, her eyes still closed. Graham smiled. He was. It happened often enough that she knew without even having to look. "I thought we talked about you being a weird vampire dude."

"I can't help it. And I didn't climb through your window, so it's different."

"Mm-hmm, that's what they all say." She yawned and stretched against him like a cat. "You're cute, so I'll let it slide."

"So magnanimous," he teased, giving her ass a playful squeeze. "According to my clock, we managed to sleep in."

"Oh? What time is it?"

"Eight a.m."

Eloise snorted. "Woo. Dream big." Her stomach, which was used to having breakfast much earlier in the morning, growled. "Any chance there's somewhere to eat in this town?"

"Nowhere at all. You're going to starve."

"I knew it. This entire trip was a ruse to bump me off. You lured me in with good sex and lots of snacks, and now you're going to let me waste away in this mansion like Mrs. Havisham."

Graham laughed. "That doesn't even make sense. You haven't been jilted, and you don't own a wedding dress, I don't think. And Miss Havisham didn't starve."

"Fine. It's more Poe than Dickens, but I'm hungry. I can't be expected to be brilliant on an empty stomach." She twined her arms around his neck and fixed him a gaze so melancholy it would have melted the heart of pre-ghost Ebenezer Scrooge. "Feed me and tell me I'm pretty."

"You're gorgeous. And if I can find a way to convince myself to leave this bed when you're all over me, I promise I'll feed you."

Graham leaned in for a kiss, but only felt air. Eloise had scrambled off the bed and was dashing for the bathroom.

"I can be ready in twenty minutes!"

"Why does it take so much longer when we're at home?" he shouted after her.

"I have a reputation to uphold back home," Eloise shouted back from inside of the bathroom, and then came to the door, her toothbrush in her mouth and his shirt brushing her knees. She'd twisted her hair into a floppy messy bun on top of her head, and the rush of affection Graham felt nearly bowled him over. He leaned forward, wondering if the besotted grin on his face looked as dopey as it felt. "I have to look cute there. Here I can look like an unkempt troll."

"You look cute now."

She rolled her eyes, but he saw the smile that she was trying to fight off. "Stop it."

"I mean it. You're adorable."

"You're only saying that because you don't have your glasses on."

"Then I'll take a picture so I can get a better look," he said, reaching for his phone.

"Don't you dare—Graham! Delete that right now!"

"Not a chance. This is going to become my wallpaper." Graham quickly locked his phone, in case she got any ideas. "Go get ready, or I'll take another picture."

"I'm going to find a way to get you back for this," Eloise threatened. It was hard to take her seriously with her mouth full of toothpaste.

"Promises, promises."

Despite her threats to look like an unkempt troll, Eloise looked, to Graham's eyes, just as good as she always did. She had pulled her hair into a ponytail, swiped on some mascara, and put on a simple, navy blue dress with little white daisies dotted over it.

She seemed more herself after getting some sleep, too. They talked easily as he drove them down to the breakfast place he'd picked out, holding hands over the center console. This felt normal and right. He could now confidently chalk up her strange behavior yesterday to being overwhelmed and tired.

"Waffles?" Eloise asked after they had been seated on the back patio, with the sound of the ocean and the squawking of seagulls for ambience.

"Waffles," Graham confirmed, picking up his menu. "Every single dish has waffles."

After years of brunch dates, he and his friends had probably tried most of the breakfast places within a twenty-mile square radius of Los Angeles. This place was one of his favorites. The menu reminded him of what would happen if a cooking competition had a waffles-themed episode. They'd even managed to sneak waffles into a salad. Plus, they had six different kinds of mimosas permanently on the menu and rotating seasonal options that Jordy loved.

"What do you get?" Eloise asked, turning the menu over. Her eyes widened. "Oh my god, there's more."

He grinned. "I'm partial to the chicken and waffles. You really can't go wrong with a classic. Plus, they use an herb waffle for it that is just…" He sighed happily. "Really, anything on the menu is fantastic."

She snorted, shaking her head. "I think you feel more deeply about these waffles than you do about me."

"They are pretty fantastic waffles—" Before Graham could finish the rest of his joke, his phone began buzzing in his pocket. He was determined to ignore it, but it was distracting. And since Eloise was talking to their waiter who had showed up to see if they wanted anything to drink, it couldn't hurt to check it.

Athena's picture was on the screen, and his thumb hovered over the decline button. But then the call ended, making his decision for him.

That had been simple.

"And for you?" their waiter asked.

"Can I get a—" His phone began vibrating again. Getting one call from Athena wasn't out of the ordinary, but two calls, back to back, with no voicemail, was highly unusual. "Uh, coffee. I'm sorry, I've got to take this."

"What?" he hissed, he got to the opposite corner of the patio where there weren't currently any diners to take the call.

"Oh, now you answer my calls," Athena deadpanned. "Does

no one at that rinky-dink hotel you own know how to deliver a message?"

Graham bristled. "It's not rinky-dink."

"Pretty defensive for someone who wanted nothing to do with the place a few weeks ago."

"I'm not defensive," he snapped, and pinched the bridge of his nose. The snicker on the other end of the phone wasn't appreciated, but he had earned it. "I'm not defensive. Things have just...changed a little since we last spoke."

"Mmm. Because you're fucking her?"

"How—"

"Jordy told me." Athena said. "Said you brought her to meet the family. Are things serious? Do you still want to sell the place?"

"My mother is in Italy," Graham said, stalling. "She didn't meet the family."

"Those boys are your family. Now stop avoiding the question: do you still want to sell?"

Graham would have paid good money to have been anywhere else, having almost any other conversation, than trying to have this discussion with his attorney when the person his answer mattered to most was sitting a few feet away. He'd been avoiding talking to Eloise about the future. Both the hotel and their relationship status were in flux. Graham had been hoping this trip would provide some clarity, to let him know if he could fit the pieces of his life together.

"I don't know," he finally answered.

"Well, figure it out. Overcharging you to field bids is losing all its sparkle."

"Is that why you called? To ask me about Eloise and the hotel? Because I'm not paying for this phone call when I'm going to be seeing you socially tonight at the game."

"No, I actually called because of Russell Brooks. If you had returned my calls—"

Cold fury spiked through him at the name. "What about Russell Brooks?"

"He's trying to get on your board of directors, Graham. He's been going around town courting votes."

Graham froze. "What? But there isn't a spot available on my board of directors. All the seats are filled."

"Rumor has it someone is going to step down. I had Chelsea run this down, and it seems legit."

"Who's going to step down?" he demanded.

"I don't know. It depends on who you talk to. My money is on Krager. He's been going on a lot of overseas business trips, if you catch my drift." Athena sighed. "I don't want to say I told you so, but I *told* you not to mess with Brooks last year. Do you know how badly he could fuck things up for you if he got on your board?"

Graham didn't need to be told. He was acutely aware of the control the board had over the company. "Yeah, I know," he said. "What am I supposed to do about it? Can you do anything?"

"I heard something, I called. What Brooks is doing is not illegal, just shady. You know, his usual MO. My suggestion? Circle your wagons and get your board in line."

Graham mumbled a goodbye. His brain felt like a beehive. How had this happened? What was going to happen? One month. He had taken his eye off the ball for a mere handful of weeks. And because he was weak—so easily distracted by a pet project that had mostly been decided by his dick—his company was in jeopardy. Russell couldn't technically take it away from him, but if he got on the board, it was game over for all his plans for the future.

Who did he call first? Who was the weak link in the chain

that could be pressured into stepping down, and how did he get back ahead of Russell?

Graham didn't remember eating breakfast. He didn't know if he'd talked to Eloise during the meal. He barely registered her confusion when they ended up back at his house right after. There were things to be done, and they needed to happen quickly. He went straight to his home office and closed the door behind him.

At the end of an unsatisfactory call with his corporate lawyers, Eloise stepped into his office.

"I just talked to our contractor," she said, looking down at her phone. "The painters are behind schedule on another job and don't know if they're going to make it to us on time."

"I don't care."

She continued, scrolling through something on her phone. "The good news is we've got the paint already—"

"I don't care!" Graham snapped. "I'm dealing with shit that actually matters."

The silence that followed swallowed the room, eating up all the available air. Then, in the quietest voice, Eloise said, "Okay, then."

A faint alarm bell went off in the back of his brain, trying to tell him something was wrong. But then his phone rang, so he pushed it aside to deal with later.

CHAPTER THIRTY-ONE

Eloise didn't know what Graham was doing in his office, but it didn't sound good. Occasionally she heard muffled shouting through the door, but he never came out. The lunch she made for him sat uneaten on the kitchen island, and the little fantasies she'd been cultivating about how the rest of this vacation might go withered and died on the vine.

There was at least time to get all the last-minute *Claymore Abbey* ball stuff organized. New dance cards were designed, messages about accommodations and activities were answered, and she was just settling into the message board when a presence over her shoulder made the hair on the back of her neck stand up.

"Whatcha doing?" Peter asked, leaning over the back of the couch to look at her computer.

Eloise jumped out of her skin. "Fuck! Don't do that!"

He had the decency to look mildly chastised, but he wasn't going to win any awards for the performance. The grin twitching at the corners of his mouth gave him away. "Sorry. I tried to say your name, but you were absorbed. What's so interesting?"

Rabbits recovering from a near death experience had slower heartbeats. It took a few deep breaths to calm herself, but Eloise tilted the screen towards him. "It's a *Claymore Abbey* fan community."

Delight lit him up from the inside out. "No way. Can I look?" He didn't wait for an answer, instead hopping over the back of the couch and bouncing on the cushion next to her. Eloise passed him her computer, morbidly curious about his response to the show he'd briefly been on roughly a decade ago.

"I can't believe this exists…I mean, I can, but no one lets me look at this stuff."

"No one lets you?" Eloise had to laugh. The idea that anyone told Peter Green "no" was ridiculous.

"My assistant and my therapist told me that it's not healthy for me to engage online. They're right. I hate it, but they're right." Peter shrugged, his eyes scanning the screen. "I can't believe people are still mad at my character."

"Oh, it's a whole thing. If they'd just killed you off, we could all move on, but the hope that Christian comes back and rescues Amanda from certain spinsterhood springs eternal."

"I actually was supposed to die," he told her. "It was going to be this incredibly tragic young love affair. I worked on the writers every day until they changed it."

"Would you ever go back?"

He nodded emphatically. "Oh, absolutely. And we've tried, but there have been scheduling conflicts, or it wasn't the right time in the story, so on and so forth." Peter dug in his pocket for his phone, and swiped through some photos before handing it to Eloise. "Francie and I get lunch or dinner every time I'm in London. That's her baby, Calla."

There was Peter, beaming at the camera, holding a real-life cherub with the chubbiest cheeks Eloise had ever seen on an infant. Next to him was Francie Weston, who played Lady

Amanda on *Claymore Abbey*. It was always a bit disorienting to see her in modern clothes and makeup. That they were still friends all these years later was sweet.

"Got beat out for godfather by that prick Everett Blythe," Peter said, and then added, "I promise you he's not actually a prick, I'm just bitter." Before Eloise could ask any questions about the man that played Lovingford, Peter pointed at something. "Is that you? Little Teapot?"

She flushed. "Yes."

"Why Little Teapot?"

"When I was little, my grandpa called me his little teapot because I was short and stout. That nickname spawned a teapot collection that is collecting dust in my parents' garage, and here we are. Little Teapot."

"That's adorable. When I was little, my grandma taught me to make a bone-dry martini. I don't know what kind of screen name that would spawn."

"Viscount of Vermouth?" Eloise offered and Peter's head fell back as he laughed. It felt good to make someone laugh after the day she'd been having.

"That's good." He handed her back her computer and slapped his hands down on his thighs. "We need to get going soon. Where's our Graham Cracker?"

Eloise closed her computer, pushing down the persistent ache of disappointment that bubbled up when she thought about how her little vacation had been going. "He's, um, working."

"Can never get away from those emails," Peter joked, standing up. "I'll go get him and we can go."

She stood, fixing the skirt on her dress and trying to fix a few flyaways when she heard a loud thud, like something had been thrown at a wall, and then Peter was back. He hooked his arm in hers and started leading her to the garage.

"He said to go without him. He'll meet us there." The statement was so smooth that if she hadn't spent most of her day sitting on the couch by herself, she would have believed it.

"It's okay," she said as they backed out of the garage. Peter's car was nice, but chaotically messy on the inside: empty coffee cups in the cup holders, abandoned sweaters and jackets in the backseat, scripts at her feet.

"What's okay?" he asked, not even glancing at the street before plunging into it. Eloise remembered now what Graham had said about Peter's driving, and she gripped her seat, like that would somehow keep her safe.

"Graham's not coming to the game. You don't have to lie to me."

"He'll be there," Peter insisted, rolling through the stop sign at the bottom of the hill they'd just flown down. An alarm in the back of her head went off, asking her if she had updated her life insurance policy.

"He won't. And it's okay. I'm going to go to the game, try to enjoy the experience, and then I'm going to go back to my life. He probably won't even notice I'm gone until he goes to bed."

"That's not true—"

"It is," she cut him off. "And it's okay." How many times did she have to say that before she believed it? "I have a lot to do back home, and he has a lot to do here. It's been a fun few weeks, but if this is what it's going to be like, I can't do it."

Peter's hand slipping into hers took her by surprise. She had been very pointedly not looking at him, because she was afraid if she saw the pity she could feel radiating off of him, she would cry, and she was determined not to cry over a man who had ignored her for the better part of two days. But when he gave her a comforting squeeze, it was impossible to stop the lump from forming in her throat.

"I'm sorry," he said, and Eloise concentrated on the fact that they had just zipped through what had definitely not been a green light to keep herself from falling apart.

It was not lost on her that, in a moment when she was doubting everything she thought she'd known about the relationship she'd been in for the last few weeks, she had just passed a billboard with the face of the person comforting her and holding her hand.

What a bizarre turn her life had taken. No one would believe her if she told them. Hell, she barely believed the last two days. Sometimes she thought this was all a dream and she would wake up back in the hotel, with Graham's bare chest pressed against her back, his arm curled possessively around her middle. That she somehow hadn't once again become the girl that was good enough to fuck, but not worth much effort beyond that.

Anger mixed with the sadness that had been sitting on her chest like a cement block. Anger at Graham, for making her believe that he wanted more beyond a few weeks of fun between the sheets. Anger at herself for falling for another man who hadn't promised her anything. All of that anger added to the weight of unbearable sadness that she was somehow right back where she had started: alone, broke, and unsure of how she was going to keep her hotel going.

Those were tomorrow problems. First, she needed to survive Peter Green on a California freeway.

CHAPTER THIRTY-TWO

It had been hours. Hours of phone calls, emails, and text messages, and Graham was no closer to undoing everything that had transpired in his absence.

The board believed he'd been negligent. Or that was the conclusion Russell had led them to. They weren't going to vote him out, because a sudden, major shakeup of leadership made stockholders nervous. But a change in board membership? That was barely a blip on the radar. In fact, wouldn't having an experienced businessman like Russell on the board promote confidence?

Graham almost wanted to admire Russell's patience. This coup must have been simmering for months under the surface, directly beneath his nose. Russell had waited for the perfect moment to strike, and when Graham's back was turned, he had flipped the board in his favor. Easy as that.

Well, maybe not as easy as that. Graham suspected there was some blackmail going on to get the retiring member to step down. He had been evasive on the phone about his reasons for leaving, and "retiring to spend more time with his grandkids" didn't sound like something he would do.

Graham leaned back in his chair and raked his fingers through his hair for the thousandth time that day. There was nothing else to do, and he had wasted an entire day chasing down every avenue he could think of to change the inevitable. A day he should have spent with Eloise.

Fucking hell. He was an idiot.

He'd missed the game. In all the years he had been friends with Jordy, he had never missed a home game. So that was two people he'd let down. And he'd thrown his stapler at Peter earlier. Make that three. Graham wondered if it was too late to call Sam so that he could go ahead and hurt everyone he cared about on the same day.

There was a brief rap on his office door, and Peter let himself in, casually picking up the stapler that had bounced off the wall by the doorframe earlier. It was probably a good thing his aim was shit.

"Had a bit of a day?" his friend asked, holding out the stapler to him. Graham took it, the tops of his ears heating with shame.

"It's been...a challenge."

"Don't be cute." Peter sat down on some important papers, but telling him to move seemed like a bad idea. "You reached a level of asshole today I didn't think you had in you. I mean, you've always been a workaholic, but this was beyond anything I've seen before."

"I know," Graham said weakly.

"Do you? Do you really know?"

"I've got a pretty good idea," he said, unable to meet Peter's eyes.

"Whatever you think, take it and multiply it by ten. That should get you in the ballpark."

Graham winced.

"Um, Peter? Can I talk to Graham for a minute?"

They both looked at the doorway, where Eloise was standing, wearing leggings and an oversized cream-colored sweater, her arms wrapped tightly around her middle. Her posture reminded him of the night he had picked her up off the side of the road, like she could hold all of the bad things in if she gripped hard enough.

"Of course," Peter said, hopping off the desk, giving her shoulder a squeeze on his way out.

Graham stood and started to come around his desk, but Eloise shook her head, briefly holding out her hand.

"Don't. This is easier if you stay over there."

The unmistakable catch in her voice made his chest constrict. "Eloise—"

"No, I need to say this, and then I've got to go."

"What do you mean go?" Graham was positive his heart had stopped entirely waiting for her answer.

"I'm going home. Tonight. The lady at the airline was really nice about it." Her lower lip trembled, and she swallowed, forcing a tight smile. "I've got a lot to do back there, and you've got a lot to do here. Mallory's going to pick me up from the airport. So it's all figured out."

"Nothing's figured out," Graham insisted, scrambling to find the right words. "I know today wasn't great—"

Eloise shook her head, her gaze fixed on his feet, even as he willed her to just look him in the eye. "Today. Yesterday. I'd say out of sight, out of mind, but I was right here. What happens when I'm a thousand miles away? Your company is important. I can understand that. The hotel is important to me." Her chin wobbled, and when she pressed her lips together, he took a step towards her. Eloise took a step back. "I'm fine. Maybe if things were different, or our timing was better...but I don't see how this works out."

"What about our deal?" He was drowning and grabbing at

anything that would bring him back to the surface. This couldn't be the end of it all. "You promised after the ball—"

"I can hold up my end of our deal. Email me any offers. I'll look at them."

"And then you'll reject them."

That gave him a perverse sense of hope. If Eloise wouldn't sell the hotel, he had something to hold onto. They would still have to occasionally have to talk to each other. Decisions had to be made. Checks had to be signed.

"Maybe. Maybe not. Someone once told me that I could buy a cute little bed-and-breakfast with my share of the sale." She shrugged. "Or I'll keep it, and we go back to how things were before."

"You were fucking broke."

"I'm still fucking broke. But I'll be fine. We'll all be fine."

"Eloise—"

"You won't have to do a thing. Maybe someday I'll even be able to send you a check with your share of the profits."

"I don't want the money!" He wanted to cross the room, to take her into his arms and hold her until she changed her mind or missed her flight, whichever came first. But his legs felt like they were made of lead, and there was no moving. "Don't go. Please."

She wavered. Graham was certain he saw the flicker of uncertainty cross her face, but then she pushed it away, shaking her head again. "We need some space. Both of us." Her phone chirped with a notification. "That's my ride."

All the things he wanted to tell her—needed to tell her— tried to come out at once and got stuck behind the lump that had formed in his throat. He opened his mouth several times, trying to get anything to come out, but nothing would. Eloise did her best to give him a smile, but she had to press her lips together at the end.

"Goodbye, Graham."

Helpless to stop her, each echo of her footsteps caused a crack in his aching heart. The click of the front door closing behind her broke him, and Graham sank to the floor.

Peter found him on the floor, laying on his back, looking at the ceiling like it held the answers he so desperately wanted. He'd already cried, but it hadn't helped. She was gone and he was exhausted.

"I don't want a lecture," Graham croaked.

"Wasn't going to give one." Peter laid down next to him, close enough that their shoulders touched. The silent support he wouldn't have been able to ask for. Graham blinked as fresh tears filled his eyes. How did he have any left?

"How am I supposed to survive this?"

"Define 'this'."

Graham let out a shaky breath. "Being in love."

"You think you're in love?"

"God, I hope so. Because if I'm not, then the real thing is actually going to kill me."

Could he die of a broken heart? Because it seemed improbable that all the shards that were masquerading as his heart could possibly keep beating. He kept replaying the last thirty-some odd hours in his head, finding all the moments he could have turned things around and hating himself for not doing it. And the look on Eloise's face when she said goodbye, when she had finally let the carefully constructed mask fall, would haunt him for the rest of his life.

For a few weeks, he had been happy. In the same way darkness couldn't be measured without light, he hadn't noticed how unhappy he had been until he met Eloise. And she was gone, taking all her light with her, plunging him deeper into darkness because at least before he hadn't known that he was miserable.

"Have you ever been in love?" he asked.

"Once," Peter answered. A small smile, somewhere between rueful and fond, tugged at the corners of his mouth.

"What? When?" In all the years they had been friends, it occurred to Graham that he had never known Peter to date. There were plenty of rumors that swirled around, and he did nothing to dispel them by being a casual, equal-opportunity public hand-holder, but they were just rumors.

"I was nineteen. I had just wrapped *Claymore Abbey*, and I was living in London at the time. She was perfect."

"And did you feel like carving your heart out with a dull butter knife when it was over?"

"Even I'm not that dramatic."

"What happened?"

"I was young. Overly confident it would all work out in the end. I let her walk away with my heart and my favorite sweater." Peter rolled onto his side. "If you love her, you owe it to both of you to figure out what it is that you want. I'd give it all up tomorrow—my career, the fame, the money—if I could have a second chance."

"It's not that simple."

"Isn't it?" He sat up. "Stop making it complicated. Do you love her? Yes or no."

He didn't need to think about it. "Yes."

"Then get your fucking shit together and go get her back."

"She said she wanted space." Graham pressed the heels of his hands against his aching eyes. "What if she's really done? What if I screwed this up beyond what I can fix?"

"Then I'll find you a butter knife."

CHAPTER THIRTY-THREE

Graham yawned and finished his cup of coffee. He hadn't been able to sleep. His bed felt too big without Eloise taking up the other half—and the middle, and his side. She could really move in her sleep. Instead of sleeping, he had tried to find some way out of the mess he had created. Which had led him to a building he hadn't visited in thirteen years.

Across from him, Russell's assistant looked up from what she was typing.

"I'm sure he'll be with you in just a few minutes," she promised, her bracelet catching the overhead light. Graham recognized the bracelet. Athena had purchased the same gold and diamond vine bangle for herself to take the sting out of turning forty. Either Russell paid his assistant very well—which was about as likely as the Pacific Ocean becoming an ice-skating rink—or he was still fucking his employees.

"I can wait."

Making Graham wait was part of the game.

"Do you want some more coffee?" she asked, already standing and adjusting her black pencil skirt. Graham didn't. That had been his second cup, but he held out the mug she had handed him when he had first arrived, and she hurried forward to grab it.

Not a career executive assistant, he decided. She was too eager to please. There was a casual indifference she hadn't mastered yet, and likely wouldn't master before Russell either grew tired of her or the current Mrs. Brooks caught wind of the affair.

"Just a suggestion," Graham said when she came back with the cup of steaming black coffee. "Don't wear the jewelry he gives you to the office. This wife isn't very understanding."

Her cheeks burned scarlet as she went back to her desk and discreetly put the bracelet in a drawer. The phone trilled once, and she picked it up, murmured an affirmative, and then looked back at Graham.

"He's ready for you."

Being made to open the door was also part of the game. He wasn't important enough to be let in, and they weren't cozy enough for Russell to welcome him into his office. At twenty-years old, it had been intimidating. At thirty-three, it was irritating.

"I was wondering when you'd show up." Russell didn't bother to get up or offer Graham a seat across from his behemoth dark wood desk.

"I've been busy," he answered, sitting down in one of the leather chairs. The couch against the wall would have been more strategic, but he could only imagine what had happened over there. The chairs, he noticed, were an inch or so shorter than they should have been, so he was ever so slightly below Russell.

Subtle.

"I'm going to assume this is about the open board position?"

"Nah," Graham replied dryly. "I wanted to discuss sports. A

little father-son bonding time." Russell's eyes narrowed ever so slightly and it gave him a rush. "But since you brought it up..."

"There isn't much to discuss." Russell settled back into his chair with an exaggerated casualness. "You're backed into a corner with nowhere to go. This is checkmate, Graham. I've won."

The yawn he stifled was entirely genuine, but it made Russell bristle. To him, it was another move in the game they played. It was a game Graham had grown tired of in the last forty-eight hours.

What was the point of it all? The schemes, the posturing? This pissing contest they had been in for the last thirteen years had only brought him headaches and misery. And money. It had brought him a lot of money. Graham didn't doubt that without the spite that had kept the fire burning in his gut to succeed, he would have given up or sold out years ago. But what he had gained paled in comparison to what he had lost. There was no amount of money in the world that made him feel as content as he did when he watched Eloise scowl at the computer in their shoebox sized office, and no business deal had ever given him the same rush as her smiling at him from across a crowded room.

Or an uncrowded room.

Any room, actually.

Everything Peter had said on the floor of his office the night before slid into place, like a key in the correct lock, and clarity hit Graham like a hammer. None of it really mattered. The money, the company, his never-ending feud with the man who shared half of his DNA. He never stopped because it was never enough to fill the deep, aching void he felt. But for a few, wonderful weeks in a creaky old hotel with loud pipes and a louder furnace, he had felt whole.

He didn't need a solution where he kept all the pieces. His father could have the entire board, for all he cared.

Eloise was all that really mattered.

"You know what, Russell," Graham said, standing up. "This has been an extremely illuminating conversation. Thank you."

"Extremely illuminating...You just got here."

"I know. But there's a lot to do when you step down."

"Step—step down? Where are you going?"

Graham was already halfway out the door, but looked back over his shoulder. Russell's neck was red, and there was a worrying vein throbbing at his temple. Was that sort of thing hereditary? He almost asked, because he hoped this would be the last time he ever saw his father, but he had wasted enough valuable time.

"I'm going home."

———

Graham tossed his keys on the counter, his entire body humming with excitement. Now that everything seemed clear, he wanted to put his plans into motion as fast as humanly possible. There was a lot to do, and he had a million phone calls to make, but he had a kind of soul-deep certainty he had never experienced before. This was what he was supposed to be doing.

From the corner of his eye, he spotted Peter sitting on the couch, his headphones on, doing something on his laptop. If anyone was going to be proud of him for the decision he had made, it was going to be Peter.

"What are you doing?" Graham asked, putting his hands on Peter's shoulders.

Peter jumped, his laptop jostling precariously on his lap.

"Nothing!" he squawked, angling the screen away. "It's weird porn, okay? Super, super weird porn."

Graham raised an eyebrow. "Really? On the couch?"

"It—oh, fuck it." He sighed dramatically and tilted the screen for Graham to see. A very familiar website was on the screen. "I couldn't help myself, okay? Eloise showed me the site, and I needed to know what people were saying about me."

In the upper righthand corner, a message notification appeared.

"You're messaging people? Peter!"

"It's okay!" Peter clicked on the mail icon and a very, very familiar screen name was there. "It's just Eloise."

"You're talking to Eloise?" It came out as a prepubescent squeak. It was a miracle he could speak at all, because in front of him was the final confirmation that Eloise and Teapot were the same person.

> Little_Teapot: Your assistant is going to put parental controls on your laptop after they find out you're on here. And I will NOT tell you about the fanfic. No. I can't be responsible for introducing you to alllll of that.

"Oh, come on. How bad can fanfic be?" Peter started to type out a response.

Graham's brain, meanwhile, acted like dial-up internet in the nineties: lots of buzzing and beeping, and it was taking too long to connect.

If Eloise was Teapot, that meant that he had actually known her for about a year. She had always been the one he wanted to talk to in the middle of the night, the one that never failed to make him smile when he was having a bad day. And maybe on some deep, subconscious level, he had always known.

Somehow it made what he'd done so much worse. He'd hurt the woman he loved *and* his friend.

How would she feel when she found out? Would she be happy? Relieved? Angry? Would it make any difference to her at all?

"Graham Cracker."

He inhaled sharply, surprised by the sound of Peter's voice. "Hm?"

"I said, I am talking to Eloise. Is that a problem? Has something changed since last night? Do we still need a butter knife?"

Something had changed since last night. A lot had changed in the last few hours. And in the last few minutes, his entire world had tilted on its axis and was only just beginning to rotate properly again. His plans began to shift and change.

"Peter, there's some stuff I need to tell you, and I need you to promise to remain calm."

"Are you dying?"

"What? No. Why—"

"You asked me to remain calm. What else would send me into a tailspin?"

Graham took a deep breath and told Peter everything. From the first time he had watched an episode of *Claymore Abbey* on TV after Edgar had died and he couldn't sleep. To his deepening obsession, and then innocently joining the fan community. He told him about the first time he'd talked to Eloise online, and even pulled up the thread for him. How they had been messaging each other for the better part of a year, and how part of the reason he had agreed to help Eloise with the hotel was because he had hoped to meet her online persona at the ball, and then that he had fallen in love with Eloise herself long before he realized she was Little_Teapot.

Peter, to his credit, remained calm the entire time. When Graham was done, he nodded, absorbing all the information.

"Why didn't you tell me you liked the show?"

Graham gave him a look. "Because you would have asked a lot of questions. You get really weird when I like one of your projects."

Peter nodded. "This is fair. So, there's a ball? With costumes?"

"There's a ball. With costumes."

Peter nodded again, opening up a new tab on his browser. "Perfect."

"I'm scared to ask, but why is that perfect?"

"You'll see."

CHAPTER THIRTY-FOUR

Their relationship was going to end the same way it had begun: with an email.

Which was exactly why Eloise couldn't bring herself to open the message from Graham just yet. She wanted a few more hours where she could pretend that she hadn't retreated instead of sticking up for herself. A few more hours where she hadn't ruined absolutely everything that was good about her life.

Well, almost everything.

"Here." Sybil set a mug of steaming tea next to her laptop. "It will make your throat feel better."

After Mallory had picked her up at the airport and dropped her off at the hotel, Eloise had gone to her room and realized that she couldn't stay there. Remnants of Graham were everywhere. His laundry was mixed in with hers, like they were going to do it when they got back on Friday, and the book he'd borrowed from the library was on his nightstand, waiting for him to return.

Eloise had managed to hold it together the entire journey back to Crane Cove. She hadn't cried in the car on the way to the airport, or on the flight, even though the couple sitting next to her were returning from their honeymoon. But Sybil answering the door in her too-large red cardigan, her brown eyes soft with understanding, broke her wide open.

Once the tears started, they didn't want to stop. The sobs eventually subsided, but her eyes would not stop leaking tears. She fell asleep sandwiched between both Morgan sisters in Sybil's bed.

In the morning, Eloise had tried to work. She really had. But ten minutes into work she looked to her left where Graham normally sat in their cramped office to ask him something, and her heart cracked open all over again.

When would he stop haunting her hotel? Because she kept thinking she saw him out of the corner of her eye, or she could feel him standing behind her, but when she turned, no one was there.

Hours of frayed nerves later, Eloise gave up and told the front desk she was going to go work at Stardust, and to call her there if they needed anything. It was only marginally better, because as locals drifted in and out, they stopped to say hi, ask about the hotel, and inevitably ask where Graham was. Had they really been that attached the last few weeks? And when had he ingratiated himself to the community so much?

She smiled as best she could and told them that he was in Los Angeles. It was the truth. And it hurt every single time.

The tea Sybil had given her was liberally dosed with honey. And Sybil was right. It did feel good as it slid down her throat, soothing and sweet.

"How's it going?" Sybil asked, sitting down across from her.

Eloise's first instinct was to push it all down, to put on her usual smile and assure Sybil that she was fine. That her marathon crying session the night before had been a fluke and that her tender heart wasn't as bruised as it seemed. But pretending things were okay didn't make them okay, and she was exhausted from the effort of keeping up appearances.

"Honestly? Shit." She clutched the mug tightly in her hands, not caring that it was at the tipping point of being uncomfortably hot. "The last year has been a disaster."

The walls she put up to keep everything contained came crumbling down all at once. It flowed out of her like a river breaching its dam: Edgar, the dire financial position of the hotel, how she had been living there, her strange online friendship, what had happened in LA.

Eloise wiped a tear with the sleeve of her black polka-dot sweater, sniffling. Crying in public was beyond embarrassing but couldn't be helped right now. Once she started crying, it was hard to stop. "Do you want to know something crazy?"

"Besides the fact that you've been conversing with a stranger on the internet?" Sybil's tone was dry, but her expression was soft and teasing.

"I wanted it to be Graham." Her lip trembled. "That somehow we had always been meant to be and it would be a funny story we got to tell our kids someday. I was even suspicious for a minute, but I think my heart wanted it to be true too much." In response, her heart throbbed, and Eloise rubbed her sternum, like she could massage the pain away. "I don't think I've ever actually been heartbroken before. This sucks."

"It does," Sybil agreed, pushing up the sleeves of her red cardigan. "But you'll survive."

"I need to be more like you. You'd never let a boy break your heart."

"You'd be surprised. We are all fools in love." Sybil pressed on before Eloise could ask her what that meant. "Let's focus on what we can control. Is everything on schedule for the ball next weekend?"

"No." She groaned. "I got a call from the painters yesterday.

They won't be able to make it until Thursday. Which doesn't work because most people arrive on Friday. So I've got to find a way to paint the rooms before Wednesday. With no money to hire help. And I have to unpack all of the new linens that arrived while I was gone. Alone."

"Do you have the paint?"

"Yeah."

"Perfect." Sybil stood, picking up Eloise's crumb-filled muffin plate. "I think we should be able to finish before Wednesday."

"Who is we? You and me? Because it is logistically impossible for us to paint the entire hotel in less than a week. Not unless we take massive amounts of meth to stay awake."

"I've got to make some calls, but you're forgetting something really important."

"You've recently come into possession of a time machine?"

"No. That you're loved. People want to help you, if you'd let them."

It was less of a lecture than Eloise had been expecting. But wasn't that how it always worked? The things she put off because she was afraid of the outcome were never as bad as she thought they would be.

With that thought fresh in her mind, she opened the email from Graham.

Subject: Thoughts

Eloise,

I've been doing a lot of thinking since you left. I think we need to have a serious conversation, but I don't want to do it over phone or email. I'll be back in town after the ball. We can talk then.

Graham

What the hell did that mean?

She reread the email three more times, each time drawing a different conclusion. He definitely wanted to break up. He wanted to get back together. He was being held at gunpoint, and this was his coded message for her to ignore the kidnappers' demands and call the police.

Why wasn't there a sign-off? No "hope you made it back safely" or "I miss the hell out you, please don't leave me like this." Not even a "best" or "regards."

Eloise hit reply, about to ask what he meant by "serious conversation." She stopped.

Whatever he meant, she was not going to respond to that vague message. All she had left was her pride, and she clung to it like a life preserver. She couldn't bend again. Bending led to breaking. She wasn't going to let Graham break her more than he had.

Instead she checked to see if Peter had written her back yet. His chaotic energy bled into everything he wrote, and it had been a bright spot in her day to talk to him, even if it made her wonder if Graham knew or cared. There was no new message from Peter yet, but there was one from someone else.

> Foolproof42: I don't know if you're going to be there, but there's a Claymore Abbey ball in Crane Cove, OR. I'll be there, looking tall, dark, and devastatingly handsome.

A few weeks ago, the idea of Foolproof42 being at the ball, threatening to look handsome, would have given her excited butterflies. The feeling she got knowing he would be there wasn't bad, but it wasn't the same.

> Little_Teapot: I'll be there, but I never dress up. I'm looking forward to finally meeting you. It will be nice to have a friend there. I really need one after the week I've had.

Foolproof42: Why do you go if you don't dress up?

Eloise hesitated for a moment, and then replied.

Little_Teapot: I work at the hotel. And I don't have a dress. The ultimate wallflower.

Foolproof42: If you had a dress, what would it look like?

That was an easy question to answer. She had daydreamed about this for years.

Little_Teapot: Something like Olivia's ball gown from the end of season five. But purple instead of blue.

Foolproof42: Periwinkle. That's your favorite color.

Little_Teapot: It is. Make sure to come find me. I'll be watching from beside the potted plants.

Foolproof42: I think your wallflower days are numbered. See you Saturday.

CHAPTER THIRTY-FIVE

"This place is adorable. It looks like a movie set."

Graham adjusted his hat, which was a terrible disguise, but they were supposed to be incognito. Something Peter seemed to have forgotten as he turned in a slow, fascinated circle, admiring the quaint beauty of Crane Cove's historic downtown district. Nothing conspicuous about a stranger who looked suspiciously like one of America's most beloved actors wearing a purpose-fully nondescript hat standing in the middle of the street taking pictures.

"What are you doing?" Graham asked.

"My mom is always looking for locations for future projects. Imagine the revenue a movie could bring to the town." Peter paused with his camera pointed at Stardust Coffee. "Do we have time for a cup?"

"No. We have a schedule."

A schedule that had been crafted with military precision, planned down to the minute. One that would work, as long as everyone else kept to the timing. It had taken all week to devise that schedule. The longest week he could remember, because a week without Eloise felt like an eternity. He missed sharing his days with her, working with her, laughing with her. At night he barely slept because he would wake up reaching for her, only to find cold sheets where her warm body should be. So, this meticulous plan had to work. It didn't have time for Peter's side quests. The rest of his life depended on it.

"But there's coffee," Peter protested, glancing longingly over his shoulder as Graham gripped his elbow and pulled him down the sidewalk.

"I will get you a cup somewhere else. But not there." Graham cast a cautious glance over his shoulder, positive he'd see Sybil glaring at him through the window.

Peter stopped, planted his feet, and stared at his friend. "What is so scary about a coffee shop?"

"Who said I was scared?" With a mere twitch of his eyebrow, Peter telegraphed his disbelief, and Graham sighed, adjusting his hat again. "The owner hates me, okay? I'm not ready to face her. I'm missing protective equipment."

"You went toe to toe with titans of industry, and you're scared of a woman who runs a coffee shop?" A grin spread across his face, and he turned to walk back. "I have to meet her."

"No, no, no." Graham grabbed him again, forcing him in the opposite direction of Stardust Coffee. "We are not going to poke the dragon lady today. You're here to help me, remember? You can't help me if I'm dead."

"What about mostly dead?"

"You're not funny."

"I'm delightful and charming. *Vanity Fair* said so."

"Your publicist paid them to say that."

"Inger would never. Maybe for Sam, but never for me."

———

Eloise checked her schedule. On time to the minute. The day was flowing flawlessly, even better than she had hoped for in her wildest dreams. The ballroom was decorated, guests were checked in, and Amara had even indulged her in ten whole minutes of last-minute fussing over the menu. She even had the decency to pretend not to be annoyed when Eloise worried that they wouldn't have enough cucumber sandwiches.

Thanks to a small army of volunteers, the hotel looked the best she had ever seen it. The usual suspects showed up to help: Connor, Kiki, Mallory, Chase, and Cole. But then more people showed up. The historical society. The bird-watchers. Dale. Bitsy and Greg McMahon. People Eloise had only ever met in passing. All of them picked up a paintbrush, or changed linens, or cleaned. A few times, she had needed to step into her office to cry for a few minutes because she was overwhelmed by the outpouring of love and support. They believed in her and wanted her to succeed.

Longing tugged at her heart as she scanned the remaining tasks. Graham would have loved the color-coded masterpiece.

She missed him. Oh, how she missed him. It had taken a few days for the hurt of their disastrous trip to Los Angeles to fade, but once it had, she had been left with two indisputable facts.

The first was that she had been part of the problem. The past week had shown her that when she needed something, she needed to ask for it. The help that she had needed for so long had always been available, but no one knew she needed it because she hadn't said anything. The same was true for what had happened on their trip. Graham had never minded her asserting herself before. He had encouraged it. And when she saw him again, she was going to apologize for not speaking up, for running away when she should have stood up and fought.

The second thing she knew, with perfect clarity, was that she loved him and wanted him in her life. Eloise didn't know what that would look like yet, but it was what she wanted, and she was determined make it work. If that meant long distance, so be it. A life without Graham's single-dimpled smiles was not a life she was interested in living.

"Schedule says it's time to go," Annie announced, plucking Eloise's schedule from her hands and replacing it with her jacket and purse. "Fairy godmother time."

Her cousin Annie had offered to come immediately when she had called her crying the previous weekend. It didn't matter that she had school or that the drive from Seattle was long. Eloise had even heard the jingle of keys before she had managed to convince her that it wasn't necessary. Mid-week, Annie had told her that she was coming down for the ball to act as her moral support through the event. Plus, she was still fighting with Jake and needed a break from his bullshit.

"Where on my schedule does it say 'fairy godmother time'?" Eloise asked, reaching for the paper that Annie effortlessly held over her head. She was four inches taller and used every one of those inches to her advantage. "I need that."

"It might not be on your schedule, but it's on mine." Annie said, tapping Eloise on the nose. "You cannot meet your mystery man looking like you've been frantically running around all day."

"I have not been frantically running around all day. It was a controlled power walk."

"That doesn't make your point the way you think it does." Annie handed off the schedule to a passing staff member. "You have sixty seconds before I toss you over my shoulder and carry you out."

"You wouldn't."

Annie put a hand on her hip and cocked her head to the side. "Try me."

Eloise put on her coat with all the enthusiasm of a child

being told to go to bed. "I don't need to be fairy-godmothered. I need to be here to make sure everything keeps running smoothly."

"Eloise, love of my life, angel of my heart," Annie began, wrapping an arm around her shoulders so she couldn't turn around and steal her schedule back. "You have left your staff with a schedule a toddler could execute. Stop arguing with me."

"What does being fairy-godmothered even mean?" she asked when they were halfway back to Sybil's house. It was still too hard to be in her old room.

"We're going to do your hair and your makeup and put you in one of the pretty dresses you own."

"That is a pretty pathetic fairy-godmothering."

"Beggars can't be choosers. You didn't hear Cinderella bitching about her midnight curfew, did you?"

Eloise snorted, looking out the window as a dark blue sedan passed them, headed toward the hotel. The week apart must have been longer than she thought, because she could have sworn she saw Graham driving with Peter in the passenger seat. If she was seeing him where he wasn't, Monday couldn't come soon enough.

———

Sybil staunchly refused to take down her Halloween decorations until after Thanksgiving. This had less to do with resisting the creeping start date of Christmas, and everything to do with pissing off Edith Nelson, who lived across the street. Because the only thing Edith loved more than gossip was Christmas. From November first until Black Friday, their opposite sides of the street looked like the Griswolds versus the Addams Family.

"Eloise!" Edith called from her front yard, her wave nearly

synchronized with the inflatable Frosty the Snowman she had put up.

Eloise hadn't even made it two steps out of the car. She dug down deep for a friendly smile.

"Hi, Edith," Eloise called back, waving to the older woman. "Great weather today."

It was a beautiful day. The sun was shining, the air was crisp, and there wasn't a threatening cloud in the sky, just the cute, fluffy white ones.

"Gorgeous. It's supposed to rain all next week, so got to get my decorations out while I can." Her laugh was so forced that Eloise wanted to wince in sympathy. "A man with a large package was just at the house. Do you know what that was about?"

Annie snorted, covering the sound with a cough.

"A large package?"

"Yes. It was absolutely massive." She shook her head in disbelief, silver curls bouncing.

From her left, Eloise heard Annie make a choked noise.

"No idea," she said quickly. They needed to exit stage left. Now. "Well, it was great talking to you, Edith. Have a wonderful day." She pushed her cousin toward the house.

"I want to know more about this large, absolutely massive package," Annie said in a stage whisper, trying and failing not to giggle.

"You are a doctoral candidate. Pull it together."

"I am allowed to laugh at old ladies accidentally euphemizing penises, Eloise."

Eloise rolled her eyes and let them inside. The interior of the house was balmy. Sybil came around the corner from the kitchen, a mug clasped in her hands, a blanket around her shoulders, and her red hair in a tousled bun.

"I thought you were resting." Eloise frowned. Sybil had

woken up with a horrible cold that had knocked her absolutely flat. She hadn't even gone into work that day, which was unheard of. The world could be ending, and Sybil would have gone to work.

"The doorbell woke me up," she mumbled, sipping her tea. "Something got dropped off for you."

"What was it?" Eloise asked, hanging her coat up by the door.

Sybil shrugged. "Don't know. Mallory got it."

"The case of the mysterious package continues." Annie wiggled her eyebrows, grinning as she headed for the stairs. "I want to see what it is."

"Don't take this the wrong way," Eloise said to Sybil as they slowly climbed the stairs together, "but you look like shit."

"Ha ha," she deadpanned, sipping her tea again and wincing as she swallowed. "I feel like shit."

"Well, at least we'll all be out of your hair tonight. Any exciting plans?"

"I'm going to chug enough cold medicine to put me into a light coma."

"Sounds like a party."

Mallory was waiting at the top of the stairs, dressed for her shift at the hotel, bouncing on the balls of her feet.

"Could you two go any slower?"

Sybil responded by holding up her middle finger.

"I thought your shift started later? Did Ian call? Is everything okay?" A million disastrous possibilities about what could have happened in the ten minutes since she left the hotel flashed through Eloise's mind.

"No, it's fine—I mean, I'm assuming it's fine." Mallory grabbed her hand, pulling her down the hallway toward the guest room where she had been staying. "I didn't want to be rushing to get ready later."

"Why would you be rushing?" The prickly sensation that there was something going on that she wasn't aware of tickled Eloise's stomach. That suspicion was confirmed when she entered her room and saw what was hanging on the closet door. She gasped.

A periwinkle ball gown, with short, delicately puffed sleeves, and glittering beadwork woven into the lace along the sweetheart neckline. A cluster of small, pale pink and ivory silk roses were sewn on to each shoulder. The voluminous skirts were left unadorned, except for the lace hem.

It was a near perfect recreation of her favorite Olivia gown.

Her fingers trembled as she reached out to touch the silk gown. "Mallory, who dropped this off?"

"I don't know. Some guy who looked like Peter Green."

The thud of ceramic hitting the floor made Eloise jump.

"Shit." Sybil bent over to pick up her mug, tea soaking into the carpet. "It's fine. It just slipped."

Eloise looked up at Annie, her heart racing. "Did you do this?"

Annie smiled and put her hands on Eloise's shoulders. "Cinderella, it's time to get you ready for a ball."

CHAPTER THIRTY-SIX

"Should I have shaved? I feel like I should have shaved." Graham ran his hands down his face, the week's worth of growth scratching his palms.

"No, no," Peter reassured him. "The beard is dashing and debonair. It says 'I'm miserable without you and I haven't slept all week.' Which is true."

"So, it's not Tom Hanks in *Castaway?*"

Peter took a half step back to study him. He looked perfectly at home in the long-tailed wool jacket and silk waistcoat, while Graham couldn't stop trying to loosen the constricting collar of his matching outfit.

"No. I think you cleaned it up nicely."

Graham sighed, resisting the urge to tug at his collar again. His stomach was so twisted it could have doubled as a knot-tying manual.

The ballroom glittered, the light of hundreds of electric candles catching the crystal chandeliers, casting a warm glow throughout the room. A botanical garden's worth of flowers had been smuggled in, along with an ice sculpture for the refreshment table, and a twelve-piece chamber orchestra. Costumed attendees marveled at the transformation, the decor far and above anything they had previously experienced on the usual shoestring budget.

"She's late," Graham remarked, struggling to keep the tremor out of his voice. The rest of his life hinged on the night going well.

"She'll be here," Peter answered, his eyes sweeping over the room. "I still think you should have let me rent the champagne fountain."

"We went from a quartet to a twelve-piece band. I had to draw the line somewhere."

"You drew the line at peacocks for the courtyard. You didn't need another line."

Movement by the ballroom entrance caught Graham's eye. His heart stuttered and his breath caught, but it wasn't Eloise. He wiped his sweaty palms on his trousers. He needed to intercept Eloise as soon as she entered the ballroom, before she thought some other stupid asshole was Foolproof42 and dazzled him with her brilliant smile and big, blue eyes. Because he wasn't the only tall, decently attractive man in the room, and he had purposefully tried to throw her off the scent by lying to her about when he was coming back to town.

"If you'd let me rent the horse and carriage, she'd be here by now."

"Not helping," Graham grumbled.

"Let's go over this. What happens if she had decided in the last week that you're not worth the effort and she would rather move on?" Peter asked, turning his attention away from the bustle of the ballroom and focusing on Graham. "If all of this was for nothing, what are you going to do?"

"Butter knife."

"I'm being serious."

"Fine. Havisham."

Peter rolled his eyes. "Dickensian gallows humor aside..."

"Peter, I am two seconds away from a panic attack, I look like I belong in *A Christmas Carol*, and in the span of a week, I have uprooted my entire life. Let me have my dick humor."

"Dickensian."

It was clear to Graham that if Peter had gone to regular school, instead of being homeschooled with tutors, he would have been shoved in a variety of lockers, trashcans, and janitorial closets. The urge to punch him in his pretty face was strong.

"Hey, boss." Mallory's sudden presence at his elbow made Graham jump. She handed him a glass of champagne. "For your nerves."

"Aren't you supposed to be at the bar?" Graham asked, trying to not accidentally crush the stemware as his hand automatically tightened.

"I was helping set up the champagne fountain."

Graham wheeled on Peter, who was slowly backing away. He held up his hands in defense. "It is not my fault she's late. You were supposed to be occupied and too happy to notice that I may have gone ahead with the champagne fountain."

"For what it's worth, I think it looks cool," Mallory said, and Peter nodded rapidly. She took a better look at him, understanding dawning on her. "Hey! You're the delivery guy. Wow. You are a dead ringer for Peter Green."

Maybe not that much understanding.

"I'll have to tell my mother," Peter said. "She'll be so proud."

Graham sighed. "Peter, this is Mallory. Mallory, this is Peter."

Mallory's eyes widened. "And your name is Peter, too? Whoa."

"No, Mallory, *this* is Peter Green."

Mallory blinked up at him, then looked at Peter, then back

at him, then back at Peter. "Holy shit. How much money did you spend to get him here?"

Graham pinched the bridge of his nose. "Peter is a friend."

Peter grinned. "He made me promise to never tell him how much I spent on the ball."

"Your sister promised to murder me if I came back to town. Any chance she's available?" Graham asked, forcing himself to sip his champagne instead of tossing it back in one gulp.

Mallory chuckled. "She is currently conked out on cold medicine. Maybe she can pencil you in for tomorrow."

Graham's return quip died on his lips. All air and rational thought left his body in the same rush because Eloise was standing in the entrance of the ballroom.

She was radiant.

It was a phrase Graham thought was applied too liberally to the general population. How many people were truly radiant? But Eloise, standing in the doorway, her cheeks flushed, soft berry lips slightly parted, a few curly tendrils of hair escaping from her updo, was radiant. She glowed. A bomb could have gone off behind him and he wouldn't have noticed because she held every inch of his attention.

The beading on her dress glittered as she slowly surveyed the room, taking it all in. Her brow furrowed ever so slightly, and she looked up at the tall brunette next to her and asked a question. That had to be Annie. He had only seen her in photos, like the one on Eloise's desk and on the university's website where he had tracked her down to recruit her for this entire fiasco.

Eloise's big blue eyes grew wide as she locked eyes with Graham from across the room.

It was like stepping off a curb that was a little higher than he had anticipated. His stomach fluttered, his breath hitched, and his chest felt too small for everything it contained. The weight of missing her, of staying away from her, of not talking to her because she had wanted some space lifted, and Graham couldn't feel the marble floor beneath his shoes as he floated toward her.

For the last week, Graham had thought of, refined, and practiced what he was going to say to Eloise when he saw her again. But standing in front of her, his mind was a swirling, incoherent mess of emotions that all wanted to come out at the same time. And with the traffic jam in his verbal processing center, all that came out was a small, two-letter word.

"Hi."

CHAPTER THIRTY-SEVEN

It wasn't fair. It simply wasn't fair.

Eloise looked beautiful. She knew that. It was an undeniable fact. Her hair was braided, tucked into an updo, and being held in place by an obscene amount of bobby pins. Her gown fit perfectly, and Mallory had done something with her eyeshadow to make her eyes look bigger and bluer.

But Graham? He was glorious.

The rest of the room—which had been transformed in her absence into some kind of decadent, expensive dream—faded away when she saw him. He was so handsome in his black evening suit that it hurt to look at him.

And he had a beard.

Graham was a habitual shaver. It had been part of their morning ritual, jockeying for position at the sink while he shaved and she brushed her teeth. One of them easily could have waited, but it had been fun. Her teeth had never been cleaner because she drew out the process to watch him make those precise strokes with his razor.

How had his week gone if he had a beard?

He started walking towards her. Half of her brain wanted to retreat, and the other half wanted to pick up her skirts and run to him, flinging herself in his arms to find out exactly how that beard would feel against her face as she kissed him senseless. With all the mixed signals, her feet remained firmly rooted to their spot, her heart trying to beat its way out of her chest.

It really wasn't fair. He looked even better up close. Tall, strong, and commanding in black and white. A shocking amount like Lovingford.

And tired. So very tired.

The pale purple shadows under his eyes betrayed a week of poor sleep that probably mimicked hers.

"Hi," he said quietly.

Eloise blinked up at him. After a week apart all he could come up with was "Hi"? She had expected more. Well, she hadn't expected him to be here at all, but he was. So, she didn't know what she had expected, but it wasn't "Hi."

Graham cleared his throat, color rising from the high collar of his shirt up to his cheeks. The longer the silence drew out, the redder he got. Eloise wondered what he was waiting for, and then Annie's finger jabbed her in the side, though the poke was muffled by the layers she wore.

"Hi," Eloise said in return, because it was all she could think of.

The deafening silence of unsaid things began to grow again when Peter filled the empty space between Annie and Graham. He rocked up onto the balls of his feet, and then back on his heels, looking between Eloise and Graham, and then at Annie.

"Are they just staring at each other?"

Annie nodded. "I'm having flashbacks to middle school dances."

Peter held out his hand to Annie as the band began to play the opening strains of a waltz. "Shall we set a good example?"

"I'm going to step on your toes," she warned as she placed her hand in his.

"Follow my lead, and you'll glide like a swan."

That made Annie light up. "You know, a lot of these dances remind me of bird courtship rituals..."

Her lecture on the sex lives of birds faded as Peter guided her toward the dance floor. Eloise wondered if he would be able to get a word in before the dance was over. No one could out-talk Annie once she started talking about birds.

"I was going to do that," Graham complained, and Eloise looked up to see him frowning.

"You were going to ask Annie to dance?"

"No! I mean—fuck. Goddammit." He groaned, and Eloise caught his hand just before he could drag it through his perfectly brushed hair. Not that she was opposed to his hair being rumpled. She just wanted to be the one doing the rumpling.

"I'm teasing," she soothed, and his shoulders relaxed. "You look tired."

"I'm exhausted. It's been a very long, weird week."

"Do you want to go sit down?" she asked, pointing to some open chairs lined against the perimeter of the ballroom.

Graham shook his head. "No. I didn't spend all week twirling Peter around my living room to be a wallflower."

"You twirled Peter around the living room?"

"I needed to learn how to dance. He wouldn't let me use the broom, and I wasn't going to use Jordy's blowup doll."

Laughter burst out of Eloise with the force of a confetti cannon. It couldn't be helped. Her imagination was working overtime with all the juicy possibilities. Graham dancing with some haggard blowup doll that had probably been trotted out for every Phantoms' bachelor party for the last fifteen years was easily her favorite, followed by Graham scowling as Peter corrected his posture.

Eloise dabbed at her eyes with the edges of her fingers, hoping she hadn't smudged her mascara by laughing too hard. As her fingers came away clean, she noticed that her skirts were squished against a pair of long, trouser-clad legs, and her forehead was resting against a starched shirt that had been placed over a warm, strong chest she was intimately familiar with. During her laughing fit, she had instinctively fallen against Graham. Her body wanted to be near his and, as soon as her mind was occupied, had made it happen.

She took a deep, steadying breath, and his scent wrapped around her like a warm blanket. It was comforting and so familiar, like coming home after a long time away.

The small smile he gave her when she looked up was hopeful but cautious, and just enough to make his one dimple faintly appear.

She'd missed that dimple.

"Do you want to dance?" he asked. "I'll try not to step on your toes."

"Can you even find them under all this fabric?" Eloise joked, and his foot tapped hers in response. She grinned. "Ah. Already trying to get under my skirts."

"One thing at a time." Graham winked, and her stomach did a double backflip. "So, dance? Yes? No?"

Eloise looked at the couples gliding gracefully across the dance floor, colorful skirts twirling. Peter skillfully covered his wince with a smile when Annie stepped on his foot, and she could see him tell her to relax, which would never happen. Annie was a Price. Prices didn't know how to relax, especially when they weren't good at something.

"Next song," she told him, and he frowned. "What? What's wrong?"

"I only learned the waltz. The next song may not be a waltz."

"Peter let you get away with only learning the waltz?"

"I'm a slow learner."

"We'll only get half a song," Eloise pointed out.

Graham shrugged. "Half a song with you is better than an entire song with anyone else."

How was a girl supposed to say no after that?

———

"I'm sorry about your toes."

"They're fine."

"Are you sure they're not broken? You were limping."

"Would it make you feel better if I took off my shoes and socks so you could inspect them?" Graham teased, draping his jacket around Eloise's bare shoulders.

The November night was clear but cold, the cloudless sky dusted with thousands of stars and a fat, bright moon. Eloise pulled Graham's coat tight around her body, nestling into the residual warmth that clung to the silk lining. They had retreated outside to a stone bench in the courtyard where they could watch the ball through the tall windows. Inside, Peter was asking wallflowers to dance, and his current victim managed to go pale and blush vividly at the same time. Graham must have seen it too, because he chuckled and stretched his long legs out in front of him, flexing his poor, abused feet.

"I wasn't expecting to be that bad," Eloise apologized. Again.

"I'll learn to move my feet faster."

She was shocked. "You want to do that again?"

"With you? Absolutely." Graham shifted, turning toward her, and Eloise's heart skittered, every internal organ following suit shortly after. The too familiar silence took over again, and just when she couldn't stand it any longer and was going to fill the space with more meaningless chatter, Graham found his words.

"I hate that I hurt you and made you feel like you were unimportant to me. I was an asshole. A complete and utter asshole, and I'm sorry. You are everything to me, Eloise. Absolutely everything. I love you so much that sometimes it feels like my heart is beating outside of my body. I want to make us work. I—"

It wouldn't have mattered if he finished his apology, because her brain was stuck on one little four-letter word: *love.*

He loved her, and he wanted to make things work. That was all she needed to hear. It was all she had really wanted after she had done her own postmortem on their situation. If they wanted to make things work, they could, no matter where they lived or what they did.

So, Eloise launched herself at him, muffling whatever he was going to say next with a kiss. His lips were as good as she remembered, soft but firm and immediately yielding to her. She was so happy she could have floated away like a balloon, but his arms wrapped tightly around her, crushing her against his body.

God, he felt good under her hands.

"I love you too."

"Thank god." His tongue slipped into her mouth, and she felt that delicious slide all the way down her spine. Her fingers tangled in his hair, trying to bring him closer, cursing her gorgeous dress because she couldn't crawl all over him without messing it up.

"I should have told you how I was feeling," she said against his lips, rushing the words out so she could keep kissing him. It had been a long fucking week. "I should have said something instead of letting it build up. I'm sorry I left."

"I would have left me, too." Graham sat back, panting, and cradled her face in his hands, pressing light kisses in a line from her forehead, down the bridge of her nose, and then her lips. "The whole thing was a fucking mess."

Eloise took a few deep breaths, and the increased oxygen to her brain let her think. "What even happened?"

He sighed, smoothing his hands over his hair, repairing some of the damage she had done in her frenzy to kiss him. "My father happened. He threatened to worm his way onto my board and—you know what. It doesn't matter."

Eloise's eyebrows shot up. That had to be a joke.

"How could it not matter? Your father, the only person I would push into traffic, interfered with the board of your company? Why are you not freaking out? I'm freaking out."

He rubbed the back of his neck, looking at the wall, the sky, the ballroom, anywhere but at her. "I, um, made the decision to step away from my company."

Eloise gasped. Of all the things she could have imagined, Graham leaving his business had been somewhere in the bottom third. He had worked so hard to build his company. To abandon it because of that worthless piece of shit seemed wrong.

"You can't let him run you off," she told him, jumping to her feet. This needed a plan. Some kind of action. "I won't let him run you off. There has to be an option besides quitting."

"Rumple." The nickname took a bit of the edge off and warmed her insides. She had her hands on her hips—well, more accurately her waist because her hips were hidden beneath nineteenth-century underpinnings—trying to look stern, but Graham was looking up at her with the kind of tender affection that made her heart ache. He took her hands off her hips and held them. "He didn't run me off. All he did was speed up a decision I was going to make eventually. Being here with you made me realize how unhappy and unfulfilled I've been. Even if you didn't want anything else to do with me, I couldn't keep going on like I had been. So, really, this is all your fault, and you're stuck with me now."

"You gave it all up?"

"What was I giving up?"

"Your house, your friends, your billion-dollar company. You're giving all of that up to live in a hotel room in a small town with shitty cell reception?"

"The house is easy to give up. You're not there, therefore I don't want to live there. My friends are rich enough that they can buy plane tickets if they want to come see me, and I can do the same, so I'm not giving them up. As for the company, I've done more with it than I ever thought I could. I'm retaining just enough stock to be a major pain in the ass at the annual share-holders meeting, but I have felt so incredibly light since I decided I was done. It's the right decision." Graham ran his thumbs over her knuckles. "We are not going to live in a hotel room, though. I'm going to buy a house, and after an appropriate amount of time, I'm going to ask you to move in with me."

Eloise was overwhelmed but she felt as light as a bubble.

"What about an inappropriate amount of time? Could you ask after an inappropriate amount of time?"

A smile lit up his entire face, and Eloise's chest didn't feel big enough to contain her heart. Graham was staying. He was buying a house and staying. They could get coffee from Sybil every morning before going to work, and then go to barbecue night every week with their friends. She would finally have room to rescue her teapot collection from her parents' garage.

"There is one little thing we need to discuss," Graham said.

Eloise nodded. "Selling the hotel."

"Okay, there are two things we need to discuss." He frowned at her. "What do you mean selling the hotel?"

"Fair is fair. You mostly held up your end of the deal, so I was going to hold up mine. I'll hear any offers you've gotten on Monday. I mean, you're technically about to be unemployed and trying to buy a house. We shouldn't ignore any possible revenue streams."

It took everything she had not to laugh at Graham as he gaped at her. She could hear the cogs and gears in his brain grinding with the effort it took for him to realize that she was, mostly, joking.

He shook his head in disbelief, his voice light with laughter. "I can't believe I almost fell for that. When did you get a poker face?"

"I've been practicing." Eloise grinned. "So, if it wasn't the hotel, what did you want to talk about?"

"Your friend."

That wasn't really a surprise.

"Sybil will eventually forgive you," she assured him, combing her fingers through his hair. "Especially if you buy me a house with a really big closet so I can get more shoes."

"You can have any kind of house you want to hold as many shoes as you want, but I mean your other friend."

"Chase?" Eloise snorted and rolled her eyes. "He's been on your team the entire time. He kept telling me to call you all week to patch things up."

"Okay, you have too many friends for this to work." Graham took a deep breath and then said, "Foolproof42."

The name sent a quick bolt of dread through her.

"He doesn't mean anything, Graham. He's just a friend. I mean, yeah, at one point I had a strange, *You've Got Mail* crush on him, but—" She stopped rambling, her brain catching up to her mouth. "Wait. How do you know about Foolproof42?"

"I'm Foolproof42."

Eloise stared. She looked at him hard. Studied every small twitch of his face to see if he was lying to her.

And then she remembered the first time they had watched *Claymore Abbey* together, when, for the length of an episode, she had wondered if he could be Foolproof42. It had seemed too far-fetched. What exactly were the odds that the mysterious man she'd had a crush on was the same man she had been falling in love with?

"You're Foolproof42?"

He nodded.

"Tell me something only he would know."

Graham looked up at the sky, thinking. "You had a cat named Cupcake that ran away when you were in seventh grade, but after watching the episode of *The Office* where Dwight mercy kills Angela's cat, you strongly suspect your sister tried her hand at euthanasia to see what would happen."

That was a story she had only ever told Foolproof42. It had come up during a discussion about the merits of having pets, and because he was an anonymous stranger, it had felt safe to divulge her theory about Cupcake. People tended to get nervous if they thought their doctor was a cat murderer. And if Graham knew that very specific story, that meant...

"Oh. My. God."

"I was shocked, too," he said, helping her sit down on the bench before her legs gave out.

"How long have you known?"

"I suspected for a while, but I knew since Friday when you were talking to Peter online." Eloise was still processing the information, but she must have been quiet for too long because he asked, "Are you mad?"

"No. No." She shook her head, all the emotions of the past week mixing with strange relief and overwhelming her. Tears pricked her eyes, and she dabbed at them with her fingers, trying to stop them before they really started. "I...I just really wanted it to be you. I had some suspicions, but it seemed...I wanted it to be you."

Graham brushed a stray curl out of her face. "I wanted it to be you, too."

CHAPTER THIRTY-EIGHT

"Have I told you how much I love you?" Graham murmured against Eloise's neck as they stood at the perimeter of the dance floor. He held her close against him, the crinoline beneath her dress half squished between them, half pushed out in front of her. It might have been clingy, but he didn't care. She was a dream he was afraid he would wake up from if he let go. The longest week of his life was over, and the rest of his life stretched out before him.

They'd had a long talk in the courtyard. About where they had gone wrong, how they would work on their relationship and themselves so it wouldn't happen in the future. He couldn't promise he wouldn't occasionally be an asshole, and she couldn't promise that she wouldn't shut down from time to time, but they agreed to call each other out when they saw it happening. None of it felt like a burden or a sacrifice because being with Eloise was worth every ounce of effort.

She tilted her head to give him better access to her neck with a dreamy sigh. "Yes, but a girl never gets tired of hearing it."

"I love you."

"That's a statement, not an accounting of your affections," she laughed.

"I love you so much," he amended, nipping at her earlobe, "that I learned how to waltz. Poorly, but I did learn."

"Mmm. ...In your defense, your dance partner has the grace of a foundered elephant."

"I think we're getting better."

Their subsequent dances had gone marginally better than their first one, though Graham couldn't help the sting of jealousy he got when he saw Peter effortlessly holding conversations while dancing. Talking while dancing seemed impossible when he needed to concentrate to count his steps and steer them around other couples.

"When you start at rock bottom, the only direction is up." Eloise rested her head back against his shoulder. "Do you think anyone would notice if we snuck off?"

She said it so casually that Graham almost assumed she was tired and wanted to go to bed. Nearly. But then he caught the heated look in her blue eyes and most of the blood required to operate his brain rushed south.

Eloise wanted to go to bed, but not to sleep.

"As long as we make it back before the fireworks," he told her, turning them around and nudging her towards the door.

She planted her feet and he barely resisted the urge to toss her over his shoulder like a sack of obstinate potatoes. "Wait, there's going to be fireworks?"

"Yes. It was supposed to be a surprise to cap off the night. Scoot, Rumple."

It was amazing how quickly a highly motivated woman could move in a cumbersome dress.

No sooner had the door to their room had clicked shut behind them than Eloise had a firm grip on the lapels of his jacket, pulling him down to meet her for a deep, hungry kiss. A week's worth of longing and a lifetime of promise were wrapped up in the scorching slide of her tongue against his as they stumbled toward the bed. Graham was burning from the inside out, his fingers fumbling with the multitude of buttons on his ensemble; he barely knew where to start because he wanted it all off and he wanted it all off now.

And he hadn't even gotten to the problem of Eloise's dress.

"How long do we have?" she asked, scattering his thoughts as her teeth scraped his bottom lip.

"Not long enough," he rasped, shrugging out of his coat and tossing it toward the chair in the corner.

There had been a plan for their first time after their separation. A slow seduction where he worshiped her body the way she deserved and he desperately wanted. But there was no way in hell he was going to turn down a chance to be inside of her sooner, logistical nightmare be damned.

"It takes forever to get in and out of this. Any ideas?"

Ideas? How was he supposed to have ideas when his brain was being run by his cock and balls?

Graham took a step back, like some kind of physical distance would restore functionality to his brain. Every season, *Claymore Abbey* had a dressing montage or two to remind viewers that getting dressed in the time of Queen Victoria had been a process. Undoing the dress wasn't an option. He doubted he would ever get it back on correctly, or in a timely fashion. This was more complicated than changing a tire in a NASCAR pit stop.

"Bend over the bed," he directed, slipping his braces off his shoulders. Eloise did as she was told, and he had to give one thing to corsets: they really emphasized the natural curve of her waist. Of course, he would have preferred her naked, but as a last resort, this wasn't bad. When he was an old man in a nursing home, he was going to look back on this moment fondly.

The condoms were still in the nightstand where he had left them, and Graham took one out, placing it on the bed by her hand. He finished unbuttoning his shirt and pulled it free of his pants.

"Later, I'm going to eat you out like you're dessert," he promised, compressing the crinoline that gave her skirts their shape so it was bunched up at the base of her spine. White linen crop pants greeted him—drawers, he remembered the name now—and to his surprise and delight, they were split open at the crotch.

And Eloise wasn't wearing any underwear underneath them.

"Are you ready for me?" he asked, relishing the needy whimper he drew from her as he easily slid two fingers inside of her. Always hot and wet, his Eloise.

"Fuck." She rocked back against his hand. "Hurry. Please."

"We've got time."

Graham trailed kisses down her exposed skin, starting at the top of her neck and working his way down her spine, vertebrae by vertebrae, until his lips met silk. It wasn't a lot of space, but he cherished every centimeter.

"What should I do to you?" He licked the sensitive spot behind her ear and she shuddered, her cunt squeezing his fingers. "Should I fuck you fast? Slow?" His teeth scraped her pulse. Another fluttering gasp. "Hard? Soft? Or should I make you come on my fingers instead of my cock for being so impatient?"

Fuck, he hoped she didn't pick the last option. He wanted her clenching around his cock and not his fingers when she finally came.

"I want—oh, fuck—Hard. Fast. Cock. Now."

That was enough for him.

Eloise whined when he withdrew his hand. With slippery

fingers Graham undid his pants and yanked down the zipper. They dropped to the floor, pooling around his ankles. The condom he had strategically placed on the bed opened with a bit of fumbling, and he rolled it down his shaft.

"Spread your legs more," Graham directed, finding and circling Eloise's clit with his thumb. The sound of her breath catching as he found just the right spot to touch her made his cock throb. For the rest of his life, he was never going to get tired of hearing that sound.

She complied, her stance widening, and he fit his cock at the entrance to her body.

It took one thrust to seat himself completely within her. The hot clasp of her cunt nearly undid him. Fast was definitely going to be a box he could tick if the tingles that shot down his legs at the first squeeze were any indication.

The way he saw it he had two options: slow himself down or speed Eloise up. And with the way she was sliding herself up and down his cock, the latter seemed much more likely than the former.

"That's a good girl," he encouraged, kissing the curve of her shoulder. "Fuck yourself on my cock. Make yourself come."

"F-uck," Eloise moaned, her cunt clenching. "Keep talking. Holy shit."

So, Graham did. He told her every filthy thought he had ever had about her. The way he loved that she wore mostly skirts and dresses because it meant that at any moment he could push them up and fuck her. How he was deeply enamored with her leggings because it meant he could watch her ass as she walked in front of him. He found her clit again while he told her that their rendezvous in the second-floor supply closet was his favorite memory to masturbate to.

That sent Eloise over the edge. She cried out, her body tightening under and around him. The pressure that had been incessantly building since he drove into her burst, and Graham came shortly after, his entire body tensing and shuddering. His thighs quivered as he caught his breath.

Graham looked at the clock on the nightstand. They needed to clean themselves up and get back downstairs soon, but it was hard to care about anything when he was buried up to his balls.

"Who needs fireworks after that?" Eloise asked, her voice slow and satisfied.

"Glad it was good for you, too." Graham kissed one of her flushed cheeks, and then her temple. "I love you, Eloise."

"I love you, too."

———

"Are you sure you can't stay longer?" Eloise asked as she hugged Peter tightly the next morning.

"I wish I could," he said, squeezing her in return. "But contracts and film schedules don't wait for anyone. Well, sometimes they do, but my assistant and my agent have assured me this is not one of those cases. I thought Dempsey was going to have a fit when they had to switch my plane ticket from LAX to PDX."

"Because there aren't any non-stop flights to Heathrow from Portland on Sundays, and you aren't great with connections," Graham reminded him from his seat by the fire.

It had been a late night, and he was very tired, a little sore, and so happy he kept touching the corners of his mouth to make sure he wasn't smiling like an idiot.

After the ball had ended and the last table had been put away, Graham had taken Eloise back to their room, stripped her bare, and kissed every inch of her body. The second time was less hurried than the first, but the collar of his quarter-zip sweater was turned up to hide the hickey she'd given him in her enthusiasm. Not that he cared if anyone saw it, but she cared and her concealer hadn't quite covered it.

The rain tapped against the stained glass, and Graham wished he was still curled up in bed with Eloise, cocooned in their shared warmth, but after everything Peter had done for him the last week, he at least deserved a send-off.

Graham frowned as one tiny, little detail occurred to him. "How are you getting to the airport?"

Peter smiled. "Your car service."

Eloise and Graham shared a look.

"What car service?"

"The one we definitely have," Kiki cut in, swooping in and pushing a cardboard carrier full of coffee cups into Graham's hands. She extracted a tall cup and handed it to Peter, beaming. "It's a special service we offer to VIP guests."

"We have VIP guests?"

"Very funny." Peter glared at him as he tipped the coffee cup to his lips. His eyes widened, and he pulled the cup away from his mouth, holding it out to stare at it. "What is this?"

"Coffee?" Kiki frowned, reaching out to take the cup back. "Is something wrong with it? I didn't know what you'd want, but—"

Peter pulled the cup close, cradling it against his chest. "Don't you dare take this. It's perfect."

"We'll send you some beans," Eloise promised, finding the cup with her name on it, and then bending closer to read the remaining cup. "Hm."

Graham lifted it to his eyes and sighed. In thick black marker, Sybil had scrawled "Fuck You" on his cup. He wondered how long it would take for him to get back to "Prince of Darkness."

"Did you have to tell her this was for me?" Kiki shrugged in response, and he passed the cup to Eloise. "Take a sip. If she poisoned it, she'll feel bad if you die."

"She didn't poison it," Eloise chided, making a big show of taking a drink. "There. Do you feel better now?"

"Yes, I do." Graham kissed her forehead. "Now I just need to wait fifteen minutes to see if you start foaming at the mouth."

She rolled her eyes. "Yesterday it was 'I love you.' Today it's 'Here, drink this and see if you die.'"

"And you make the absolute best guinea pig."

"Seriously, how is this so good?" Peter took off the lid of his cup and inhaled deeply. "This isn't coffee. This is heaven in a cup."

"We might never be able to get rid of him now," Graham whispered in Eloise's ear and she jabbed him in the ribs with her elbow, but her lips twitched.

"If you're looking for a new job," Peter said to Kiki, "I could use a second assistant."

"Stop trying to poach my employees." Graham glared at Peter. "Kiki, can I talk to you?"

She followed him over to stand beneath the grand chandelier, worrying her dark red bottom lip between her teeth.

"We're not really starting a car service," Kiki said quickly. "It was just something I said because, you know, a chance to be in a car with Peter fucking Green for two hours and—"

"Kiki." Graham put his hands on her shoulders, bending slightly so they were eye level. "Calm down. I'm not mad. You're not in trouble. We are absolutely not starting a car service."

Her body relaxed, but her eyes remained wary. "So why did you want to talk to me?"

"I have an idea."

Once he had decided that his life was wherever Eloise was, and Eloise would likely always be with the hotel, his entire future had opened up before him, clear as day. He had plans, and this was the first step in making his plans a reality.

"I want to pay for your school," he began, holding up a finger when Kiki opened her mouth to say something. "Hear me out first. In return for paying for your college education, I want you to get some kind of business degree so you can start training to run the hotel. You're basically the night manager already, so consider yourself promoted. Eventually you'll become the assistant manager, and someday, general manager. We've still got some details to hammer out, but I want you to know that no matter where we go or what we do, you've got a job with us."

"You mean that?"

"Absolutely. I see a lot of potential in you, Morticia. If you need time to think about it, I unders—"

Kiki threw her arms around his neck, her shoulder jabbing his windpipe as she pulled him into a crushing hug. "I don't need to think about it. I accept. You're stuck with me now, Lucifer."

"I'm glad," Graham wheezed, and hugged her back.

CHAPTER THIRTY-NINE

"I've changed my mind," Graham announced as he entered their office an hour after they had said goodbye to Peter. "Sybil didn't poison this. No, that would be too easy. Death by decaf."

"She can't hate you too much," Eloise soothed, not looking up from the cleaning supplies order form she was filling out. Owning a hotel could be so glamorous. "She didn't ruin your grand romantic gesture."

She had gotten a good laugh out of hearing that Sybil had told him to fuck off when he had called to ask for her help in pulling off the *Claymore Abbey* ball surprise. Apparently Graham had called nearly the entire town, from Chase to Edith Nelson, who was supposed to distract her if she got to Sybil's house too early and saw them dropping off the dress. The amount of effort he had put into the operation was sweet.

"That wasn't my grand romantic gesture," he said, leaning against the doorframe.

That caught Eloise's full attention. "How is a Victorian ball gown not a grand romantic gesture?"

Graham shrugged, a sly grin hiding in the corners of his kissable mouth. "That was romantic, but I don't know about grand."

"There was a champagne fountain."

"Peter went off script for that."

"Fireworks."

"Okay, so it was both grand and romantic, but when was I ever going to get another opportunity like that?"

"Next year?" Eloise offered.

"It was hard enough to keep something from you when you were completely in the dark."

"You'll just have to learn to be sneakier." She grinned at him, and her stomach fluttered when he grinned back, his dimple appearing.

"Come with me," he said, inclining his head out of the office. "I've got another surprise for you."

Her heart kicked into high gear. She stood, tugging down the hem of her burgundy skirt. "What is it?"

"If I told you, it wouldn't be a surprise," Graham reminded her, tipping her chin up when she met him in the doorway to give her a tender kiss. "But if you can guess before we get there, I might tell you."

Eloise felt that simple kiss all the way to her toes. And as much as she wanted simple to become hot and heated, soreness be damned, she wanted to know what her next surprise was more. So, she took his hand and let him lead her out through the lobby.

"Is it a pony?"

He snorted. "Not yet. I'm saving that for the next time I screw up."

"You might want to start making a list. I have a feeling you'll screw up a lot." Eloise squeezed his hand. "Is it a new car?"

"No, but we should get you one. I have nightmares about you breaking down and then getting hit by a semi-truck when you're walking on the side of the road because there's no cell phone service around here." He shuddered.

"Wow. That was incredibly specific and morbid."

"Maybe we should get you a satellite phone, too."

Graham stopped in front of the closed doors to the bar. Eloise frowned.

"My surprise is in the bar?"

"It is. So it is most definitely not a pony or a car."

A wild idea occurred to her, and she put her hand over Graham's to stop him from opening the door.

"Graham...are you planning on proposing?"

He stared. She stared back. And for what felt like an unblinking eternity, they stood there and looked at each other.

"Eloise," he began slowly, "if I was going to propose in the hotel, it would be under the chandelier on a sunny day because when the light hits the stained glass just right, it looks like you're underwater. That's your favorite spot."

Warmth flooded Eloise. It made her chest ache and her cheeks burn. Of course he wasn't going to propose, it was too soon. But the fact that he had thought about where he *might* propose in the future made her love him even more. She wrapped a hand around the back of his neck and pulled him down to her for a kiss.

"I love you."

"I love you too. And I do have a proposal, just not the kind that ends with a diamond ring."

Eloise was surprised when Graham opened the door. She wasn't sure what she had been expecting, but it wasn't for the bar to look exactly the same. The only thing that was different was the addition of three easels with blank poster boards on them set up in front of a table.

"You know you could have made something called a Power-Point, right? We wouldn't have even needed to leave the office."

Eloise sat in the chair that Graham pulled out for her. "Didn't you own a tech company? Get in on the ground floor with apps?"

"Not the same experience. Trust me."

This had to be what it felt like to be on *The Price Is Right* before they revealed all the prizes. Her mouth was a little dry, her skin tingled, and all her excess energy came out through her bouncing leg. Graham turned the first board over and Eloise forgot how to breathe entirely.

It was the hotel. Their hotel. But it had been recreated in one of those fancy interior design rendering programs, with fake guests and plants that she hoped were fake because no one ever remembered to water the real ones. The lobby had been reimagined in a few different themes and color schemes.

It was the most beautiful thing Eloise had ever seen.

Until he flipped over the next board.

By the time he got to the third board, Eloise's eyes were so clouded with tears she couldn't see exactly what it was. The idea for a soaking tub and separate shower in the suites had sent her over the edge. In her wildest dreams, she had imagined maybe half of what she had seen on the boards.

"So, the idea is—Eloise, why are you crying?" Graham sounded horrified. She couldn't make out the finer points of his facial features at the moment.

"It's just so beautiful," she croaked. "This might be better than a diamond ring."

"It's going to be a lot more expensive than a diamond ring."

Graham brought her closer to the boards and explained his plans to her as he held her, her back against his strong chest, because the interior design plans were too pretty to view from anywhere but up close. It really was like he had peeked into her brain. Each detail was something she could have sworn she had only mentioned in passing, if at all.

The renovation would take time. Graham didn't sugarcoat that part. They would keep working at a reduced capacity for at least the next year, assuming there weren't delays. It could be shortened, but they would need to completely shut down the hotel, and he knew she wouldn't want to do that. Though it was tempting.

There was a business plan, too. A spiral-bound, laminated business plan with the updated logo and branding on the cover.

And there were tabs.

Graham looked slightly terrified when she burst into tears all over again.

"If you don't like it, it can be changed..."

"Don't you dare. It's perfect." She ran her hand reverently over the cover again, steeling her jaw as her chin began to wobble again. "This is better than fireworks and diamonds."

Graham kissed the top of her head. "You're the rest of my life, Eloise. You can have anything you want, as long as I get to have you. Even the pony."

Until the day she died, Eloise knew she would wonder how she possibly could have gotten so lucky to have Graham. She would marvel at how the whole universe had conspired to bring them together. He was the stranger who had become her friend, the frustrating man on the other side of an email who had somehow become the love of her life. Every choice she had made, everything she thought had been a mistake, clearly led to this man and this moment.

She tried to beam up at him, to pour all of her love into a smile, but most of it just trickled down her face as the happiest tears.

"The rest of my life," she agreed. "And after."

"After?"

"Because if I die first, I'm absolutely going to haunt you."

EPILOGUE

Graham Thatcher was on a mission. A mission to get his fiancée to leave work on time.

He would have had better luck landing a Mars rover from his living room.

The last year had been chaotic, and that was putting it kindly. But as he walked through the lobby, he was incredibly proud. The Crane Hotel was painted, polished, and as impressive as the glittering chandelier in the lobby. It was spectacular. Not that he was biased. And they were on the cusp of being successful.

The previous spring, he, Eloise, and Kiki had pounded the pavement at college job fairs, finding staff for the summer season, and trying to poach any promising hospitality majors from the big hotel chains. There had been a stretch of time on that road trip where he was convinced that Kiki survived entirely on sour gummy worms, spicy chips, and a variety of flavored seltzer waters. Graham had also become addicted to her spicy chips, and they kept a case of them stashed in the manager's office. Eloise had tossed up her hands and only complained about how much space the box took up on days ending in Y. She hated the box so much that she had moved it one day in May, and almost given him a heart attack because he had hidden her engagement ring in it. It was the only place he could think of that she wouldn't look, and his frantic search for it had ruined most of his planned proposal. It still took place under the chandelier in the lobby, but it had been in the middle of a shouting match about where they were going to store the box of chips.

The only part that had gone to plan was her crying when he showed her the antique diamond and sapphire ring he'd chosen for her.

Graham had underestimated how busy they would get in the summer. Eloise told him that it wouldn't have felt so awful if they hadn't been juggling construction, too. There hadn't been a day he hadn't sat at the front desk to take the brunt of complaints, feeling more like Lucy from *Peanuts* every moment. He pasted a smile on his face, but Eloise had taken away his coffee can with "Advice 5 Cents" away, which made it a lot less fun. A few people had actually patted down their pockets for change first.

The Cranberry Festival had been wonderful, and not just because it meant they all got to take a deep breath as the brunt of the tourist season passed and the renovation officially wrapped up. Food, carnival games, and a top of the Ferris wheel makeout that had gotten them whistles and cheers from the car below. Graham had enjoyed flipping off Chase and Cole.

The door to the office was slightly ajar, and Graham opened it slowly. Eloise was sitting at her desk, stuffing papers into folders, her forehead creased in concentration. Her dark hair was twisted into a bun, and the gray herringbone sheath dress she was wearing made her look like a cross between a pinup and a librarian.

He loved it.

Not that there wasn't much he didn't love about Eloise.

He rapped his knuckles lightly on the door, and chuckled when she jumped. She shot him a glare that was void of any real malice.

"You're late," he reminded her, tapping his watch.

She sighed, shoving more paper into folders. "I know, I know. But I'm almost done with the welcome packets for the engagement party, and I wanted to finish them up before going home."

It took only a few steps to reach her desk. Their office was the only place in the hotel they hadn't renovated. There were too many good memories in the small room. If they had more time, he would have liked to make some more good memories in the room, but they were on a schedule.

Graham put his hands on her shoulders and began to trail kisses from the tender spot behind her left ear to the inviting curve of her neck.

"They're not going to be here until next week. Can't it wait until tomorrow?"

She shivered and he got a hot rush as goosebumps rose on her chest. "No. Because the wellness retreat folks show up tomorrow. And that's going to be a high-maintenance thing." Eloise tipped her head to the side to give him better access to her neck. "Crap. I need to talk to Sybil about the coffee bar..."

Graham grabbed her periwinkle sticky notes and a pen, scratched "Sybil. Coffee." on one, and affixed it to the screen of the computer. "Tomorrow, love of my life. We have plans. Remember?"

Eloise sighed. "I feel like this is my fault for saying we needed to do date night more often."

"It absolutely is," Graham said, taking her coat from the hook on the wall and holding it up for her to slip into. It was his second December in Oregon, and to a former Californian, forty-five degrees still felt too cold. "And we have a schedule tonight, so chop-chop."

"I still can't believe Peter planned us an engagement party." Eloise slid her arms into her jacket.

"Believe it."

Peter had been organizing the party since before Graham had proposed. Getting all their schedules—and the correct occupancy for the hotel to host the function—had been the worst game of Telephone Graham had ever played, but they had pulled it off. Eloise's family had never visited Crane Cove, and they were going to see the hotel in its Christmas glory.

Eloise scribbled a note to Kiki to double-check the towels in the block of rooms for the wellness retreat and hesitated once more before leaving the office. Graham trailed behind, unabashedly staring at her ass as she walked ahead of him.

Dinner. Sex. *Claymore Abbey* season premiere. It was his idea of a perfect night.

The drive home was filled with speculation about what was going to happen in the opening episode.

It was season ten, and the writers had left them with lots to chew on during the finale of season nine. Because British television seemed to operate on an incomprehensible schedule, fans had been left waiting for answers for over a year.

The juiciest bit was Meryl and Heston had been caught in an extremely compromising position during Annabelle's come-out ball. It was innocent, but it looked terrible. Whether or not they would, or even should, get married to save her reputation had been a hot-button topic on the forum, followed closely by the identity of the mysterious American that had been hinted at all through season nine. And once Amanda told her parents that she was putting herself firmly on the shelf because she couldn't stand being on the marriage mart any longer, fans were chomping at the bit for the new season.

"Ryston is not going to throw himself on the matrimonial altar!" Graham insisted with as much gusto as he could manage without descending into a full-on shout.

He turned the car into the driveway of their house. The pale blue Victorian with the white gingerbread trim was one of the oldest surviving homes in Crane Cove. Eloise had sighed wistfully as they drove the storied Lilac Lane when they were house-hunting, and Graham would never tell her how much money it had taken to convince the previous owners that they wanted to move closer to their grandchildren in Poughkeepsie. Annie teased him mercilessly about being a penguin, except instead of pebbles, he gave Eloise properties.

"He could!" Eloise fired back. "He could offer to marry her instead of Heston. Everyone wins then."

"No one wins in that situation. Especially Meryl." He took her hand as they headed up the brick walkway to their front door. "I'm telling you, the hate-fuck consummation of her and Heston's marriage would blow anything else out of the water."

Eloise tossed her head back and laughed. "Oh my god. You went there!"

"It could happen. I'm just saying, a bunch of streaming shows have really pushed the envelope in that department."

"If we see a Meryl-Heston hate-fuck on *Claymore Abbey*, I will watch *Breaking Bad*."

"Bring on the special license," Graham cheered.

"No. No." Eloise pointed her finger at him, her precious face twisted into a scowl that was meant to be menacing. It was adorable. "Hate-fuck. The bet is for a hate-fuck. Not just getting married."

"So, what if they don't hate-fuck? What do you win?" Graham asked, grinning at her.

Eloise thought for a moment as he unlocked their front door. "You have to wear the jacket in public."

"No."

"Yes."

She didn't need to elaborate which jacket she was talking about. Six months ago, a box had been delivered to the house, and wrapped in tissue paper was a silk bomber jacket with his name embroidered on the left side and "Brunch Bros" stitched across the back. Graham adamantly refused to wear it, and because his group of friends had not been all together since they'd gotten them, it had been a moot issue.

It was an excellent forfeit, and with a disgruntled huff, he nodded his agreement.

"Perfect." Eloise hung her coat up on the hook by the door. "Now, first things first. I know the plan was to have dinner, sex, then *Claymore Abbey*"—she turned and moved her hair off her neck—"but I was thinking we switch up the itinerary and have sex, dinner, then watch. Can you unzip me?"

———

"Has Sam ever considered writing a cookbook?" Eloise asked as she dished up two plates of hoisin glazed pork chops and roasted broccolini. She still couldn't wrap her head around the fact that she called a rock star for dinner recipes.

In the last year, she had gotten close with Graham's friends. Peter had been working too much to visit since the first ball he had attended, but both Jordy and Sam had come to check things out individually.

Sam had been fascinated that over half of the town's population had no idea who he was, and he had been looking at land around town to build himself a cabin to get away from it all.

And Eloise had loved introducing Jordy to Chase. She thought her giant ex-boyfriend was going to drop like a felled tree in the presence of the quarterback he had idolized for so long. The joy she got from the look on Chase's face when he met Jordy was closely followed by Jordy's face when he did the math on how old the twins had been when he had started playing for the Phantoms.

"No. I think the recipe book he made for you for your birthday is the closest we'll ever get," Graham said, reaching inside the fridge to grab the pitcher of sangria he had made for the premiere.

Their fridge was covered in an assortment of photos, magnets, and even a few postcards from Mallory's travels. It was a stainless-steel monument to everything they loved. Someday they would frame their favorites, like the picture of the boys at opening night of the *Emma* musical, which had won Peter a Tony Award for playing Mr. Knightley, or when he and Eloise got the keys to their house.

"Did he find a spot for the cabin yet?"

He shook his head, pouring two full glasses of sangria. "No. But speaking of property, I had an interesting conversation with Ed Gilbert today."

"Ed Gilbert from Parks?"

"Bingo. I guess the department is looking to offload the lighthouse."

Eloise could tell when Graham was trying to back into an idea the long way. "You want to buy it, don't you?"

A guilty blush colored the tops of his cheeks. "I thought it could be an interesting addition to our portfolio."

She wrapped the soft cotton of his T-shirt in her hand and pulled him down for a kiss. Even after all the kisses they'd shared, each one sent an electric sizzle down her spine.

"I want a presentation by the end of the week. If you do it naked, I might be more inclined to sign off on your project."

"You drive such a hard bargain."

"Someone has to keep you in check."

They arranged themselves on the couch, because they had spent too long in the bedroom to have dinner before the show started. Not that Eloise minded. No, she didn't mind at all. Not when screaming orgasms were involved.

"So, the bet is for a hate-fuck," Graham reminded her as he turned on the television. "If they hate-fuck, you have to watch *Breaking Bad.* If they don't, I will..." He sighed heavily. "Wear the fucking jacket in public."

"I would like to amend this to very specifically include the coffee shop."

Graham's eyes widened, and he shrank back. "No. Absolutely not. Sybil will never let me live it down. That's *years* of ridicule, Eloise."

It had taken a full six months for Sybil to warm back up to Graham after he made Eloise cry. Six months of him being suspicious every day that she had swapped his coffee with either decaf or a quad-shot heart attack in a cup. And then, one sunny May morning, she wrote his actual name on the cup instead of some variation on Satan, and that had been that. Since then, they had bonded over murder podcasts and sci-fi novels. Graham had thought she would like the *Emma* musical after seeing an old edition on her bookshelf, but she had teared up and left the room during the bridge of Peter's ballad "If I Loved You Less."

"Then you better hope you're right. Any last guesses on the identity of the mysterious American?"

"No, but if it creates a love triangle with Annabelle and Captain Goddard, I'm not watching anymore. Those two might replace Olivia and Lovingford for me."

Eloise gasped. "They've been together for less than three episodes and one waltz."

"And I would die for them."

The season picked up right where the last one had ended.

Meryl was pacing anxiously in the greenhouse while Amanda tried to calm her down and their father shouted at Heston in the study, threatening him with everything but a duel if he didn't marry her. And then the butler knocked on the door, and what happened next made Eloise scream.

Peter, sporting a beard, was shown into the study.

Christian had returned to *Claymore Abbey* after ten long years. And he was no longer a penniless stable hand.

"He's the American!" Graham shouted, pointing at the TV. "I talked to him yesterday and he didn't say anything!"

"It's official. The writers are trying to kill us."

ACKNOWLEDGMENTS

I knew the dedication for this book before I knew how the book would end. Keyed Up would not have been possible without my friends who steadfastly championed me through the process. However, these acknowledgments are the part I've been putting off the longest. How do you compress the depth and breadth of your love for someone into what is, essentially, an Oscar's speech? I can already hear the orchestra playing me off the stage.

For my friends who have been around the longest: Joanne Machin, Michelle Kallman, Liz Zerkel, Stacey Turner, and Heather Novak. You poor souls heard the earliest rumblings of these stories and told me my first few chapters weren't a flaming pile of garbage. Thank you.

For my friends that kept me going when it got hard: Kate Emery, Eliza MacArthur,Megan Cousins, Livy Hart, Hannah Bird, Marni Gesinski, Esther Reid, Meghan Lloyd, Nellie Wilson, Lee Hall, Lara Hodo, and Kelsey Bowman. You've gotten more screenshots than anyone should ever get. Your love and guidance was invaluable.

For all my early readers whose excitement kept me going: Carline, Sarah, Jennie, Kesslan, Rita, Kim, Kristen, Tamara, Andi, Margaret, Nadia, Emma, and Morgan.

For my editor, Sarah, who understood my vision for this book and helped me make it come true. I'm so grateful for your guidance and wisdom. You're an evil genius.

For my cover designer, Mia Heintzelman, who is the most

gorgeous person inside and out. You distilled paragraphs of ramble into four cover designs that took me weeks to choose between. Thank you.

And finally, my husband, Daniel. This book would've been done ages ago if you could leave me alone for longer than twenty minutes. The way you love is an inspiration and there's a little bit of you in every hero I write. I love you.

ABOUT THE AUTHOR

Sarah is a Pacific Northwest based romance writer who would call herself "indoorsy". When she isn't traipsing around the country for work, Sarah enjoys buying more books than she can ever read, drinking an irresponsible amount of coffee, and not respecting her bedtime.

Find her on Instagram @remarkablysarah

sarahestep.com